The Moneybag

By

Sam Skinner

This book is a work of fiction. Places, events, and situations in this story are purely fictional. Any resemblance to actual persons, living or dead, is coincidental.

ISBN: 1-4033-2767-X (e-book)
ISBN: 1-40332-7680-8 (Paperback)
ISBN: 1-4033-2769-6 (Dustjacket)

Library of Congress Control Number: 2002091826

This book is printed on acid free paper.

Printed in the United States of America
Bloomington, IN

1stBooks - rev. 07/29/02

Dedication

To Ellen Frary Skinner and Billie Castile Skinner.

Acknowledgements

Jean Brackens, Jean Carlstedt, John H. Skinner
and Nancy Wilkens.

Chapter One

Tuesday, January 16 - 11:45 P.M.
Old Town Alexandria, Virginia

Denise James breezed out the double front doors of the restaurant having just had her way with the full menu and wine list on Treasure Chest Bank's tab. Still inside were her division head and three die-hards, all certain to drink until told to leave. Everyone else in the Real Estate Finance Division had already gone home, and it was high time she did too. She didn't envy the final four their certain hangovers for whatever pleasure remained in abusing the bank's credit card into the wee hours.

Outside, the air was freezing. Her gloved hands drew her hat snug over her ears and pulled the strap of her coat tight as she turned up King Street, the eighteenth-century thoroughfare running west from the Potomac River. All the quaint shops were closed at this hour, the faux-candles of their colonial facades flickering a faint orange glow. Along the sidewalk, gas lamps cast a Victorian sheen to the street below.

There weren't many people out, and after she turned onto Fairfax, she was alone. Here the street narrowed between clapboard townhouses, some dating back a hundred years. Trees in the sidewalk cast shadows through a canopy of leafless branches from the occasional street lamp overhead. She pressed homeward, watching the street and listening to the metal buckles of her shoes jingling like spurs. Thank God for pantsuits, she thought. Hate to be wearing a skirt on a night like this.

Sounds to the left made her turn her head.

A man was running through a service alley bisecting the middle of the block, a streetlight at the far end silhouetting his form.

She stopped.

The man stole a glance over his shoulder. Against the light she could see he gripped something across his body. When he turned back, he took a few more strides and lurched to one side, reeling out of control, and would have fallen had he not caught the corner of a building with his arm. A moment later he emerged from its shadow

1

holding the object in one hand and reaching for his stomach with the other.

Two silhouettes rounded the far corner under the light.

"Freeze!" shouted one.

The man kept running.

"You! Freeze!"

The man stopped and whirled around.

A shot cracked out. She flinched. Twice more he fired as those in chase jumped to the sides of the alley.

The man turned toward her and ran. She could hear the labor of his breathing before she could see the exhaustion in his face. He was desperate, lungs gasping.

"Hey!" she called. "This way!"

He saw her for the first time, her arm pointing down Fairfax Street.

"This way!" she said. "Next block!"

He was going to pass to her right to make the turn. The bag was in his left hand, the gun in his right.

She turned her left hip to the apex of the man's turn and leaned back on her right foot. A half step short of where she wanted him to be, she shifted forward and launched her right leg in a wide arc. Snapping her knee straight, she planted her instep into the center of his stomach, grunting on impact, right hand flailing the air above her knee, every ounce of strength focused.

The man's torso halted as if he'd slammed into a fence rail. Extremities, gun, bag, and stomach contents flew. She withdrew her leg and he crumbled at her feet. Clutching his stomach, he rolled to one side and curled into a ball, eyes scrunched shut.

She leaned over from behind his head, the smell of gunpowder and vomit rising. He looked Hispanic, wore a scruffy goatee, and had a mouth full of crooked gray teeth.

The men from the alley trotted up.

"You got 'em!" panted one.

They were police officers, guns drawn.

Both leaned over at the waist, hands on knees, mist filling the air above them like that from spent racehorses.

She turned from them to gaze in wonder at the goateed man. She hadn't thought to do anything, couldn't believe what she'd just done. It was as if she'd been a spectator watching someone else.

One of the officers stood straight. She saw his nametag— ROBERT ARMSTRONG. He holstered his gun and fastened its safety strap.

"Wind's out," he declared.

He looked about thirty, fair skinned, thickset. He wore the uniform of the City of Alexandria Police Department under an un-zipped winter coat. His chest heaved.

"Yeah," panted his partner in a high voice. "His win'."

This officer didn't look big enough to be in uniform, an impression not changed when he straightened his back and looked at her. He was short and spare, a weak moustache adding little age to his boyish face. She caught his nametag— STEPHEN JOHNSON.

The goateed man began dry heaving, his body attempting to void an already empty stomach.

Armstrong asked, "You okay?"

"Yeah," answered Johnson. "Never been shot at."

Armstrong looked at him in surprise. Their eyes met. Armstrong motioned for him to put away his weapon. The automatic looked gigantic in Johnson's hand as he lifted it high to his holster. Denise smiled to herself and thought: toy cop.

The officers caught their breath, little concerned with the goateed man's plight. They hadn't returned fire after being fired upon, and seemed content to watch him retch. When Armstrong could speak a complete sentence, he leaned to his epaulet-mike and pressed the sender.

"Twelve-Charlie to Com-Three. We have suspect in custody. South Fairfax between Duke and Prince on Fairfax at number two-one-two."

"Acknowledged, Twelve-Charlie," a radio voice crackled. "Two-one-two South Fairfax. Assistance arriving."

Armstrong pulled out a pen and pad.

"What's your name, ma'am?"

"Denise James."

He wrote it down.

"Boy! That was somethin'!" said Johnson.

"Thank you. I don't do this sort of thing all the time."

They smiled.

Johnson kept his eyes on the goateed man while Armstrong went to the automatic in the street.

"Beretta ninety-two," he announced.

Johnson said, "Those shots are going to mean mandatory jail time, brother. Five years minimum."

"You're under arrest," said Armstrong walking back. He pulled on latex gloves and searched the man where he sat. Johnson watched, his hand on his pistol. No weapons, money, or identification were found.

"Jesus! Lookit that car," said Johnson. "That's awful."

The fender and hood of a Mercedes parked near the alley's entrance steamed with a chunky brown liquid.

"Serves the bastard right," muttered Armstrong.

The goateed man breathed easier now. He sat up for the first time. Armstrong cuffed him where he sat, hands in front. Both officers helped him to his feet where he stood a good six-two, dazed, and unsteady. Johnson held his elbow while Armstrong looked him over, shining a flashlight near, though not in, his eyes. Armstrong asked, "Do you know where you are? Where are you? What's your name? Are you feeling okay? Are you hurt anywhere?"

Nothing.

Denise thought the officers' conduct quite good under the circumstances. The man looked helpless, and his insides were scrambled, but he'd shot at them, and she could well understand their desire for a little off the record nightstick practice.

"You have the right to remain silent..."

The man glared at her throughout Armstrong's recitation.

"Do you understand these rights?"

"I say no-ting. I wan' lawyer." Then to Denise, "We meet a-gang, puta!"

He held up his cuffed hands, pointed his finger at her face with a two-fisted pistol grip, and dropped his thumb like a cocked hammer.

Denise broke into a smile, extended her forefinger to her mouth, and blew away imaginary smoke from shots just fired.

"Maybe so," she said twirling an invisible gun and slapping it into an unseen holster at her hip. "But tonight, the angels win."

Johnson cackled a high-pitched laugh.

Police cars pulled up, three of them. Pulsating red, blue, and white strobes cast a nightclub atmosphere to the alley's exit. Armstrong reported to one of two plainclothesmen.

There had been a drug bust at the waterfront. Armstrong and Johnson had chased this man from the river. He'd shot at them in the alley. This woman disabled him with a kick. The suspect had no ID.

The goateed man was read his rights a second time in front of the plainclothesmen. Knowing the ropes, he asked for an attorney and said nothing more. Two uniforms placed him in the back of one of the cars and secured his handcuffs to a chain on the floor.

"Turn off the lights," the plainclothesman in charge ordered in a husky voice. He was in his forties, about five-eight, and had a large distended stomach. "Did anybody touch anything?"

"No, sir," said Armstrong. "The gun's in the street. The bag's by the car."

"Take pictures of the gun and tag it into evidence." He pointed to two uniforms. "Go find the shell casings in the alley and mark them."

Denise stood to one side with Armstrong and Johnson while officers unwound and strung up POLICE LINE - DO NOT CROSS tape. A photographer snapped pictures.

"I'm Detective Scaleri," said the plainclothesman to Denise. "That was some kick you did. That guy must outweigh you by a hundred pounds."

Scaleri emanated the odor of a chain smoker.

"Thank you, Detective. It surprised me as much as it did him."

Scaleri pulled on latex and watched the scene, shifting his weight from one foot to the other. Denise wondered if there was a rule against smoking while an investigation was in progress.

When the photographer said he was done, Scaleri sent him to take pictures of the spent casings in the alley.

"Okay. Let's see what we got."

Scaleri lifted the tape, stepped to the curb, and bent to the plastic bag beside the Mercedes. All movement stopped as he unwound the twist-tie and placed it in an evidence bag held by the other plainclothesman. Scaleri bent low over his stomach, lifted the edge of the plastic with a pen, and looked inside.

"It's paper!"

The second plainclothesman looked too.

5

"Shredded paper," he said. "No drugs."

They stood and turned to the suspect in the car who held up his hands to the length of the restraining chain and flipped them the bird.

"He's a fuckin' decoy," said Scaleri. "Somebody else got it."

Scaleri went back under the barrier tape with the expression of a sour stomach. He looked down the alley, at the Mercedes, at the suspect sitting in the car, and at Denise. He pulled out a pack of cigarettes, drew one, and gripped it between his teeth.

"All right," he said. "Wrap it up. Take the bag. Leave the tape." He pointed at two uniforms, irritation in his voice. "Stay here till I call you. Armstrong. Johnson. You're with me. You too, Miss. Back to the park. Maybe they got something there."

The Potomac River, two dead-end streets, and the Strand surround Waterfront Park, a rectangular field with trees and bushes dotting its sides. Dead quiet after midnight most of the time; now it teemed with police and flashing lights.

Denise was asked to stand by to make a statement. She waited beside an area bounded by barrier tape inside of which were two cars and into which few ventured. Uniformed officers with flashlights and nightsticks probed bushes in the park while other officers talked in low voices among themselves. A helmeted team of twenty dressed in riot gear fell into formation, mounted vans, and drove off. Feeling cold standing still, she walked up the Strand, her shoes crunching frozen grass. No one paid much attention to her. She passed along a line of police cars parked against the curb. Each contained a single man sitting in the back. None looked happy.

"Denise James?"

She turned expecting to see a police officer.

"Yes?"

A man in a trench coat smiled at her.

"I'm Dan Mattison, Channel Three Action News."

"Oh! I've seen you on television."

He leaned close enough for her to smell his cologne.

"I understand you apprehended one of the suspects shooting his way out of tonight's raid. Would it be all right if we did an interview with you?"

"Here?"

"No. Not here. Could you come with me, please?"

She followed him to a Channel Three van, a cameraman waiting beside it.

"Would you mind answering a few questions?"

"Sure."

The camera light made her blink. Mattison spoke in his broadcast voice.

"Would you tell us what happened and what you did just a few minutes ago, Denise James of Alexandria?"

She faced the camera and spoke in a rush, arriving quick at her encounter with the goateed man.

"... and he went down, and the police officers ran up the alley and—"

"Mattison!" a voice shouted. "You know better than this!"

Two policemen ran up. The speaker was tall and well built, not negotiating.

"Shut it down and get to the press area."

Mattison thanked her, signed off, and the cameraman put down his equipment.

"You guys suck blood," said the officer. "You know the rules."

"Yeah, yeah," said the cameraman.

"We'd like to get your statement now, Ms. James," said the officer in a politer tone. "Please come with us."

He led her to the barrier tape, started a Dictaphone, and recited the date and time. He asked for her name and address. Then he let her speak without interruption while the second officer stood by.

More news teams arrived and were ushered into the media holding area at the far end of the Strand. The line of squad cars with unhappy men drove away. Cruiser lights were turned off. Spectators watching from the sidewalk were told there was nothing more to see and encouraged to leave. Few seemed willing.

From a distance, sirens approached.

Two black sedans rounded the corner at King and drove as close to the barrier tape as they could get before going silent. All the officers stopped what they were doing to watch. The newcomers got out, and the shortest man among them strode to the officers in charge.

"Who is that?" Denise asked.

The officer switched off the recorder.

"That would be Commonwealth's Attorney Roody Packwurst. Looks a lot smaller in person than he does on TV, don't he?"

"From your height he must."

Packwurst had dark hair slicked flat against his skull. His suit looked shiny, his shoes polished. Detective Scaleri was among those in the group around him, but said nothing, his face a scowl.

In short order, Packwurst gathered what information he needed and moved to the television lights in the media area. Mattison wasn't in the crowd as far as she could see, and the Channel Three van was gone.

Packwurst spoke with his feet on the curb, the cameras in the street. He held his head high and used his hands to point to the barrier tape over his shoulder. When he finished, he walked away along the top of the curb, not stepping to the street until he was out of camera range. He gesticulated at the officers again. Then he and his entourage left, sirens on. The media began packing their equipment. Spectators started to disburse.

The officer with Denise turned on his recorder and resumed asking questions. Who attended dinner with you? What time did you leave the restaurant? What route did you take? Where is your car parked? How many shots did you say the man fired at the officers? Where did you learn to kick like that? She began to shiver.

"Well, that's it," he said at last. "We may have some follow-up questions, so you might get a call, but for now I think we're done." He seemed pleased and nodded to his partner.

"Good," said Denise. "I'm freezing. When's it okay for me to leave?"

"As soon as Detective Scaleri says it's okay. Shouldn't be too long."

She could see Scaleri standing with a group of uniformed officers not far away.

"Well let's go ask him."

The officers went with her.

"Excuse me. Detective Scaleri?"

He looked at her with faint recognition, his mind somewhere else.

"May I go home now, please?"

The interviewing officer held up his recorder. He said, "She's Denise James. I got her statement."

8

Scaleri looked at her. "Yeah, okay," he said without much thought.

"You're good to go, Ms. James," said the interviewing officer. "That was great what you did tonight. Thanks."

"You're very welcome. And thank you." She shook his hand. "Let's not do this again any time soon, okay?"

"Yeah," he said. "Once is gotta be enough."

On course for home yet again, she walked up Union Street past the now closed restaurant where she'd dined so well earlier. At King, she made sure of her direction, not at all registering its lack of pedestrians or moving vehicles. Her thoughts were on her chances of ending up in the Channel Three dumpster preempted by the necessity of putting on the Commonwealth's Attorney. He'd have told the reporters how much dope there was, how many police officers were involved, and how the city had arranged the ambush. All the same, she imagined what it would be like to sit with Michael at breakfast and watch herself on television. Her husband of five years was hard to impress, but this would do it.

She quickened her pace. The street was deserted. When she came to the alley, she saw that the officers who'd been ordered by Scaleri to stay by the barrier tape were gone. Here was the spot where she'd sucker-punched the man. God he was big. One perfect kick she'd practiced a thousand times and he was down. She couldn't have done it better, not in a million tries.

Her eyes wandered up the alley. Light from the opposite end refracted off the buildings and invaded the shadows. Against the wall where the man almost fell, she saw a line of trash bags.

Epiphany!

The man could have switched bags!

He didn't lose his balance and right himself against the building. He could have dropped the bag he was carrying and picked up another one. Then the police came around the corner. They didn't see it.

She walked into the alley.

The ground was dirt, spotted with small stones. To the right was an open area for tenant parking. Plastic bags and trashcans were laid out against the wall.

9

She pushed the first bag with her foot. Shredded paper. She pushed the second. Paper again. The third bag lay flat, and her toe met a hard object. She laid her heel into it, and the bag scraped along the ground. With her gloves, she felt a solid surface through the plastic. Her foot told her the remaining bags were like the first two.

Drugs!

This was the bag the police thought they had when Scaleri opened the one with shredded paper.

She stepped back to think.

The best thing to do would be to leave it where it was and go get the cops. But she couldn't leave a bag of drugs outside for just anyone to pick up, could she? No way was she going to carry it all the way back to the river. Her car was a block away at most. Better to drive it back.

She felt for handles through the plastic, found them, and lifted. The bag was heavy, almost too much to carry. Heading back the way she came, it banged against her knee in an awkward rhythm against her stride, her free arm swinging.

This was going to be a pain in the ass to explain to Scaleri, she told herself. They'd keep her till dawn.

Fairfax Street was vacant when she exited the alley and headed toward Duke. Her forearm ached. Here she was in the middle of the night hauling what felt like a half-ton of illegal drugs through the semi-lit streets of Old Town when she should have been home long ago. Maybe she could avoid all the hassle, wait till morning, drop the bag at the nearest police station's front door, ring the bell and run. Not good. They might have a surveillance camera over the entry. A hospital could use some of the drugs no doubt, but they probably had quality control procedures against doing that.

At Duke, she put the bag down and walked around it. Tree trunks and low-hanging branches obscured part of her view, but no one was on the street. Some townhouses had lit exterior lights, others not. Few showed any windows lit from within. Those that did were faint. She stood a moment and raised her head to the sky. She took a deep breath and continued with her other arm.

The air around her became a vacuum as she trudged along, her world compressed into a concentration of the moment, on keeping one foot plodding ahead of the other. The pattern of bricks in the sidewalk grew hypnotic, and she raised her head to look around, to see if anyone was watching.

By the time she arrived at her Firebird, she felt she could go no further. Breathing hard, she picked her keys from her purse and pressed the remote entry. It took both arms to heave the bag over the fender into the trunk.

Damn!

She closed the lid and got behind the wheel. Despite the cold, she could feel moisture prickle the scalp under her hat. She was tired and wanted to go home. It wasn't her job to pull an all-nighter and track down the cops and give them the evidence they couldn't find.

Her hand shook inserting the key.

Muscle fatigue?

Or fear.

She started the engine and took a long look at herself in the mirror while it settled.

Decision time.

Villamay, a Residential Subdivision

She punched the garage-door remote, backed the car inside, turned off the engine, and re-closed the door. The dashboard clock read two-thirty. She popped the trunk-release, went to the back bumper, and lifted the lid.

The bag lay there like a bloated slug, scuffed and torn.

She twisted the long end of the yellow plastic tie and slid it back over its stays. She peeled back the plastic to expose a black canvas bag. It looked new. She pulled the zipper across its top.

Inside were rows and rows of hundred dollar bills.

Chapter Two

She closed the trunk, and looked over the car's roof as if putting the bag out of sight might put it out of mind. Seconds ticked as surprise passed, her hands holding steady on the lid.

There had to be a million dollars in that bag.

Her gut impulse was to pack up and make a beeline for the coal country of West-By-God-Virginia with Michael and the children. That was a terrible idea. She had to get hold of herself.

She went through the laundry room to the kitchen and flipped on the coffee maker. Her watch showed two thirty-three.

As she stared at the brown liquid dripping into the pot, the image of SWAT teams and drug gangs flashed through her mind. Her stomach lurched. They might be on their way right now if the bag had a tracer.

She took off her gloves and coat trying to imagine what could go wrong if she searched the satchel. Exploding dye?

Taking a penlight from a drawer and a pair of ski goggles from the laundry room closet, she picked up her gloves and headed for the garage. The timer bulb was out, and she used the flashlight to find her way to the trunk and open it. The bag was still there, the musty smell of currency rising to mix with that of the car's engine. This was no dream.

She held the flashlight in her mouth to put on the goggles and gloves. Lifting the bag with both hands, she placed it on the bumper, holding it there by the pressure of her knees against the rear of the car. She pulled the sides wide, stopping to gape at the bills before spreading the outer plastic across the trunk floor.

Was it counterfeit?

Pulling out a bill, she held the penlight behind it and examined the thin strip to the left of the portrait. Over and over she read USA 100 right side up and upside down. Not a teller by training, she thought it was real and slid it back in its wrapper. She riffled each bundle before tossing it onto the trunk. She marveled at the sheer numbers, each bundle bound with a tan wrapper printed $5,000 in brown or $10,000 in yellow, each bill carrying Ben Franklin's Mona Lisa smile.

The bag's weight forced an awkward bend to her knees and put pressure on her thighs and back. Her breath grew into a cloud of fog. Moisture condensed inside her goggles, and she had to tilt her head to one side to see what she was doing. At any moment she expected to be sprayed with purple dye.

At last she was done, the money a huge pile. She took off the goggles, closed the lid, and carried the bag into the laundry room where she took out its plastic bottom, turned it inside out, felt the seams, and explored the material until she was satisfied there were no foreign objects.

Back in the garage, she repacked the money, stacking it in piles inside the bag so it fit. It had a smell all its own: heavy, inky, and unclean.

In the kitchen, she poured a mug of coffee and sat. Now she had time to think.

There had to be a couple of million dollars out there. Some lawless gun-toting hardcore criminals knew they were missing big bucks, and they were going to want it back in the worst way. If she turned it in like the Good Samaritan she always thought herself to be, well that would be the good and proper thing to do. Then what? Then the money would disappear into the bureaucracy's black hole. She didn't like bureaucrats much, government bureaucrats least.

Who knew she had it?

The man who switched bags knew. As soon as he learned the money was missing, he'd guess who had it. Then the gangs would find out. Nobody in an organization like that was going to write off a bag full of hundred dollar bills without a good hard search. But what could they do? File a complaint?

The cops knew the money was missing too. That's why they were poking around in the bushes. Would they think the drug dealers got away with it when they couldn't find it?

A drug deal has two sides: the suppliers have the drugs; the buyers have the money. The idea is to exchange, but in this case, the cops had a sting set up at the right time and the right place. Somebody snitched.

The cops would have waited until the drugs and the money were swapped so they could arrest everybody in sight. If they raided before the exchange, some clever lawyer might get the buyers off. It's still not a crime to carry around a trunk full of cash if it can be explained.

If her man was the supplier, he'd have arrived with the drugs, and his side might not know how much money was in the bag, at least not to the dollar. Maybe she could keep some of it? Three or four of those bundles might not be missed.

Wrong.

They'd miss it. They didn't start this business yesterday. They'd know how much money was supposed to be there.

Even so, anyone could have picked up the bag, and she could always give it back.

Maybe she could keep it all, justify it as a reward. She could've stepped around the corner and let the man pass. Tired as he was, the cops would never have caught him after the switch. In another block, he'd have tossed the shredded paper aside, and the officers would have stopped chasing him to get it. They would never have discovered the real bag in the alley.

Well, the man she'd decked wasn't going to be back on the street any time soon. The cops would hold him without bail for those gunshots.

Anyone could have gotten the bag. A neighbor might have checked the alley after the shots. Anyone walking by could have picked it up. One of the cops left at the scene could have taken it. Maybe the garbage guys would pick it up in the morning.

Now there's a good thought.

The garbage was set out for pickup. Maybe they'd take everything in the alley, and the whole thing would resolve itself in a few hours. That's why the money was inside a garbage bag on garbage night, so if the deal blew up, the money could be hidden with that night's garbage. Her man had to know those bags would be there, so his escape route had to have been planned. Someone in the gang was supposed to go back and pick it up. She might have missed him by minutes. It was even possible that when the retrieval came up empty, the man's own gang would suspect him of a double-cross.

She smiled.

Keeping a pile of cash like this was a comforting thought. She and Michael had a mortgage, car loans, credit cards, and the children's college costs to pay. As a parent, she had a duty to provide for the family's support, and here, so to speak, was a golden opportunity. Cash like this would take the financial worry out of living.

What would Michael say?

Precise and analytical, more often than not, Michael had a different take on the same set of facts than she did. He worked with computers, designing programs for Data-Now in Springfield. Good at math, he thought in straight lines, A to B to C. He claimed she lived on emotion. It was emotion that had gotten her the Firebird, a car he'd insisted was unfit for a couple with two small children. Then trade your BMW for a van, she'd told him.

She took the stairs two at a time and turned on the bedroom light.

"Michael! Get up! I have something to show you."

Michael James stood barefoot and shivering in the garage, all patience having left him the moment he quit the warmth of the house.

"The floor's freezing, Denise. What is it?"

She lifted the trunk's lid.

His head fell forward. Brown hair fell across his forehead. Hazel eyes blinked. Whatever he'd been expecting, this wasn't it. He reached out a hand. She stopped him.

"Don't touch. Just look."

He stared.

"Is this part of your magic act?"

"No. It's real."

Her answer turned his eyes sharp. He sensed crimes unknown.

"You robbed Treasure Chest?"

"Of course not. Come inside."

He drank coffee while she told him.

"Well," he said when she was done. "Why would you bring home a bag you thought was full of drugs?"

"That's fair. I was tired of hauling it around, and didn't want to answer any more questions. I figured I'd turn it in later. At the time, I just wanted to come home." She gave him her best little girl smile. "Driving back, I wanted to taste it, to see what the cops on TV taste when they cut open a bag and put it on their tongue. I know that's silly, but I wanted to know if it was tart, or salty, or whatever. I couldn't do that if I took it back right away."

She couldn't tell how he was taking this.

"Most of all, I wanted to show off."

"That was a mistake. What if you'd had an accident, or been pulled over? How would you explain what was in your trunk?"

"I'd fall on the defense of being tired and emotional, and tell the truth. I'd gotten the drugs off the street, it was late, and I wanted to go home."

He seemed to dissect whether or not he thought that might have worked.

"No one knows you have the bag?"

"I can't see how. No one saw me take it."

"And you're the only one who saw the man switch bags?"

"That's right."

"But the man knows what he did with it. He'll guess you took it."

"True."

"There must be two million dollars out there."

"Might be."

He brushed his hair back behind his ears with both hands.

"Let's count it," he said.

Michael wore shoes, a coat, and gloves to count out stacks of fifty thousand dollars from the bundles. He lined the money in neat rows across the trunk floor, its space taking up much less room than the tossed pile she'd made.

"How much?" he asked when the bag was empty.

"Sixty-three times fifty thousand is three million one hundred fifty thousand."

He stared at the rows of cash. "It's nice to have a fortune at least once in your life," he said more to himself than to her.

She watched him repack the bag, picking up stacks six to eight inches thick with both hands and laying them on their sides like books. Good God, it was a lot of money, all hundreds.

"The bills look used," she said.

He zipped up the sides of the bag.

"Come out of the cold and tell me what happened again, sugar. In detail this time. Every fact."

They went inside.

16

She began with leaving the restaurant and ended with waking him up.

"So the money was in a garbage bag," he said. "The trash collectors might pick up everything in the alley." He tightened his lips. "They'll search the landfills, of course. It'll take time, but they'll do it."

The sight of all that money was pulling at him.

"We have two children, Michael. We both have careers that'll grow, and we're making ends meet well enough. Let's admit it to ourselves. We have little motivation to run a risk like this. People with guns will be looking for it."

He shifted in his chair. A chess player by nature, he was used to dealing with facts. Before deciding anything, he wanted to see every piece on the board, know how many squares the board had, and know the capabilities of each player. Secrets and bluff were alien to him. She was the poker player, the banker who used intangibles as well as facts to gauge a borrower's willingness to repay a loan in tough times.

"We could wait a few days," she said. "See what happens. If there's a whiff of suspicion, we turn it in. If nothing happens, we keep it. That leaves us uncommitted. Then we could waterproof the bag and bury it, wait five years until the whole thing's a distant memory. It would be our little secret, our hidden treasure."

"The drug dealers and the police are looking for it right now, sugar. Where do we hide it? The house is no good, and you can't ride around with it in your trunk."

"You'd consider keeping it?"

"In theory. You're the magician in the family. Come up with a foolproof hiding place. Maybe a storage locker in a bus station?"

"Storage lockers have master keys and get inspected more than you think. We can't mail it anywhere without the risk of it being opened."

"Why don't we just bury it like you said?"

"Because we have to be able to get it fast to turn it in." This would take careful thought. "The best place to hide anything is in plain sight."

He considered the question without offering a suggestion.

"Not having a dire need for money throws suspicion from us," she said. "But I'll be questioned again."

17

"Can you handle it?"

"You mean lie to the police?" She looked at him. "I'm not sure."

He ran his index finger from his eyebrows down the length of his nose and off its tip, a telltale she thought meant indecision.

She said, "I'll keep it in the trunk until we come up with something better."

He offered no reaction.

"This is a big opportunity and a big decision, Michael. If we turn it in right away, what will we think of ourselves down the road? A chance to make a fortune comes our way and we bail out in a few hours?"

He gave her a weak nod.

"Think about it this way," she said. "If every person in the world could be in our position right now, a lot of them could figure out a way to keep it. All we have to do is figure out how any one of them would do it."

"Well I guess a day might not hurt," he said without much enthusiasm. "Just to watch the news and see what happens. We can decide as we go along."

"If either of us wants to turn it in, it's over. We do it. If I tell you to take the money to an orphanage, you have to get it and turn it in, and vice-versa. Mutual veto power. We can't tell anybody, parents and friends included. And we can't spend any of it. Not until we both agree."

He nodded.

Affirmation from Michael, however reluctant, gave her reassurance. They weren't leaping ahead with their eyes closed; they were feeling their way forward with their toes. She hadn't been sure how he would react, and now he was calling her "sugar" for the first time in, well, she couldn't remember the last time.

Chapter Three

Dressed for work, Denise and Michael were feeding Tommy and Sydney at the kitchen table when the Channel Three news broadcast began.

"Good morning everyone, I'm Brad Casey. Today is Wednesday, the seventeenth of January, and these are the top news stories.

"City of Alexandria police last night intercepted a drugs-for-money exchange on the Old Town waterfront. According to Commonwealth's Attorney Roody Packwurst, Alexandria police arrested five suspects and confiscated approximately fifty-five pounds of illegal drugs near midnight in an ambush at Waterfront Park. Seventy officers participated in the raid, the largest on record, and a local woman is credited with apprehending one of the suspects. Dan Mattison has the exclusive."

"Thank you, Brad," said Mattison standing in the dark in his trench coat. "Alexandria police have confirmed seizing illegal drugs they value at seven million dollars here at Waterfront Park. Five suspects were taken into custody during the raid, and police continue to search the neighborhood for others still at large. Seventy officers, including SWAT team personnel, participated according to Commonwealth's Attorney Roody Packwurst. And, in a Channel Three exclusive, a local woman is credited with assisting in the arrest of one of those apprehended. I spoke with two officers earlier this morning who witnessed the encounter."

Standing side-by-side, Robert Armstrong dwarfed Stephen Johnson, their names captioned at the bottom of the screen.

"The suspect ran from the park down this alley," said Armstrong turning and pointing behind him. The picture telescoped over Johnson's head to eliminate light from the far street lamp and increase contrast in the shadows.

"My partner and I were in foot pursuit," Armstrong continued. "The suspect shot at us, and we took cover. When he got here, where we're standing, a woman took him down."

The picture pulled back to the officers.

"I've never seen anything like it," said Johnson, his voice excited. "She kicked him right in the stomach!"

"The suspect had fired shots," said Armstrong. "He could have shot her."

Back to a close-up of Mattison.

"Who is this woman, and what did she do? Her name is Denise James of Alexandria, and I spoke with her last night just after the incident."

And there she was, her name at the bottom of the screen. Cold air painted roses in her cheeks, and her dark hat and coat lent contrast to the whiteness of her skin. Mascara made her eye color hard to see, but overall, she was pleased with her first appearance on television.

"Would you please tell us what happened and what you did just a few minutes ago, Denise James of Alexandria?"

"I'd left a business dinner and was walking to my car to go home. I saw a man running toward me down an alley, and two policemen came around the corner and shouted for him to stop. The man shot at them. The officers took cover, and the man ran at me. I kicked him in the stomach, and he went down, and the police officers ran up the alley—"

An editing cut eliminated the arrival of the police censor. Mattison ended by saying, "That is a remarkable story, Denise James. Thank you very much."

Mattison was back live-feed.

"Police are withholding the names of all suspects now in custody. As more information is released, we'll keep you informed. Back to you, Brad."

"Thank you, Dan," said Casey. "Commonwealth's Attorney Roody Packwurst was present at the waterfront supervising what appears to have been a well-planned operation. He is expected to make a formal announcement concerning the raid later this morning. Channel Three will provide highlights at noon."

The picture changed to a burning building.

"A fire occurred near Bailey's Crossroads last—"

Michael muted the set. He started to say something when the telephone rang. He picked it up.

"Hello?"

Listening, he turned to Denise.

"You saw it?"

Tommy demanded a slice of jellied toast.

"That's true," said Michael. "Here, let me let you talk to her."

He covered the receiver.

"It's Gus Gordon. Sees all, hears all. I don't know when he sleeps."

She took the telephone.

"Hi, neighbor. You're the first person to call."

"I was just watching the news," his eighty-year-old voice said. "That gunman could have killed you."

"Ah, but he didn't now, did he? The sight of a woman must not have seemed threatening."

As she watched Michael pour coffee, she detected what might have been a hint of jealousy crossing his face. He wasn't used to playing second string.

Gordon said, "He's got to be mad as hell at you."

"No doubt about that. You should've seen the look he gave me while they were reading him his rights."

"That's a crazy thing to do at your age, young lady. You're just a kid."

"Twenty-six and full of fire, Gus. But listen, we have to get the children ready. Give my regards to Rosemary, would you?"

"Be careful, Denise. Hate to lose you."

"We'd hate to lose you too, Gus. Thanks for the call. I'll be careful. Talk to you later."

"Okay. Bye."

"Bye."

The telephone continued to ring. They let the recorder pick up the calls while Denise got the children dressed and Michael watched the news. When she came downstairs, he reported she'd been mentioned by name on Channels Five and Nine.

"And?"

"So far, so good. You're a super-star, sugar. May I touch you?"

"Anywhere you like, big boy."

He gave her a kiss. "I think you deserve a reward."

"A certificate of appreciation from the city would be nice."

He bent to her ear.

"I meant something that fits into the trunk of a car."

"I know what you meant," she whispered, and kissed him.

21

They locked the house and loaded the children into Denise's car. Michael drove to Data-Now. Denise dropped the children at childcare, and then drove herself and the moneybag into a world about to make her its darling of the moment.

Northern Virginia

Nick "The Knife" Rivera was bullshit. His drug buy in Alexandria had been intercepted, his money was gone, he didn't have the dope for his distributors, three of his men were in custody, and the cut-house was too hot to use. More important, the loss of cash and profit would delay the purchase of a parking garage for which he was committed at the end of the month.

Rivera owned two legitimate businesses, a janitorial cleaning service and a chain of dry cleaning outlets. What he wanted was another cash enterprise to launder money, hence the parking garage.

The raid was a financial setback, nothing more. He'd negotiate a delay in the closing date for the garage and figure out what happened. There was an informant, had to be, and his gut told him his counterpart in Baltimore might be responsible. Honor among thieves was not what it once was, and probably never had been what it was cracked up to be, so he suspected his supplier up the line might be trying to take over territory at his expense.

The car couldn't be traced. Those arrested couldn't implicate him because their knowledge was compartmentalized into that portion of the business for which they were responsible: pick-up, cutting, and delivery. Even if filled with truth serum they couldn't name names they didn't know, especially his. The procedure was cumbersome and expensive, but safe.

Rivera calculated it would take five or six runs to make up the cash he'd lost, and that assumed Murphy hadn't been busted. If he had, a new source would have to be found that could maintain the price and quality to which his customers had become accustomed. That would take time.

Six runs to Baltimore to break even, and he couldn't attempt another until the snitch was exposed. He'd ask around on his end, and meet Murphy in a day or two after things settled. The snitch was out there somewhere. Perhaps Johnny Murphy himself.

Baltimore, Maryland

Johnny Murphy operated four legitimate restaurants as well as a wholesale drug distributorship south from Baltimore. Cocaine and heroin came pure from overseas into the port. Pills came from Pennsylvania. Synthetics and designer drugs were manufactured on Maryland's Eastern Shore.

More experienced and higher up the distribution chain than Nick "The Knife" Rivera, Murphy felt insulated from being stabbed in the back by one of his own men. He'd known them too long. Rivera, and people at his level, made sales at retail and had to collect when a buyer couldn't, or wouldn't, pay. Sometimes that took muscle. Knowing what would happen to them, users sometimes got desperate before they got hurt, so Murphy guessed the informant had to be on Rivera's end. Still, he would run down a list of those who knew the details of the sale. No doubt Rivera would do the same, and they'd meet face to face in a few days.

The J. Edgar Hoover Building

Special Agent in Charge Eric Peabody Kludge stood in front of a picture-screen in a briefing room, his eyes scanning everyone as they quieted. At six-three, he carried a hundred and sixty pounds on a rail-thin frame. A sixteen-year veteran, and a lawyer, he'd been posted at FBI Headquarters for four and a half years, charged with implementing cross-state drug interdictions.

"For the benefit of those not up to date with 'Operation Flytrap,' I'll provide a summary."

Lights dimmed, and a slide projector threw up side-by-side full-face and profile photographs of a well-groomed white male twenty-five to thirty years of age.

"Four weeks ago, the Bureau wrapped up a gambling ring in Oakton, mostly football and basketball for high rollers. Seven were arrested, Jason McCullough here being one. He's a high school graduate, two years college. He's married and has four children. He manages an electronics store.

"Wanting more, he got greedy, and he got caught. He had a lot to lose, and he offered a deal if we went soft. We agreed to listen. He said he'd put us onto a regular drug run from Baltimore to Alexandria, one of the big ones.

"We already know distribution at this level is done through vertically integrated chains in large dollar amounts. The structure is compartmentalized, so it's hard to identify the players in the upper levels. A single run could involve a couple of million dollars. State lines would be crossed.

"The benefits to the Bureau were numerous. We could work our way up and down a regional artery from both ends. Charges against all involved would be based on the value of the collateral seized, and this would be an all-Bureau operation. No one at DEA, or Treasury, or ATF would know about it until it happened.

"McCullough was called for the sale, and he called us. His team went to Baltimore and picked up the package. McCullough planted a tracer in the bag, a mandatory condition per his agreement. Then they drove to Old Town, same car, same people, same everything. We had agents on site and mobile units prepared to follow."

A street map transparency replaced McCullough's picture.

"Here was the situation at eleven-forty last night. The money was on the ground between two decoy bags in front of three men representing the suppliers. The buyers were examining the drugs. There were nine individuals altogether.

"At this point, Alexandria police blockaded the automobiles, and their SWAT teams moved in. They did a fair job of it, even by our standards. When they crashed the party, the suppliers picked up the bags and ran, attempting to play hide-the-ball with the money."

Kludge was pleased to see no smiles.

"The police seized the money, the drugs, two automobiles, and five of nine possible suspects."

"How much money?" asked Special Agent Marv Iacob.

"We estimate two and a half million, but we haven't talked to them, yet."

Kludge looked back at the screen.

24

"The bottom line is that Alexandria knew enough to be at this site with enough manpower to effectuate a seizure of the majority of the collateral. The squealer has to be our informant, Jason McCullough."

Heads around the table nodded.

"Much as we'd like to have McCullough right now, he's being held by the Alexandria police. The Bureau intends to contact the city, obtain access to McCullough, and exercise forfeiture."

"They're going to try to keep the money," said Special Agent Jack Olsen.

"Not after I get through with them," said Kludge. "This was our case. We have precedence. They interfered, without knowledge perhaps, but all the same, they interfered.

"No blame for last night's failure can be attributed to the Bureau. We did everything according to procedure. If Alexandria hadn't jumped the gun, we would have been on our way to rolling up a major artery on both ends. If I hear Roody Packwurst say anything negative about this—"

He let the agents' imaginations complete the thought.

"Any questions?"

"What about McCullough's immunity agreement?" asked Olsen.

"Bad faith on his part," said Kludge. "He'll get sixty months minimum."

Office of the Commonwealth's Attorney

Roody Packwurst held out his arms as if hoping they'd be filled.

"It was right in our hands, Joan. We got the dope and the dealers, but where's the fucking money?"

Chief of Police Joan C. Harris and two captains stood at attention in front of Packwurst's desk.

"Roody," said Harris. "As far as we know, we've accounted for all three bags. We've halted today's trash pickups and organized a wider neighborhood search. This is going on as we speak."

"I gotta get the goddamn money to wrap up the case, Joan. I want forfeiture. I've called a press conference. I want to say I have the money."

Packwurst leaned his chest against the edge of his leather-topped desk.

Harris said, "No one was injured, Roody. By all measure it was a successful open street ambush."

"It's only successful if we find the fucking money!"

"We're looking." Her exasperation showed. "We got the important part. The drugs are off the street."

"How much are they worth?"

"Somewhere between six and seven million."

"Stick with seven."

"Sir?" interrupted a voice over the intercom. "FBI Special Agent Eric Kludge for you."

"Tell him I'll call him back"

"He says it's about last night."

Harris and the captains watched Packwurst pick up the telephone.

"Roody Packwurst."

"Eric Kludge, here."

"Morning, Eric. What can I do for you?"

"With regard to the drug seizure conducted by the Alexandria Police Department last evening, are you aware you interfered in an ongoing FBI operation?"

Packwurst sat back in his chair.

"How is the Bureau involved?"

"Have you examined the drugs?"

"They've been inventoried. They're in lock-up."

"Our tracer's in the bag, taped inside the zipper."

Packwurst was silent.

"I can provide you with its serial number," added Kludge.

"A tracer?"

"Look, Roody. I want to work with you on this. Let's put a good spin on it before the media gets wind of our involvement."

Packwurst was thinking fast.

"Of course we'll work with you, Eric. We apprehended five people. How many of them are yours?"

Kludge believed elected law enforcement officials deficient in basic investigative technique, their prime concern being reelection. Packwurst was validating his theory.

"None of them. Our operation was set up by an informant."

Shit, thought Packwurst. He had an informant, too.

Kludge probed. "You acquired all the collateral?"

"We have the drugs and the cars. We're still looking for the money."

Kludge flattened his voice.

"You don't have the money?"

"Nobody had it. All we have are decoy bags."

Alexandria's raid hadn't been so successful after all, thought Kludge. Forfeiture couldn't occur until the money was found. Still, he wanted to know what Alexandria knew.

"Nothing on this has been released to the media has it?"

"Nothing about the money. I have a press conference coming up. I don't want a treasure hunt on my hands."

"Keep it that way," said Kludge. "We'll give you the standard seventy-two hours to continue with your investigation. We'll be available for consultation if you request it. If you haven't made progress by that time, we may consider taking over the case. In any event, we'll need to meet, go over the details. You show us what you have, and we show you what we have."

"Okay."

"I suggest you keep our involvement low key for now. At the appropriate time we'll say this was an FBI-Alexandria operation under the Joint Inter-Governmental Agency Drug Interdiction Agreement, JIGADIA, I believe it's called. Don't tell them you haven't found the money."

"Of course not."

"And here's another idea that might do you some good. We understand a woman disabled one of the suspects. Her name is Denise Elizabeth Lang James of Alexandria. We did a check on her. She's clean. The best way to handle your press conference may be to say as little as possible about the investigation itself and build up the woman. Let the press feed on her."

Packwurst already knew the woman was clean. She'd been checked out at the scene while she was waiting.

"Sounds okay," said Packwurst. "I have to get ready for the press, Eric."

"Let's plan to meet here Saturday afternoon."

Why did it always have to be at their place, thought Packwurst. And on a weekend no less?

"Talk about the woman, Roody. We'll work out our understanding when we meet."

Kludge hung up.

Packwurst put the receiver down and looked up at the uniformed officers.

"Our raid upset one of their operations," he said. "They want to see us on Saturday. Find the money before then so we won't have to go."

"Yes, sir," said Harris.

Channel Three ran its Dan Mattison interview with Denise James every half-hour. Five other channels broadcast Packwurst's interview standing on the curb the night before during which he'd named her. Just after nine o'clock, Channel Three released its tape to the majors. By ten, CNN ran excerpts in its headlines.

Chapter Four

Saturday, January 20
The Hoover Building

Special Agent in Charge Eric Kludge had Special Agents Jack Olsen and Marv Iacob, two administrative aides, and a stenographer with him before he entered the conference room where Commonwealth's Attorney Roody Packwurst, Chief of Police Joan Harris, two captains, and two aides were waiting. After introductions and handshakes, the FBI sat on one side of the table, Alexandria the other.

"Thank you very much for taking the time to join us here today." Kludge's delivery was formal, unemotional. "I know how important a Saturday afternoon is, and I appreciate your indulgence."

Heads across the table nodded.

"What do you have?"

Packwurst leaned forward. He said, "I'll let Chief Harris bring you up to date."

Harris wore a fresh-pressed uniform with full citations. Her features were gothic, ebony eyes, heavy liner, white skin, and black hair pulled into a bun at the nape of her neck. In her late forties, she'd earned respect as a no-nonsense chief who went by the book and protected her turf.

She opened a file, and handed out a dozen plans of the Alexandria waterfront. When everyone had a copy, she began.

"We've interrogated all suspects, interviewed the officers involved, reconstructed the scene of the raid, and searched the red-lined area of the map I just gave you. We've concluded there were four members of the drug supply team from Baltimore and five members of the drug buying team from Northern Virginia. We arrested three suppliers and two buyers, five of nine. According to our informant, Jason McCullough, the buyers were supposed to bring three million one hundred fifty thousand dollars in hundred dollar bills. The money was in a canvas carryall inside a trash bag. It would weigh approximately seventy pounds. When we closed in, the bag was on the ground beside two decoy bags in front of the suppliers. We

29

have fifty-five pounds of drugs and value them at approximately seven million dollars."

"From the list you faxed," said Kludge, "it's closer to five."

Harris let that pass.

"Each of three men on the suppliers' side picked up a bag and ran. There was considerable confusion. It was dark, there is extensive tree cover, distance had to be crossed to reach the suspects, and the suspects themselves scattered."

She referred to her notes.

"All three bags believed to have been beside the suppliers' car were located. All contained shredded paper. One McCullough had, one was abandoned on the north end of Waterfront Park, and the third was taken into evidence on Fairfax Street from the man the woman disabled. Those arrested have been segregated, Mirandized, and questioned. Only McCullough has talked. His bag was a decoy."

Kludge began writing.

"The seized automobiles are registered to corporations, both of which reported stolen vehicles the next morning. Our neighborhood search located twelve other bags containing shredded paper. All these bags have been tagged and taken into evidence.

"All captured suspects have been identified by fingerprints. They were armed and have priors. We've issued a warrant for Clayton Stevens, the supplier who escaped. McCullough gave us his name. The two buyers have said nothing so far."

She closed her file.

"And that's where we are."

"Well," said Kludge. "It's a one hundred percent success except you're missing four suspects, three of whom remain unknown, you have no leads up or down the distribution chain to Baltimore or Alexandria, and you're missing three million one hundred fifty thousand dollars that could be used to purchase more drugs."

"The investigation is not yet complete," said Packwurst in defense. "If the suspects are in the area, we'll find them."

Kludge changed his tone.

"Your intentions are admirable, Roody. Alexandria has done an outstanding job on this. You've carried the ball a long way."

Personal concessions complete, he turned to his agenda.

"The Bureau proposes a symbiotic relationship from this point forward using the best capabilities of both the local police and the resources of the United States government. I'm sure we can agree our facilities are larger and have more capabilities than yours. You, on the other hand, have a better chance of locating and apprehending fugitives within your jurisdiction.

"I propose maximizing our combined abilities and obtaining optimal results. Up to now, the Bureau has stayed out of your investigation to give you a free hand, as per the rules. Now it's time to join forces, pool knowledge, and clear the case."

Kludge looked to the elected politician for confirmation.

"Of course," said Packwurst.

"The Bureau will allow you to make all arrests and prosecute suspects within your jurisdiction. If the fugitives have fled your jurisdiction, the Bureau will apprehend them and prosecute them under federal law. Be mindful that the Bureau's press releases and public information will mention the Commonwealth's Attorney and the City of Alexandria in the most complimentary of terms."

Packwurst looked at Harris and smiled. He said, "That's acceptable. How can we help you, Eric?"

"First, prepare all physical evidence in your possession for pickup Monday at noon. This includes all photographs, crime scene evidence, copies of arrest reports, files on those arrested, fingerprints, internal reports, witness reports, everything involving the case.

"Second, have the five suspects transferred into our custody."

Before Harris could protest, Kludge said, "You arrested them for crimes committed within your jurisdiction, and the Bureau respects that. We agree to return them into your custody for prosecution within, say, three weeks."

That quieted Harris.

"Third, the same with the drugs you seized. We'd like our lab to examine them. Their origin may provide leads to the supply route into Baltimore or the location of their manufacture.

"Fourth, we want Jason McCullough under a special arrangement. He has an immunity agreement with you that we will respect. However, he may have violated federal law.

"Fifth, we want the automobiles you impounded.

"Sixth, we want the names, addresses, and social security numbers of all police officers at the waterfront site, and all officers and personnel used in supporting roles during the night of January—"

"You *don't* suspect our people of taking the money?" snapped Harris.

Kludge looked at her without expression. He turned to Packwurst.

"This is standard investigative procedure, Roody. It's nothing personal."

"We can do that."

Harris glared across the table at Kludge.

"Seventh, you should provide the names, addresses, and telephone numbers of all businesses and residents within the designated red-lined area of your map."

"That's a big job," said Harris.

Kludge ignored her.

"And eighth, you are to continue to keep our involvement in this investigation low key for the time being. That's it."

"Fine," said Packwurst. "We can do that."

Harris asked, "What information do you have for us?"

"Nothing at this time."

"Nothing?" said Harris. "You have no information at all? We're working under the outlines of the JIGADIA agreement and the symbiotic relationship you just talked about, aren't we?"

Packwurst put a hand on Harris's arm.

Kludge said, "We have not yet engaged ourselves in the case."

Harris didn't believe that. With visible control she looked at Packwurst and said, "We can have the drugs, cars, evidence, and suspects ready. Copying the files and getting the names and addresses will take more time." She looked at Kludge. "I'm sure the Commonwealth's Attorney can arrange for delivery when the documents are complete."

"That's acceptable." Kludge looked at his men. "Have I neglected anything?"

Special Agent Iacob looked at the eight checked items on his notepad and said, "No, sir."

"Thank you very much for coming," said Kludge. He stood in dismissal, a Grim Reaper smile on his lips. "We look forward to working with you."

After the Alexandria team departed, Kludge told the agents, "We can still pick up both ends of the distribution chain if we go all out on this when we get their evidence. Flytrap may not have worked the way we planned, but we can salvage it. And I want McCullough. He crossed state lines to betray us. He's ours."

In one of two automobiles driven by Alexandria aides, Roody Packwurst and Joan Harris sat in silence as if suspicious the FBI might overhear anything said within the confines of the District of Columbia. After they crossed the George Mason Bridge, Harris said, "Roody, we've given them everything we have. They aren't giving us anything."

Packwurst gazed out the window, his expression blank. He said, "If the FBI can arrest the at-large suspects, get the money, and roll up both sides of the operation, so much the better. We'll get credit for it. We ran the raid."

"I hate giving up suspects and evidence with nothing in return."

He looked at her, his eyes questioning. "It's the politic thing to do, Joan. Besides, can you carry the investigation any further than where it is right now?"

She sighed. "Not without a break. The well's gone dry."

"Then let those high-and-mighties have a crack at it."

"You know they're going to forfeit the money to their side if they find it. They won't share that any more than they share information."

"We'll get part of it," said Packwurst. "At least enough to cover the cost of the raid."

She looked ahead.

"I doubt it," she said.

Sunday, January 21

The City of Alexandria released the names and mug shots of the five captured suspects in time for broadcast on the local evening news. All those arrested were reported in solitary confinement at the Alexandria Jail, apparently abandoned by the beneficiaries of their chosen profession. The man who'd polished the top of Denise James's shoe was identified as Victor Barracks: six feet two, two hundred and twenty-five pounds. Viewers were given a tip-line number if they had any information regarding the four suspects still at large.

Villamay

The telephone rang.
"Hello?"
"Is this Michael Sidney James?"
Pinpricks ran down his neck.
"I'm suspicious of anyone using my full name. It reminds me of John Wilkes Booth or Lee Harvey Oswald. Who is this?"
"Mark Logan, United States Secret Service."
"Secret Service?"
"Mr. James." The voice was monotonic. "Am I catching you at a bad time?"
"No. Not really."
"Good. If it's convenient for you, my associate and I would like to meet with you and your wife, Denise James. Is she there with you now?"
"Yes."
"We can be there in a few minutes."
"May I ask what this is about?"
"We have a proposal for you and Ms. James. It's one I think you'll like. We can discuss it when we meet. Say in about fifteen minutes?"
"All right. We'll be here."
"Thank you very much, Mr. James. You won't be disappointed."

Michael found Denise putting sheets on the crib mattress.
"That was the United States Secret Service. At least that's who he said he was. Two agents are on their way over here right now. He said we'd like what they have to say."
She fluffed Sydney's pillow and laid it on top of the blanket. For the moment she couldn't imagine a connection between the Secret Service and the moneybag. Might be a practical joke.

She said, "My father says to be on your toes any time you hear the words, 'Hello, there. I'm from the government and I'm here to help you.' We'd better hide the silver."

Michael answered the door holding Sydney. Denise and Tommy stood beside him. Two men in gray suits looked at them from outside, both in their mid-thirties, thin, and fit. One face held a faint smile.

"Mr. and Ms. James?"

"Yes," answered Michael.

"I'm Mark Logan, United States Secret Service." Both held out ID's. "This is my associate, Keith Potter. May we come in, please?"

"Sure." Michael opened the door and pointed the way to the living room.

Logan showed even white teeth as he entered. With a receding hairline, alert blue eyes, and ears that lay flat against close-cropped hair, he had the clean look of an accountant, neat and organized.

Potter had round puffy lips, a silicone implant gone awry. He looked dour, as if wishing he were somewhere else. It was in his eyes, a vacant, disinterested indifference to his surroundings.

When they were seated, Logan began.

"Thank you very much for seeing us on such short notice."

Denise smiled.

"And you have two lovely children."

"Thank you," she said.

Cards were handed over. One read: MARK A. LOGAN - AGENT - PUBLIC RELATIONS. The White House was the address with a 202-telephone number. The other read: KEITH W. POTTER - AGENT. Both were embossed with the seal of the United States Secret Service.

"Michael and I have cards too," said Denise. "But we suppose you already know who we are."

Logan smiled. Potter remained unreadable.

"I'll come to the point so as not to take up your time," said Logan. "The President of the United States needs your help."

Tommy and Sydney quieted in the conversational gap that followed.

"How?" asked Denise.

35

Logan generated another smile, pleased at her reaction. He sat upright and put his hands on his knees.

"The President of the United States would like you to be his guests in the Visitors Gallery of the House of Representatives this Thursday evening for his State of the Union Address."

This statement brought a silence long enough for the children to look at their parents as if something might be wrong. Denise thought a practical joke was unfolding, a good one. Her division head was famous for this sort of sophisticated string along, and she took a long look at the purported agents.

Tommy waved an arm at Logan. "Who are they, Mommy?" he asked.

"They're our friends from the government, honey. They're here to help us."

"Go on," said Michael.

Logan looked square at Denise.

"Due to your assistance in the capture of a suspected drug dealer fleeing a police raid, the President would be pleased if you would show him the courtesy of allowing him to present you to the nation as an example of pro-active citizenry. If everyone were as self-aware and responsive as you, homeland security would be much improved."

He withdrew a videocassette from his pocket.

"This address, as always, is televised. You'll be seated with the First Lady and other dignitaries in the House Visitors Gallery. Basically, the President will describe what you did and introduce you. You stand and wave. This video contains excerpts from the last six presentations to show you what it's like." He held out the tape.

"You've prepared this very well," said Denise. She took the cassette.

"You'll get to meet the President and the First Lady, you'll have official photographs taken, and there will be gifts to memorialize the occasion. Does this sound like something of interest to you?"

Denise said, "If you could excuse me a moment, I'd like to call the number on your card and verify you are who you say you are."

"That's fine," said Logan. "Please feel free to do so, Ms. James."

She got up and went to the kitchen, leaving Michael and the children with the agents. Logan asked how old the children were, what their names were, and what they liked to do. Michael answered in monosyllables. He was trying to hear what Denise was saying.

When she returned, she carried a tray of soft drinks.

"They're legit, Michael."

She placed the tray on the coffee table in front of the agents.

"They are?"

He looked at them with new respect.

"The man described them to me. And the number on the card matches the one in the phone book."

Logan thanked her for the refreshments, though neither agent drank.

"There are some things we need to go over concerning this invitation," said Logan. "First, the Service has conducted, and is continuing to conduct, a background check on you and your family."

Tommy tried to look at his shoulder blades.

Denise said, "Not that kind of back, honey."

"Please understand, the President wishes to avoid being embarrassed by introducing you as a hero if it turns out you are something else. So far, everything appears to check out. But if anything does come up, the President reserves the right to cancel your appearance under any pretext, or for no pretext at all."

"Of course," said Denise.

She looked at Potter sitting knees wide apart, hands on the chair's armrests, his face expressionless.

"Second, while your appearance is not top secret, we don't want it broadcast you're going to attend. We want your first public exposure to be when you're seen sitting in the gallery. So, please keep this to yourselves."

"We can do that," said Michael.

"Third, this is a respectful and solemn occasion, a part of one of the most important speeches of this administration. We need assurances from both of you that you will treat this occasion with the seriousness and dignity it deserves. This means you will not criticize or make negative statements concerning the speech, the Congress, the Judiciary, the Cabinet, or the Executive."

They said they understood.

"Now, think about this very carefully. Do either of you know of anything, anything at all, that, if it became public, could be cause for, or that you think might be cause for, concern by the White House or the President?"

The Jameses looked at each other.

"I don't think so," said Michael.

"Do speeding tickets count?" asked Denise.

"Yours are okay," said Logan.

Denise said, "The James family Michael comes from isn't related to Jessie James."

"We know," said Potter. He sounded disappointed.

Michael looked at him and realized the depth to which they'd already been investigated. He said, "Yes, I suppose you would."

Potter held his gaze.

Denise said, "Of course we'll agree, Mr. Logan, Mr. Potter. We'd be delighted to attend."

"Are there any questions either of you have at this time?" asked Logan.

"Do we bring the children?" she asked.

"Yes. We encourage it. You have a beautiful family."

"Thank you."

"Then it's settled." Logan stood. "Thank you both very much. The Office of Protocol will contact you with details about the time and place, and answer any further questions you may have."

Monday, January 22
Tysons Corner, Virginia

Nick "The Knife" Rivera and Johnny Murphy met in the food gallery at the Tysons II Mall as the lunchtime crowd dwindled. Rivera's bodyguard and Murphy's man went through the concession lines while the two bosses talked at a table for four.

"My sources for merchandise remain firm," said Murphy. "The price won't change."

"Good," said Rivera.

Johnny Murphy was shiny bald on top, a fringe of gray around his ears. Ruddy complexioned and stout, he looked like a middle-aged barkeep in one of his restaurants.

"What have you found out?" he asked.

The bust had been in Rivera's territory so Rivera was responsible for local intelligence.

"They didn't get my package."

Nick Rivera was Guatemalan, second generation, a little accent. Dark and wiry, a bushy moustache and acne-scarred cheeks were his outstanding features apart from gold jewelry.

"I didn't think they got it," said Murphy. "They've been too quiet."

Rivera's eyes challenged Johnny Murphy, prime suspect in the loss of his money.

"Where is it?"

Murphy threw him a blank expression.

"I don't know. I'm in the dark as much as you."

Rivera wasn't sure he believed that. Murphy's men had the money when the raid started, and if they'd gotten away with it, Rivera wanted half, share-and-share-alike.

"Holding out ain't gonna work."

"No one's holding out, Nick."

Rivera drew his coat aside and exposed the hilt of a sixteen-inch knife inside a leather sheath.

"Then where the fuck is it?"

"Don't threaten me, Rivera. I'll cut you off."

Rivera leaned across the table, neck chains swaying.

"Who got it?"

"I think the snitch has it," said Murphy.

"Who the snitch?"

"I assume it's someone on your side. It was in your territory, with cops on your payroll, and you trade in retail. You have a lot of customers and a lot of potential enemies. I have one customer. You."

"The snitch is on your side."

"Why would you say that?"

"Because I make my men reliable." He patted the hilt of his knife.

"Through threats? No one is reliable, Nick."

"None of my men talk. All yours have."

"My men don't know anything."

They sat taking the measure of each other across the table.

"You want to wait," said Rivera. "Hope the rat show he-self. See someone spend too much money. I got property to buy!"

39

"It's business, Nick. I have to absorb the loss just like you. If you need money, go to a bank and get a loan like everybody else."

"Whoever got the money, whoever squeal, is personal."

"Do you have any suggestions?"

"I suggest nobody cross Nick Rivera."

Rivera's bodyguard and Murphy's man arrived with food.

"That's not very helpful," said Murphy.

They ate in silence and left minutes later.

The cover of *Time Magazine* displayed an artist's rendering of Denise James doing Bruce Lee on Victor Barracks. *Newsweek's* cover carried her full-face portrait superimposed on an urban night scene. Multi-page spreads in both detailed the story with pictures of the alley, the stained car, the Alexandria waterfront, and Denise sitting at ease in her Treasure Chest office. A former aircraft carrier pilot, now a reporter, christened her NAFOD: No Apparent Fear of Death. Women's groups voiced support for women in combat.

Editorials discussed citizen participation in law enforcement and drew contrasts between defensive reaction and vigilantism. Denise's involvement was judged reactive and well handled. A banker and a woman, she'd been in the wrong place at the wrong time and had done the daring, though not recommended thing. The consensus was the country could stand to have more like her. Victor Barracks rated a mug shot.

Wednesday, January 24
The Hoover Building

As was his habit, Special Agent in Charge Eric Peabody Kludge entered the conference room when he was informed all attendees were waiting.

"You say you've got something?"

"We do," said Special Agent Olsen.

Everyone present was connected in some way with the Flytrap task force. Special Agents Jack Olsen and Marv Iacob coordinated field investigation. Assistant United States Attorney Paul Fleming provided legal assistance. The remaining team members were lab technicians, analysts, and administrative assistants, all of whom had had access to the City of Alexandria's evidence for forty-eight hours.

Kludge sat. A television/VCR unit was on. Olsen pressed the remote. The picture was a view of an alley taken in full daylight.

"This police video was taken where Barracks was apprehended by the woman." Olsen freeze framed the picture. "Barracks was chased down this alley running toward the camera's position." He pressed the remote and the picture zoomed tighter toward the street beyond. When the image stopped expanding, Olsen freeze-framed it.

"This was taken on the morning of January seventeenth, as per the counters at the bottom of the picture, and is official City of Alexandria evidence. You can see Lee Street at the far end. Notice the yellow police ribbon partway down the alley surrounding this area on the right." Olsen outlined the ribbon with a pointer. "Against the wall are trash cans and garbage bags."

Everyone focused on the area inside the tape.

"There are five bags and five cans." He pointed them out, and stood back from the screen. "Does everyone see them?"

Everyone did.

Olsen removed the tape and inserted another.

"This was taken by Channel Three after Barracks was captured. It's a recording made by Accumulation from the actual broadcast aired during the morning news on Wednesday, January seventeenth, taken maybe thirty minutes after the event itself."

Officers Armstrong and Johnson appeared, light shining from a lamppost on Lee Street behind them. As the picture tightened down the lane over Johnson's head, the light at the far end went up and out of the frame, enhancing the small amount of illumination from the camera's light, and casting a dim glow onto the objects in the alley. At maximum zoom, Olsen stopped the tape.

"This picture shows the same area of the alley as the first tape. The images are indistinct around the bags. You can see partial outlines, here and here."

Those around the table leaned forward and squinted.

"This video has been analyzed by our lab, and they have completed an enhancement of this segment. Conrad Peterson will provide you with details."

41

A tall thin man stood up, all bones, angles, and Adams apple. Among other things, Conrad Peterson was the pixel expert for the FBI lab.

Unhurried, he opened a file and distributed copies of a photograph. He then removed a poster board that had been facing the wall behind the television. It was a blowup of the image he'd distributed.

"I know your time is valuable," said Peterson. "I'll be brief."

He turned to the blowup on which could be seen one side of the alley, the building, and the row of trash bags and garbage cans.

"This is an enhancement of the night video you have on the screen. I won't bore you with the details, but each pixel of this picture has been digitally enhanced to bring out its contrast. The frame I'm holding, and what I handed out, is what the video would look like if there had been more light."

Everyone could see that the video and the distributed picture were of the same scene, the picture displaying a green, night-vision look.

"As you can count, there are six trash bags in this area."

A murmur of consent arose.

"Note the positioning of the bags, five upright, one on its side. Now, look again at the first video."

The daylight tape was re-shown and freeze-framed. Behind the police tape were five bags, all upright.

"The enhancement of the Channel Three tape, every frame of it, will match this picture and delineate six bags in the alley."

Olsen said, "We believe it's probable the sixth bag is the moneybag, and that it disappeared between the time Channel Three took this video just after the incident, and the time the Alexandria police took their video the next morning."

Kludge made a temple of his fingertips at his mouth.

"Assume this is the moneybag," said Olsen. "Barracks runs into the alley with it and swaps it for a decoy. If that happened, the paper inside Barracks's impounded bag will match shreddings in these other five bags." He pointed to the bags in the daylight video. "We're checking that out now.

"Barracks rounds the corner into the alley and is out of sight for a few seconds before the police catch up and see him. During that time, he could've exchanged bags. When the police order him to stop, he turns and shoots, making them jump to the side. Then he runs into the woman. If hoof-beats are horses, another member of the gang came back to the alley and picked up the money sometime before dawn. Zebras have to include police officers Armstrong and Johnson, who could've rounded the corner and seen the bag exchange when Barracks made it. Another zebra is the James woman. She could have seen the switch before the police came around the corner. Maybe they all saw it."

Kludge wrote names under columns headed HORSES, ZEBRAS and UNICORNS.

"Unicorns have to include any neighbors looking out windows, any vagrants, a homeless person sleeping in the alley, any passersby, someone on the television crew, another policeman, anyone who happened to get lucky."

"What are the chances *that* bag is the money?" asked Kludge.

"Analysis believes it is over eighty percent," said Olsen. "We'll know more when we fully examine the paper in Barracks's bag and interview the zebras."

"The obvious thing is to get the answer from Barracks," said Kludge. "He knows whether or not he had the money. Is he talking?"

"No," said Fleming.

Kludge looked to Olsen. "Is that everything?"

"Yes."

"Good job in a short time everyone," said Kludge. "Jack, Marv, and Paul stay. Everyone else, thank you."

When Kludge was alone with Olsen, Iacob, and Fleming, he said, "Walter Christian tells me we have a group of trainees on standby down at Quantico. They need their final exam. I also found out this James woman and her family will be attending the State of the Union speech tomorrow night at the Capitol. We can kill two birds with one stone, eliminate the woman and graduate three new agents. It'll set it up with Walter."

Olsen said, "There's not much time to get organized on our end."

"That's life, Jack. This is a real-time exercise."

"Right."

Kludge looked to Fleming. "Do you see any problems, Paul?"

"Not as long as it's undetected. They can't leave the air they breathe inside that house."

Fleming's diction came out slow and mushy, as if he struggled with a speech impediment; this in sharp contrast to the distinguished white-haired sophisticate of fifty-two he otherwise appeared to be.

"And nothing found there can be used as probable cause for a warrant," he added. "If they do find something, we'll have to use these tapes here to get a warrant and do it all over again. I want to be very clear on that."

"Understood," acknowledged Kludge. "It'll be transparent. Let's meet again tomorrow afternoon to go over where we are."

Kludge looked at the agents.

"We've made considerable progress in a short time. Good catch on that sixth bag being missing in the video. It puts us on the right track. Anything we've forgotten?"

No one offered anything.

"Good." Kludge stood. "Until tomorrow, gentlemen. Good hunting."

That Evening

Fifteen children and their attendant staff watched Denise take the handcuffs from Richard Dykstra at Shelby Carter's tenth birthday party. The atmosphere was sedate compared with that of typical nine- and ten-year-olds, for these children lived in "1911 Center," named and endowed by an Arlington physician for the year in which his only child had been born with Down's.

Approaching forty, Dykstra was the only single man in *Magic Central*. With beady eyes and a pointed nose, he looked like a weasel. Denise suspected he harbored a crush on her. As such, she'd troweled on his makeup thick and fast to be done with him. No one called him "Dick," though she thought he was.

Dykstra had already completed his act pulling multi-colored handkerchiefs from his sleeves. Despite a few glitches, he'd received a hearty round of applause; so forgiving were these children. Good or bad, they enjoyed every performer.

Her trick was new and required an assistant. Dykstra had jumped up.

"Now, Richard," she said. "Are these handcuffs solid? Are they steel?"

Dykstra jangled them and clicked the shackles through the hasps.

"Yes they are. Solid steel."

"Now please examine the lock."

Dykstra picked up a padlock from the prop stand. He held it up to the children and ran the bolt in and out so they could hear the sound of metal against metal.

Denise held out her arms.

"Please be sure I have no hidden key, and place the handcuffs on my wrists."

Clammy fingers massaged hers too long, then clamped the bracelets tight against her bones.

Pain shot up her arms.

She forced a smile.

"Please examine the box."

All eyes turned to the polished wooden box Dykstra picked up from the stand. As they did, Denise lowered her arms in front of her cape.

The box had two wrist-sized holes at either end. A hinge divided the back, and a clasp in front was set to accept a padlock. At her direction, Dykstra rapped the wood with his knuckles so everyone could hear its solid sound. Steel cut against skin as she pulled a handcuff key from a thread inside her cape.

"Hold the box open."

He did so, and she held up her arms to the audience.

"Now, boys and girls, I'm going to put my hands inside the box, and Richard is going to close it and lock it with the padlock."

With her arms in the holes, her elbows sticking out the sides, Dykstra closed the lid with a clap. He turned to pick up the padlock, rushing her. Tendons snapped across bone as she manipulated the key across her wrist into the left handcuff. Dykstra snapped the lock closed.

"Next, we need the Magic Cloth."

Dykstra plucked it from the tray and flourished it in front of Shelby Carter and the girls in the front row. Their eyes grew wide at

45

its purple color. Denise twisted her wrists to turn the key and force the left cuff. It opened.

Dykstra draped the cloth over the box giving no time for error. She switched the key to her left hand and opened the right side, gathering the cuffs and key into her left hand. Dykstra straightened the cloth and stood aside. With her right hand, she felt for the "V" in the hinge pin that would open the box.

"Now please watch carefully, boys and girls. My hands are encased in steel inside a locked box. There's no way to get out. Right?"

The children smiled agreement and chimed, "Nooo..." in chorus.

She raised her arms.

"Abracadabra!"

She pushed the hinge pin to the side, the rear of the box released, she grabbed its wrist-hole with her right hand as her arms came free, and gravity snapped the box lid shut. Facing the children, she held the handcuffs in one hand and the still padlocked box in the other.

Applause began after the Magic Cloth settled to the floor.

Michael drove home in the Firebird. Denise rubbed cream into her wrists.

"There was no need for Richard to do that," she said.

"The kids loved it, though. Nobody noticed a thing."

She hadn't told him what happened until they'd gotten the children into their seats and he'd started the car. She didn't feel he appreciated how hard it had been to complete the escape without showing the pain of each twist and turn she'd had to make.

He said, "Why don't you get some of those safety-cuffs you were telling me about? You'll never have to worry about that problem again."

"He's always doing things like this, Michael. He acts like a juvenile sometimes. Anyway, I don't see how I can make them work. The key has to be turned backwards to set the shackles. They can't be preset."

"Then volunteer to assist in his act. Sabotage him."

"I'd never assist him. Besides, he's a solo standup, and it's not proper etiquette. What he did was just mean-spirited. It's not a fault in the trick."

They cruised in heavy traffic for the next few miles. In the back seat, Sydney was asleep. Tommy talked to an imaginary friend. They turned off Route One into a residential section leading into Villamay.

"I can't believe you haven't told anyone about our secret," he said.

"Oh? You mean the one the Secret Service doesn't want us to tell or the other one?"

"The Secret Service one. You have such loose lips sometimes. It's a wonder you've kept it a secret."

She felt the heat from that.

"I can keep a secret."

"I hope you can, sugar. I've been worried about it."

"Why would you worry?"

"Because you couldn't wait to tell me about the *m o n-e-y*."

"You mean I shouldn't have? I love you, Michael. I should be able to tell you anything."

He kept his eyes on the road.

"Wouldn't you have told me?" she asked.

"Well—of course—of course. I would have told you as soon as you told me."

He turned into their driveway. The garage door began rising.

"Here we are," he said as if to change the subject.

He eased the car into the garage.

"Be sure to put my seat back where it was," she said and got out.

Chapter Five

Thursday, January 25
United States Capitol, Washington, D.C.

Denise and Michael arrived with the children and Sydney's paraphernalia bag at the designated door on the House side of the Capitol Building at half past seven, as per instructions from the Protocol Office. They identified themselves with photo ID, passed through a metal detector, and were shown into a waiting area by an escort.

Sydney wore a frilled cream-colored toddler's dress, and she clung to her mother as if to a life preserver, the crowd being what it was. Tommy was dressed in a blue blazer and gray slacks, his blond hair parted and held in place with spray. He walked beside his dad. Michael wore a charcoal pinstripe, white shirt, and red tie. Tall and athletic, he looked every bit the twenty-first century Lancelot ready for presentation by the king to the court for dragons-well-slain, even though his wife had done the actual slaying. Denise wore navy blue wool over a medium-gray turtleneck, understated, accented by a single strand of pearls.

The Lifetime Achievement Award winners and their entourages arrived, two aged actresses and an actor, easily recognized. They stood in the center of the room and greeted those who approached, which happened often.

The Jameses sat alone on a bench to one side under a portrait of a severe nineteenth-century congressman. They watched as the room filled with people they did not otherwise know.

Villamay

The drive-by car passed the house first.

A minute later the command van pulled to a stop across the street. On its side was stenciled NORTHERN VIRGINIA SECURITY above a telephone number. Two men carrying clipboards and wearing dark-green jumpers left the van and walked to the house with the tired gait of a long day. They carried ID matching the names sewn on their jumpers, and a receptionist was standing by to confirm their employment at the telephone number on the van. All wore two-way headsets.

The Northern Virginia Security company man whose shirt read "George" stood in the front yard while "Vern" rang the bell. They'd already checked for any alarm systems of record and found none. No one answered the door. They circled the house looking for electronic contacts, exterior lighting, and motion detectors. They made notes on clipboards.

The team didn't expect to find any doors or windows unlocked, but one never knew. A target's front door had been found open on one occasion by this very team. They spoke to each other and to the command van over the com-system. A security company decal in one of the front window was from a service with whom they'd already checked. Homeowners often posted stickers for non-existent security systems, but to make such a ruse effective, fake contacts in sight on the windows had to be installed.

The house had three entries: the front door, a side door, and a rear sliding glass door. The slider would be the easiest access except for the pins whose looped chains could be seen from the exterior. Passing through both frames, the pins eliminated the sliders for access. Without them, the glass could be lifted out of its tracks and removed. The front door was exposed to three houses across the street, though mature landscaping shielded its flanks. The side entrance was visible only from the house next door.

"We gotta do it the hard way," said Vern.

The side door had a five-pin deadbolt. Vern gave instructions to George, who took both clipboards to the truck and returned with a toolbox.

This was one of Quantico's crack lock-picking teams, the best of the Bureau. Still, the time allocation for entry was forty-five minutes.

"Starting now," said Vern.

He lit a wick on a lamp, and passed a blank key over its flame. When hot, he inserted the blank in the lock, worked it back and forth, and withdrew it for examination by the light of the wick. The marks of the pins on the blank's edge could be seen. Vern would file the blank at those points, and reinsert the key until each of the pins fell into place.

At 8:07, the lock yielded.

"Success."

The van driver glanced at his watch.

"Thirty-two minutes."

One at a time, Vern and George returned to the van, and were replaced by two agent-trainees designated "Bill" and "Jim." Trainee "Gene" was sent next, then Team Leader "Art." In the darkness, anyone watching would have had to have been observant indeed to notice four people instead of two at the house.

At 8:12, the search began.

The Capitol Building

Sydney, Tommy, Denise, and Michael fidgeted on the bench while the Lifetime Achievement Award winners remained the center of attention. Elegant dresses and rich business suits passed back and forth without comment. The Jameses recognized no one but the actors, and no one introduced themselves to them. Nervous, they watched in silence.

The air above Sydney became fetid.

"Michael. She's blown a diaper."

"Flip you for it."

He pulled a quarter from his pocket and showed her its two sides, a habit born after he'd caught her handing him one of her two-headed trick coins.

"Heads," she said.

He flipped it.

Tails it was, and she picked up the diaper bag and headed to the ladies room.

On the flip-down changing table, Sydney smiled as Denise removed a well-smeared throwaway.

"You did a good one, baby. Yes, you did."

She ran water in the sink and breathed through her mouth.

Three chattering middle-aged women came in.

"Hello, there," said Denise. "Just tidying up the little one."

The women stopped talking. She could feel their eyes on her as they went about their business.

So, she thought. Here she was in the United States Capitol about to be honored by the President of the United States, and she was cleaning number two off her daughter and getting snubbed by the elite ladies of the government. Hadn't any of them been mothers?

The women completed their tasks in silence and left.

Villamay

The first phase had been to scan the house for unknown persons or pets. None were found. Then the blinds and curtains were drawn. Low lights were turned on, and digital pictures taken of each room. At first the search was broad; attic to basement, all storage space, the garage, the one car, anywhere where a seventy-pound bag of money could be hidden.

The Capitol Building

The throng of guests was ushered into a much larger marble-inlaid room topped with gold crown molding and hung with portraits of past congressional leaders. An American flag edged in yellow frill stood next to a gas-lit fireplace. Poised facing it stood a photographer with a tripod, camera, and flash.

Fit young men and women with ear-sets and twirling tubes of plastic running down their necks entered and left at a bewildering pace. Tension rose until a crier announced—"Ladies and gentlemen. The President of the United States and the First Lady."

And in they strode through opened double doors. All smiles, they walked to the fireplace and flag. Ushers formed the guests into a receiving line where aides double-checked each person's appearance. Out of place hair was brushed, shiny foreheads powdered, and ties and dresses straightened. Each group in turn was brought to the First Couple. A few words were exchanged, a pose struck, generally shaking hands, and the photographer flashed the strobe twice.

When the Jameses' turn came, both the President and the First Lady greeted them by name. The President said he was proud to make their acquaintance, and hoped they were enjoying the evening.

Denise thought they looked remarkably good. The President was taller than she'd expected, the First Lady prettier.

An aide assisted in arranging them for the camera, Michael holding Tommy, Denise with Sydney. After they said good-bye and walked off, another aide behind the First Couple announced the names of the next two guests loud enough for the Jameses to hear. The resulting greeting sounded warm and sincere. Arms ushered the Jameses to a man sitting at a table who verified their names and address for the pictures. Then they were moved along to another aide who handed them silver-paper gift-wrapped boxes.

In eight or nine minutes, the assembly line ran all the guests through the public relations machine and the session was over. The President and First Lady smiled at everyone, said their good-byes, and were gone.

"That was impressive," said Denise. "It was so smooth."

She put the gifts in the diaper bag.

"Who was that?" Tommy asked at Michael's shoulder.

"That was the most powerful man in the world, and you just shook his hand."

Tommy looked at his palm.

"Your other hand," said Michael.

Tommy looked at his right hand, unimpressed.

Michael said, "For someone about to speak to millions of people, he didn't seem the least bit nervous."

"No, he didn't, did he? Butterflies are making me float. This is all so unreal. It's like a dream."

Villamay

None of the agents had expected to find the money, and after phase one was complete, the search became a training exercise driven by textbook procedure. Computer data was copied to discs. Paper files were examined for information on vacation homes, storage facilities, bank accounts, and investments. Garage tools were examined for signs they'd been used in the past week. Books on the library shelves were riffled. Hair samples and carpet fibers were taken. Shoes were covered in plastic wrap and casts taken. Fingerprints were dusted and lifted, the powder residue wiped away with care.

The Capitol Building

A matron seated everyone in the Visitors Gallery according to a chart. Denise and Michael were shown to the front row. They got the children settled, and looked over the rail at the House Chamber. Carpeted in blue and gold, the floor was filling with the men and women responsible for running the country. The House Sergeant at Arms announced the Diplomatic Corps, the Justices of the Supreme Court, and the Cabinet. Television cameras could be seen hidden in the shadows.

Michael said, "It looks smaller in person than it does on TV."

Denise agreed.

"Daddy," asked Tommy. "When's it over?"

"Probably in an hour, son. About as long as two of your cartoon shows." He leaned to Tommy's ear. "While we're here, please sit still. We're going to be on television, and we're recording this at home so we can watch it later. You're not going to want to see yourself with your finger in your nose or your thumb in your mouth, are you?"

He shook his head.

"Okay, partner."

"What if I have to itch?"

"I'll scratch for you."

"Okay, Daddy."

The Vice President's wife was announced and entered the gallery to applause from the floor. There were still two seats vacant. Having seen the tape from the Secret Service, one had to be for the First Lady.

"Who's that second seat for?" asked Denise.

"I don't know."

Moments later, the First Lady was announced. Everyone in the gallery and most on the floor stood and applauded.

The First Lady sat next to Denise.

"It's nice to see you again, Ms. James, Mr. James, and you too, Tommy and Sydney." She looked at the squirming girl.

"Thank you," said Denise. "She wants to doze, but the noise is keeping her up. And please call us Michael and Denise."

"Thank you." She faced the boy. "Now Tommy. We're going to be on television in a few minutes. It's important to keep your hands in your lap." Her sincerity could only be taken as helpful advice.

"Michael was just speaking to him about that," said Denise. She looked at Tommy. "We're all going to help you keep still."

"Okay," said the boy. He put his hands under his knees.

"You've probably never done this before," the First Lady said, her expression changing from interest in a child to concern for the Jameses.

"You are well informed," said Denise. "We've been briefed, but I'm jumping out of my skin. If I freeze at the moment of truth, you have my permission to bop me on the head."

The First Lady laughed. She said, "Everything will be fine. We are honored to have you."

"That's very gracious of you, but it is we who are honored."

"Thank you."

"Mr. Speaker!" called the Sergeant at Arms.

"Here we go," said the First Lady. "Assume the camera is on you the entire time."

"The President of the United States!"

Applause erupted and everyone stood as the President appeared at the entrance opposite the Gallery.

Villamay

Stealth and silence were the watchwords during any mission. The only communication came over the remote units in the operatives' ears when every three minutes the time was given from the command van. At nine forty-five, the final check would begin. By ten, the exit deadline, Team Leader Art would compare each room to the continuity pictures taken earlier.

One of the trainees sat on the floor flipping through the CD's in the entertainment rack. He could hear his heart beating. The VCR unit next to his head clicked on, and he jumped with what he thought was a loud start.

He looked at the recorder, then around the room. He shook his head: glad Team Leader was somewhere else.

The Capitol Building

Ten minutes after the President entered the House Chamber, the First Lady leaned to Denise and said, "Your part is coming up."

She nodded, and looked at the President, her mouth dry. She'd been maintaining her nerves by applauding and standing when the First Lady did, and looking at the House floor to see who applauded what and who didn't applaud anything. Seldom was there universal support for anything the President said. Certain sections clapped with enthusiasm while others remained quiet. This was never apparent on television.

The President was saying, "The greatest asset America has is the character of its people. Since our founding, America has been the melting pot of the world, having created an atmosphere where ideas of every variety can become reality, where freedom and liberty reign, where tolerance of others is paramount. Regardless of gender, race or creed, every citizen in America is a patriot in his or her own right by virtue of working, raising families, paying taxes, contributing to the community, and obeying the law."

Applause.

"Proactive citizenship is more important today than ever before in our history. Tonight, we are pleased to have with us, and I am honored to present to you, a true American hero. She works at a bank in Virginia as an Assistant Vice President. During a recent drug interdiction, at great peril to herself, this fine young woman disabled an armed suspect, enabling police officers to make an arrest they might not otherwise have made.

"Ladies and gentlemen, may I present, Denise Elizabeth James, her husband…"

The floor erupted. The First Lady squeezed Denise's arm and lifted. Denise stood, Sydney's arms tight around her neck. Michael stood beside her holding Tommy, who covered both ears with his hands.

"Wave, Tommy," said Michael.

Tommy flapped a hand for an instant and put it back on his ear.

Denise nodded over the rail. Everyone around her was standing and clapping. She sat to a continuing ovation.

At last the room quieted. Everyone sat.

"That was perfect," said the First Lady.

"Thank you," said Denise.

A few minutes later, the President introduced the First Lady to partisan applause. Supporters were avid. Non-supporters provided a golf-clap at best.

When she sat, Denise said to her, "You deserve better than that, ma'am."

The First Lady smiled across the Gallery at a television camera's red light.

Villamay

So far, the mission had performed according to parameters, a fixed amount of information needing to be acquired within a fixed amount of time. Team Leader Art made a final walk-through comparing each room to the digital images to be sure everything was in proper position. He went through the house again with a "rug mop" to remove carpet marks. The lights were extinguished, and the drapes and blinds opened as they were before entry.

The team would return to their command office, trade after-action postmortems, and conclude with an analysis meeting. Nothing would be written. The next day, the digital picture and computer disc examinations would begin, but the team already knew nothing remarkable had been found. All the evidence they'd gathered would be archived. Only a personal interview with the Jameses remained.

Team Leader Art closed the side door and locked it with the key made earlier. He crossed the lawn and stepped into the van, not pulling off his latex until he closed its door. The driver started the engine. Art handed the house key to a trainee who taped it to one of the evidence bags.

Mission results would be "on hold" for five days, and considered a success only if the Jameses lodged no complaint. If all went well, in a week the FBI would graduate three new Special Agents.

The trainees thanked God it hadn't been raining.

The Capitol Building

As the President shook hands along the exit aisle after the speech, the matron asked everyone in the gallery to remain where they were until the special dignitaries could be escorted out. While good-byes were exchanged, Denise asked The First Lady, "That seat in the front row stayed empty. Who was supposed to sit there?"

The First Lady leaned forward so only Denise and Michael could hear.

"We leave a seat vacant now and then so it won't look as if we're stuffing the gallery. An empty chair sometimes has more value than an occupied one."

The Jameses nodded assurance this secret would remain so.

As the First Lady went through the exit, Michael said with respect, "I don't know when I've been so impressed by anyone."

"No kidding," Denise agreed. "She's going to have to eat live babies on television before I say anything bad about her."

Chapter Six

Early Friday, January 26
Villamay

Despite getting to sleep, Denise soon awoke. She stared at the ceiling, hands folded under her breasts as if lying in state. A drip in the toilet plinked. Downstairs, the refrigerator purred. The heat pump clicked on and off. She lost count the number of times it cycled. Next to her, Michael breathed constant in sleep.

It wasn't as much a panic attack as *a knowing* that the pendulum of fortune had swung her way as far as it could go, and now, bending to the necessities of nature, it would fall away. Declared a hero by the President of the United States, she and Michael held a secret that, if exposed, would be an embarrassment to rival that of any White House scandal, ever.

Could they do it?

More than at any time prior, they had to depend upon each other.

She prayed the authorities would believe the drug dealers retrieved the money, though nothing had been mentioned about it in the media. She worried that forensic science might have reached the point where molecules from her body could be found on the ground where the bags were switched, or that radiation in the anti-counterfeiting stripes could be picked up by satellite if enough bills were together. Maybe they'd wrap it up, say they'd won, and move on to other things. The drug dealers would be looking too, she knew, but maybe there was nothing they could do. It all went round and round without answer or end.

When the alarm sounded, she got up with none of the grogginess of first waking, the gloom of night evaporating as soon as she began her morning routine. She hurried down the stairs to get the newspaper, and begin what she knew would be a whirlwind day in the afterglow of her surprise appearance at the State of the Union Address.

Sunday, January 28
Evening News Broadcast

"City of Alexandria Chief of Police Joan C. Harris announced today that no money was recovered during the drug seizure at Waterfront Park in Alexandria nearly two weeks ago. More than three million dollars was supposed to have been at the site. She also disclosed that the FBI has now formally taken over the inquiry, and that all evidence and suspects have been turned over to the Bureau."

Monday, January 29
Alexandria

Near two o'clock, Special Agent Jack Olsen called Denise at her Treasure Chest office.

"Ms. James. If it would be possible, my associate and I would like to meet with you and go over the events of the night of January sixteenth. Just routine. We'd like to confirm a few things for the record that we've heard from other people."

"Sure." She tried to sound natural. "The whole thing's been fully reported. I can't add much to what's already been said, but I'll try."

"Well, there are a few things we'd like to clear up."

"Okay. Ask away."

"Could we perhaps stop by tonight? Would that be possible?"

"Michael and I have a class tonight. Then we have to take care of the children and get them to bed."

"When would that be over? About what time?"

"Maybe by nine."

"Can we—could we say—nine-thirty?"

"That's fine. Nine-thirty. You know the address?"

"Yes."

"All right. See you then."

"See you then, Ms. James."

"Bye."

She hung up, a storm of dread churning. She knew from the news the FBI was on the case. An interview was predictable, even obvious, and she'd missed it. Always anticipate the worst, she told herself. Hope for the best.

She telephoned Michael.

"The FBI is coming to see us at the house tonight at nine-thirty."

Several heartbeats followed.

"The FBI?"

Another two heartbeats.

"Is there a problem?" he said.

"I don't think so." She tried to sound calm. "He said they have some follow-up questions. It's routine."

"Fine."

"Let's go to class, eat, and get the children to bed first."

"Okay."

She told him her idea in the car going to the gym. He was reluctant, but she talked it up, and insisted he think about it. Her approach would take the agents out of whatever game plan they had. Besides, she liked offense. He agreed she was offensive.

"Well," she told him. "Like they say at Data-Now, Michael. Think outside the box."

Clyde Strong's Health and Fitness is a regional chain offering free weights, circuit stations, aerobics, personal trainers, obesity management, and most important for those with small children, a nursery. Tommy and Sydney knew its playroom well.

Once changed into uniform, Denise and Michael stretched out on the aerobics room floor with about forty other students until Master Joon Kim entered the room. Then everyone lined up, high ranks in front in descending order to the left. In stilted English, Master Kim congratulated Denise for her recent "martial arts expertise under fire." In the second row, she felt her face go red through the tips of her ears.

The first quarter hour was aerobics, interspersed with stretching. Then the ranks split into groups and punched torso bags.

Throughout this basic routine, Denise visualized the upcoming FBI interview. Her idea had a certain charm in that it contained a built-in excuse for a bad result that could be justified after the fact. She'd have to get Michael firmly aboard, maybe give him some lines, extend to him her own enthusiasm. The more she thought about it, the more she liked it.

The class split into belts of equal rank for forms. Denise, Michael, and three other red belts lined up with Ms. Lee, a junior instructor.

"Cha-Ryoth," Lee commanded.

They came to attention.

"Kyung-nae."

They bowed.

"Jhoone-Bee."

The students came to ready-stance; feet shoulder width apart, hands knotted in fists at their belts.

"Choong-Moo."

This was a thirty-move pattern named after a sixteenth-century Korean admiral. Students testing for black belt would have to complete this form in good order under the scrutiny of three judges, the other students, and their guests. Choong-Moo's most challenging evolution was a counter-clockwise 360-degree spin from a C-block in a back stance to a double knife-hand block in the same stance.

"Si-Jak!"

All five red belts moved as one from position to position, exhaling aloud at each punch, block, or kick, heedless of the other ranks going through their patterns around them. All eyes looked straight ahead, not staring at anything, seeing all, concentration intense. Any stray thought and the next move would evaporate.

Denise executed the back right round-kick, the left spin-side-kick, and the back left round-kick into the C-block. She jumped, turning her head to the left to lead her body around and stop as close to one revolution as she could. Where her feet landed was critical.

She undershot.

On the next move, a right spear-hand to the groin, she corrected. At the final reverse punch and *"Kihap!"* she held her position.

"Ba-ro," commanded Lee.

Return to ready stance.

"Shuit."

At ease.

Now she could look around, straighten her uniform, and listen to the critique from Ms. Lee.

"Prepare the complete pattern. Do not concentrate on perfecting one or two difficult parts. Make it flow, smooth and plastic. That is what the judges will be examining."

61

Ms. Lee took them through the exercise four more times. Denise hit the landing once to her satisfaction.

With twenty minutes remaining, class was rejoined and paired off for one-, two-, and three-step sparring.

Her thoughts returned to the interview.

Villamay

She opened the front door with a flourish to greet two men in suits and ties. Their hands held ID's. She smiled.

"Agents Mulder and Scully, I presume."

"Denise Elizabeth Lang James?"

"'Tis I, Denise James, my own self."

"I'm Special Agent Jack Olsen. This is Special Agent Marv Iacob. We're from the Federal Bureau of Investigation. May we come in?"

"Of course."

Olsen was of medium height, mid-thirties, short brown hair, pale skin, and a strong dimpled chin. Iacob was about the same age and height, looked Middle Eastern, and wore an expression of mild curiosity.

Michael arrived as the agents entered the foyer. "They're here? Great."

The agents introduced themselves to Michael, Iacob marking himself from the Deep South. They still held their ID's in their hands. Denise and Michael had tumblers in theirs. The air smelled of scotch.

"I've never seen an official FBI badge before," said Denise. She gripped the leather cover in her fingers. Olsen held firm.

"I can't let you hold it."

She withdrew her hand.

"Do you have cards?" asked Michael.

The agents handed them over.

"Come sit at the table," said Denise. She led them into the dining room. "May I get you something to drink?"

Olsen sucked in his cheeks. He said, "No ma'am. We're on duty."

"Of course you are, poor things. You don't mind if we do. We're off duty, and life has been most exciting for us lately."

They sat at the table. The agents laid files in front of them. Iacob produced a legal pad.

Denise said, "Before we get started, let's play cards. I'll go first."

She shuffled and handed one of the cards to Michael. She turned over hers. On the upper left was the blue FBI seal. The right corner proclaimed: FEDERAL BUREAU OF INVESTIGATION. In the center was the name: JAMES (JACK) OLSEN, JR., SPECIAL AGENT. The address was the J. Edgar Hoover Building, Pennsylvania Avenue, NW, Washington, D.C. The telephone number and suite number had been struck through and new ones written above.

"Here we go," she said. "Your telephone number and suite number are new, so you've been moved around inside the building because the address is the same. The card seems worn, as though you've carried it around a while. The writing is printed, not engraved, indicating cheapness. Your father works for a great metropolitan newspaper. You insist on being called Jack, whereas your father, still a low level gofer for Perry White, is known as Jimmy. You hate being called 'Jimmy Olsen.' That's why you have 'Jack' printed on your card."

Neither agent moved.

"My turn," said Michael.

His card was the same except the name was: MARVIN (MARV) IACOB, SPECIAL AGENT. The telephone number and suite number had been marked out, and new ones written above.

"The first thing that jumps right out is that the printer spelled *'Jacob'* wrong. Either that, or he was educated in the Latin alphabet, in which case there are no *'J's'*. This card also seems worn, and is printed, not engraved."

"Which leads you to what conclusion?" asked Denise. She felt giddy. She couldn't have hoped for better out of Michael.

"That they have to pay for printing their own cards?"

"Right you are," she chirped and turned to Olsen. "They provide a box, but you have to pay for reprinting."

Holding his glass in the air, Michael said, "You probably get issued one full box. If you get transferred to a different suite, you don't want to buy new cards every time. Same thing if you get a new telephone number. And that probably happens all the time knowing how big organizations work. Why, you'd end up paying a fortune if you got new cards printed every time something changed. You just update a few by hand with the new information and carry them with you."

Seconds passed.

"An astute observation," said Olsen.

"Calls for a toast," cheered Denise. "Here's to us!"

She and Michael drained glasses.

"My name is Jack Olsen, and this is Marv Iacob, with an '*I.*'"

"Oh, I much prefer you to be Mulder, and you," she pointed at Iacob, "to be Scully." She beamed a broad smile. "Those names just popped into my head the moment I saw you."

Michael laughed at that, and got up to freshen the drinks. Scotch, ice, and soda were on the sideboard.

"Are you sure we can't get you something?" asked Denise. "We have cokes, coffee, juice, tea, even that designer stuff that's more expensive than gasoline. What's it called, honey?"

"Bottled water."

"That's it."

"No," said Olsen. "We're fine, thank you. We'd like to get started if we could."

"Well, Agent Mulder, as they must say down at the FBI, shoot."

"Ms. James," said Olsen. "We are Special Agents of the Federal Bureau of Investigation here on official business. We request the respect our position merits."

Denise said, "And we are two loyal tax paying citizens in our own home after hours accommodating your immediate request for a meeting. Over one third of our income goes to pay taxes of one sort or another. Your jobs are dependent upon those taxes. In essence, you work for us." Her smile was constant, the light of alcohol dancing in her eyes. "Everything you're going to ask, I've already answered. This is still America, land of the free, home of the brave, and you are guests here in Chateau James. Are you wearing a wire?"

Olsen's expression opened in surprise. "No," he said after a hesitation. "Marv will take notes."

Iacob picked up his pen. At the sideboard, Michael dipped his fingers to the bottom of a half-filled glass behind the ice bucket.

"So," said Denise. "Word of honor from the FBI. This conversation is not being taped, transmitted, or recorded in any way except by Agent Scully here?"

Olsen frowned. "Do you have a problem, Ms. James?"

"Ha! I asked first."

"Now, Denise," said Michael. "What do we care if they're taping? You've been interviewed to death. Let them ask their questions."

He sat with fresh drinks.

Denise faced Olsen across the table.

"All right. As I said, shoot."

Iacob joined the conversation.

"Mr. an' Ms. James. Are ya'll recordin' this?"

"No," answered Michael.

"Not in enny way?"

"Only memory," said Denise. "So far I've had a memorable time."

Olsen opened his file.

"The reason for this interview is to establish the facts in this case. Let me outline what we know. Stop me if I'm incorrect or incomplete in anything."

He recounted the evening of January sixteenth. His delivery was precise, each sentence complete, no hesitations. His eyes stayed on his notes until he asked, "When you left the park, did you return directly to your car?"

"Yes," Denise answered. "I even took the same route, walked down the same streets."

"Did you stop at the entrance to the alley on the way back?"

"No."

"You went to your car and drove home?"

"Yes."

"Drove directly home?"

"Yes."

"Do you know what time you arrived here?"

"I'd guess around two-thirty."

"Did you go straight to bed?"

"What I do in the privacy of my own home is out of bounds."

"Did you walk down the alley on the way to your car?"

"No. I walked up King Street, took a left on Fairfax, and then a right on Duke. It was the same route I'd taken after I parked, only in reverse."

"After you stopped at the alley entrance, did you walk down the alley any distance?"

"I didn't stop at the alley."

"Would it interest you to know that we have a witness that says he saw you walk down the alley?"

"No, it wouldn't. I didn't."

"How do you explain that?"

"Maybe it was J. Edgar."

Olsen consulted his file. Denise drank half her glass.

"Ms. James. Let's go back to the time you first saw Mr. Barracks."

"To be precise," she replied, "I saw a man running down the alley. I didn't identify him, and neither did the arresting officers. He had no ID."

"Fine. When you first saw the man running toward you down the alley, did you notice how heavy the bag was?"

She took a swallow, thoughtful. "I don't know how heavy the bag was. I saw him. Then two people came around the corner chasing him. They were running like cops."

"How do you mean, 'running like cops?'"

"Hands out to the sides because of all their holsters and nightsticks and stuff they carry. Then they shouted for the guy to freeze."

"Fine."

"I concluded the man coming toward me must be a bad guy. Then he turned and fired a gun at the officers and confirmed how truly brilliant I am. The cops dove to the sides of the alley. The man ran at me. The rest is history."

"So Mr. Barracks ran straight down the alley at you?"

"Whoever he was ran down the alley at me."

"Okay. At no time did you see this man stop in the alley?"

"The cops were chasing him and he was running away. Do you think he'd stop and take a leak?"

Michael laughed.

66

"At no time did you see the man throw down the bag he was carrying and pick up another one?"

"No."

"Would it surprise you to know that it was the distinct impression of the two officers chasing Mr. Barracks—I mean the man you saw them chasing through the alley—that the bag he was carrying was heavy?"

"I have no idea what the officers thought."

Olsen's gaze was steady.

"Where are you going with this?" she asked. "It's beginning to sound accusatory. Is it?"

"We're just gathering information."

"Is Denise a suspect?" asked Michael.

"Not at this time. We just want to know what happened, that's all."

"Are you carrying guns?" asked Denise. "Michael and I, we're against guns in general, and we're against them inside our house in particular. You haven't brought guns in here, have you?"

"On calls like this for information gathering purposes, we usually don't carry firearms," said Olsen.

Denise leaned across the table and spoke so low Olsen tilted his head forward.

"Guns are loud, oily, and messy. Their purpose is to shoot people." She still held a pleasant smile. "It's a simple question you haven't answered. Are you carrying guns or not?"

"No. We have no firearms."

"Thank you," she said. "I feel much better now."

Michael stood to refill the glasses.

"You don't know any of the suspects that were detained, do you?" asked Olsen.

"No. They don't run in my circle."

"Do you think you could pick out the man who ran down the alley? From a line-up, I mean?"

"Sure. I got a good look at him while I was waiting for the officers."

"And he got a good look at you?"

Michael dipped his fingers into the glass on the sideboard and rubbed his palms together.

"I suppose so," Denise replied. "He wanted to bash my head in when he got up."

"Has anyone threatened you?"

She raised an eyebrow.

"Not till you arrived."

Olsen looked surprised.

"Have I threatened you, Ms. James?"

"I believe so. A threat is what I think it is. I told you I walked the same path back to the car and drove home. You asked if I would be surprised if you had a witness who saw me go into the alley. You don't have one, because I didn't. You asked if I would be surprised if the officers told you the bag the man was carrying was heavy when I know it was filled with shredded paper. I saw Detective Scaleri open it. Right now I'm feeling threatened by false accusations." She turned to Michael. "Do you think I've been threatened?"

"Sounds like it."

"See?"

She took a filled glass from her husband.

"Michael, the reason Mulder and Scully are here is because there's a bunch of money missing, and we need to be shaken up and stirred to see if it falls out of us."

Michael looked across the table. "Is that true?"

"If you're looking for the money, just ask us," said Denise. "Feel free to search the house and cars. But don't come here and threaten us."

"I assure you," said Olsen. "No threat was intended."

"Might there be anything else?" she asked. "Like don't leave town?"

"No, no. I think we're done. Is there anything else, Marv? Have we forgotten anything?"

Iacob looked at the pad on which he had written nothing.

"No. Ah believe that's everythin'."

Denise and Michael stood. The agents got up, and the Jameses followed them to the foyer. No one spoke.

At the door, Iacob said, "Y'all might could consider the benefits of a twelve-step program, Mr. and Ms. James."

"Not necessary," said Denise.

Olsen and Iacob walked down the steps. The Jameses remained in the doorway and watched the agents until the taillights of their Concorde turned the corner out of sight.

"I love goofing on the authorities," said Denise. "They're *so serious*."

Michael whispered, "This could come back to bite us, Denise."

"No, it can't. We have a perfect defense, Temporary insanity. And we found out they have no witnesses and no proof. Besides, I think it puts a little humility into them."

She closed the door.

"Did you see the bulges under their jackets?" she asked. "They had guns didn't they?"

"I don't know. They might have had empty holsters. I didn't see a gun."

She cleared the tray from the sideboard and took it to the kitchen. On the countertop was the pitcher she'd used to mix instant tea to the color of scotch, the funnel to fill the bottle from which they drank, and a real bottle for the scent glass. She filled a tumbler with scotch to the level of the scent glass and handed it to Michael.

"I'd say that was a routine interview in almost all respects." She clicked his glass. "Well done, my love."

Olsen cruised up the parkway gripping the wheel with white knuckles.

"Those assholes."

"Now don't forgit the mission, Jack. We got what we came for. One suspect down. She ain't got it, so let's move on."

"I thought that bitch was going to frisk us."

"Good thing she didn't." Iacob pulled a recorder from his breast pocket. "Ah never had a inner-view like that, but the way Ah read it, we caught 'em at a good time. They both had them a buzz goin'. They're believable, her 'specially, an' she's the one we hafta believe. You see it enny different?"

Olsen slowed for traffic.

"No. I guess not. She was never high on the list."

"But she sure was high. Ah'll write the report that way."

They arrived at the first traffic light in Old Town.

"Ah don't see the need to transcribe this word for word, d'you?" Iacob held up the recorder. "Ah'll do it from memory."

"Fine. But I'd like to rip the grin off that bitch's face. I surely would."

69

Chapter Seven

Tuesday, January 30
The Hoover Building

Kludge entered the conference room.

"Has Barracks said anything yet?"

He laid his pad at the head of the table at which Olsen, Iacob, Fleming, and two assistants were seated.

"No," Fleming answered. "He's got court appointed counsel. No one seems interested in him. Our first meeting is tomorrow, and we'll tell him there's nothing we can do. The only way he can get charges reduced is if he supplies substantial assistance."

Kludge flipped a page on his pad. "Barracks is a minor player, a delivery boy. When you talk to him, try to get him to admit he was the one who picked up the moneybag and swapped it."

"We can open the door for him on that," said Fleming. "But the question has to be structured in the proper manner for his response to have any value. When he learns the charges against him and the range of sentence, he might admit to anything to mitigate."

Kludge sat.

"There are four reasonable suspects," he said. "McCullough's gang, the two police officers, and the woman. The gang's by far the likeliest, ninety-percent plus chance. It's one of these four, or a unicorn. You interviewed the individuals, Jack. What're they like?"

"The officers seem okay. Armstrong has fifteen years under his belt and a handful of commendations. One complaint filed ten years ago and dropped. Johnson's been on the force less than two months. When we interviewed the woman, she and her husband were either drunk or well on the way. Marv and I came away believing she was just cocky because of the publicity she's been getting."

"Well, let's wind up the money part," said Kludge. "If we announce the gangs, the two cops, and the woman are suspects, then if any of the individuals report contact, we'll know the gangs don't have the money. That would eliminate the horses and leave the zebras."

Fleming filled the pause.

"Shouldn't we tell them in adva—? No, no, that's silly. Sorry I said that."

70

Iacob asked, "Do you wanna get an order to tap their phones?"

"No," said Kludge. "Not when the chances they have it are less than ten percent. We'll use informals, nothing we would use in court."

"Then why do it?" asked one of the assistants.

"Because the gangs talk to each other. They know whether or not they have the money. If they don't, they'll contact the cops and the woman. We've done their detective work. The only individual who won't report receiving a call will be the one who has it. With informals, we'll know who got called. That's the best case. Not conclusive, but it would light our way to concentrate on a prime suspect if there is one."

For a federal trial attorney like Fleming, the ideal investigation is pursuit to the point where a negotiated plea is the target's only rational option. Informal activities, such as undisclosed informants or anonymous tips, often pointed the case in the right direction, but if trial became necessary, everything presented had to be legally correct. Trials were expensive, and no one wanted a lot of work thrown out on a technicality except the defendant and his counsel, who'd be looking for errors both real and imagined.

Fleming said, "Well, if you don't need to use it in court."

"Okay," said Kludge. "I'll set up the announcement. Now, with the woman, what's the media going to say?"

"Anything they want," said Fleming back on solid ground. "We're following basic investigative procedure. It's fair to include the cops and the woman with the gangs. We're playing by the book. The gangs and these three are inside the net, and until they can be removed for one reason or another, they stay there."

"To recap," said Olsen, "the most likely scenario is we announce the three names and a week goes by. Neither the cops nor the woman calls to complain, and we get nothing from the taps. That means McCullough's gang picked up the money. There's no forfeiture. Whatever case there is goes over to the DEA, and we're out of it."

"Correct," said Kludge.

Iacob asked, "What if one of the gang members came back, got the bag, an' didn't tell ennybody? Say he's tryin' to keep it for himself?"

"That would be categorized as a unicorn," answered Kludge.

Wednesday, January 31

A week after the State of the Union Address, the media festival over Denise James began to fade. *Time* and *Newsweek* had new covers, she had no interviews not already aired, and "Dateline" had broadcast three new shows since the one devoted to her. No longer was every waking moment filled with the effects of sudden fame.

Most odd to her, the FBI interview nagged. Goofing on the agents seemed like such a good idea at the time. Now, after the noise and confusion of each day ended, it festered, keeping her from sleep. A little voice inside wondered if she might be manic-depressive, or bi-polar, or something worse. She tried her best to dismiss such self-diagnosis. The interview had to be what they said it was. It *had* to be routine. Didn't it? Agents would *have* to interview everyone involved to complete the files. Hers was done. She could move on.

Then, in her office, she received a call from her next-door neighbor, Gus Gordon.

"I thought you might like to know—I saw it on the news. It was just a few minutes ago—I think Channel Three. What's that Action News station? It was the same man as before."

Gordon had the patience for detail of the long retired, and she let him take his time arriving at the fact that an FBI spokeswoman had announced her name in the investigation to locate the missing money. Police officers Armstrong and Johnson were also named.

"You mean they declared me a suspect? An active, official suspect?"

"They sure did, young lady." His voice was that of a funeral priest. "I thought you might want to know."

"Fame becomes infamy, Gus. I get introduced by the President on national television one week, and the next week they suspect I'm a thief."

Gordon said nothing.

"Well let them investigate all they want. They'll never find where I hid it."

He laughed the shallow laugh of the elderly.

"That's what I like about you, Denise. Your sense of humor."

"Thank you, Gus. I try. And thanks for the call. It's always good to get warning before the SWAT team breaks down your door."

"Did you get the security system?"

"Excuse me?"

"You had people at your house."

"What people? When was this?"

"I don't remember. It was after dark."

"How do you know it was for house security?"

"Well—let's see. Said so on the truck. Had a sign on the truck."

"Who was it?"

"Well—it was a security company. You know, for house alarms."

"Michael hasn't said anything about it." She made a mental note to ask him. "Anyway, thanks for the heads up. I appreciate it."

"Glad to help, young lady. See you later."

"Okay, Gus. Bye."

"Bye."

She put down the phone.

Damn!

She could assume Victor Barracks had told the FBI he picked up the money. They probably had a bag description from interrogating the buyers, and the unnamed informant must have told them that the gangs didn't get the money after the raid. They had a suspect list. And she was on it.

It was over. She had to fold her cards right now and get out of the game no matter what her husband thought.

Michael's resolve to stick it out had blossomed after the raid. He'd insisted all their financial worries would be over. They'd carry on with their lives and not worry about retirement plans or stock portfolios. They'd laugh at the follies of the world, and dance and sing as if no one were watching. Then one day they'd travel the world in a champagne bucket. In one excessive fit of testosterone he claimed the money was theirs by right of conquest.

Nights had been the worst, lying there staring at the ceiling, fears magnified. She knew if she coughed it up she'd have to live the rest of her life with the knowledge that she'd been a coward who'd lost her nerve when she had the chance to spin straw into gold. She didn't want to think of herself as a coward, and she fought it off until courage returned each morning.

Now she had to pull herself together again, this time in daylight.

Things might not be so bad. She'd been named a suspect, true. But so had Officers Armstrong and Johnson. Maybe this was some sort of trick. Maybe they were trying to rattle her, make her panic—

The telephone startled her.

"Real Estate," she answered.

"Denise. What say we go to the track in Charlestown Saturday? Girls night out." It was Cathy Pfau, secretary to bank president Larry LaBelle.

"What?"

"I know this horse. Odds are seven to one."

It was winter. The tracks were closed.

"If you bet three million, you win twenty one. I want half." She started to giggle.

"Someone called me about the announcement, Cathy. How'd you find out?"

"A customer called Mr. LaBelle and told him."

"Is he smiling? Or calling people with his serious voice?"

"Hold on."

Cathy cupped the receiver.

"He says for you to come down here."

"I'm on my way."

She crossed the second floor mezzanine looking at the faces of the administrative assistants. None looked her in the eye. Word traveled fast.

"Ms. James is here, Mr. LaBelle."

Cathy Pfau put down the receiver.

"Go on in," she said.

Denise went through the door. Treasure Chest's Chief of Security Morton Mieske was seated in one of two chairs in front of LaBelle's desk.

"Why don't you close that behind you," said LaBelle.

She returned and did so.

"Have a seat."

She did, and stared into the concerned face of the President of Treasure Chest Bank. Balding, gray at the temples, six and a half feet tall, Larry LaBelle wore glasses that magnified pale brown eyes.

Genteel and Victorian by nature, his posture and tone conveyed dislike for the stress he was feeling.

"I received a call from one of our customers," he began.

"Informing you that two Alexandria police officers and I are on a short list of suspects that might be in possession of the money missing from the raid."

"Yes,"

"A neighbor called and told me. He saw it on television."

"Do you have the money?"

She looked him in the eye.

"I do not."

LaBelle inhaled a half-breath.

"That's a relief."

He bent his head forward as if in prayer to recite the party line.

"Treasure Chest wants no adverse publicity for itself or its employees. I know you've done your best to minimize the bank's exposure, and your role in this affair has been portrayed in a good light. If you don't have the money, and I asked you a direct question to get an honest response, if you don't have the money, then I don't see a problem at this juncture."

"That's good, sir. I don't have the money."

LaBelle raised his head.

"I must tell you, however, the members of the board will be discussing this, and I don't like that. In banking, we want everything quiet, steady, and dull."

"Larry," she said. "I wasn't thinking of the effect on the bank at the time of the raid."

"I would not have expected you to have been, Denise. I don't quite understand what motivated you, but I expect what you did was due in large part to the situation of the moment. It was an unusual circumstance in which to find oneself."

"So it was."

LaBelle addressed Mieske.

"If this is the situation, Morton, that Denise doesn't have the money and should not be considered a suspect, is there anything you can recommend she do in this circumstance?"

Mieske had been with the FBI for twenty years before taking his pension and retiring to the private sector. Not yet fifty, he still carried himself with the trim look of an agent: suits well worn but cared for, button-down collars, and thick-soled shoes. Economic in movement, he spoke little, but what he said was no nonsense. He'd been with Treasure Chest almost six years. Denise knew him because he sometimes joined the Real Estate Finance Division for after-hour cocktails. She liked him.

"Getting the money found would help the most," he said.

"Finding the money is out of my hands, Morton. Besides, I thought everyone assumed the drug people had it. That's been the consensus in the media."

"The media reports what it can find out, or what it can surmise," said Mieske. "That's not always what is."

LaBelle seemed to consider the implications of that. Then he said, "I suppose finding the money is outside your domain, Denise. I just wanted to hear it from you that there's nothing behind this announcement."

Mieske said to LaBelle, "She'll be in the spotlight again, Larry. This time as a suspect. Treasure Chest will be named as her employer. A flat public denial is better than any 'no comment.'"

"Of course I'll deny it. It's not true."

Mieske looked at her and ran his forefinger under his nose.

"Be careful what you say. Bureau culture is dedicated to apprehension."

"I'm not in it. I have nothing to hide."

Mieske lifted his chin and looked down his nose at her.

"As far as bankers go, you are irreverent and sarcastic, a black sheep with a tongue that gets you into trouble. Watch what you say."

She never expected Mieske to say anything like that in front of the president of the bank.

She turned to LaBelle.

He said, "Your wit does resemble that of Dorothy Parker on occasion, Denise."

Her next words were all she could bring herself to say.

"I have nothing to do with the missing money."

LaBelle's magnified eyes blinked. He said, "I believe you."

Her division head met her with a handful of telephone messages when she walked through the door to Real Estate. She flipped through

76

them without registering anything other than that they were from the media.

"Let's talk, Denise." He looked as if a close relative had died. "The FBI doesn't name suspects without good reason."

He was like a big brother to her, like he was to everyone in the division, and he wanted a counseling session.

"I can't right now," she choked. "I just can't."

She brushed by him to her office and closed the door.

"God Almighty," she swore out loud.

She'd just lied to two people she liked and respected. Now there would be never ending questions, and an FBI interrogation, this time without the niceties. Everything she ever said would be dissected, authenticated, and thrown back at her with contradictions until she lost track of what she'd said and who she was.

She fought rising tears, blinked them away.

What else could be happening? What other surprises had yet to be sprung? On top of everything else, she could feel her period coming on.

A tear rolled down her cheek.

She paced the floor to think and gather her wits. She rehearsed denials, forming phrases that sounded varied and unplanned. Deny and delay was all she could do. She had to stick with her story and buy enough time to get rid of the money. Michael could do it. He'd have to. He could leave it in a church.

Bad idea.

Even if she could convince him, he'd be watched too.

She stopped pacing, and looked out the window over barren branches and gray rooftops. The scene, quite mundane, shone brilliant in the sun. A cloud swept overhead, its shadow marching across the vista like some gathering storm. Such, she felt, was her world.

What was that saying about evil? It doesn't spring on you all at once. It comes on little by little and makes you its friend before you recognize what it is.

She gathered her things and headed home.

Commonwealth's Attorney Roody Packwurst was examining the photographs of three candidates to replace his campaign manager when Alexandria Chief of Police Joan Harris telephoned.

"The FBI just announced two of my officers are suspects in the missing money from Waterfront Park."

"Did they say my name?"

That took Harris aback. She was slow to answer.

"No, Roody. They didn't say your name. They didn't mention the city or your office. They named my officers and spoke as if the Bureau carried out the raid. Did you know about this in advance?"

Packwurst didn't like her tone.

"Don't forget who you're talking to."

"I'm talking to you, Roody. Don't you remember what Eric Kludge said about giving you and the city credit?"

That hit the right nerve.

"Now, Joan. Don't get your feathers all knotted up. My office wasn't advised there would be an announcement, much less what it would be. What'd they say?"

She told him.

Packwurst said, "Under JIGADIA, they're supposed to keep us informed."

"I know that, Roody. They've talked to everyone who was at the raid. That's the extent of their cooperation. It's a one-way street."

"Well look. We have plenty of time. The election's ten months away."

An audible exhale greeted that.

"Some year-away election may be at the top of your agenda, but it's not on mine. If you don't call Kludge, I will. I've got to protect my people."

Packwurst knew how to play hardball when he had to with appointed officials like Harris. He sensed now was not the time. She had direct public access. He didn't need a feud aired on this issue. It wouldn't play well.

"I'll call Eric," he told her. "I'll find out what's going on and what they know."

"I want my men off the suspect list, and I want them off now."

"I hear you, Joan. I'll call you as soon as I know something."

He put down the receiver.

His office had already interfered in the investigation once, and Packwurst didn't feel like crossing swords with Kludge again. Besides, until the money was found, there could be no forfeiture, and that was what he wanted, a feather for re-election. He could wait a few days and let the FBI play it out. That would give Harris time to cool off. Then he'd call that snot Kludge for a case update.

He returned to his pictures.

Villamay

Michael met Denise when she pulled into the garage with the children. He'd heard the news. He asked how she was, saw her concern, hugged her, and whispered reassurance. Anyone could have picked up the money he said over and over. The police had to think the drug dealers got it. Be strong. Gut it out. Everything will be fine.

She wasn't at all sure.

Michael was like the Asian monkey with his fist wrapped around a handful of rice inside a thin-necked jar tied to a stake who got captured because he was too greedy to let go of the rice and pull out his hand. She felt torn. He wasn't feeling the pressure she was.

No sooner had they gotten the children out of the car and settled inside the house than a television crew knocked at the front door. She felt she had to make a statement.

"I don't know anything about the money," she said in measured tones. "The bag the detectives opened was full of paper, and that's the one the man had when he came down the alley. If there was any money, I don't know what happened to it. That's all I know. Thank you."

"How do you feel about being named a suspect?"

"The investigators are doing their jobs, and I support them in that. I hope they find the money soon."

"Were you surprised?"

"I cried."

"How does being a suspect contrast with your portrayal by the President as a hero?"

"I don't have anything further to say. Again, thank you very much."

She closed the door, her mind a blur. She told Michael to watch the children and start dinner. She was going to take a bath.

Except for the nightlight, the room was dark, the children quiet in bed. Meals and baths over, nightclothes on, they watched their mother tune her guitar.

John Lennon's "Julia" was their latest favorite lullaby. The trick was the pick, striking the fifth and first strings together, then in rapid succession the fourth, third, sixth, second, and fourth, repeating and changing chords without break. The words were wistful and soft, a haunting tribute of dreamy images and affection to Lennon's mother dead too young.

Tommy and Sydney's eyes alternated watching her fingers moving along the bridge and plucking the strings, seldom looking at her as she sang. Sydney rolled on the pillow and looked sideways through the crib rails. Somnambulant rhyming words and chiming notes lulled their bodies still. Tommy's eyelids grew heavy and closed. Two times through she trailed off singing and played only the notes, ever softer, until the C major seventh coda.

"That was beautiful," said Michael.

She turned. He stood at the door.

"How long have you been there?"

"Long enough to appreciate how much I love you and why."

He had a shy, self-satisfied look.

"I hope we're doing the right thing," she said.

All sentiment left him. The mask fell.

"Everything will be fine," he said and turned away.

Later that evening, the telephone rang.

"Hello."

"Denise James," said a mechanical voice.

"Is this a real person?"

"You are Denise James. You got something that belong to me." The voice was robotic, disguised. "You got my money."

"Who is this?"

"I want it back."

She hung up.

Her first thought was that the call was a crank. Or maybe Olsen and Iacob might be trying to flush her out, might be working some sort of scheme. If someone received a call like that and didn't report it, wouldn't she appear suspect?

That would be true only if Olsen initiated the call. If the drug dealers made it, what good would reporting it do?

What would the innocent Denise James do?

She punched "*69" and wrote down the time and number. She got Olsen's card from her purse and called him. On the fourth ring a recorder answered.

"This is Jack Olsen..."

After the beep, she said, "Hello. This is Denise James." She gave her address and telephone number. "I received a call a few minutes ago from a man who said I had something that didn't belong to me, his money. When I asked who he was, he said he wanted it back. I hung up."

She gave Olsen the "*69" number and time.

"If you record all the telephone calls in the country, bring up a call from that number to this one. It's now ten after nine if you need to synchronize your watch. His voice was electrolyzed somehow. Maybe you can unscramble the call and compare his voiceprint against all the others you have on file. I think he's a dope dealer calling me because you named me as a suspect.

"And while I have you, I think you're out of line naming me and not telling me in advance. We have two little children and no protection. That guy could come over here and do God knows what. Your announcement already got me into an unscheduled conference with the president today, the president of the bank—not the other one.

"Please call me and tell me when you think you'll have this man in custody, and what you're going to do in the meantime to protect us.

"Thank you very much. Bye."

She took the stairs two at a time to tell Michael.

Thursday, February 1
Villamay

Next morning, the media was back on the front lawn. She smiled, and repeated she had not taken the money, that she would cooperate in all respects with the investigation, and that she felt honored to be on the same suspect list with officers Armstrong and Johnson. On the morning news shows, her face split the screen with two of Alexandria's finest.

That night she received another call from the electronic voice.

"Denise James. You got my money. I want it back. You, Michael, Tommy, and Sydney live on Henley Road in the brick house with—"

She hung up.

She got the "*69" information, a different number this time, and called Olsen.

"This is Denise James, again. It's Thursday, February first, eight thirty-five. I just received another call from the same person as last night saying I had his money and telling me the names of my family members and my address. I hung up.

"I would have thought you would have called me back by now about the first call last night, Mr. Olsen. Please call me."

She left her home and office numbers.

Friday, February 2
The Hoover Building

The core task force of Eric Kludge, Paul Fleming, Jack Olsen, and Marv Iacob met to update the case.

"All three individuals reported receiving calls of a suspicious nature," said Olsen. "It was the same scrambled voice calling from different public telephones. Day before yesterday, he told the woman she was in possession of something that didn't belong to her. The money. Yesterday morning, Armstrong and Johnson received similar calls at their homes. Both were on duty the night before. Our informals confirm this. The officers reported the calls to their department heads. The woman received a second call last night and reported it."

"This is a break," said Kludge. "The drug dealers don't have it."

"We are of the same opinion," said Iacob. "Paul has more."

"I do," said Fleming. "This morning, Victor Barracks, by agreement through his counsel, agreed to cooperate in return for a possible reduction of charges. No obligation on our part, unless what he says leads to the recovery of the money."

"What'll he say?" asked Kludge.

"His attorney told me he will say he took the money when the raid started, and exchanged it with another bag in the alley before the woman attacked him."

"That fits with the lab report," said Kludge. "Same type documents in Barracks's bag and the bags next to the wall in the alley. Plus, the bag Barracks had is the same type as the ones in the alley, a different manufacturer than the ones from the park."

Kludge looked to Fleming.

"Barracks says the woman attacked him?"

"That's what his counsel told me off the record," Fleming answered. "We'll have to wait until he signs a formal statement."

Olsen said, "That can't be right. Barracks walked into it, or ran into it. The cops saw it happen. If he says she attacked him, it might taint the validity of the rest of his statement."

"We'll have input before he signs his statement," said Fleming. "I don't for a minute think the woman attacked him and set this all up."

Kludge asked, "Did he say the woman saw him make the switch?"

"Not only will he say that, he'll say he made the switch before the officers came around the corner to see him do it."

"Better and better," said Kludge. "It fits."

"Yes, it does," said Olsen. "And we've interviewed all members of the Alexandria Police Department on the scene that night. While we can't be certain at this point, we believe Armstrong and Johnson can be accounted for until they went off duty. They were with the television crew for the interview at the alley after the incident, and left with the crew. During the neighborhood search, their territory was the north end of Waterfront Park. Other officers covered the area where Barracks was apprehended."

"Interesting," said Kludge. Denise James's picture was clipped to the top of her folder in front of him. "The woman doesn't fit the profile, and the house search was unremarkable. Yet everything points to her. What's she like, Jack?"

"Good looking—smart"—further diplomacy failed—"hell, Eric—she's a smart-ass. There's no other way to describe her. Husband, too. They were drinking heavy. I saw her pop three, and they'd started long before we got there. It was hard to get a straight answer out of them."

"That your opinion too, Marv?"

"It was a difficult inner-view. Neither of us thought she was a viable candidate."

"Do you think she's our man—ah, woman?"

"Either her or a grim-lin," said Iacob.

Gremlins were more rare than unicorns. A gremlin would be a vagrant who saw the switch, picked up the bag, bought a bus ticket to Laredo, and walked into Mexico never to be seen again.

Kludge asked, "Do we have any problems, Paul?"

"We're solid legally."

Kludge looked again at the picture on top of the file.

"However strange it may seem, the woman is our target, gentlemen. Start working on deep background. Keep Paul up to date. This assumes the final lab reports don't contradict anything we've said, and that Barracks's statement of facts agrees."

Olsen threw himself a modest mental party.

"Be careful. No guesses, no hunches, no chances. If she's got the money, the proverbial will hit the fan when it becomes public. Keep each other informed. Questions?"

"Estimated timeframe?" asked Iacob.

"Six to eight weeks. Take your time. There has to be no doubt."

It was late afternoon when Olsen called Denise at Treasure Chest Bank.

"I'm sorry not to have gotten back to you sooner, Ms. James. You say you've received calls of an unusual nature?"

"Why didn't you tell me you were naming me a suspect before you announced it on television?"

"We're not in the habit of notifying suspects they are under investigation."

"Instead you have a press officer announce it to the world?"

"I'm not certain what I can do about the calls," said Olsen. "You say you wrote down the numbers?"

"Haven't you done anything with the information I gave you?"

"Neither do we record every telephone call in the country as you suggest, Ms. James. I'm not sure we can help you."

She could feel her cheeks flushing.

"No, I suppose you wouldn't want to help anyone you've already labeled a suspect."

"Is there anything else, Ms. James?"

"No, Agent Mulder. You won't be hearing from me again unless—"

The line disconnected.

Denise and Michael attended class at the gym that evening. It felt good to get out on the floor and punch and kick and sweat without having to think too much about the suspect announcement or the telephone calls.

When they arrived back home, there was a message on the answering machine.

"Denise James. My partners and I are worry about the health of your husband and children. Have they been feeling okay? You take my next call if you want them to stay that way."

Michael gawked. This was the first time he'd heard the voice.

"That's the third call," she told him. "According to that, there's going to be one more. Then something's going to happen."

"And the FBI won't do anything?"

"Not while I'm a suspect."

"What are we supposed to do? Buy guns?"

"We can save this message for evidence. Maybe play it for Dan Mattison." She pulled the telephone book from a cabinet. "And we can get an unlisted number. That'll stop him from calling."

Without a sound she mouthed the words, "I'm turning in the money."

She didn't like the look he gave her. He started to say something, and she put her finger on his lips. They'd agreed not to talk in the house without a sound buffer.

He shook his head no.

85

She took the telephone book with her and left him still shaking his head.

Monday, February 5
Treasure Chest Bank

Morton Mieske appeared at Denise's office door.
"Come with me."
"What's the matter?"
"You'll need to see for yourself."
She followed him to the employee sub-basement parking garage. Bank guards were there. Mieske watched her as she walked around her car.
Green-white safety glass lay like crusted ice along the concrete around the car's fenders. Whatever remnants remained in the frames after they'd been broken looked as if they'd been routed out. Holes cratered the front and back windshields leaving them opaque and fragile. Squares of glass sat piled on the seats. The trunk was open.
Mieske said, "The lot attendant heard a car alarm go off. He came down. He got the guards. The guards called me. No one saw anything."
She didn't know what to say.
"I'd guess a sledgehammer," said Mieske. "It's a message from the drug dealers."
"But Morton, I don't have the money."
Mieske pulled his cell phone from his belt, handed it to her, and said, "Call your husband. Tell him what's happened. Ask him to meet us outside your house. Tell him not to go inside. I'll drive."

Villamay

Mieske pulled his car to the curb on Henley Road.
"Give me your front door key."
She handed it to him.
"Stay here."
He left her in the car, engine running, and went to the front door. He inserted the key, turned it, and pushed the door wide, leaving the

key in the lock. He looked inside for some seconds without crossing the threshold, then backed away to the middle of the lawn where he punched his cell phone and spoke. After he hung up, he got back in the car.

"We'll wait for the police."

"What's wrong?"

"Could be someone inside. We'll let the pros handle it."

Michael arrived by taxi and slid into the backseat.

"The BMW's windows are smashed," he said in a rush. "There's glass everywhere."

He was shaken.

"Any suspects?" asked Mieske.

"Security's there. I don't know what they know."

A K-9 unit and two police cars drove up. Mieske got out, briefed the officer in charge, and got back in the car. A German shepherd and five officers went to the front door where the dog was released into the house.

Inside the car, Denise reached over the seat and held Michael's hand. They waited and watched, palms getting sticky.

The shepherd reappeared, and the officers went through the front door leaving it open. Minutes passed.

"Why is it taking so long?" asked Denise.

"They're looking for more than people," said Mieske.

Michael leaned over the seat.

"Like what?"

"Like maybe a booby-trap." Mieske turned to Denise. "Maybe something else."

"Like clues someone's been in there?" she asked.

"Not much doubt of that."

They waited until an officer appeared at the door and motioned them in.

"It's clear," said Mieske. "We can go inside. Don't touch anything."

The foyer lay in disarray from the closet's contents. In the den, the computer, video equipment, and television had been smashed where they sat. Loose paper was everywhere, an incredible amount of paper. In the dining room they stepped over broken china and scattered

87

linen, then over cutlery, dishes, and food on the kitchen floor. The cupboards, refrigerator, freezer, and pantry were empty. Water ran between the stairway rails overhead and dripped through wet spots in the first floor ceiling. Large sections of the living room carpet pooled wet.

Going up the stairs, they were warned not to touch the handrail. In the bathrooms, officers had already shut off faucets that had overflowed plugged sinks. Medicine cabinet contents floated in the toilets. Clothing and bedding were scattered and upturned. In the children's room, the guitar was in two pieces, joined by the strings. An officer stopped Denise before she could pick it up.

"Might have fingerprints," he said.

Downstairs, they gave their statements standing on soggy carpet, surrounded by broken lamps and upended furniture. Denise noticed Michael's vacant stare at the area where the sofa had been. She supposed she had the same expression on her face. A photographer snapped pictures. Mieske looked on.

Michael asked if he could use the telephone to call the insurance agent to report the damage. Mieske said no, and handed him the phone from his belt.

An officer showed them the punched in window in the side door where a hand had reached in and turned the deadbolt. He said the damage looked like the work of a street gang paid to trash the place in ten minutes. Mieske concurred.

"Do you think there's a chance of finding them?" asked Michael.

"There's some," said the officer. "We got lab people on the way. We'll talk to the neighbors, see if anyone saw or heard anything. You never know."

Mieske asked if they had anywhere to spend the night. Michael said he'd book a room at a motel and get a rental car so they could pick up the children.

"Good idea," said Mieske. "They're going to dust for prints, run some tests. This'll take a few hours."

"Press is here," called an officer from the front.

"I want to talk to them," said Denise, her first words since entering the house.

"Watch what you say," Mieske called as she went over the threshold.

"Ms. James, can you tell us what happened here?"

"Our house and cars have been vandalized," she said in an even tone.

"Do you know who might have done this?"

"The drug dealers did it. Someone from the FBI announced my name and the names of the two police officers as suspects in the investigation of the missing money from the Old Town raid. They spotlighted us for the dealers. I've received threatening telephone calls, and I left messages about them with Special Agent Jack Olsen of the FBI. When he called back, he said the Bureau didn't aid suspects. Now our home and cars have been broken into and our things destroyed."

She lowered her voice.

"Let this be a warning to Officers Armstrong and Johnson, and their families. Agent Olsen and his team aren't afraid to set them up to further their investigation."

"Do you have the money, Ms. James?"

"No, I do not," she stated without hesitation. "If I did, I'd turn it in to be free of this nightmare."

"Do the police have any leads?"

"I'm sorry, that's all I have to say. I have to get back with my husband and figure out how to pick up the children."

She left the next question unanswered and returned inside.

Next day, children dropped at daycare, they returned to clean house. Police kept a few reporters at bay across the street, and Denise provided no comment to their shouted questions as she and Michael crossed the lawn from the driveway to their front door.

While they were still sizing up the job, Mark and Karen Stewart, parents of their babysitting twins Sarah and Terry, showed up dressed in work clothes and trailing two plastic garbage barrels on wheels. They were a welcomed addition.

Work began in the den, picking up papers and pictures and books and usable items first, then sweeping the remaining debris into piles to expose gouges in the hardwood floor.

Two men who lived down the street arrived with a boom box. Michael told them to plug it in, set it to their favorite station, and crank it up. With music playing, the newcomers picked up the console television and hauled it to the street.

More people arrived. Some came to work; some said their high-school-age children would be over after the day's last class. The side door windowpane was replaced. Someone brought a wet-vac. By mid-morning, ten people were helping with the cleanup, all unsolicited. Two couples wore "United We Stand" sweatshirts.

As work went on, Denise came to realize that if she and Michael were cleaning up by themselves, it would take days to finish, and they'd be getting on each other's nerves as the extent of damage became more evident. But with all these people helping, they made remarkable progress. She felt heart-warmed by their show of support. It wasn't a party by any means, but there was camaraderie, and with guests in the house, she and Michael were on their best behavior.

At the same time, she felt a certain shameful guilt. Here were all these people helping because they believed she and Michael were victims. That was an iffy proposition at best, since she and Michael still had the money. Well, she thought, she was a victim. If this had been a barn raising, it wasn't as if she'd burned down her own barn. Somebody else burned it down, and these people were helping her rebuild. Whether or not she took the money, she'd been trashed, and here were the neighbors come to help. All the same, she felt uneasy deceiving them.

"I'm ordering pizza!" Michael shouted from the first floor. "Place your orders. Soda and pizza for everybody."

Gus Gordon wandered by while they were eating. Thin and stooped, he sat in a chair Michael pulled up, and accepted a slice of double cheese.

"You two should have gotten that security system," he said. "Might have prevented that big pile of trash out front."

"What security system?" asked Michael.

"I forgot to ask you about that," said Denise. She filled him in on what Gordon had told her.

"I don't know anything about it," said Michael. "I never called anybody about a security system."

Denise said, "The side door where they broke in faces your house, Gus. Everyone here was at work yesterday. Did you see anything?"

"Like I told the police, Rosemary and I see pretty good, but we can't hear too good. I didn't notice anything. Rosemary says she didn't either, but her memory isn't what it used to be."

"How old is she?" Denise asked.

"Same age as me, eighty-four next February. You two ought to find out who those security people were. Their truck was out front a long time."

Piles of trash and bags of broken household goods grew along the curb. By the time the high school kids arrived, the bulk of the work was done. Washing clothes would take the rest of the day, and the carpets would need steam cleaning in places, not to mention painting over the water damage on the walls and ceilings, but everything usable was back in place. The house approached being livable again.

"We're going to have all of you over for a thank you party when we get this place put back together," Denise announced when they broke for the day. "It's wonderful what you've done for us. Thank you so much."

After everyone left and they could be themselves again, Michael asked Denise to look at the list he'd made of the damages. He was angry. The insurance claim would be impressive, and he wasn't looking forward to negotiating with the adjustor. She took the papers. He sat on the sofa bouncing his heels on the carpet.

"We should stay at the motel for the next few days," she said. "Just to get our heads back together. The cost of that should be on the list."

"Add it."

She did, and started flipping through the pages. She could see him fidgeting out of the corner of her eye.

She said, "You know, I don't agree with what Morton told us about not saying anything to the media. He might be trying to protect his old buddies."

Mieske had advised them not to say anything further about the FBI after Denise named Olsen as unresponsive. What she'd said had been quite enough. It was for this reason she hadn't spoken to the reporters that morning.

"I'd like to stick it to Olsen and his crew for this," said Michael, an edge to his voice.

"Fat chance sticking anything to anybody at the FBI. There's no higher authority."

"Well somebody made the decision to name you," he said. "Why can't we make a big stink about it and find out who it was? We might be able to sue him."

Her eyes wandered over the list and grew hard, like chipped green ice.

"That's not good enough," she said looking up. "I want to embarrass them."

Chapter Eight

Saturday, February 10
Villamay

They got their cars back with new glass Friday, and returned to their home that night. Saturday dawned sunny and mild, not a hint of a breeze. When Denise went to get the newspaper, Dan Mattison hopped from a van.

"Ms. James? Could I speak to you for a moment, please?"

"Morning, Dan."

"Would you mind answering a few questions?"

"There's a backlog of curiosity about us, isn't there?"

"Yes, there is. No one knows where you've been these last few days."

"The FBI knows."

"Yeah, and they're taking some heat over what happened to you."

"Not enough."

Mattison had makeup on, his hair sprayed. He was ready for Prime Time.

She had an idea, at least the start of one.

"I'll tell you what, Dan. Would you like an interview? Let us tell our side of the story?"

"Of course."

"Okay." She pointed to the lawn between the sidewalk and the house "Set up a table and three chairs right here with all the cameras you want." She faced him. "I'll make a statement and answer any questions you have. It'll be exclusive. You'll be the only other person at the table besides Michael."

"Your word on that?"

She delivered her answer with an alluring smile, knowing full well that in his current mood, Michael would be an easier sell for her this time than he had been for the interview with Olsen.

"My word," she said. "We'll be effervescent."

By ten fifteen, Channel Three had assembled a mobile broadcast unit, camera crew, and the requested set. Inside the house, Sarah and Terry Stewart were baby-sitting Tommy and Sydney. Mattison had everything ready, and was about to go to the front door, when it opened and Michael appeared. He crossed the lawn paying out an electric extension cord. Mattison met him at the table.

"We're ready when you are, Mr. James. And I'd like to thank you and your wife for this opportunity."

"You're quite welcome. Are you airing this live?"

"No. We're feeding it to the station. They'll tape it and use excerpts."

"Good."

Michael laid down the balance of the cord and placed a telephone recorder on the table. He said, "Since Denise is going to do most of the talking, why don't we let her sit in the middle?"

"Whatever you like, Mr. James."

"Call me Michael."

They sat, and fitted themselves with microphones lying ready on the table. A soundman tested voice volume. Behind them the front door opened, and Denise came out. She carried a tray, and walked across the lawn as if attending a garden party in St. James Park. She laid the tray on the table. On the tray were three glasses, a bowl of sliced lime, a saltshaker, napkins, and a bottle of tequila.

"Good morning again, Dan."

"Good morning, Denise."

She shook his hand, sat, and clipped the microphone to her lapel. "This is a voice test. Is it okay?"

A technician gave her a thumbs-up.

She nodded to Mattison. "I'm almost ready."

"Denise," said Mattison. "What's this about?" He pointed at the bottle.

"This is so we won't get tongue-tied. We're not used to being on television."

Michael picked up the bottle, unscrewed the top, and filled a shot glass.

"Denise?"

"Yes, please. I'm a little nervous."

"Me too. Dan?"

The odor tempted Mattison not at all.

"It's a little early for me."

"Suit yourself," said Michael capping the bottle.

94

Denise and Michael shared the shaker sprinkling crystals on the skin between their thumb and forefinger, clicked glasses, licked the salt, downed the golden liquid, and chewed a slice of lime.

"I don't think this is a good idea," said Mattison.

"Oh, it's all right," she said. "A little nip takes the edge off performance anxiety." She looked at the camera. "We're not used to this."

"You can't drink liquor on television."

"It's done all the time, Dan," said Michael. He refilled the glasses. "Cowboys come off the trail and wet their whistles. Besides, this is taped. But I understand what you're saying." He put the bottle on the ground between his and Denise's chairs. "We'll keep it out of sight."

"See that you do," said Mattison.

Michael placed the glasses behind the bowl of lime.

The mobile unit manager got a final okay from everyone, Mattison heard the "count-in" on his ear mike, and the red light on the middle camera lit.

"Good morning, everyone. I'm Dan Mattison, Channel Three Action News, here in Alexandria, Virginia outside the home of Denise and Michael James. As many of you know, Denise James became involved in a drug interdiction undertaken by the FBI and the Alexandria Police Department last January. She was hailed a hero for her role that night in apprehending one of the suspects, and she was introduced as such to the nation at the State of the Union Address. It has now been disclosed that more than three million dollars is missing from the raid, and the FBI has named Ms. James as a suspect in its disappearance. Earlier this week, the Jameses had their personal residence, you can see it there behind me, and their cars vandalized.

"Denise. I understand you'd like to start with a statement."

"Yes, I would, Dan. Thank you." She gave him a nod. "This week there has been renewed interest in what happened that night in January. I'd like to go over those events, and then allow you to ask me any questions you like."

"That's very generous, Ms. James. Thank you."

She faced the camera and began, starting with the end of the Treasure Chest dinner. Two minutes into the dialogue, she picked up the saltshaker, sprinkled, licked, drank, and chewed. Then in full view of the camera, Michael picked up the bottle and filled her glass.

Mattison leaned forward, distress on his face. Michael set the bottle on the table. With Mattison sitting on the other side of Denise, the bottle was outside Mattison's reach.

"Let it go," Mattison heard in his ear from the mobile unit manager. The attentive interviewer expression returned to Mattison's face as he sat back in his chair.

The mobile unit manager then called the station's program director.

"Cut to Mobile Three's line, Raj. We're transmitting to tape. Denise James is doing tequila shooters on her front lawn."

When the program director saw Denise take a third shot on the live feed, he called the station manager. Six minutes later, the home repair show being aired was pre-empted, and the James interview was broadcast live as breaking news. Stations monitoring Channel Three recognized its tabloid value and dispatched mobile units.

Inside the Hoover Building, Accumulation was monitoring all channels and took note of Channel Three cutting to its special report. Following procedure, Eric Kludge was called at home. He watched a few minutes, then ordered agents to Villamay as a precaution.

A half-hour into the narrative, four television stations and four Fairfax County police officers were on site. A crowd of neighbors had gathered behind the cameras, including members of the cleanup crew from Monday. Denise had had eight shots, Michael six.

"The FBI made a public announcement that I was a suspect," Denise continued. "I wasn't advised in advance. Then I received three telephone calls from someone I didn't know asking about money I didn't have. I'd like to play one of those calls if I could?"

Feeling powerless to object, Mattison said, "Of course."

Denise unclipped her mike, held it over the recorder, and pressed Play. The machine's voice said, "Friday, seven forty-seven p.m." Then came the disguised voice.

"Denise James. My partners and I are worry about the health of your husband and children. Have they been feeling okay? You take my next call if you want them to stay that way."

She put the mike back on her lapel.

"These calls scared us. I telephoned Special Agent Jimmy Olsen of the FBI and left messages asking for help. I got a call back from Mr. Olsen in which he said the Bureau was not in the habit of assisting suspects during an investigation. I asked for protection. He declined. When our automobiles and home were ransacked, we believed the taped voice was responsible."

Mattison asked her to play the message a second time.

Two Concordes arrived and double-parked as close to the crowd as they could get without blocking the street. Special Agent Joseph Stitch was already in direct contact with Eric Kludge by cell phone and began a situation report as soon as he got out of the car.

Denise was speaking.

"One of the dealers could have taken the money and not told anyone in the gang. Or the money could have been switched with another bag before the buyers and sellers met in the park."

Michael filled her glass, the bottle two-thirds empty. Feeds from the local stations were already up-linked to the networks. People in airport lounges and hospital waiting rooms watched, and a crowd stood in the street gazing at her image on the giant-screen in Times Square. The official shot-count was at the bottom of the picture. Denise had had twelve, Michael ten.

"A neighbor could have picked it up," she said. "A homeless person could have gotten it, or anyone else who walked by. There may not have been any money at the site at all. Don't forget, the Alexandria police were prepared for the raid."

Michael filled her glass.

"They knew the time and place of the sale in advance," she said.

He topped his glass.

"So, here's a big secret." Her eyes sparkled. *"There's an informant."*

The camera cropped to her face.

"Otherwise, how would the police know to be at that place at that time with all those people ready to jump out of the bushes?" She asked this thrusting the fingers of both hands at the camera as if to say *"Boo!"*

"And where was the FBI during this cooperative raid with the Alexandria Police Department under that joint JIGSAW agreement they were talking about?"

"It's JIGADIA, you dumb bitch," Kludge said into his phone.

"Who was there from the FBI? No one's said. Who's the informant? No one's said. But that's getting away from the reason we're here, because I can't solve this case."

She licked and drank. The graphic on the screen changed her total to thirteen.

Kludge asked Stitch, "What are the cops doing?"

"Nothing."

"Go see if they'll stop this."

Stitch went to speak to the patrolmen.

Denise continued. "What upsets us is the high-handed nature of the actions taken by a few FBI agents. They're *supposed* to work for *us*, you know." She held out her hands, agitated. "They've shown a decided lack of respect for innocent citizens. Even if Officer Armstrong, Officer Johnson, or I actually *have* the money, that means the other two *don't,* yet we were *all exposed* to the drug dealers."

Michael drank his shot. His total changed to eleven. He refilled the glasses.

Stitch told Kludge, "The cops won't do anything. They say they're on private property."

"How close are you to them?"

"Twenty-five, thirty feet."

"Deploy to arrest."

Stitch turned his back to the crowd.

"On live television?"

"That's right. On live television. Cite FCC violations."

"Sir. I don't think it's—"

"That's an order, Special Agent. Deploy the team and wait."

"Yes, sir."

Denise said, "We had to spend four nights in a motel for our safety because it was clear"—she licked her hand—"the FBI wasn't going to protect us"—she drank—"and had, in fact, set us up, putting us at the mercy of the drug dealers."

The graphic changed her total to fourteen. Little was left in the bottle.

"So the purpose of me saying all this is to tell the two drug gangs that the James family doesn't have the money, and to please leave us alone. For all *I* know, the FBI agents *running* this investigation have it, and they've staged this *whole* charade as a cover-up so *they* can keep the cash for themselves."

"Goddamnit!" thundered Kludge. "Arrest them! FCC violations. Go! Go! Go!"

Michael was fingering the un-squeezed lime slices in the bowl as agents moved from the crowd.

"Denise James. Michael James, FBI." Stitch stood in front of the table showing his badge. "You are under arrest for violations of Federal Communications Commission rules and regulations."

"Name them," retorted Denise

Agents circled to her rear.

"Please stand up, ma'am," said Stitch. "You too, sir."

Cameras jockeyed for position.

"What's the real charge?" asked Denise standing up.

"Please be quiet, Ms. James," said an agent behind her. He pulled her arm behind her back and snapped a handcuff on her wrist. "I will silence you if necessary."

Stitch turned around. "Shut off the cameras," he commanded.

"Don't do it, Dan," called Denise.

"You're drunk, Ms. James," said the agent cuffing her other wrist.

"I am not."

"I can smell the booze."

"We want a breath test," said Michael.

"You'll get one downtown," said the agent locking cuffs on him.

"The police are here," countered Denise. "They can test us right now."

The agent holding her arm said, "Move along ma'am, or resisting arrest will be added to the charges."

Stitch walked toward the television crews, his hands spread wide.

"That's enough. Lay the cameras on the ground, or the equipment will be confiscated. Do it now."

Denise and Michael were seen being hustled into the back of one of the Concordes before the last camera from Channel Three was turned off and the broadcast ended.

"It seems any form of common courtesy is forbidden," said Michael. "It's as if they're drugged."

Cruising north up the George Washington Memorial Parkway, Denise and Michael had received no response to any of the questions they'd posed to the agents in the front seat.

Denise offered an explanation.

"Their mashed potatoes might be spiked with saltpeter."

She'd already removed the key taped to the inside of her belt at her back. She turned it in the left cuff.

"Look at them," she said. "Vacant stares. Soft palms. Deviated palates."

"I've never heard of that," said Michael. "How can you get a deviated palate?"

The agents stared ahead mute; conscious they were being baited. A rancid odor emanated from the backseat.

Michael asked, "I wonder why they always go around in pairs?"

"J. Edgar set the standard for that with Charles Tolson. I understand they were bosom buddies, but that's supposed to be a fiction made up by the left wing."

"Baseless polemics?"

"I suppose."

By the time the car arrived at 10th and Pennsylvania, the agents were relieved to turn over their passengers to the waiting security team.

Kludge felt a cold shiver cross his neck and spread outward toward his extremities.

"Don't tell me we arrested them on television for drinking tea."

"It's probable, sir," said Stitch from Villamay. "There's a note taped to the top and bottom of the tray that says it's tea. The bottle and glasses haven't been analyzed yet, but they don't smell, and the woman wasn't falling down drunk."

"I know she wasn't falling down drunk!"

Kludge leaned back in his chair. To make any charge stick, the tea would have to be replaced with tequila, and a positive Breathalyzer test produced. If pursued that way, the case would become a swearing contest. The woman would call expert after expert to testify that if she'd consumed that much alcohol in so short a time, she'd have been face forward on the table.

He was going to become the Bureau's village idiot for this. The media would turn him on a spit for weeks.

"Okay," he said. "Send the evidence to the lab. If the bottle is tea, we'll charge them with what we can. I'll have Paul Fleming meet us downtown in my office in an hour."

The Hoover Building

Two agents stood in the center of a waiting room watching Denise and Michael sit on a sofa. One wall from waist to ceiling was thick glass behind which were reception stations and the building's exterior windows. The other walls were off-white, decorated with the Department of Justice-FBI seal and a color photograph of the President, his official portrait. Keypad interior entry doors were on opposite sides of the glass. Video cameras hung in corners from an acoustic tile ceiling. A metal detector stood to one side as if placed there as an afterthought.

"So this is FBI World Headquarters," said Denise. "I love what you've done with the place. What do you call this style? Neo-Federalist Plain?"

The agents faced them, feet apart, immobile.

Michael asked, "How long does it take to get booked into these accommodations?"

"It will probably be a few minutes more, sir," said an agent. "Please be patient."

They waited, asking a flood of questions. Was the wall in front of reception protected all the way to the floor with bulletproof glass, or were the receptionists susceptible to being shot at by intruders who aimed at the drywall underneath? Was the ceiling protected? Couldn't someone reach over the grid and drop a grenade on the other side? Besides, how could anyone with a weapon get this far into the building with all the security they had downstairs? And what was so important about the receptionists anyway?

Like palace guards, the agents didn't move.

Denise asked if it was true American spy satellites had cameras with enough resolution they could identify the fingerprints of people holding their hands in the air during a holdup. Michael pointed out it would be the holdup men whose fingerprints they would want, not the people being held up. Denise seemed perplexed by this; then admitted it had been a trick question. Wasn't it common knowledge the government knew whether O. J. Simpson was guilty or not because they had it all on tape from spy-in-the-sky cameras and chose not to disclose the truth in order to keep the technology secret?

An hour passed before a side door opened and four men entered.

"Mulder and Scully!" A smile swept Denise's face. "It's wonderful to see you." She and Michael stood.

"We'd love to shake hands, but…" She turned to show her wrists.

Eric Kludge sighed.

"I think you can remove those."

One of the agents reached into his pocket, but before he could produce the key, the Jameses brought their arms forward, two sets of handcuffs dangling from their fingers.

Silence.

"I'm sorry," said Denise. "Did you mean for him to do it?" She pointed to the agent and looked at Kludge. "You said 'you' and I thought you meant 'us.' Sometimes I'm not very good with personal pronouns. What did you think he meant, Michael?"

"I thought he meant us."

An awkward moment followed. Kludge stepped inside the aura of tequila and took the handcuffs.

"Well," he said flat-voiced. "Would you join us in our conference room. There are things we need to discuss."

"Lead on," said Denise.

"I'm going to have to ask you to step through this metal detector before we go any further," Kludge told them. "Please remove all personal items you may be carrying."

Michael emptied his pockets into a plastic bowl held by Iacob and walked through the arch. From the bowl, Iacob picked up a perfume atomizer. He shook it, and sprayed the air.

"So, this is how y'all got the smell," he said.

"You can keep it," said Michael. "It's almost empty."

"Mine too," said Denise handing him hers. She walked through the detector.

In front of one of the interior doors, an agent cupped the keypad so only he could see, punched buttons, and swiped his neck-card to click the door open. They walked a long corridor, an area of partitioned workstations, an elevator lobby, and another hallway before they entered a conference room.

"Please be seated," said Kludge.

Everyone sat.

"I'm Special Agent in Charge Eric Peabody Kludge of the Federal Bureau of Investigation."

If he anticipated a reaction, he got none.

"You were very cute this morning with your tea and tequila trick."

"Thank you," said Denise.

"You knew it was on television?"

"We knew it was being taped," Michael answered. "Has it been aired?"

"Yes."

Denise said, "I hope you're humiliated for the way you treated us. Would you have done what you did if the three suspects had been FBI agents?"

"That's beside the point."

"Then switch houses with us until the money's found."

Kludge ignored her suggestion and turned to the man on his right.

"This is Assistant United States Attorney Paul Fleming. He's with the Department of Justice. I'll let him speak."

Fleming fingered his pen, not the least hurried.

"There are a number of charges that can be brought against the two of you."

"Then book us," challenged Denise.

Fleming spoke in such a slow rhythm it was easy to interrupt.

"After careful consideration on our part, we hope not to have to do that at this time."

"How inconsiderate of you," said Denise. "You have nothing to charge us with except something you make up."

"If I could please finish?"

He waited until she nodded.

"As I said, we would like not to have to charge you with anything at this time. There are, however, a number of serious felonies the government could bring against you, including conspiracy and obstruction of justice. But we think we have a fair way to settle all this, and I'd like for you to listen to a proposal I am about to offer."

103

Michael asked, "Do we need an attorney for this?"

"You do not need legal counsel as long as we do not pose questions for which you may need legal advice. You may listen to the proposal I am about to offer you without such aid."

"Then shoot," said Denise.

Fleming picked up his pad, stood, and returned his chair to the table, standing behind it. He projected dignity and poise. He looked at Denise for a moment, then bowed his head and read.

"First, our discussion with you, this negotiation, is verbal between us, and is confidential between yourselves and us only. In addition, you agree to say nothing negative or derogatory to anyone regarding the Bureau, the government, its actions, its employees, or its representatives.

"Second, you both hereby agree to cooperate fully with the existing investigation to determine the location of the missing funds from the attempted drug sale of January sixteenth. This will consist of debriefing sessions to be done at mutually convenient times.

"Third, you will disclose to us all real property you own, any real property you lease, and all other personal property within your possession, and you will allow us entry to same.

"Fourth, you will submit to a blood test.

"Fifth, you agree to be fingerprinted and photographed for our files.

"Sixth, you will apologize to the public for your actions of today in language to which we will all agree."

He looked up.

"Is that all?" asked Denise. "Only six things?"

"That's it," said Kludge. "We think this is a very fair resolution. In return, we will not press charges against you. This neutralizes the situation for everyone."

"My, my," said Denise. "Such a weighty decision requires careful consideration and sober thought. My head's still spinning with tea."

"You'll need to agree now, or we'll withdraw it," said Kludge. "You're both smart people. You don't need to shoulder the cost of an attorney or the bad publicity if we go the other way."

Denise turned to Michael.

"Would you like to go belly-up under Mr. Flaming's demands and have them run right the hell over us? Or should we make a counterproposal?"

"Counter it."

"All right, Mr. Flaming. Here's our proposal."

"It's Fleming."

"That's what I said. Flaming. I'm from Ohio. The accent's different."

She leaned forward and addressed the decision maker: Kludge.

"Here's our deal. You apologize to the two police officers and their families, and to us, for exposing us all to the drug dealers without notice. You provide around-the-clock protection until the missing funds are found, or until we feel safe. That goes for the officers too, if they want it. You show us all the evidence you have that points to me taking the money. This includes anything oral or written, infrared photographs, psychic readings, everything. Also, you have to reimburse our insurance company for what they have to pay, and reimburse us for the deductibles we have to pay, to repair the damage your actions caused to our property. If the police officers got vandalized, them too. And we want it in writing and made public."

She turned to Michael.

"Anything else?"

"They have to drive us home."

"That's right. We don't have a ride."

Kludge seemed to hold his breath. Fleming stared at his legal pad. No one moved.

"Jack," said Kludge. "Take them to booking and hold them." Kludge walked to the door and turned to face them. "You'll need legal counsel now." He left the room.

"Lead the way, Mulder," said Denise. "By the way, Mr. Flaming. What are the charges?"

Fleming said to Olsen, "I'll see you downstairs, Jack."

In Eric Kludge's office, Paul Fleming's position never wavered.

"You can't charge them with anything I can make stick, Eric. This thing is on national news. We're swamped with calls asking us what we're doing with them. They were introduced at the State of the Union. They're high profile, and they fooled us, fooled us good. They may not have intended it to go this far, but that's the result. To protect the Bureau and the integrity of this investigation, let's just drive them home."

Kludge had his back against the wall doing his best to maintain composure.

"If you don't agree with me on this, Eric, I'll go to Assistant Director Penes. I mean it. The networks have already announced what was written on the tray. If we drag this out, we're going to make the damn woman look like Robin Hood."

"Those assholes made us look like idiots," Kludge said under his breath.

Iacob said, "We might could keep after the woman, Eric. Nothin' keeps us from workin' the case. The way Ah see it, it's her or a grimlin. Let's keep at it. Give her a few weeks to get comfortable an' make a mistake. Time's on our side. Let's finish the profile, an' spring it on her when we're good 'n' ready."

Kludge wavered. "How do we handle today's mess?"

"Have someone say we were trying to protect the public," said Fleming. "We saw two people on television drinking tequila straight out of the bottle. We sent agents because the woman is a suspect in a federal case. The agents didn't know she was drinking tea. On their own initiative they moved in to protect the public good. It was Saturday morning. Kids were watching cartoons. But ha! It was only tea. Make it sound like we're good sports not charging them with anything."

If Fleming went over his head, Kludge knew blame would fall on him alone. If he went along with Fleming, his career might be singed, but not over. The best scenario would be to spread responsibility and have Olsen and Iacob convince Stitch to say he'd acted on his own in making the arrest. Stitch could then count on Kludge to return the favor big-time down the road.

"Okay, Paul. Let them go. We'll need that announcement in time for the evening news."

"Fine. I'll do up a draft. But have someone drive them home now."

Olsen said, "Get the agents that drove them down here to do it."

The days that followed were filled with debate about the front lawn arrest, but the public affairs office at the Department of Justice declined further comment after its initial "protection of the public good" statement. Since the automobile of Officer Johnson and the home and automobile of Officer Armstrong had been vandalized, credence was lent to out-of-bounds behavior. If an arrest at the "Tea Party" had to be made, the consensus was local police should have made it, not the FBI, whose actions came to be viewed as reactionary in order to halt negative comments being made about the Bureau at the time. The FBI's job was to protect against terrorist threats, not arrest private citizens drinking anything on their own property. A prominent mental health expert did question why upwardly mobile parents with two small children and promising careers would place themselves before the cameras in such a farce, and suggested their psychological fitness as parents be examined. Youth was cited as an excuse. Editorial cartoons abounded and talk show hosts feasted. The FBI cat had been belled, and the cat would just have to live with it.

Behind the walls of the Hoover Building, Eric Kludge formed a new task force, and kept them busy sharpening knives.

Jason McCullough was the only arrested suspect to make bail. He did so the third week of February. Three days later he missed his first appointment with his probation officer, and the court issued a warrant, a fact reported by the press. Perhaps in retaliation for his betrayal of Operation Flytrap, perhaps in response to questions still hanging unanswered from the Tea Party, Paul Fleming's office named McCullough as the Old Town raid informant. Public opinion then speculated that McCullough, along with other unknown accomplices, had somehow recovered the money.

For Johnny Murphy and Nick "The Knife" Rivera, it was a long way out of a hole three million dollars deep, and the moment Jason McCullough was exposed as the snitch, shipments between Baltimore and Alexandria resumed. Fueled by public speculation on McCullough's role in the raid, Rivera became convinced Johnny Murphy had conspired with McCullough to take the money in an effort to hemorrhage his operation and force him out of business.

In Villamay, after taking precautions, Denise began to feel storm clouds clearing.

Chapter Nine

Two Months Later - Tuesday, April 10 - 8:10 P.M.
Villamay

(SEAL)

U. S. Department of Justice
United States Attorney
Eastern District of Virginia
1421 Courthouse Square
Alexandria, Virginia 22314

VIA HAND DELIVERY

Denise Elizabeth Lang James
5958 Henley Road
Alexandria, Virginia 22307

Dear Ms. James,

This letter is to advise you that you are a target of a federal grand jury investigation in this district into allegations that you engaged in theft, tampering with evidence, conspiracy after the fact, obstruction of justice, drug trafficking as an accessory after the fact, racketeering, lying to federal agents, impeding a federal investigation and income tax evasion in violation of Title 18, United States Code, Sections 2B1.1, 2X1.1, 2D1.1, 2J1.2, 3C1.1, 3C1.1(3)(g), 3C1.1(4)(b), 3C1.1(4)(c), 2E1.1, 2T1.1, 2T1.6 and related statutes.

This office expects to request the grand jury to return an indictment of you in due course. If, however, you are interested in resolving potential criminal charges against you by means of a pre-indictment plea agreement pursuant to which you would provide complete and truthful cooperation with the government, your attorney should contact us at this address as soon as possible. Please be advised that any cooperation by you would necessarily include your complete and truthful testimony with respect to yourself and your co-conspirator, should he be prosecuted.

If you are interested in exploring the possibility of such a pre-indictment plea agreement, please have your attorney contact us within ten days of your receipt of this letter. If we have not heard from you by that time, we will assume that you are not interested in such a plea agreement.

Very truly yours,

OLGA G. FAIRCHILD
UNITED STATES ATTORNEY

By: *Richard Paul Fleming, III*
Bruce Carpenter Lee
Richard Paul Fleming, III
Assistant United States Attorneys

ccs: Special Agents James Olsen and Marvin Iacob

"I can't imagine ending a letter like this with 'Very truly yours.' It's like, 'Greetings! Your mother is dead. Have a nice day, The Morgue.'"

Denise handed the single sheet to Michael. Special Agents Jack Olsen and Marv Iacob stood in the foyer.

Olsen said, "If there is an indictment, the charges may be refined from those specified in the letter."

Michael's eyes scrolled down the page. "This is a Xerox signature."

"It's official under the rules," replied Olsen.

Michael frowned. "Let me get this straight. No charges have been filed, and no indictment has been issued, and you're here scaring the wits out of us with this letter?"

"I suggest you take it to an attorney at the earliest possible time," said Olsen. "This is a criminal matter. You should be advised by a criminal attorney."

Denise had become lightheaded after her initial comment on the letter. Colors looked pale. With just enough sound to be audible, she said, "I don't know any attorneys who are criminals, Mulder."

"Ms. James," said Olsen much too fast. "My name is Olsen, Jack Olsen. Not Mulder. Your silliness is inappropriate under the circumstances."

She breathed deep.

"You never objected before," she said. "Since you insist on formality, you were christened James, the familiar is Jack, the pejorative—Jimmy. From now on, you'll be Jimmy Olsen. That should be all legal and proper, not a violation of Section two-twenty-one-D-four of the United States penal code."

"D'you have enny questions on this matter, Ms. James?" asked Iacob not straying from federal agent mode.

She looked to Michael, who shook his head.

"I don't think so," she said.

"Thank you, Mr. James, Ms. James," said Iacob. "We will leave you now. We have other appointments."

Olsen had his hand on the doorknob. "This is serious business. You should take it seriously."

The agents left.

Denise telephoned Morton Mieske and read him the letter.

"You need an attorney."

"Do you know anyone for something like this?"

"I'd call Moses Hirschfeld or Vartan Antaramian. Their firm is by the courthouse in Alexandria. Give me a day. Then call."

She wrote down the names.

"Thank you, Morton."

Two days later, Moses Hirschfeld accepted her call. He asked her to fax the letter. He set an appointment date, and told her to bring her checkbook.

Friday, April 13
Alexandria

Antaramian, Hirschfeld, Crawley, Hanes, Garfield & Smith, PC maintained offices a short distance from Courthouse Square, the brick and stone complex that supported the federal courts and attendant facilities, including branches of the Department of Justice and the Federal Bureau of Investigation. At the agreed time, Denise presented herself to the firm's receptionist as being available for her appointment to see attorney Moses Hirschfeld at his convenience. She was shown into his office, and the door closed behind her.

In his early fifties, Moses Hirschfeld stood about five-seven. He had light olive skin and wore round glasses in front of alert hazel eyes. Clean-shaven and dressed in a suit that looked tailored in Savile Row, he appeared well scrubbed, almost disinfected. His office was Queen Anne, a carved cherry desk with two matching chairs in front, a sitting area with a sofa and end tables opposite, all on a three-tone carpet, the pattern of which fit the room. Not a file or paperclip could be seen.

Hirschfeld introduced himself and invited her to have a seat in front of his desk. He sat in the chair next to her, and asked her to outline, "Only the facts of which you are aware that are known to the government in this instance."

He listened for the next three-quarters of an hour, asked few questions, and agreed to representation. He produced a two-page engagement letter he would use "to evidence my legal representation on your behalf when I meet with the Department of Justice to discuss this matter."

She wrote a check to the firm for five thousand dollars.

Tuesday, April 17

"Come in, Denise," said Moses Hirschfeld. She entered the main conference room of the firm. "This is my partner, Vartan Antaramian. I have asked him to join us for this session."

Antaramian stood and smiled showing even white teeth. He was heavier and darker than Hirschfeld, and his top shirt button was undone. No color-coordinated handkerchief protruded from his pocket, and his palm was dry when she shook it. Hirschfeld had yet to offer her his hand or allow a full look at his teeth. She liked Antaramian right away.

An assistant offered coffee or soda. She declined. Hirschfeld invited a paralegal to take notes. She came in and closed the door.

"I have asked Vartan to join us this afternoon because of the seriousness of the potential charges with which you may be faced as indicated by this letter." He held it up. "Two heads are better than one."

"And you're the top two heads on the letterhead around here."

"Yes," said Hirschfeld not missing stride. "At this time we are not going to ask you, and you are not to tell us, whether or not you committed the act or acts for which you are being threatened with federal action. We will present to you what the government has on this matter, and outline for you the parameters of danger we feel you face. Then we will ask you to consider what we have said, and to get back to us with how you wish us to proceed. We do not want you to say anything at this point that might put us in an untenable position at a later date."

"All right."

Denise already knew that if she told Hirschfeld and Antaramian she took the money now, she'd be stuck with that position. Her counsel could not permit her to say under oath something they knew to be false. They were officers of the court, and could not knowingly suborn perjury.

"Also," said Hirschfeld, "we advise you not to discuss this issue with anyone, not your husband, or family members, or outside advisors."

"That's because they become witnesses against you," said Antaramian. "Even your husband can be compelled to testify against you."

"Okay."

"No discussion with any members of the media," continued Hirschfeld. "Let us do the talking for you."

"All right."

He opened a file on top of which were handwritten notes.

"The target letter recites certain charges the government believes it can process into an indictment against you."

"It's called a 'target letter?'"

"Indeed. When the government believes someone is guilty of a crime, they may issue a target letter, a letter like this one." He held it up. "Its purpose is to induce a plea. You are the target."

Antaramian said, "Local law enforcement prosecutes crime. The Department of Justice prosecutes people."

"And they are prosecuting you," said Hirschfeld. "I have seldom seen them so focused. You have made them very angry. They like nothing better than to pursue someone with a high profile that has made them look bad in public. They will never admit it, and we will never be able to prove it, but that near arrest at your home stung certain members of the Federal Bureau of Investigation to the extreme."

"So I taunted them, and showed them looking like a bunch of bozos, and they're getting back at me?"

"Perhaps. Perhaps not. In any event, the Department of Justice is pursuing you with enthusiasm. Maybe not as hard as someone who killed an agent, but the people on the task force believe they are on a mission from God."

"They have a task force?"

"Yes. It is called 'Mousetrap.' You are the mouse."

Hirschfeld let that sink in.

"Mousetrap is led by Special Agent in Charge Eric Peabody Kludge. He has been at FBI headquarters for four years and has shown himself eager to make his mark. He reports to Assistant Director Roscoe Penes, regional head of Criminal Investigation. Special Agents Jack Olsen and Marv Iacob are doing fieldwork and directing at least six other agents, plus technical support teams.

"They have assembled a dossier on you that includes income tax returns, credit reports, military history, gun permit status, DMV status, state corporation commission name searches, passport status, location of safe deposit boxes and bank accounts, and the names, addresses, and telephone numbers of all close relatives. It includes anything they can obtain through government channels, and it is considerable in volume. They have pictures of you going to and from your home, office, and your children's childcare center. I was impressed."

If they were expecting a reaction, she tried not to provide one.

"They have witness reports, lab reports, videotapes, and evidence analysis. It appears as if Olsen and Iacob have been working this case full time."

"Have either of you done business with them before?"

Antaramian answered. "We know Eric Kludge by reputation. He believes political campaign contributors should be prosecuted for bribery."

"I met Kludge after the Tea Party."

"We are glad he is not the judge," said Hirschfeld. "The agents who came to your home, Olsen and Iacob, are new to this firm's experience."

"But not unknown in the industry," added Antaramian.

"The industry?"

Antaramian gave her a sly smile. "Criminal justice is an industry just like banking, or automobile manufacturing, or anything else."

Hirschfeld continued. "The charges they have outlined in the target letter relate to their belief that on the night of January sixteenth you retrieved a moneybag brought to Waterfront Park that contained three million one hundred and fifty thousand dollars, and that you have hidden it in a location unknown. This money was the purchase price for drugs seized earlier in the park.

"The government has an interview transcript taken by agents Olsen and Iacob indicating you told them you did not have possession of this bag, that you did not venture into the alley, and that you do not know the location of this bag."

"You always call the prosecution 'the government.' Not the 'people?'"

"That is the correct term in the industry."

Hirschfeld turned the page.

"Now let us go to the basis of their case and the evidence upon which it is founded. The Alexandria Police Department's source of information concerning the time and place of the exchange came from an informant, Jason McCullough. Two decoy bags filled with shredded paper were on site. The drugs and money had already been exchanged, and everyone present was waiting while the merchandise was being examined when the trap was sprung. Five of nine suspects were apprehended, along with fifty-five pounds of illegal drugs. The police believe they seized all three bags. However, no money was found, and they initiated a search of the area without success.

"The FBI became involved a few days later, and the City of Alexandria turned over all evidence to their task force. After pixel enhancement, the task force is able to show that one bag, seen in the Channel Three video taken the night of the raid, is missing in a video taken by Alexandria police the next morning. Vartan and I have seen these tapes.

"Early in the investigation, the task force believed the suppliers returned and retrieved the money. To eliminate them, the task force authorized the release of the names of the two police officers and you as suspects. All three received threats and suffered vandalism to property. That told the government the drug dealers did not have the money.

"The Department of Justice informed us that the man you stopped, Victor Barracks, will testify as part of a plea agreement with the government that he picked up the moneybag and ran with it from the park. He will testify you saw him exchange bags in the alley, and that he made the exchange before the police came around the corner in his pursuit.

"All neighbors were interviewed. No one saw anything. If anyone heard shots, they returned to bed when the excitement was over. All bags within the alley were taken into evidence, checked for fingerprints, and content. A third bag, found north of Waterfront Park, was discovered to be of the same manufacture and contained the same type of shredded paper as that in Jason McCullough's bag. The bag you saw the police open was made by a different manufacturer than the other two captured in the raid. The paper inside it matches shredding found in other bags in the alley, all being documents from a legal firm fronting on Duke Street. Fingerprints on the bag Barracks had match prints found on the bags in the alley. These prints match an employee at the legal firm. Bag type matches, content matches, prints match. The other two bags from the waterfront do not match these.

"From information supplied by McCullough, the task force apprehended the supplier who fled with the third bag. His name is Clayton Stevens. He claims he picked up a decoy and discarded it to the north where it was later found.

"The task force has interviewed all police officers involved, plus the television crew who made the video with Armstrong and Johnson the night before, to establish the location of Armstrong and Johnson from the time they went through the alley until well after their shift was complete. They have constructed a time-line that shows the officers were together, and except for taping the interview, they did not and could not have returned to the alley to retrieve the money.

"Jason McCullough made bail and fled. The government believes he had no opportunity to have acquired the money. They believe he has become a fugitive because his role as a government informant was exposed."

She started to say something. Hirschfeld held up his hand.

"That is the gist of the evidence supporting the statutes cited in the target letter. We will discuss these statutes now.

"If the government pursues you through trial and convicts you on any of these counts, you earn the corresponding sentence under mandatory minimum sentencing guidelines."

"I earn it?"

"You are a first time offender for purposes of this discussion. If you go to trial and are convicted on all charges outlined in the target letter and lose, we calculate the sentence range under the guidelines equates to six hundred and four to seven hundred and fifty-two months. Since you put the government to the time and expense of trial, prison will be medium-security at least. Combined fines total twenty-seven million dollars."

Hirschfeld, Antaramian, and the paralegal focused their eyes on her. She looked at each in turn; sensing from the paralegal's expression that one of the attractions of her job was the pleasure of watching someone else in trouble. The Germans had a word for it, the joy one feels at someone else's misfortune, though she couldn't recall it at the moment.

"Surely there's some good news," she said.

Antaramian's eyes twinkled. "Although bankruptcy will not discharge the fine, the law is quite clear that the balance of any unserved sentence is commuted and any unpaid fine waived when you die."

"How thoughtful."

She really did like Antaramian.

"Here is a section by section computation."

Hirschfeld handed her a list of columns and numbers.

"Now," said Hirschfeld. "If, in fact, you did not take the money, Vartan and I, this firm, or any good attorney, will tell you to reject any plea the government may offer now or in the future. If you have the money, you may ask us to approach the government and determine what kind of arrangement we can negotiate. If you produce the money and cooperate by admitting everything, it is my feeling they would drop all charges but one. The sentence could be as low as three to four years in a minimum security facility and the payment of a fine between two hundred thousand and four hundred thousand dollars."

Pure voyeurism etched itself in the paralegal's face.

Denise said, "This is a heart attack, gentlemen. Let me repeat so you're sure I understand. All the evidence is circumstantial."

"True," said Hirschfeld. "However, if the government proceeds against you, it is our contention they are near to proving their case."

"So the best case scenario is I produce the money and get three to four years in jail, plus pay a fine of up to four hundred thousand dollars?"

Hirschfeld said, "Our rough estimate at this time. The actual sentence and fine could differ substantially."

"Or worst case, I decline to give back the money because I didn't take it in the first place, I go to trial, lose, and get fifty to sixty years plus a fine of twenty-seven million dollars?"

"There are many factors to consider," said Antaramian. "Sometimes a client believes he is innocent, yet he decides it's best to plead guilty to a lesser charge to make the matter go away. The client may have a family. The client may be unable to afford the cost or strain of trial, and most of all, even though he believes himself to be innocent, there is a lot of gray area out there. He may feel he can't afford to take the chance of going to trial and losing. We never recommend this. However, any sentence coupled with a plea and cooperation is substantially less than after losing at trial. To protect the rest of his life and the welfare of those around him, he may decide to plead to a lesser charge when faced with a known downside floor versus an unknown bottomless pit."

"Are you saying the government is harder on people who go to trial and lose?"

Hirschfeld said, "Vartan and I are both former prosecutors. If a guilty verdict is rendered, the judge feels free to impose the maximum sentence. Make no mistake. If you lose at trial, sentencing is harsh."

"Are you saying I could plead guilty, not turn over the money, and come out better than going to trial and losing?"

"It would be difficult to negotiate from that position," said Hirschfeld. "You could pay the fine from the money, complete the sentence, and retain the balance. The government would not see merit in letting you retain the money."

"But I don't have it."

Hirschfeld said, "You could, of course, go to trial and win. That is always a possibility."

Antaramian smiled at that. He said, "Yes, Moses. Winning at trial is sometimes most fortuitous."

Hirschfeld grinned without parting lips. He looked at Denise.

"So let us examine that possibility. What evidence do you have to support a position that you did not take the money?"

The two learned counsel well practiced in the criminal arts looked to their client for the exculpatory evidence that would make their job easier.

"I don't have it."

"Did anyone see you walk down Fairfax Street the second time?" asked Hirschfeld.

"Not that I know of."

"Did anyone see you arrive home?"

"No. And I didn't stop for gas or get a traffic ticket or make any stops." She looked at the ceiling as if seeking advice from above. "If there were video cameras on the street or in the alley, Kludge would have the tapes. What kind of evidence do I have to have?"

"Someone who can account for your time until the next day when the Alexandria police video was taken."

"Like if I'd taken Dan Mattison home to meet Michael?"

Hirschfeld said, "Did anyone see you get into your car and drive away?"

"I don't think so."

"Was the street well lit?"

"No."

Antaramian offered a suggestion to Hirschfeld.

"We could get our investigators to canvas the street. See if anyone saw her get in her car empty handed."

"Wait a minute, gentlemen. This isn't France where the defendant is presumed guilty and has to prove himself innocent. They have to *prove* I'm guilty."

The attorneys looked at each other.

"Do you want to tell her?" asked Antaramian.

"You tell her."

Antaramian sat up, eyes steady.

"A cornerstone of the American judicial system is that the accused is presumed innocent until proven guilty. This principle is taught from middle school on. It's a lie. The truth about the system of justice as it is practiced is that it doesn't matter whether a person is innocent or guilty. What matters is whether he gets convicted.

"The penal population of this country is over two million. With less than five percent of the world's population, we account for twenty-five percent of the world's inmates. Now, the vast majority of those two million are guilty. But some are innocent, ten to fifteen percent according to some studies. But they were convicted. They believed they were innocent, and had faith in the system, had faith in what they'd been taught in school, and only realized their lives had been nine-elevened when the verdict was read.

"Some couldn't afford adequate counsel and were bulldozed by the machinery of the government or the ineptitude of their overworked and underpaid public defender. Others tried to stay within a reasonable budget and shunned private investigators, forensic examiners, scientific testing, the cost of whatever was necessary to defend themselves to the max. Some were convicted because witnesses perjured themselves, or co-conspirators lied in exchange for lighter sentences. The question isn't guilt or innocence. The question is whether or not a person gets incarcerated, and if so, for how long. That's the real world."

Denise felt run over. They sounded as if they knew what they were talking about. She didn't know what to say.

"What we would like to do from here," said Hirschfeld, "is let you think about this for the next forty-eight hours. Examine yourself. Then tell us your preference. Plead it out, come up with convincing evidence we can take to the Department of Justice, or decline to plead and prepare for possible indictment."

"Ms. James," said Antaramian. "During the Battle of Britain, the British government had no fixed budget for the war. If they lost, there would be no United Kingdom. You are fighting the same type of battle."

"What if they find the money?"

"If the money is found, we will try to convince them to drop everything," said Hirschfeld. "If they find it on someone they can blame with legitimacy, those chances are good. If the money appears without explanation at FBI headquarters, I do not sense from them that this will go away. They will think you have given it up anonymously."

"They've made this a blood feud because of the Tea Party, haven't they?"

"If you don't offer a plea," said Antaramian, "they're going to present reasonable cause to a grand jury. It may include an indictment against your husband as a co-conspirator after-the-fact. You won't even know about it."

"Jesus."

"All accepted prosecutorial procedure," said Antaramian. "As I said, the Department of Justice doesn't solve crime. They investigate individuals and organizations they suspect until they uncover a crime they can prosecute."

Antaramian nodded to Hirschfeld.

"Once an indictment is handed down, it will be announced to the media with great fanfare. Hero turns thief is what they will say. You should be prepared for the worst."

"But don't they have to find the money? In a murder trial don't they have to have a body? A murder weapon? Motive, means, opportunity?"

"No," said Antaramian. "There doesn't have to be a body or a murder weapon. They don't have to find the money. They have to convince a jury. The motive is you wanted the cash. The means is you picked it up and took it home. The opportunity is you were there when the money disappeared. All other suspects have been eliminated. As I said, it's whether or not you get convicted."

Hirschfeld said, "There are five judges in the Eastern District of Virginia. There is one in particular we would prefer to hear this type of case. He feels the government has become highhanded of late. There are two judges who think the government is always right." He opened his hands palms up. "If you should draw one of those?"

"I see."

"Think over these questions carefully, Ms James," said Hirschfeld. "What you decide will affect the rest of your life. Do not underestimate the United States government. It has the legal authority to imprison its own citizens for many years, even put them to death. At the same time, it can release an individual from incarceration for no apparent reason. No individual has that depth of power. It merits respect."

She found herself in a dead-end corridor after turning the wrong way out of Antaramian, Hirschfeld, Crawley, and the rest of them. She backtracked, and waited at the elevators without punching a button, getting on only when someone else got off. Head down, she wandered the lobby between marbled columns until she happened upon the exit.

Across an open field stood the main courthouse building, brick and stone, solid and intimidating. She guessed Kludge and his crew were in there somewhere. They hadn't accepted the Tea Party as evening the score. They'd plotted and schemed while she'd deluded herself into believing everything was going to be all right.

Now she had to find a way to dump the money so it wouldn't snap back and bite.

Villamay

Tommy was doing a credible job on a pile of picked chicken, sweet corn, and Tater-Tots. In the high chair, Sydney finger-painted ketchup across her plate between hand-fed bites. Michael listened to everything his wife said, more sanguine than she thought necessary.

"They made a point of scaring the be-Jesus out of me."

"That's what this is all about. Scare tactics. Psychological warfare."

"Isn't that what people tell themselves before they get God-smacked?"

"I don't mean to downplay it, sugar. I'm just saying that since you don't have the money, you can't do anything but decline."

They'd agreed not to talk openly in the house, but this wasn't helping. If he was acting, she wanted a sign. Without a wink or a nod or any reassurance, she thought he was serious.

"They can't prove I took the money, but I'm the only one left. And they have a grudge against me because of the Tea Party."

"That was fun."

From his expression, she could tell he wasn't acting.

"I have to get back to the attorneys in a couple of days, Michael. I can't plea to anything because I don't have the money. What am I going to do?"

He gave her the look he reserved for an unappetizing meal.

"I don't know. I'll think about it."

The children were fussy getting ready for bed. She felt unfocussed, relieved to get them settled under the covers. No guitar tonight, not in the mood. She read them a story. When their eyes closed, she turned out the light.

"Come upstairs," she called from the landing.

Michael stroked a final computer key and got up.

She had the shower running when he came into the bathroom. She closed the door.

"We have to turn in the money," she told him.

"How?"

"I'd like some ideas. I'd like you to come up with something."

"Look, sugar." His shoulders slumped. "I think it's an empty threat."

"Not for me."

"Well, listen. The letter is a Xerox. It's not even legal. The agents who took the heat from the Tea Party are behind this. They were reprimanded, and they're getting back at you. That's all."

"And those agents got the whole FBI to put on a show for Moses Hirschfeld? *Get real!*"

"You're overreacting."

"No, I'm not. We agreed it only takes one of us to decide to give it up. I'm scared, and I'm giving it up."

"That's premature without a plan. We can afford to wait. I'm not sure what they're doing is legal."

"*Kristallnacht* was legal. Anything the government says is legal— *is* legal."

What he said next confirmed his agenda.

"Think about it, Denise. We have three million one hundred and fifty thousand dollars in cold, hard, cash." He chanted it out. "With that kind of money, our troubles are over. Just knowing it's there should keep you going. Have some guts."

"And what if I'm indicted?"

"Then we give it back."

"How? You haven't offered any suggestions, much less a practical one."

"We could give it to the First Lady."

That wasn't helpful.

"They have to find it in a place they overlooked, Michael. Do you think there's anywhere in Old Town they missed? Or even better, they have to find it on a drug dealer from the raid. Do you know any?"

His silence made her think the blood in his veins was as cold as the water running down the drain.

"You'd better come up with a way to give the money back, or you're going to be indicted too."

She left him with the shower running.

Thursday, April 19
The Hoover Building

Paul Fleming, Jack Olsen, Marv Iacob, and two aides were assembled in the conference room awaiting the arrival of Eric Kludge. Fleming had instructions to call a meeting as soon as he'd heard from Hirschfeld.

Kludge came through the door.

"What'd she say?"

"And good afternoon to you too, Eric," said Fleming.

"I haven't got a lot of time."

"Have a seat. This won't take long." Fleming adjusted the position of the file in front of him for no apparent reason. "You'll like what I have to say, but there are some things we're going to have to decide."

Kludge sat.

"I received a telephone call from Moses Hirschfeld, counsel to Denise Elizabeth Lang James, advising me that after advising his client of the evidence we have against her, and after his client's careful consideration of the matter and all its ensuing consequences, she has chosen to reject any proffers from this office."

It was as if the Holy Spirit had passed through the room.

Fleming added, "We have a free hand."

A keen observer would have been pressed to notice a change in the face of Eric Kludge. His eyebrows might have been seen to rise a quarter millimeter, and perhaps the left corner of his mouth. Olsen and Iacob had toothless grins. Fleming showed teeth.

"Good," said Kludge.

By giving the woman a chance to come forward via the target letter, the Department of Justice had followed the law in a humane manner. She had declined, as was her right. Now, despite all the positive publicity surrounding the drug bust and the entertainment ratings of the Tea Party, she would feel the weight and power of the federal judicial system according to established rules properly implemented.

"I have one suggested change to the profile," said Fleming. "I believe it would be better if someone from Alexandria made the announcement. From a perceptional standpoint, if we do it, it might appear vindictive. If we get them to do it, the woman can't say it's us."

"Good idea," said Kludge. "I need to throw Packwurst a bone. Apparently his chief is fixated those two cops are still official suspects."

He turned to the field agents.

"Assume the woman will be talking to the media. She has an inside lane to Dan Mattison at Channel Three, and she's been riding a wave of popularity. Everyone on our team has to be professional at all times. Assume the press is listening to everything we say."

"That's true," said Fleming. "This is a celebrity case."

The direction and tone of the investigation settled, the core members of the Mousetrap task force spent the next two hours reviewing the attack profile. At the meeting's conclusion, Kludge summed up the attitude he wanted.

"Let's put that split-tail in a vise. I want a half-turn every day until she starts to leak. Then I want a quarter-turn every day until she pops. I don't care how much she screams."

Chapter Ten

Wednesday, April 25
Villamay

Denise left Treasure Chest as usual, picked up the children, and drove home. As she pulled into the driveway, four men in suits exited a van parked across the street. Her heart jumped when she saw them.

"Why if it isn't Jimmy Olsen and Marvelous Marvin Iacob," she said arms wide. "Have you come to inspect the repairs we've made since the drug dealers busted up our house?"

"Denise Elizabeth Lang James," said Olsen. "This is a federal Search Warrant executed by Judge Gerhard Ehrlich." He tapped his finger against the edge of folded documents as he stopped in front of her.

"And it's good to see you, too, Jimmy."

She held out her arm to shake hands. Olsen made no move to shake it. Denise made no move to accept the warrant. Olsen lowered the papers to put them in her hand. She raised her palm as if to examine it for offending dirt. Olsen dropped the warrant across her lifeline.

"You have been served. Please stand aside."

This was superfluous in that she was not in the way of Iacob and two other men as they passed by going through the garage.

She opened the papers and read. The warrant covered the house and cars. Olsen stood beside her.

"Are you here to keep me from committing suicide?"

"I'll keep you company."

"Do you mind if I get the children out of the car?"

"Go ahead."

She retrieved Tommy and stood him beside her. Then she picked up Sydney and closed the door.

"Of course you know," she said in that ever-pleasant tone she used to goad authority figures, "I'm going to have to start calling you Agent Mulder again."

No reaction.

She carried Sydney and led Tommy into the house through the garage. Three agents wearing latex were taking photographs. She and the children sat on the living room sofa. Olsen watched them.

"Mommy," said Tommy. "What they doing?"

"They're from the government, honey. They're here to help us."

She turned to Olsen.

"May I call my attorney, please?"

"Go ahead."

She dialed Hirschfeld and left a message with the service that a search warrant was being executed at her home. She asked for a call back.

"How about I call Dan Mattison at Channel Three?"

"I don't think so."

The telephone rang. She answered it.

"Hello, Moses. That was fast."

"Ms. James? Dan Mattison, Channel Three. This conversation is being recorded. Did you know you've been named the prime suspect for having taken the money from the drug raid in Alexandria?"

"No."

"Commonwealth's Attorney Roody Packwurst is holding a press conference right now. He just announced it. Do you wish to comment?"

"I'm happy to report that as we speak I'm participating in a search with Jimmy Olsen of the FBI. It's for our house and cars, a warrant signed by Judge Gerhard Ehrlich. So far, we haven't found anything except lint balls in hard to clean places."

"The FBI is there? Not the police?"

"It's Agents Mulder and Scully, a.k.a., Jimmy Olsen of Superman fame and Marvin Iacob of undetermined origin. They've brought two accomplices to aid and abet. There's no one here from the police. Why don't you come over for a live report? Crime-busting in action."

Station policy was not to interfere with an active investigation in progress. Reporters could observe from across the street. That was it.

"Ms. James. Did you take the money?"

"No. I've said no a dozen times. I don't have it and didn't take it."

"How do you feel about the investigation right now?"

"I support the government in all it's doing. I want to be free of this as soon as possible." She lifted the sofa cushion and looked under it.

"As a matter of fact, I'm helping with the search." She spoke to Olsen. "It's not in the sofa." She picked up a pillow and fluffed it. "This feels normal. How big is it? Can it fit into something this size?"

Mattison cut in. "Could we get an interview when the search is over?"

"Let me pass on that. I don't know how long this'll take. I've got dinner and baths and getting the children to bed, not to mention all these agents underfoot."

"Thank you very much, Ms. James. I'll call again, if that's all right."

"Okay. Bye."

"Bye."

She hung up.

Michael came through the garage, his arms full of grocery bags. He saw an agent.

"Who are you?"

"FBI, sir. Please have a seat with your wife in the living room."

He leaned around the corner and saw Denise on the sofa.

"May I put away the food before the ice cream melts?" he asked.

"Okay," said Olsen. "Watch him."

"How about I help?" said Denise.

"Please remain where you are, Ms. James." Olsen called to the kitchen. "Just put away the perishables, Mr. James. Then join us in here, please."

"Always so polite," said Denise. "Is that how you pacify your conscience as you trample people's lives?"

"Your rights are being protected."

"Let's not discuss rights. You harass to the point where the law says you have to stop." She smiled. "Your hypocrisy shows no bounds."

No response.

"I'll take that as agreement."

Michael said from the kitchen, "It's not just those they harass within their legal rights, sugar. It's their spouses and children. They're affected too."

"Ah, but the government is sure to say it's not them harassing spouses and children. The person who's the target and might have

128

broken the law is the party responsible for the family's plight, not the government. The government is just enforcing the law. Isn't that true, Agent Mulder?"

Silence.

"We'll have to assume he's gone deaf, Michael."

"Mr. and Ms. James," said Olsen. "Please be quiet."

"No can do," said Denise as Michael came from the kitchen and sat beside her. "You and your band of un-merry men make your living from our taxes. That gives us the right to tell you what we think any time we want, even while you're searching our home. And just to make sure you're complying with all the politeness statutes, may I ask how long you intend to be here with this search?"

"As long as it takes."

She reached into her jacket for the digital recorder she used for site inspections, held it up, and turned it on.

"We're recording, Wednesday, April twenty-fifth, at about six-forty in the evening. FBI Special Agent Jimmy Olsen is conducting a search of our home.

"Mr. Olsen. Would it be permissible for me to fix dinner for my three year-old son and one year-old daughter, please?"

Olsen knew this was a legal recording. He was being dared to deny a request reasonably made.

"Of course, Ms. James. Please feel free to feed your family."

Perfect. No sarcasm. No feeling.

The telephone rang.

"You're recording all our calls now, right?"

Olsen didn't answer.

"Hello?"

"Hello, Denise."

"Moses! Thanks for calling. Four agents are here with a search warrant. They've taken pictures, and they're going through all our stuff."

"Have they done anything you would consider unreasonable?"

"They won't let me call Dan Mattison."

"No, I do not suppose they would. As we discussed, you and your husband can now expect increased pressure from the government. In all likelihood your office at Treasure Chest will be searched tomorrow. Other activities will occur in sequence until they find the money, or you are indicted."

"We're prepared for that. We're letting them do their thing."

Hirschfeld said, "Let me give you a portable number. If you need me, call." He gave it to her. "How are you feeling?"

"The entertainment value of watching our tax dollars at work has never been greater."

"A person in your position should be anxious. Not entertained."

"A clear conscience, Moses. A clear conscience is the best defense. Besides, I'll be back in the news. Dan Mattison called me."

"Do not talk to anyone from the press, Denise." His voice was stern. "Do not talk to the agents. Do not talk to anyone. You create witnesses against yourself. I have already instructed you on this."

"Okay, okay. If I need you, I'll call. Anything you hear on the news was what I said before we had this conversation."

Hirschfeld breathed an audible sigh.

"I will let you know how much damage you have caused yourself."

While Olsen watched the family eating, the agents searched unconstrained by time or covert need. Paint covering access panels to bathroom plumbing was scored at the seams and unscrewed to expose the interior. HVAC covers were removed and their vents peered into with flashlights. Furniture was flipped, poked, and prodded.

After dinner, Denise requested the children's bedroom be completed so she could get Tommy and Sydney to bed after baths. The agents complied. An hour later they heard the string tempo and floating words of "Dear Prudence" as she lulled her children to sleep.

"Very nice," said a young agent as she drew the children's bedroom door closed behind her.

"New guitar," she said.

Michael was asked to move his car onto the driveway to provide access to the attic via the garage's pull-down stairs. Two agents were up there quite a while searching storage boxes, fingering insulation, and crawling through the under-roof area above the main structure's second floor. The cars were searched last.

By eleven, the agents were packing tools and equipment. Iacob snapped shut boxes containing the evidence they were taking: the pantsuit and coat she'd worn the night of the raid, three pairs of shoes, a hairbrush, dirt samples from her car, and fingerprints. The house looked disheveled. Denise was eager to see them to the door.

"Thank you so much for an evening of sprightly repartee, knee slapping fun, and scientific education. Too bad you couldn't find what you were looking for, though I'm glad you're going away disappointed."

The agent who'd complemented her singing hid a smile as he went out the door.

"And please don't come again," she added in that same happy hostess tone. "It wasn't a pleasure having you."

Olsen stopped under the entry light and handed Michael a receipt for the evidence.

"Good-bye," he said, and walked after the others.

"I'm going to nail that wise-ass bitch," said Olsen after he'd started the van and gotten underway. "Her office, eight o'clock."

"The signal's clear as a bell, Jack," said Iacob. "Ease up. Nobody 'spected to find anything inner house for Pete's sake."

The agent who'd hidden his smile, a new man, then committed a near mortal sin for anyone career-pathing through the Bureau.

"She's not going to have hidden the money in her office, Jimmy."

The other agents were stunned.

Olsen eased up on the gas and let the van coast. Speed drifted down until he feathered the brake, gliding to a gentle stop along the side of the road. He eased the transmission into park, and unbuckled his seatbelt. He turned to the backseat, looked the agent square in the face, and in a conversational voice said, "What did you say?"

Everyone held his breath.

"I said, 'She's not going to have hidden the money in her office, Jimmy.'"

He said it without hesitation, loud enough for no misunderstanding.

"I apologize for the 'Jimmy' part. It won't happen again."

He looked straight at Olsen.

131

"See that it doesn't."

Taking his time, Olsen turned forward, re-buckled, changed to drive, and pressed the accelerator.

Everyone breathed.

"We'll be there when she arrives," said Olsen. "We'll go down each item and execute the plan. It's only a matter of time."

Lying in bed, Denise stared at the ceiling, toilet-drip plinking, refrigerator purring, air handler cycling, nerves flayed. Beside her, rhythmic breathing emanated from Michael. She wondered if he'd taken a pill. Neither had mentioned anything about the money since the agents left.

She assumed he had a plan. He must have a plan. He had to have a plan and he wasn't sharing. He wanted the money, no doubt about that. He wanted the money more than he wanted her or the children.

But what could she do? She'd be watched twenty-four seven now. She wouldn't be able to light the fireplace without them rushing through the door to see if she was burning the money.

A customer of hers, a developer facing the dire prospect of bankruptcy, once told her that no matter what happened to him, he always had alternatives and attitude. His attitude was that he would get through his troubles as best he could and accept whatever came. He'd keep sifting alternatives until he found one that worked, or a combination that worked, and he'd never give up along the way. If he ever ran out of alternatives, he still had his attitude.

She'd already examined every alternative. She could get rid of the money in a hundred different ways and Kludge and his task force wouldn't stop. About all she had left was attitude. If she didn't do something soon—

Dear Lord, she prayed. I got myself into this, and I need to get out. I was greedy. Please tell me what to do. I can't trust Michael. He doesn't care about the children or me. He's going in a different direction. All he cares about is the money. Please have mercy. Please forgive me. I'm in a bad way, and I need help. Please tell me what to do—there has to be an answer—has to be—

If she'd had X-ray vision, she would have seen the metal box strapped to a truss in the attic above the ceiling at which she was staring. Spliced into the house electricity, this receiver captured and recorded transmissions from voice-activated microphones located in, and powered by, the light sockets in the kitchen, living room, basement, and master bedroom. At intervals it transmitted short-wave bursts to a receiving station at the field office on Leesburg Pike. Once in place, the system was maintenance free.

The bugging had gone without a hitch except that in the living room and master bedroom, lamps that had been plugged into the top outlets were now plugged into the bottom ones.

Neither Denise nor Michael ever noticed.

Chapter Eleven

Thursday and Friday, April 26 and 27
Alexandria

After a search of her Treasure Chest office, Larry LaBelle and Denise's division head shut themselves behind closed doors. Michael called to tell her Olsen and Iacob were interviewing his superiors at Data-Now. Neighbors Gus Gordon and Mark Stewart telephoned to say they'd been contacted for interview appointments at home. The day spun itself into a fever compounded by sleeplessness and stress.

When she got home, Michael wore the same stone face he'd had that morning. It didn't change when she got him in the bathroom with the shower running.

"What's your plan, Michael? I know you have one. What is it?"

"You're paranoid."

"No, I'm not. What are we going to do?"

"We sit tight."

"I'm tired of hearing that. We didn't turn it in when we had the chance. Now it's too late."

"It wasn't the time."

"It's never the time. Now we can't do anything. The FBI's out there watching."

He shifted his weight to his other foot. He said, "We've had a flood and a search. The money's safe where it is. Don't lose your nerve."

"I'm not worried about my nerve. I'm worried about my sanity."

His expression hardened.

"Get used to it."

Friday morning, agents served a search warrant on Treasure Chest for access to her safe deposit box. Every commercial lender and administrative assistant on the mezzanine averted their eyes as Denise carried her box to a room where Olsen and Iacob examined its contents.

Just after three, Cathy Pfau called and said Mr. LaBelle wanted to see her.

"He said for you to bring your keys and pass."

She felt sick.

She was going to be fired.

"I'll be right there."

Chief of Security Morton Mieske sat in front of Larry LaBelle's desk. She closed the door without being told.

"Good afternoon," she said.

"Please have a seat," said LaBelle.

She took a seat.

"Denise. There is no easy way to tell you this, and I wish I didn't have to say it to you. The bank is concerned with your situation as regards this FBI investigation. Until the matter is resolved, it is the decision of the bank, after careful consideration of all options available to it, that until further notice, you are to be placed on administrative leave with pay."

They waited for her reaction.

"I'm doing all I can to prove I haven't done anything wrong, Larry."

"Believe me, this is difficult for all of us. None of us like what is happening. You have an exemplary record here at Treasure Chest Bank, and you should view this decision as a sabbatical. It won't be counted against vacation, and as I said, you will be paid."

"What did they say to you?"

"I shouldn't tell you this. They asked me not to. But I do feel an obligation to you as a member of the Treasure Chest family. They disclosed to me the nature of some of the evidence they have accumulated in this investigation."

"What evidence?"

"I'm sorry, Denise. I can't tell you that." The discomfort of discharging this duty weighed heavily on him, and he dropped his head. "I was asked to say nothing."

"Larry?"

She waited until he raised his eyes.

"What do you think I should do?"

His chair creaked as he leaned back.

"I think you should discuss this with your legal counsel. That's the best advice anyone can give you, and the best advice you can take."

"Thank you."

"I've always liked you, Denise. Everyone does. I hope this ends happily for you. I've asked Morton here to assist with the transition. You know Morton, of course."

"Yes."

Mieske nodded.

"Morton will take your keys and pass and ID, and let you gather your personal effects. He will then escort you to the garage."

"That's fine."

"There's nothing personal in this, please understand that above everything."

"I know. The bank is protecting its shareholders." She stood. "I'll be happy to talk to anyone upstairs to ensure an orderly transition."

"I would expect nothing less, Denise."

"Will someone call me when my status changes?"

"I will call you myself."

She laid her bank keys, parking pass, and Treasure Chest ID on LaBelle's desk, choosing to surrender to the president rather than the policeman. They shook hands.

"I'll put out a memo to the staff for you," said LaBelle.

"Thank you, Larry." She turned to Mieske. "All right, Morton. Let's do it."

She led him along the mezzanine past its workstations and offices and up the back stairs to Real Estate. Her coworkers said not a word, barely giving her peripheral looks. They were protecting their careers, distancing themselves from looming scandal. The office search the day before had spooked them, and Cathy Pfau must have made a call about what was going to happen in LaBelle's office. Now, here among friends, she'd become invisible.

Mieske watched her pack a copy-paper box with pictures and personal items. It took no more than a few minutes.

"How much trouble am I in, Morton?"

"Loads."

She closed the drawers and looked over her desk.

"I won't touch the computer. Have someone else turn it off."

"Fine. That everything?"

"I think so."

"Let's go."

She carried the box across the bullpen. She felt pathetic leaving like this, unable to bring herself to say anything while under security escort.

At the elevator, Mieske punched the button.

"Larry had a hard time with the agents," he said. "You've made some people downtown mad as hell. That's a big mistake. They target people, you know. It's as if they put a picture on the wall and say, 'First one that can nail this guy gets a promotion and a raise.' Then they put the target through the wringer. They're doing it to you."

The elevator arrived and they got in. Mieske pushed lower level two.

"I didn't take the money."

He didn't look at her. "You did as far as the task force is concerned."

The doors opened onto the lower-parking lobby. The garage was quiet, too early for employees to be leaving. This was as far as Mieske was obligated to take her.

"You know, I bounced around a lot in the Bureau. Finally, I just got out. Good law enforcement officers, good judges, the ones that can do their jobs day in and day out and sleep at night, they look at justice different than I did. To them the law rules with a capital *"L"*. If a person breaks the Law, he's a criminal and pays the penalty prescribed by Law. They don't see people as flesh and blood, just statistics. I never got used to it."

She sensed this was difficult for him, a confession he seldom made.

"And then there's your case. You've pissed them off, the worst thing you could do. They're out to get you. I can see it in their faces, in their eyes. I've been there and done it myself."

"Why? What have they got?"

"I won't say. But they know you have the money. They've been working this case a long time, building it, polishing it, refining it. A lot of good criminals become bad fugitives and they're squeezing your juice until you make a mistake. Time works for them in a case like yours."

"If the *'they'* is the FBI, why did Roody Packwurst make the announcement I was the prime suspect?"

"You're the only suspect. Kludge doesn't want the public to see only the Bureau. But the task force is directing everything. They're just giving Packwurst camera time. He's a politician. He'll owe them."

"So you're saying Kludge is out to get me. He thinks I have the money."

"God help you, Denise. You do have the money."

That was blunt, even for Mieske.

"I see. Kludge knows I have the money, and he's made legitimate attempts to get it, the target letter and the search warrants for example. What else can he do?"

"He can push the envelope further than you think. He knows how to do it."

She thought this quite honest of him.

"Morton, you've been a good friend. Let me ask you something."

"Sure."

"If you were me, and you had the money, what would you do?"

Mieske lifted his chin and narrowed his eyes.

"I'd cut a deal through your attorney and turn it in. You got no other choice."

"And what if you didn't have the money?"

"If you don't have the money, that means a gremlin or a unicorn took it. You and I and Eric Kludge know they don't exist."

"You didn't answer the question."

"Not having the money is not an option."

Even in the faint light, the pupils of Mieske's eyes were the size of pinheads. He was waiting for an admission. She wondered how big her pupils were.

He said, "If you don't have it, God help you."

The spell was broken.

"Listen, I gotta get back. You take care."

"You too, Morton. Thanks. You were a big help that day with the car and the house. I felt I was in good hands."

"Sure." He pushed the button. "Do you have a gun? Have you taken the course?"

"No. I have small children and don't like guns. Is Kludge going to shoot me?"

"I was thinking of the dealers who lost the money. They play by different rules."

"Oh."

The elevator arrived and Mieske got in.

"Morton?"

He faced her from inside the cabin.

"Do FBI agents always carry guns when they're on duty?"

He gave her a quizzical look. "It's a rule," he said. "See ya."

"Hope so."

The doors closed and he was gone.

Those sneaky bastards, she thought. Olsen lied when he said he and Iacob didn't have guns that first interview. If he lied about that, he might lie about anything else he thought he could get away with. When it came right down to it, he was no better than she was when it came to the truth.

She pulled her keys from her purse and started toward the far end of the garage where her car was parked. Her footsteps echoed between concrete walls.

Mieske seemed to know the players and a lot about what was going on. He might be working with the FBI right now to tighten down the screws on her. Maybe he was playing the good cop.

She punched the lock release, dropped the box in the trunk, and went around to get behind the wheel.

No, she decided. Mieske was a better person than that. He wouldn't—

"Dough moo!"

She jumped, startled to the core, and turned to see a man in a brown baseball cap coming around the vehicle next to hers. He had a tense face and a goatee like Victor Barracks. A pistol pointed at her from six feet away.

"Gay een," he ordered.

Recovering the barest of wits, she opened the door and got in the car, heart pounding.

A second man appeared on the passenger side and opened the door. He slid in beside her and jabbed an automatic into her ribs.

"Star day car wang he tail jew," said the man at her door. "Dry wear he say. Dough say no-ting. Jew unner-stang?"

She put her hands on the wheel where they could see them.

"Yes."

He closed her door and left her with her passenger who backed to the middle of the seat, changing the gun to his right hand. He was short and chunky. They waited. When he heard the engine of another car start, he pointed at the ignition with the gun. She saw its hammer was cocked. She started the car.

They exited Treasure Chest past the booth attendant who idly raised a hand of acknowledgement to a car he recognized. Outside, the chunky man directed her west on the stop-and-go streets of Old Town. She scoured the streets for a Concorde, any Concorde, her mind racing.

These were drug dealers taking her somewhere to make her give up the money. If she told them where it was, would they let her go? She'd seen their faces. She could identify them. If she took them to it, would they let her go knowing she had little to charge them with if she took it in the first place?

The chunky man kept his eyes on her, and pointed with his gun which way he wanted her to go. They crossed Washington Street and turned left toward Richmond Highway South. The automatic was two feet away across the man's stomach. She thought of slashing at it with her right hand, braking, and making a dash out the door. Her eyes flicked from the road to the mirror to take him in.

He knew what she was thinking. He was ready.

They crossed the Capital Beltway. All she could see on her bumper was the car driven by the man in the baseball cap.

If she refused to give up the money, killing her wouldn't get it for them, and that's what they wanted. They'd kill her if she gave it up.

She followed chunky man's directions and pulled into the driveway of a house off Fort Hunt Road. The car driven by baseball cap pulled to the curb. Baseball cap got out and assisted chunky man in escorting her from the car up the walk. The front door opened without a knock. They marched her inside and sat her in a chair, the only furniture she could see.

"Three million one hundred fifty thousand dollars," said a third man standing behind the door. He was small and wiry, gold chains and bracelets around his neck and wrists. He took three steps to the chair and thrust his wide flat nose inches from hers.

"Is my money! I wannit back!"

He spoke with an accent, his lips spitting out words and spittle from beneath an organ grinder's moustache. His breath stunk.

"I don't have the money," she said. "I've never had it."

He stared at her long and hard.

"Take her downstairs."

Chunky man pulled her up by a wrist, his grip crushing. He could snap her arm if he chose.

Bare bulbs lit the floor below. Chairs surrounded a heavy wooden table topped with glass ashtrays. A trashcan sat to one side. The air smelled of beer and cigarettes from an all night domino game.

"Sit."

Baseball cap repositioned a chair. Chunky man pushed her down on its seat.

"I ain't gotta lotta time, baby. You gotta tell me quick."

From behind, chunky man's fingers dug under her collarbones making her wince.

"You doan tell me where is my money right now, I gonna hurt you."

"I don't know where it is."

He drew a huge knife from a shoulder holster and held its blade in front of her so close she couldn't focus on it. She looked at his eyes, not with defiance, but with an expression that told him she knew he was going to cut her.

He slapped her across the face, left palm, then backhand.

She saw it coming and rolled left and right. The blows hit, but weren't focused. Like chunky man, he was right handed.

He drew the blade back and forth in front of her face.

"Good looking white girl like you, I gonna cut up you pretty face." He backed away, sliding the knife into its sheath. "But first, I gonna do you." He looked at baseball cap. "Put her on the table."

The men lifted her from the chair and sat her on the end of the table. Chunky man pulled her jacket backwards and off. Baseball cap popped the buttons of her blouse, tearing it open with both hands. He grabbed the cups of her bra and yanked, shredding the material. Chunky man pulled her blouse and bra free, slammed her back against

141

the table, and held her there. Baseball cap pawed at her belt, unzipped her, and pulled her suit pants and panties to her ankles before fumbling with her shoes. At the side of the table, chunky man held her shoulders flat.

Lifting her head, she saw raw lust in the face of knife man. He'd stepped from his pants. He took her ankles in his hands and raised her legs to the saddle position. Baseball cap pulled at his belt. Knife man handed him an ankle, then stroked her.

"Nice," he said. "No noise. Tha's good. I hate it when they fight and scream."

He flicked on a cigarette lighter and held it between her legs for a better look. He whistled satisfaction.

"You doan tell me," he said extinguishing the light, "maybe we see burning bush after."

She felt him bump against her. Baseball cap held her left ankle. Chunky man had his arms across her shoulders. He stared slack-jawed as knife man lined himself up. Baseball cap sidled down the table for a better look.

"I have to pee!"

Three sets of eyes darted down, knife man took a step back, pressure on her shoulders eased.

She shot her left hand across her body and speared fingernails into chunky man's eyes. He released.

She was off the table.

Wide eyed, knife man covered his groin with his hands.

Stepping left, she clotheslined a ridge hand to his exposed throat catching him flush.

Baseball cap had dropped pants, hobbling him at the knees. As he reached down, she right-crossed an open palm to the point of his nose.

She became aware of their wounded cries. If she gave them any time at all, rage would overcome pain and shock. The first one who recovered would kill her.

Chunky man, who'd given her driving directions at the point of a gun and held her down on the table, was turned to the side, hands on his eyes. From behind him, she punted the inverted "V" between his legs. His body rose from the floor and keeled over face first, his head meeting the floor with the sound of a dropped melon.

Knife man clutched his throat, eyes shut, for the moment unable to breathe. Without pants or shoes, he still wore socks. She gave his proverbials a solid right-handed slap. His body wretched, his legs collapsed.

Baseball cap, who'd abraded her skin ripping off her bra, no longer had his cap. He was bent over, leaning his shoulder against a support pillar, blood running through his fingers. She picked an ashtray from the table and crashed it down on the back of his head. He fell without a sound.

She dressed in pants, jacket, and shoes, picked up her underclothes, made sure she had her keys, and ran up the stairs as fast as she could.

Being alone for the next hour going home, changing clothes, and picking up the children insulated her from any visceral reaction to what had happened. She was on a mission, conscious of maintaining calm and getting through what she had to do. She wondered when shock would hit. Inside a cocoon of denial, activity propelling her forward, she could have kept going through dinner and bedtime as long as it was just she and the children. But then Michael came home.

She told him sitting in the living room, the children crawling over them, anxious with hunger. He was quiet, letting her talk at her own speed, taking it all in. When she was done, she felt drained. This is shock, she thought. This is what shock feels like.

Michael looked apoplectic, not even searching for something to say. Then his digit counters started running. She could tell from the change in his face. He turned his head and looked at the corner of the room.

"They were going to kill you," he said.

"If I'd told them where the money was—yes."

He faced her.

"I just want to be free of this, Michael."

"And you haven't told the police? You haven't reported this?"

"Do you think they'd believe me? I came home and changed clothes, then picked up the children. Does that sound like what a normal person would do after what happened?"

Sydney stood on her lap and put her hands on her mother's cheeks. Denise picked her up, trying not to show irritation. She sat her on the cushion beside her.

"Stay there, Sydney. Please."

She turned to her husband.

"I think I should call Moses and see what he thinks."

Sydney crawled across her lap.

"Please fix dinner and take care of the children." She stood and put Sydney on the floor. "I'm going to take a bath."

By the time the phone rang with Hirschfeld's return call, the water in the tub was growing cold a third time.

"I first advised the US Attorney's Office of your encounter," he reported. "Then I informed the City of Alexandria and the Fairfax County Police Departments. Alexandria has jurisdiction due to the fact that the kidnapping occurred in Old Town. They are sending detectives to the Treasure Chest parking lot to investigate. Fairfax County has jurisdiction because the address of the house to which you were abducted is in Fairfax County. They are sending an armed team to the address you gave me in hopes of apprehending the abductors and for the same investigative purposes."

Hirschfeld's disinterested delivery calmed her more than had the warm water.

"Both Alexandria police and Fairfax police will interview you tonight. They are on their way to take your statement as we speak."

She gritted her teeth at that. She wasn't in the mood to answer questions. Talking about it meant reliving it.

"I spoke with Special Agent Olsen from the Federal Bureau of Investigation and apprised him of this afternoon's events. He advised me that federal agents are at this moment watching your home. Their plan was to follow you from your place of employment. Apparently you left earlier than anticipated."

"Larry was supposed to send me home closer to five o'clock?"

"Perhaps."

That seemed plausible. LaBelle had a tendency to get unpleasantness out of the way as soon as he could.

"Ask your husband to walk the street in front of your residence and note any vehicles displaying government plates."

144

The doorbell rang.

"Someone's here, Moses." She sat up sloshing water. "I have to get out of the tub." She pulled the plug.

"Fine."

The way he said it, she wondered if he was married.

"Denise. While I cannot be certain, it is my opinion that you are safe for the moment. The government will be visible watching you. Those responsible for this crime are in disarray. You must consider yourself lucky to have survived such an encounter. However, you must be wary. It is my feeling that whoever did this is now more dangerous to you than prior. Talk to the police. Tell them all you know about the events of this afternoon. Do not talk to the media."

"Why not?"

"The crime should be reported to the proper authorities because it is an assault against your person. Tell the police what you know, and let them tell the media what they choose to release concerning its events."

"Don't you think it would be good to announce I'm under government protection?"

"You are not. You are under government surveillance. There is a significant difference. The government desires to assure itself of your location, not your safety. You should rely on local authority for personal protection. Discuss that with them."

Chapter Twelve

Officers from Alexandria had joined those from Fairfax County by the time she came downstairs. She described the tailing car, told them the number on the house, and drew a sketch of its location. The kidnappers were Hispanic, and she gave a description of each as best she could remember. About the guns she had no idea what they were other than automatics. Asked at length how she overcame three assailants at the moment of assault, she acted it out on the kitchen table while an officer clocked her on his watch.

"You're saying it took no more than fifteen seconds to disable three men?"

"That's right."

"You hit each of them twice? Six blows in fifteen seconds?"

"Yes."

"Uh-huh."

Alexandria wanted to know the parking lot procedures at Treasure Chest. How did the tailing car get to the employee parking level? She didn't know. They'd have to ask the attendant. Fairfax wanted her torn clothing for DNA testing. She supposed they'd match threads from buttons in the basement to substantiate her story first. They scraped traces from her fingernails despite her telling them that after her time in the tub any skin from chunky man's face was long gone. She telephoned Hirschfeld, and he spoke to the Fairfax officer. When the officer hung up, he promised increased patrols during the day and a car on duty outside at night.

After the officers left, she took Michael upstairs and turned on the shower.

"Those men are going to come after me for what I did to them, Michael."

"I know." He sounded convinced this time. "While you were soaking, I locked the house and checked the windows. We'll be fine. The cops are out there. You did good, sugar. I'm proud of you."

He gave her a hug around the shoulders, their first affection in some time. She held him close.

"The thing is, I wasn't that scared. I was alert, and thinking about what to do, and what might work. They would've killed me if I'd given them what they wanted, and they would've made me miserable until I did. I thought about what Mr. Kim taught us about men. Eyes, throat, groin, in that order. Then escape. It worked."

"And I'm glad it did, sugar." He pulled back so he could see her face. "The best thing for you to do right now is to get a good night's sleep. You're safe, and if anything happens, I'll lay down my life for you."

"Just this once?"

"For once and for always."

She hugged him for that.

Nothing concerning the abduction appeared in the media. Despite Hirschfeld's advice, she thought this strange, and not quite right. Kidnapping and assault were newsworthy, and the public could help. Whatever investigation was underway, it was proceeding outside the public eye.

A police car arrived at dusk each evening, and the officers were invited inside to use the facilities before Michael turned out the lights. Different officers came to the kitchen for coffee the next morning.

Two surveillance vans stayed outside as well. One followed Michael. The other tailed Denise when she ventured out. No contact with the vans' occupants was attempted.

A few days later, a woman from Fairfax County telephoned with the results of the investigation so far. The house off Fort Hunt Road had proven empty and clueless, under lease from a fictitious partnership, rent paid in cash. Baseball cap's car could not be identified by color and make alone. A plate number was needed. No DNA was recovered from her clothing or fingernails, and nothing resulted from urgent care facilities or hospital emergency rooms advised to be on the alert for Hispanic males requiring specific treatment.

However, the woman did provide Denise with a website address and passwords. She could now scroll photographs fitting the description of the suspects from her home computer. If she recognized anyone, she was to call. The passwords would be changed in a week.

Denise hadn't known such a system existed, an in-home capability designed to ease the burden of an overworked bureaucracy and entertain victims without tying up police personnel. It could also be a trap. The server could tell which pictures she'd scanned, and if she looked at a few and stopped, suspicious minds might think her story suspect. She started at the top of the index, and scrolled through its gallery of drug dealers and suspected drug dealers. They were a seedy lot, well-tattooed, frightening to look at, and there were a lot of them.

She found him on the fourth day.

Wide flat nose, acne-scarred cheeks, younger, and without a moustache, the man staring at her was the one with the knife. Five feet five, one hundred forty pounds, nappy hair, all the photograph needed was age and hair-relaxant. Charged with "intent to distribute" six years before, the case had been dismissed for lack of evidence.

She almost printed the picture before considering it might be noted in a data log somewhere. She wrote down his name: Valentin Machado Margarida de Rivera, American citizen, alias "Nick" Rivera.

That evening, as soon as the children were in bed, she took Michael into the bathroom and ran the shower.

"I know who the gang leader is. His name is Nick Rivera."

"From the mug-shots? Are you sure?"

"I'm sure."

"Have you told the police?"

"Not yet. Listen. He's got to be homicidal after I slapped him like that. If they arrest him, he won't have to make bail to send his gang after the only witness against him: me. If I don't say anything, he may not do anything. What do you think?"

Eyes unblinking, he stared at nothing. She could almost see the flowcharts running. He might not have her open-sky imagination, but in think-mode, he could run any number of possibilities to their logical conclusions.

"Better keep it to ourselves," he said.

"You think?"

"If you accuse him, and they arrest him, he's got nothing to lose. As it is, he doesn't know you reported it. All these people you've been scrolling through have records. That's how he'll think you'll find him. If he hears the cops are looking for him, he'll know you reported it. Don't name him, and he may think you didn't report it. The more time goes by, the more he'll cool off."

"Well, what do you think about this? Let's track him down. Find out where he lives. Then we can—"

"Do what? Kill him?"

"No, no." She put her hand on his chest. "We're not going to kill anyone. I was thinking of giving him the money."

"Give *him* the money?"

"It's what he wants. He'll go away. We'll get him to tell Kludge he had it the whole time as a condition. Then we're out of it."

He looked as if his winning lottery ticket had passed through a heavy-bleach wash.

"I haven't come all this way to give up the money!"

She'd half expected this reaction. As if scolding a child, she said, "What have you done in all this, Michael? I'm the one who brought the money home. You haven't offered a suggestion since night one except to keep it, and now I've been kidnapped and nearly killed. Not even that fazes you."

"I just—I mean—we have a good chance to keep it, that's all. I'd never give it to *him*."

"Would you rather kill him or give him the money?"

She knew this was a good question. He viewed life as sacred.

"Neither."

"Either—or—, Michael. Kill him? Or give him the money?"

Go deaf or go blind? Suffocate or drown? Gas chamber or hangman's noose? He didn't answer. He couldn't. He could never choose between bad choices. Not since she'd known him.

"We'll be fine, sugar. Just hang in there. I know it's tough, but we can do it."

"I know. Get used to it."

They'd always been able to work out their differences in the past. Not this time. He'd been committed since he'd counted the cash. Or maybe it was then that he'd begun to change. Maybe that first morning he'd promised mutual veto in good faith, and from that point, he'd grown adamant to keep it at all cost. As well as she thought she knew her husband, she didn't, and she felt trapped in an inextricable web of her own making. Even if she could find this creep Rivera, she was powerless to get the money to him without being discovered.

She turned off the water.

"Never mind," she said and left him there.

The first week of May, Jason McCullough was captured. He'd checked into a motor court outside Dover, Delaware and missed seeing himself on "America's Most Wanted." The manager didn't, and she called the hotline. State troopers arrived and asked her guest for identification. He said his wallet had been stolen. They escorted him to barracks headquarters where fingerprints proved his identity. After three days questioning and no money found, McCullough was cleared of that part of the mystery. Extradition proceedings began. The manager got her picture in the paper.

As the ensuing weeks passed, Denise became less frustrated with Michael. No news from Hirschfeld was good news. All the bad news seemed to be over. They'd been vandalized, searched, and investigated, and still had the money. She exercised more often, and took afternoon naps with the children. She visited her construction projects, and she and Michael hosted a cookout on the patio for the neighbors who'd helped clean up after the vandalism. For his birthday at the end of May, she gave him the latest computer voice-recognition application and a bottle of tequila.

In early June, both Fairfax County and Alexandria informed Denise that all effective leads in her kidnapping had been exhausted, though the case would remain open. The patrol car would no longer be present throughout the night, though increased patrols would continue. Further information would be provided as it developed. Like the investigation into their vandalized home, after an initial case-status report, she heard nothing more.

She became relatively comfortable during the lazy daze of June, her night terrors and daytime paranoia fading. Michael took her to dinner at the Mount Vernon Inn for her birthday and presented her with a silver picture frame for their photograph with the First Family. Nothing was happening, and she came to believe he might have been right after all. She imagined a morning not far off when she would step out to get the newspaper and not see the surveillance vans on the street. She even let Michael make love to her again.

Thursday, June 28

Dread returned with a call from Moses Hirschfeld.

"Witnesses are being subpoenaed to testify before the grand jury in your case. This is a very bad sign. It means their intent is to obtain an indictment against you. There is no way to construc this event otherwise."

"How do you know this?"

"Paul Fleming called. He has subpoenaed six witnesses. What he wants is to make a final proffer for a plea."

"I have nothing to offer them. Nothing."

"Denise. It does not hurt to listen. In fact, it helps me get information I do not now have. I want this meeting. You cannot be hurt, and I can learn more about the evidence they have against you."

"If I agree to meet, doesn't that tell them I'm more guilty than if I refuse?"

"Not at this juncture. I think it is safe to say you will be indicted. Your defense will have more information by attending this meeting than by not attending."

"Can't you go and get what you need without me? These self-important government types rub me the wrong way."

"The Department of Justice will not meet unless you are there."

She felt a hole in her stomach.

"You think this is best?"

"It is best if you want a defense. We get a free look at their evidence. If you have any questions, you ask me, and I will ask them."

"When do they want to meet?"

"Two o'clock today at Courthouse Square. I have already confirmed it."

"You're pretty sure of yourself, aren't you?"

"If you say no, I will be at your home in thirty minutes to do everything short of kidnapping to get you to attend this meeting. It is vital. Meet me at quarter to two at the side entrance. There are things we need to discuss. Do you agree?"

"I've already been kidnapped once. I didn't like it."

"Then it is agreed?"

"Yes."

"Good. I will see you there."

Courthouse Square

She suspected the government had told Hirschfeld more than Hirschfeld had told her. There was a certain edge to his voice. Her uneasiness was not dispelled by the first words he said after she sat with him in the lobby.

"Denise, I must emphasize to you in the strongest of terms that I would never want you, or any client of mine, to admit to something they did not do or that is not true. I do whatever the client tells me to do. Having said that, I do not know exactly what the government has to offer, but I know them well enough to tell you they have something more than what they had last time.

"What I want to do is listen to their presentation. They are going to put on a show. Do not say anything. Keep the expression on your face neutral at all times. We will excuse ourselves to discuss necessary matters. I expect they will show us the evidence they have, tell us what charges they are prepared to present to the grand jury, and then tell us what terms they will proffer in exchange for a plea to lesser charges. The reduction will be substantial.

"Now, it is my sense you are not going to change your mind about whether to plead or not. I am looking at this case as a trial. As I have told you, I live to try cases. If you instruct me to go in that direction, I will give you an engagement letter for services that contains an hourly rate and a fixed price. The fixed price means you pay the fixed amount and I never keep a timesheet. If the case goes on for twenty years, that is all it takes for my firm to represent you for the duration. Appeals do not count. If you pay the flat rate and plead, it is still the flat rate. Some clients prefer to cap the monetary risk of a defense. It is your choice."

Hirschfeld removed his glasses and wiped them with his handkerchief. He didn't take his eyes from her.

"With the results of today's meeting, I should have a good idea how to structure a defense. Plus, you will have all the information you need to decide if you wish to move in a direction different from the course you have now set. I am prepared to take your direction either way. Again, it is your decision."

He put his glasses back on and looked at his fingernails.

"I must tell you, I once had a client who insisted on going to trial despite overwhelming evidence against him. I could not dissuade him. I told him it was my strongest recommendation that he negotiate a plea. If he chose not to take my advice, fine. That took the responsibility from my shoulders. I could defend him and lose with a clear conscience."

He looked at her as if she should say something.

"Now, I am not saying that you are in that position, Denise. I am not saying that at all. I am saying listen to their presentation, and then we can discuss it afterward. Fair enough?"

She wondered if whether she chose the fixed price or the hourly rate would tell him whether she was innocent or guilty. A fixed price might mean she was innocent and going to trial. An hourly rate might mean she was guilty and she was leaving all options open.

"How did your client come out? You won, right?"

"He received nine years. He could have had six to twelve months on a plea."

They rose and presented picture ID's to a receptionist seated inside what looked like a glassed-in movie-ticket cage. Their names were written on a roster, and a call was made upstairs to Assistant US Attorney Paul Fleming's office. The receptionist prepared VISITOR clip-on tags with their names hand written. An airport detector checked them for heavy metal. No cell phones, radios, recording devices, cameras, beepers, or pocketknives were allowed. Hirschfeld had his briefcase X-rayed. When they were safely through security, a marshal led them to a bank of elevators where they were told to wait for their escort.

A set of elevator doors opened. A heavyset woman stepped out. Her crossed forearms looked as if they were filled with cottage cheese.

"Paul Fleming," she said.

Denise offered her hand.

"How do you do, Paul? I hope life turns around for you now that you're wearing women's clothes again."

The woman was unimpressed.

Hirschfeld frowned.

Ignoring Denise's hand, the woman swiped a card through the elevator callbox and pressed up. The doors opened.

"Follow me please."

"I'm sure I can't walk like—"

"Denise!"

"All right, all right." She held up her hands. "I'm not saying anything from here on unless they start shooting."

On the second floor they wound their way through a dizzying array of desks, corridors, open space, and partitioning. Arriving through this labyrinth at a door, the woman opened it and stepped aside. Assistant US Attorney Paul Fleming, Special Agents Jack Olsen and Marv Iacob, and two other men were seated on one side of a long conference room table. No one shook hands.

"Good afternoon," said Hirschfeld. He motioned Denise to a chair.

This was a large room with a second table against the wall. Its top was covered with objects in transparent plastic. Trash bags were lined under it. In the center chair at the main table sat Fleming. On either side of him were Olsen and Iacob. On either side of them were the two men whose duties and identities remained unknown.

Fleming began in his slow mushy monologue.

"Thank you for coming today, Moses. What we would like to do, and we don't do this kind of thing very often, what we would like to do is present to you the totality of the evidence we have accumulated in this case in an effort to avoid having these proceedings go any further. We will next present to you the charges that could be brought against your client. Then we are going to outline the two basic charges at the core of the indictment, and we will make a proffer to you for a plea between the government and your client in which a substantial reduction of the sentence could be recommended. And let me say this, in case there is any confusion on the part of your client. The government believes what happened was not premeditated.

Things just got out of hand. We don't believe your client is a bad person, and we'd like to help her out if we could."

He paused.

"Are there any questions so far?"

This was to Hirschfeld.

"No, Paul. Please proceed."

Fleming opened his file, and a detailed reconstruction of the January events began. Fleming read his presentation, a dry run for trial. The evidence was at his rear. When Exhibit Number One was named, Iacob stood and withdrew a pair of white cloth gloves from a plastic envelope and put them on with care, as if they were gossamer and easily torn. Six people watched this ritual, designed, Denise thought, to intimidate the accused.

As each item was specified in Fleming's narrative, Iacob verified its tag, then pointed to it, or picked it up. The unidentified men sitting across the table seemed to have no apparent function other than to keep Denise from leaping the table and destroying the evidence, which was all circumstantial anyway and known to the defense.

That is until three o'clock.

"In examining the area of the alley in the location we believe Exhibit Number Five originated, Exhibit Number Five being the bag containing the shredded paper from the legal firm located along the alley, an imprint of a shoe was found."

Denise remained still.

"A cast was taken of this imprint and is identified as Exhibit Number Twenty-nine." Iacob held up a clear plastic bag, a shoe mold inside.

"The imprint of this shoe matches the left shoe, Exhibit Number Thirty, of a pair of shoes found in Ms. James's closet during the evening of April twenty-fifth in the course of a legal search of her residence." Iacob held up an unadorned brown shoe. "A lab report, Exhibit Number Thirty-one," Iacob produced it, "concludes that the cast of the shoe found in the alley matches that of the shoe found in Ms. James's closet."

Conscious not to move, Denise watched Fleming.

"Further examination of the scene in the alley produced two hairs, light-brown in color, Exhibit Number Thirty-two." Iacob picked up a small bag. "These two hairs found in the alley match samples found in

155

a hairbrush at Ms. James's residence during the same April twenty-fifth search, Exhibit Number Thirty-three. A lab report, Exhibit Number Thirty-four," Iacob held it up, "concludes the two hair samples of Exhibit Number Thirty-two are genetically identical to the hair of Exhibit Number Thirty-three using DNA testing.

"It is the government's contention that the exact match of the shoe imprint taken in the alley, Exhibit Number Twenty-nine, with that of Ms. James's shoe, Exhibit Number Thirty, and the DNA match of hair found in the alley, Exhibit Number Thirty-two, with hair found at the Jameses' home, Exhibit Number Thirty-three, establishes it as a fact, that, contrary to Ms. James's numerous earlier statements, outlined in the exhibits we have already enumerated, she physically was present in the alley at the location identified in the affidavit signed under oath by Mr. Barracks indicating where he left the money." Fleming referred to side notes, perhaps confused by his last sentence. "I'll add to that later that this is Exhibit Number Twelve, in which Mr. Barracks states he entered the alley with the money and exchanged it for a bag filled with shredded paper, completing the exchange before the officers came around the corner in pursuit, and before Ms. James attacked him."

Denise met the pause that followed with indifference.

"Please continue," said Hirschfeld.

"We have also obtained an affidavit, Exhibit Number Thirty-five," Iacob held it up, "from a resident of Duke Street, who says she was a witness to seeing a woman walking along the street who resembled Ms. James and who was carrying a large bag at around two o'clock on the night of—I mean the morning after—the raid." Fleming made an edit on his text.

"May I see that?" asked Hirschfeld.

Iacob got the nod from Fleming before sliding the document across the table. Denise appeared disinterested. She looked from Fleming, to Olsen, to Iacob, and back to Fleming.

Hirschfeld said, "This says that a certain Irene Blucher was walking her dog and passed a woman going in the opposite direction carrying a bag. The woman was the one she saw on television identified as Denise James. Ms. Blucher's dog is a Dalmatian."

"Yes," said Fleming. "We have an eyewitness to Ms. James leaving the alley in possession of the money within the proper timeframe."

"This says Ms. Blucher passed the woman on the north side of Duke Street, and that Ms. Blucher said hello to her."

"That's correct. And Ms. James said nothing in return."

Hirschfeld reread the three-page document.

"How old is this woman?" he asked.

Fleming looked to Olsen who said, "Sixties."

"So," continued Fleming. "We have reconstructed the totality of the events of the night and early morning of January sixteenth and seventeenth of this year, and we feel that when we take this to trial we can obtain a conviction on eight federal counts against Denise Elizabeth Lang James, and three counts against her husband, Michael Sidney James."

No one now expected to see any reaction from Denise.

"All these counts are outlined in this draft indictment." Fleming slid a three-quarter inch packet across the table in front of Hirschfeld. "The short story is, we believe that with this evidence and these witnesses, we can prove to a jury beyond a reasonable doubt, in fact, beyond a shadow of a doubt, that Denise Elizabeth Lang James committed violations of the statutes cited in the indictment that could merit a prison sentence in a medium- to high-security federal penitentiary for a combined term of between eight hundred and forty-one and nine hundred and seventy-two months, and payment of fines of up to twenty-seven million dollars. We also believe we can obtain a conviction at trial against Michael Sidney James, who we believe conspired with his wife Denise Elizabeth Lang James, aided and abetted her after the fact, and obstructed justice in cooperation with her after the fact. Upon conviction under current guidelines, he would be subject to a term of incarceration of between one hundred and eighty-seven and two hundred and five months, plus fines totaling up to nine million dollars."

Hirschfeld had not yet touched the draft indictment.

Fleming went on. "In order to avoid trial, and to make all of this go away for everyone involved in the best possible way, we would like to proffer to your client the following plea agreement terms.

157

"First, she pleads guilty to Counts One and Two. These are the theft and obstruction of justice charges. The guideline sentence for these charges is incarceration for a period of between one hundred and eighty-one and two hundred and twenty-five months, medium security. There would also be a fine of two hundred and twenty-five thousand dollars.

Hirschfeld began writing.

"Second, Ms. James must turn over the three million one hundred fifty thousand dollars."

Fleming waited until Hirschfeld looked up.

"This is the minimum the government will accept."

Hirschfeld used his pen to push the draft indictment to the center of the table.

"Your client may earn the government's promise to consider a possible reduction in the plea to the two charges I mentioned earlier coupled with a possible recommendation for a reduction of sentence by doing what I just said, plus the following." He read from a list.

"First, cooperate fully and completely in all future debriefings regarding this matter.

"Two, apologize to the Alexandria Police Department, the Commonwealth of Virginia, the Federal Bureau of Investigation, the Department of Justice, the news media, and the American people. Wording for this apology will be agreed upon in advance.

"Three, agree to keep confidential the terms of the Plea Agreement and the Statement of Facts, which will be sealed in perpetuity.

"Four, agree not to write a book, or sell book or movie rights to the story, or any aspect of it, nor in any way profit from this incident or its aftermath. If she does, any proceeds will be garnished at the source and paid over to the United States government. This will also cover international copyright agreements.

"Five, she agrees to do nothing and say nothing derogatory about the United States government or any federal, state, or local employees, jurisdictions, or agencies.

"Six, she will not make any public appearances, gratuitous or otherwise, concerning any aspect of this incident or these proceedings."

He looked up.

"This will, of course, be more precisely spelled out in formal language we will work out in both the Plea Agreement and the Statement of Facts."

Hirschfeld said, "What is the maximum sentence reduction we can expect under this agreement if it is acceptable and abided by?"

"Let me make this perfectly clear. And I'm glad she's here so that there is no misunderstanding, because I know you already know this, Moses." Fleming cleared his throat.

"The government is not promising your client anything. If she cooperates fully and completely, and does all the things she says she's going to do under the agreement, the government will consider making a recommendation to the court for a reduction of sentence. There is no *quid pro quo*, no promises whatsoever. She could conceivably do all the things she's supposed to do, and the government might not make a recommendation to the court for a reduction of sentence at all. If the government chooses to make such a recommendation for a reduction of sentence, the court is not obligated to grant it. The judge will ask her under oath if she has been promised a reduction of sentence in consideration for her plea. She must say she has not, which is true. She has not. She's just going to have to trust us on this. We do it all the time, and I have not known us not to grant a recommendation for sentence reduction when the defendant has fulfilled his or her part of the bargain. But there can be no promises. As I said, she's going to have to trust us."

Hirschfeld said, "What is the best case?"

"Sixty months."

Fleming let that sink in before he added, "Which, with ten percent off for good behavior and ten percent in a halfway house, is forty-eight months. And we can make it a minimum-security facility, no cells, no bars, no fences. We can even try to get her into one of the better camps."

"What about the fine?"

"Still two twenty-five."

"Why still? Why anything?"

"She can afford it," said Olsen. "We have to get something out of her."

Hirschfeld said, "Your proffer is to turn over the three million one hundred fifty thousand, serve forty-eight months, six months in a halfway house, and pay a two hundred and twenty-five thousand dollar fine. Can the fine be paid over time?"

"We know we'll have to work something out along those lines," said Fleming. "She doesn't have that much apart from the three million right now."

"Is that the complete package?"

"There's a three year probation after release, but that's standard."

Hirschfeld finished writing and said, "You do not have to answer this question, but I will ask it anyway since I know grand jury subpoenas have been issued. If this proffer is rejected, when do you expect the grand jury to hand down an indictment against my client?"

Fleming didn't hesitate. "In a week to ten days."

All eyes but Hirschfeld's turned to Denise.

Hirschfeld asked, "Do you anticipate a Post Indictment Restraining Order on assets?"

Fleming seemed not to have considered this. "No, I don't see why we would. She hasn't spent any of the money that we can see. She's got it hidden someplace. That's all we need right now is the three million back."

"What about the charges against Mr. James?"

Again, there was hesitation. "We can discuss that. If she agrees to the terms as we've outlined, we may agree to consider dropping charges against him, or proffering a substantial reduction."

The door on the left opened, and Eric Kludge entered the room. Another man followed, mid-fifties, thin like all of them. By government standards he was well dressed, a tie-coordinated handkerchief protruding from his breast pocket. He carried a tall cup of designer coffee, whipped cream foaming out a hole in its plastic top.

The seated men acknowledged the newcomers with "Hello, Erics" and "Good afternoon, Roscoes." The new man set the cup on the table and closed the door behind him. Kludge went to a chair on the government side, and the newcomer sat at the head of the table.

"Where are we?" He pulled the top off the cup.

Fleming answered. "We've reviewed the case in full, made the proffer, and answered the questions Moses has asked so far."

The newcomer took a sip.

"Are there any further questions, Moses?" asked Fleming.

"No."

"Perhaps you'd like time to discuss this proposal with your client. You may do so in the lobby downstairs, or here, if you like." Fleming looked at his watch. "It's three thirty-five now. Say, by four o'clock? Then we can all call it a day and go home."

Hirschfeld looked to Denise, who pointed to the man at the head of the table.

"I'm sorry," said Fleming. "Denise Elizabeth Lang James, this is Assistant Director Roscoe Penes who heads up the division under which this investigation is being conducted."

She spoke.

"I knew I'd be addressed as a person at some point." She sounded relieved. "I'm not a potted plant, although the tape of this meeting might cast doubt on that." She stood and addressed Assistant Director Penes.

"So you're the man in charge." She went behind Hirschfeld to the Assistant Director's chair. "Well, I'm Denise James, and I'm pleased for you to meet me." She held out her hand and smiled.

Penes was unsure she'd misspoken. He hesitated.

Denise looked at Fleming. "You know, I haven't been addressed as Denise Elizabeth Lang James ever, not even when I got married. Do you remember how Princess Diana jumbled Charles's sixteen names during their wedding vows?"

Her manner was so engaging, her voice so eager to please, a cordial effort to lift the conversation from its most serious subject of one-and-a-half hours to a lighter-side event they could all recall, that Roscoe Penes emitted a weak smile and raised his hand to meet hers.

Denise withdrew before their fingers touched. She faced Fleming.

"Of course, I was too young to remember that. But I saw the video."

Speaking in the same lighthearted tone, she turned back to Penes.

"Well, Sub-Deputy-Under-Assistant-Vice-Buffer Roscoe Penis." Her eyes danced. "We've had such a lovely one-sided chat here, your devil's acolytes and my attorney. They've laid out their case, but I don't need time to respond. It's rejected. Go ahead and indict."

She turned toward Hirschfeld. As her left arm swung back, her fingertips caught the top of Penes's cup and sent the froth-topped concoction splashing across his chest. The Assistant Director sucked in a hiss. The government side of the table jumped to its feet.

Denise turned to Penes, his hands up, his knees out. He looked down his tie in shocked disbelief. She stepped to him, plucked the handkerchief from his breast pocket, and began smearing cream across his coat.

"Here let me spread that around for you."

"Get away!" he yelped thrashing a dog paddle at her with his hands. "Get away you fucking bitch!" The backs of his knees shot the caster chair against the wall as he stood. Coffee rained.

"You did that on purpose!"

"I did not," she replied smiling. "Check the videotape." She pointed to a black half-globe in the ceiling. "Do a slow-motion replay. I assure you it was a chance event, fortunate yes, but all the same, an accident. Like Mr. Flaming says, trust me."

Roscoe Penes snarled. "You reject our offer, you won't be wearing that grin for long." He snatched the handkerchief from her hand and left slamming the door behind him.

"And thank you for stopping by," said Denise.

She turned to the men standing across the table.

"I think our work here is finished. Do what you like to me, but my husband has nothing to do with this. To indict him to get to me is cruel. No one would be around to raise the children. You indict him, and you'll live to regret it. That's not a threat, it's a promise, so govern yourselves accordingly."

She gathered up her purse.

"Come on Moses, let's find someone to lead us out of here."

To his credit, Hirschfeld waited until they'd exited the building before he turned on his client.

"Do you have lead plumbing? There is no defense in the world that can save you now. You just threatened officers of the United States Government!"

"Now, now, Moses, just relax. People have told me all my life I'm weird or worse, and they're right. I just can't help it. Especially with these bureaucrats filled with the power of their position. They don't seem human. Imagine trying to coerce a deal like that so we can all call it a day and go home safely to bed. Let's take a walk. Where'd you park?"

"I must withdraw from representation."

"Nonsense. Where'd you park?"

"I could have negotiated their proffer to one count."

"No longer necessary. Where'd you park?"

"Across the plaza."

"I'm in back. Let's go to your car, and you can drive me to mine."

They headed toward the front of the courthouse.

"You lawyers must talk to each other all the time about how stupid us clients are. Now you've got a great story for the next bar association meeting you have in St. Croix."

Hirschfeld kept pace with her rather brisk stride.

"I'm going to lay my hands on all the ready cash Michael and I have and bring it to your firm. The government is going to slap a restraining order on us no matter what they just said. Within the week I'll bring you a cashier's check on the order of fifty thousand dollars. It's all we have.

"Next is the defense. That night in January it was dry and the ground was frozen. There's no way a footprint could have been made anywhere. Get the official weather readings from some reputable US government agency. Put their own expert on the stand and have him say the ground was so frozen it would've had to have been heated with a blowtorch, drenched in water, and stirred to make a footprint like the one they claim they have. And I'll bet they only have one cast of one shoe, not thirty casts of police boots tromping all over the place."

She bubbled enthusiasm.

"The next thing, check the pictures and videos from that night. They have a plain brown shoe. I don't wear brown shoes with that blue suit. I wear black Guccis with brass buckles that jingle when I walk. I remember hearing them that night. If I can show the shoes I wore don't match the ones they enter into evidence, they have some explaining to do."

They arrived at Hirschfeld's Cadillac and got in. He started the engine to cool the car's cabin.

"Find out when they say they found the hair in the alley and what evidence they have that proves when and where they found it. I'll bet that evidence didn't turn up until after the search of our house. The same thing with the date they took the shoe mold. It has to be dated after the search of our house. And there was no woman walking a Dalmatian. There may have been someone who saw me on King Street or Union Street, but there was no one on Duke between the alley and where I parked the car."

Hirschfeld put the transmission in gear. He headed for the rear of the courthouse.

"Start looking for pictures of the shoes I was wearing and the dates the evidence was taken. Find out how reliable this witness Blucher is, and get proof the ground was frozen like a rock."

As the car turned at the bottom of the slope, she pointed out her car. Hirschfeld pulled in behind it and faced her. He shook his head.

"You are, as some people would say, a piece of work, Denise. Now that I am somewhat calmer, I must tell you that your cavalier attitude is inappropriate to your present situation. This has become very serious. If what you say about the evidence is true, and you can provide proof, that means the government has gone to illegal lengths to prosecute you. Some of the people with whom we just met may face prison. Do you realize to what extent they will go to avoid exposure? And God help you if you have the money."

"God help me if I have the money?" she laughed. "What if I don't? You said yourself it doesn't matter whether I took it. And Fleming and Kludge don't care either. I've been targeted. They've declared war, and their rules of engagement are to put me in prison no matter what."

"If what you say is true, that appears to be the case."

"So let's build evidence for a frame-up, hold it for trial, spring it on them after they've presented their case, and send some of them to jail. They broke the law."

"It would be more politic to present our proof in advance of trial so they may withdraw the action without embarrassment."

"That's Attorney Moses Hirschfeld's self-interest talking. You have to deal with these people after I'm gone no matter how it turns out. That strategy protects your career. I need to save my life, and if they broke the law, they need to be punished."

Hirschfeld removed his glasses and rubbed his eyes.

"Let me leave you with this thought," she said. "I will fight. I will fight with everything I have. The government is threatening me with made-up evidence. To add pressure, they're threatening Michael. And they want a six-figure fine because they have to get *something* out of me?"

He put his glasses back on.

"We'll make it look like a lay-down. Then when they've given themselves all the rope you need, you pull the handle, and they drop at the end of a noose they've knotted. You'll be famous, Moses. Keep that in mind when you give me the fixed price for your fee. We're not rich, and the publicity will give you national exposure. There's value to that."

"We could have done all this without your having made such a scene."

"I couldn't help it. They can't prosecute me with false evidence."

"That is not true. False evidence appears in court quite often. However, it is rare that it is so proven." Hirschfeld pursed his lips. "I will contact our investigators and begin work on these points. In the meantime, you must learn impulse-control. If this behavior occurs again, I promise you, I will resign from representation."

She smiled, kissed her hand, and patted his cheek.

"I'll bring you a check as soon as I can."

Two Weeks Later - Wednesday, July 11
Villamay

The telephone rang just as the evening's weather report finished highlighting flash flood warnings from a front invading the region from the northeast.

"Moses Hirschfeld here. A grand jury indictment against you has been issued. It is being signed as we speak."

"What about Michael?"

"My source indicates you are the sole subject."

"We'll see."

"You will be served with the indictment tonight. I informed the Department of Justice that you would self-surrender to the US

165

Marshal's office by ten o'clock tomorrow morning. They indicated that would be acceptable."

"I doubt that. It's dark and it's raining. They'll want to parade me in front of the media."

"They tell me otherwise. You may self-surrender."

"Again, wait and see. What about the restraining order?"

"If they have one, like the indictment, it has to be signed by the judge and served upon you before it takes effect."

"I'll call you after they get here."

Waves of rain were crashing against the sides of the house when the doorbell rang. Michael went into the bathroom. Denise answered the bell.

"Mulder and Scully! And a minion too! I knew we'd be seeing each other again soon."

"Denise Elizabeth Lang James," said Olsen above the din. "I am serving you with an original signature federal Indictment and an original signature Post-Indictment Restraining Order."

The minion produced documents from under his coat. Olsen handed them to her. The papers were wet from the exchange. The minion had to have been the courier. Olsen and Iacob must have been waiting outside for the documents to arrive.

Olsen said, "Numerous federal charges are outlined in more detail within the body of the indictment. I believe you have ten days to turn over your vehicles to the government."

She leaned forward.

"We have to forfeit our cars before we're convicted?"

"We know Mr. James is home. We need to serve him as well."

She turned around and called, "Michael? Personal delivery at the front door."

"I'm in the bathroom."

She faced Olsen.

"He's indisposed." A gust of wind sliced across the front of the house. She waited for it to pass. "He's not feeling well with all these rumors about indictment. I believe he's quite ill at the moment."

Olsen said, "We must complete proper service of these documents and get back to our office."

"I'm sure his needs outweigh yours, and the way things are going in there, you might outweigh him straight up very soon. Besides, he was in there before you arrived, and you didn't call ahead. Can I accept them for him?"

"No. They must be served in person."

"Suit yourself. Why don't you"—Olsen took a step forward—"wait outside until he's ready?"

"Wait?" said Olsen. "Out here?"

"Yes. Out there. Your service of these documents requires no common courtesy on our part. And let me remind you, us Jameses were pretty slick with our Tea Party, weren't we? Michael might try to make a run for it out the back. You wouldn't want to look silly again, would you?"

"This will only take a moment of his time."

"There's no lightning. You're in no danger. If you didn't bring umbrellas, you lack forethought. Do you have a search warrant?"

"No."

"Did you just serve me with a federal indictment?"

"Yes, as per the law."

"Did you just tell me we would have to turn over our cars leaving us with no transportation?"

"Yes, as per the law."

"Now, I ask you. Is that polite?" She almost closed the door. "Don't forget the back. My money's on Michael in a footrace leaping the fences. He knows the neighborhood, and you don't."

She closed the door and locked it.

The agents stood in the cascade, wind snapping their coat-straps against the material.

The courier said, "I got a bad feeling about this."

"Go around back," Olsen ordered. Then to Iacob, "Get the ponchos."

Twelve minutes later, Denise opened the door. Olsen and Iacob stood in the driveway draped in olive drab, hoods up. Both came forward.

"He says he'll be a few more minutes. He just wanted you to know."

The agents gawked at her, water streaming down their faces.

167

"Hey! Ponchos!" she exclaimed. "Good thinking! Hate to confuse an umbrella with a rifle during a shootout. Bravo for brains, boys!"

She closed the door.

Michael appeared after another quarter hour, by which time Olsen had become irate beyond extreme. The poncho, like his coat, was water-resistant, not water proof. His shirt was stuck to his back.

Warm and dry, Michael stood in the light looking not the least bit ill. The agents walked to the door and served him with the documents.

"You boys are very brave to come out in weather like this," he told them. "There's enough water out here to put out a jet engine. Your mothers must be proud of how you turned out."

Papers served, the courier was recalled from the back.

"Olsen lied." Denise held up the restraining order. "I've read this twice, and it says we're prohibited from selling or transferring title to the cars. We don't have to turn them in."

Thursday, July 12

Television trucks arrived early in Villamay under a clear morning sky, the air cool and dry from the system that had passed during the night. At eight o'clock sharp, as if choreographed, two Concordes and a van pulled to a stop at the curb. The occupants disembarked, assembled, and approached the front door. Denise and Michael watched them on Channel Three.

"Denise Elizabeth Lang James and Michael Sidney James," said a small bald man.

"Yes," they said.

He identified himself by name and title.

"You are under arrest pursuant to federal Indictment Number Seventeen-zero-one dash twenty twenty-seven-A." He read Miranda, and they acknowledged understanding it. "May we come in?"

Michael led them into the house.

"We will try to do this as efficiently as we can, Ms. James. These officers are from the United States Marshal's Service." He waved a hand in their direction providing no names.

Denise was told to empty her pockets and remove her watch, jewelry, and belt. A female marshal patted her down and fingered the collar of her blouse and the seams of her clothes with care. Did she require any life sustaining medication? No.

"Ms. James, we are going to handcuff you and shackle you at this time. We can make this pleasant, or we can do it the hard way."

"By all means, make it pleasant."

"There are news media out front. We can provide you with a hood if you like, or you may use your jacket when we take you to the van."

"Secrecy's not necessary. They already know who I am."

He turned to Michael. "Mr. James, you are free on your own personal recognizance until arraignment."

From a satchel, a uniformed marshal removed a confusing mass of chains and began unraveling them. With surprising dexterity he girded Denise's midsection and locked her wrists into a box at her waist. A separate chain connected the box to leg shackles.

"She's ready," said the marshal.

The small bald man bent to her ankles and forced the shackles as tight as they would go. Pain screamed up her legs as steel bit skin against bone. He did the same to her wrists.

"We're ready. Move out."

The front door was opened. Marshals on both sides propelled her down the steps. The ankle cuffs gouged her flesh as her Achilles tendon and lower shin worked against the metal, the too-short chain snapping taut with each stride. The pace was so fast she couldn't keep up, but the marshals braced her at her elbows to make sure she didn't fall.

"Where are you taking her?" Michael called from the front door, Sydney and Tommy at his side.

Denise was lifted into the vehicle and seat-belted into place. The van doors were closed. The cameras shifted to Michael.

"If you won't tell me where you're taking her, how is this different from a kidnapping? She's been kidnapped before you know. The drug dealers did it. Have you sunk to their level?"

"US Marshal's office, Courthouse Square," said the small bald man.

"Thank you."

The vehicles drove away.

Courthouse Square

Denise was taken to the controlled access receiving area of the main courthouse building. She was assisted from the van and escorted through an antiseptic corridor of green linoleum, pastel green cinderblock, and stark fluorescent lighting. Arriving at a bench, she was told to sit.

Forty minutes later the handcuffs and leg shackles were removed, leaving her wrists red and ankles raw. She was strip-searched, though not probed, and stood naked while two matrons examined every stitch in her clothes. Forms were completed, fingerprints, mug shots, and a breath-test taken. Lunch was a ham sandwich and soda. She thanked the marshal who brought her the food and apologized for not having money to pay. He told her meals were on the house for guests. She said he shouldn't judge character by the size of tips and drew a sympathetic smile.

By one o'clock, she'd sustained thirty minutes of activity and three and a half hours of wait. She sat with others in a row of cells.

"James, Denise Elizabeth Lang," called a marshal late in the day.

"Here."

He opened the cell, and she followed him along a series of green corridors through an exit-door. A brown-carpeted reception room under warm incandescent lights was on the other side. Eric Kludge and Moses Hirschfeld were there.

"Sign this," said Kludge thrusting out a document.

"What is it?"

Hirschfeld answered. "It says you acknowledge being released into my custody, and that I am responsible for assuring your presence at arraignment."

She signed.

Without enthusiasm, Kludge placed the paper in a manila folder. He looked gray and drawn, not at all well.

"What's the matter, Kludge? Has FREE PROZAC DOT COM run out of pills?"

"Denise!" snapped Hirschfeld taking her arm. "Come along before you do yourself more harm."

They headed toward the exit. He spoke to her under his breath.

"The press is outside. Your husband announced your Treasure Chest kidnapping. Concern has arisen that the event has been suppressed. Let me do the talking."

He guided her through the revolving door to the sidewalk and addressed the cameras with the barest of facts. Yes, Ms. James had been kidnapped in April. Please contact the authorities for further details. An investigation is in process. No further comments will be made.

They asked Denise to say something.

"Let me talk, Moses."

With clear worry in his face, Hirschfeld stepped aside.

"You can confirm everything with the City of Alexandria and Fairfax County. I'd just like to make a statement to the drug dealers. I don't have the money. You kidnapped me, and I escaped. We're even. Please leave me alone. I don't know who you are, and I've been told the police have no leads. Why don't we just live and let live. Call it—"

"Thank you," interjected Hirschfeld. "That will be all for now. My client has had a trying day. She now wishes to rejoin her family."

He locked her elbow in his and led her away.

Chapter Thirteen

Monday, July 16

The James family met early with Moses Hirschfeld and Vartan Antaramian at their office. At nine-fifteen they crossed the plaza and passed through security on the ground floor of Courthouse Square. Antaramian led the way to the eighth floor, where they sat in pews behind the bar in a high-ceilinged courtroom.

The judge's chair sat behind a raised wooden altar, the witness stand and jury box to the right. Two tables flanked a central lectern and microphone. Elderly bailiffs in gray slacks and blue blazers chatted with clerks. The gallery filled.

At nine-thirty sharp, a bailiff announced court was about to begin and no further talking would be permitted.

The room settled into quiet.

A door on the left opened exposing green tile and cinderblock. Four handcuffed men in worn gray body jumpers with PRISONER stenciled on the back were ushered in and seated on a bench against the wall.

"All rise!" announced a woman on the left.

Everyone stood.

The Honorable Emil N. Smert was announced, his black robes swaying as he mounted the steps to his high throne from a door on the left. Smert's height was hard to judge, but once seated, he was imposing. Perhaps in his late fifties or early sixties, he had salt and pepper hair atop a round puffy face.

"Oyez! Oyez! Oyez!"

The woman declared the name of the court and opened the session for business.

Judge Smert wasted no time nodding to the clerk to call the first matter. He disposed of the prisoners by denying bail and sending them back through the side door into the green digestive system of the judiciary machine.

"Case Number Seventeen-zero-one dash twenty twenty-seven-A. United States versus Denise Elizabeth Lang James and Michael Sidney James."

A murmur rose from the gallery as the case was announced. The defendants, their children, and their counsel went through the bar to the table on the left. Assistant US Attorney R. Paul Fleming, III and two others stood behind the table on the right. Introductions were made. Hirschfeld waived reading for Denise; Antaramian did the same for Michael. The defense pleaded "Not guilty, Your Honor," for each client, Denise first. Trial had to begin before November 16th to comply with the hundred-and-twenty-day speedy-trial rule. The prosecution stated their presentation would take a week. The defense estimated four to six days. Three weeks starting September 18th were reserved and docketed for trial.

Discussion turned to bail. Ten thousand dollars self-recognizance was requested and accepted for Michael. For Denise, bail was demanded in the amount of five hundred thousand dollars. Hirschfeld stated Ms. James was employed, owned a home and car, was married, had a three-year-old son and a year-old daughter present in the courtroom, and there could be little reason to suspect her of being a flight risk. Ms. James was prepared to tender her passport to the court. The charges did not involve violence. Ms. James has expressed her innocence from the beginning. She has been viewed as a heroine by the media. The President introduced her to the nation as such. If she should be so unwise as to become a fugitive, it would be easy for authorities to apprehend her as famous and well known as her face had become.

The government promised clear and convincing evidence that Denise Elizabeth Lang James had indeed made off with the missing three million one hundred and fifty thousand dollars and was capable of running quite far with it.

Smert looked at the children, picked up his pen, and appeared to write. He said, "Ms. James, you are free on you own recognizance, ten thousand dollars personal bond."

When dismissed, Hirschfeld and Antaramian escorted the Jameses to the US Marshal's Service and the Probation Office for processing.

Back at their offices, Hirschfeld spent the balance of the day going over strategy for Denise while Antaramian searched for separate counsel for Michael.

The Jameses arrived home in possession of their passports.

Monday, July 23
Alexandria

A week after arraignment, Michael met with his attorney for the first time. In his fifties, Arnold Porter had a full head of black hair, a six-foot-four frame, and a laid-back manner. Antaramian had forwarded the indictment to him, and he knew the gist of the case from the media. Like most attorneys in an initial interview, he did most of the talking, telling Michael up front he did not need to know certain information.

"There is evidence not favorable to your wife in this instance. As far as I know, there is no evidence, circumstantial or otherwise, to tie you to conspiracy. I'm not talking about knowledge you have. I'm talking about evidence the government knows."

"They can't have any evidence tying me to the money. Denise says the evidence against her is—"

Porter held up his hands. "That pertains to her case, not yours. I'm here for your defense. Denise's attorney will handle Denise."

"All right."

Porter relaxed into his chair.

"The government is going to do its best to convict your wife. One of the tactics they will employ will be to isolate her from everyone around her, including you. They'll assume she confided in you until that possibility is reasonably eliminated. If she did confide in you, they will want your testimony at trial against her."

"I didn't think a spouse could testify against a spouse."

"A husband cannot be made to testify against his wife under most circumstances. He can if he chooses to do so. If the judge believes you are a co-conspirator in a case with a co-defendant who is a spouse, you would do well to assume the judge has the power to compel you to testify."

"I see."

"The government's strategy will be to proffer a reduced sentence, perhaps immunity, in exchange for your testimony as a witness at trial against your wife."

"They extort like that?"

"They do, indeed. They squeeze as hard as the law allows. They want no risk, or as little risk as possible when they go to trial, and believe me, they are prepared to take your wife to trial. They won't agree to a plea unless she accepts medium-term incarceration. Vartan tells me he doesn't expect your wife will agree to that."

"True. But if I have no evidence to offer, nothing to incriminate her with, then I have nothing to bargain with."

"You have less to bargain with than if you'd seen your wife with a suitcase full of cash. However, the government must still leave open the distasteful possibility that an indicted individual might be innocent. They believe the probabilities are high that she told you about the money. They are convinced she has it, and they believe you to be a close, loving couple. They believe she would want to impress you, to seek your advice. To move them away from that belief, you'll have to do everything possible to prove she didn't tell you about it."

"Like what?"

"A polygraph."

"A polygraph? Is that legal?"

"Not in court. But the government has great faith in it. They use it all the time."

Porter leaned forward.

"Here's the crux of the matter. You say you have no direct or indirect knowledge that your wife took the money. If she did, she's kept it from you."

"That's correct."

"It's early in the case. Consider this. In a few weeks, maybe a month, if there is no further evidence against you than there is now, we will offer the government what they want. What they want is to have you testify against your wife, or eliminate you as a viable witness for them. If they eliminate you as a witness, you are not a viable defendant. I'll go to them and say that in exchange for immunity, you will testify as to what you know. You'll take a polygraph. You'll take a series of polygraphs until the government is satisfied that what you're saying is the truth."

Michael took in a deep breath. "I can do that."

"At the moment, I want you to consider this only as a possibility. The case needs to mature if we decide to engage such a strategy. I believe the government might accept the proposal because it throws you on their side of the fence. The other possibilities are to convince the government to drop charges against you for lack of evidence, convince the judge to view a summary judgement for dismissal in a favorable light, or win in open court before a jury. For the moment, I want to wait and see if any further evidence comes out against you. If not, then I'd like to arrange a meeting with the US Attorney's Office to see what they have and feel them out."

"Do you think I'll be all right?"

"I never want to give a client false hope. I would say that based upon what I know at the present time, and if there is no further evidence against you, you stand a fair chance of being acquitted at trial. What I want you to think about in the next few weeks is the polygraph. Have you ever had one?"

"No."

"Don't. If we go that way, I want to say it's your first time. I'll be there to be sure it's administered fairly."

"All right."

"In the meantime, I need you to execute an engagement letter and fee agreement to make my representation official." He handed over papers. "Antaramian, Hirschfeld has already transferred ten thousand dollars to my client account as an initial retainer."

Porter leaned back and watched Michael read the papers and sign.

"Don't discuss this case with your wife," he said taking the papers back. "Don't discuss it with anyone, especially the media."

"How do you think her case looks?"

"That's between her and her counsel."

"I'm not asking so I can sue you. What do you think?"

"I think your wife has an uphill climb."

While Michael was at Arnold Porter's office, Denise called her parents for a loan. All of her and Michael's ready cash was in the hands of their attorneys, and the restraining order froze all other assets. She needed money for legal fees, a lot of it. If she hadn't given their savings to Hirschfeld before indictment, she would've been forced to apply for legal services through the public defender's office. That might still happen if what Hirschfeld had on retainer ran out before she could replenish it. It chilled her to think a person could scrimp and save, have money in the bank, and if the government imposed a restraining order against it, he couldn't use his own funds to pay for legal counsel of his own choice. A millionaire subject to a restraining order would be forced to take his chances at the wheel of fortune in the public defender's office.

She told Palmer and Linda Lang she didn't have the raid money, and all negotiations with the government had failed. She'd have to fight it out in court. Legal representation would be expensive. She had good counsel, and they were working hard. She didn't mention the evidence was manufactured, not on the telephone.

Lying had become easier since January. At first she'd felt a storm of guilt saying she knew nothing about the money, almost as if a sign flashed *"LIAR!"* on her forehead. But the more she said it, the easier it flowed, the less her conscience twitched.

She wouldn't have to lie on the stand though. Trial wouldn't get that far. At the conclusion of the government's case, Hirschfeld would enter the brass-buckled shoes and proof she'd been wearing them that night and demand dismissal. Until then, all she had to do was keep telling the same story with an honest face.

Telling the lie to Palmer and Linda this time was different though. She was asking for *their* money, *their* retirement savings, for a child they'd raised, who knew she was guilty. This time telling the lie was almost more than she could stand. If something went wrong, she wasn't sure she could live with the shame.

Palmer said he'd need a week or two to raise the money. She was to call when she knew the amount.

That evening, standing beside a pay phone on Route One South, Nick "The Knife" Rivera punched a number on his cell phone. The call was picked up on the second ring.

"Yeah," answered the driver of a car in Villamay.

"You ready?"

"Yeah."

In the car's backseat, a second man cradled a beat-up rifle. The muzzle was taped to a two-liter plastic bottle spray-painted black, crude, but effective for one shot. A rasp lay on the floor to sanitize the barrel before the rifle was dismantled and dumped.

"You seen the FBI car?" asked Rivera.

"They have vans," said the driver. "I walked the block and saw them."

"Good. I make the call, now."

Rivera held the portable against his shoulder as he lifted the receiver off the pay phone. He laid a scrambler on its mouthpiece, deposited coins in the slot, and dialed. He put the cell phone to his right ear and the pay phone to his left so the driver could hear what he was saying.

When the telephone rang, Michael was reading a frog and princess story to Tommy and Sydney, their eyes already closed. He got off the chair and picked up the line in the master bedroom. He heard Denise say, "Hello."

"Denise James."

It was the synthesized voice.

"How'd you get this number?" she asked.

"We ain't even, you bitch. You still got my money."

The driver started the engine.

"You're insane," she told the voice. "The FBI's recording this. They're triangulating your position right now."

The driver slid the transmission into gear. The car eased down the street.

"That don't matter, you fuck! I can get you any time I want, and the FBI can't do nothin' 'bout it. You run, you die tired."

The rear window was cracked six inches from the top. The car slowed at the lot line.

"Ready," said the driver to Rivera.

The passenger took aim, his left shoulder propped against the backseat.

"I show you," said Rivera. "Now."

The driver said, "Now," and the rifle spat.

Michael heard a sound like a rock hitting a windowpane.

"You give me the money or you dead!"

Michael heard the line click off. Denise hung up. He put the receiver down, checked that Tommy and Sydney were asleep, and went down the stairs.

"What was that?"

No answer.

He looked around the room

"Denise?"

The front door opened and she rushed in.

"Someone shot at the house."

"What?"

"The curtain jumped." She went to a front drape and pulled it aside to expose a spider-web hole in the glass. She pointed across the room. "A bullet went into that wall." He followed her arm. She crossed the room. "It was the drug dealer. The same man as before. He said he would kill me." She scanned the wallpaper pattern.

"The drug dealer shot at our house?"

"Here's where the bullet hit." She pointed at a hole under the crown molding.

"So you ran out the front door? They could have shot you!"

"Not likely." She faced him. "It was a demonstration. The car was rounding the corner when I got outside. The FBI guys are still sitting in their vans."

Michael stared at her a moment.

"Goddamn them!" he said bolting to the door. "They've got to protect us better than this!"

Two agents came inside. They examined the window and the hole in the wall, found the exit hole on the other side, and pointed out a gash in the kitchen ceiling.

No, they had not heard or seen a shot. One agent went back to the van to report. When he returned, he suggested Michael contact Fairfax County as this incident fell into their jurisdiction. The van team's role was surveillance, not protection. Denise asked to see their ID's. They complied. She wrote down their names. The agents returned to their van.

Denise called 911, then Dan Mattison's air-mobile number.

"Hi, Dan. It's Denise. I have another exclusive for you."

A Channel Three Action News truck stopped across the street from the James house. A cameraman got out and walked toward the nearest van. Mattison followed. The camera's light came on and began recording.

The driver turned the ignition, put the van in reverse, backed into a driveway, and exited down the street. Behind the Channel Three truck, another engine started. The second van pulled out too.

In their living room, Denise and Michael faced a camera, Fairfax County police examining the wall at their back.

"I received another telephone call," said Denise. "The same man as before told me I had his money, and he wanted it back, or he would kill me. Then he said something like, 'If you don't believe me, watch this!' Right on cue a bullet came through the window." She pulled the drape and the camera zoomed in on the starred hole. "It went across the room and hit that wall." An officer pointed at a quarter-inch hole near the ceiling. "Michael was upstairs with the children when it happened. I was sitting in this chair." She sat in it.

"Then what happened?" asked Mattison.

"We decided to tell the FBI," Michael answered.

"How could you do that?"

Denise said, "We have our own agents watching us around the clock. We can get them any time we want by going out to their van."

"Is that what you did?"

"I did," said Michael. "Two agents came in. They said it was a bullet."

"They told Michael to call the police," said Denise. She stood. "I couldn't believe it. Here was a shooting right in front of them. They're first on the scene, they tell us to call the police, and they go back to their van."

"Special Agents Duane Bower and Bruce Wadler," said Michael.

"Channel Three can confirm two vans left the street when we arrived," said Mattison.

Denise propositioned the camera.

"Have an excellent job evaluation Agents Bower and Wadler."

"What can you tell us about the indictment in your case, Ms. James?"

"On the advice of counsel, I'm not supposed to say anything about the investigation or the case for fear it will be misconstrued, misinterpreted, or God forbid, used against me in a court of law."

Tuesday, July 24
The Hoover Building

"That *twat* is making fools out of us."

The FBI Director had dressed down Roscoe Penes, who'd dressed down Eric Kludge, and it was now Eric Kludge's turn to dress down everyone on the Mousetrap task force.

"Seeing the woman led away in front of her children was bad enough. The way the kidnapping came out, it makes it look as if we're covering up something no matter how many times we say it wasn't our jurisdiction. Now we look like idiots again with this bullet through the window. She's becoming a fucking folk hero, for Christ's sake!"

He took a deep breath and lowered his voice.

"Let's keep ourselves out of the news for the next twenty-four hours, shall we?"

No one smiled.

"Now, with that in mind. What's the latest we have on Denise Elizabeth Lang James?"

Olsen reported first.

"Except for that one conversation, she hasn't said anything we've sourced that would lead us to believe she or her husband know anything about the money, not even pillow talk. That one conversation was deemed inconclusive."

"What was it again?"

Olsen referred to a transcript, opening it at a yellow sticky.

"She'd just finished telling her husband about the kidnapping. He says, 'They were going to kill you.' She says, 'If I'd told them where the money was, yes.' There's a pause. She says, 'I just want to be free of this, Michael.' He says, 'And you haven't told the police? You haven't reported this?' She says, 'Do you think they'd believe me? I came home and changed clothes, then picked up the children. Does that sound like what a normal person would do after what happened?'

He put down the transcript. "We've all listened to it, plus profilers, shrinks, and legal. It's a 'conjectural if' statement. It can't be construed as proof."

He saw from Kludge's expression he'd better move to something positive.

181

"The following actions will be taken to shift public opinion our way. We spoke yesterday with Treasure Chest, and we should get something out of that. Statements from those suspects apprehended in the raid, including those of McCullough and Barracks, are ready to be released. This should inform the public that the underlying evidence against her is strong. That's about all we can do until she makes a mistake."

Kludge looked to Fleming.

"What about legal?"

"The defense is trying to dig up exculpatory evidence. I don't think there is any. Our case is firm, and we got the judge we wanted. The best thing that could happen is we find the money with her prints all over it."

Kludge turned back to Olsen who said, "We're interviewing out-of-town relatives again and assembling a wider list of friends, neighbors, and acquaintances. High school and college classmates are being located to see if she's kept in touch with any of them. If anyone else has suggestions, I'd be pleased to add to the list."

Kludge said, "What about church, her husband's friends, merchants around the bank where she works, her real estate customers?"

"Neither attends church. Her husband's friends are being checked. Merchant interviews turned up nothing. All bank customers we've contacted consider their relationship purely business."

"Credit?"

"Run every week, nothing unusual. It's as if she's tucked it away somewhere and is waiting until the heat dies down."

"What about the Internet?"

"She gets fan mail. We're monitoring that as well as postings on other sites."

"You know her password?"

"'Glassflag.'"

"What's that supposed to mean?"

"Don't know."

"Still no dirty laundry?"

"No. Both appear to be consensual heterosexual monogamists. Profiling considers their sex mechanical, hers in particular. It's in the tapes."

Kludge turned to Fleming who said, "The next move we expect is a call from Arnold Porter requesting a meeting on behalf of his client, Michael James. This should occur after the case gets a little further along, about a month before trial I should think. We have a good idea what we want to do with him when the time comes. I believe we can arrive at an arrangement that will take the smirk off her face."

Kludge asked the question he wanted answered.

"If we went to trial right now, how would we come out? No wishy-washy legalese, Paul. Percentages. What's the percentage we have of getting a conviction?"

"A percentage?" Fleming leaned back, hands behind his head. "We have Judge Smert. We have a footprint and hair. We have an eyewitness, though a weak one. May not even call her. But we don't have the money. I'd say it's fifty-fifty for conviction. If we can find the money or produce one more piece of hard evidence, it should be over."

Kludge spoke to Olsen.

"You and Marv, push it that way."

"We'll have something this afternoon," said Olsen.

Kludge asked, "What about the call?"

Olsen said, "It originated from a pay phone. We're working with de-scramblers, but I don't think we'll get anything, and it won't take us where we want to go with the woman if it does. The dealers agree with us. She took it. Our job is to watch her for the money, not protect her from the dealers. She's going to have to take her chances with them."

Chapter Fourteen

Tuesday, July 31
Alexandria

Bank president Larry LaBelle summoned Denise to Treasure Chest and told her that because of the indictment and pending trial, the bank felt it necessary to further separate itself from her. He advised the obvious: if convicted, her employment would be terminated; if acquitted, Treasure Chest would consider rehiring. This had been an agonizing decision for the board. In any event, August 15th would be her last day with pay.

All those arrested except Jason McCullough, still in Delaware pending extradition, pleaded guilty and were sentenced under negotiated agreements. Victor Barracks and his driver went to state prisons. The others went to federal penitentiaries because they'd crossed state lines.

Barracks's Affidavit and Statement of Facts turned up verbatim in the *Washington Post* from a "reliable source." An "unnamed official" was quoted saying the bag Barracks had when captured matched those of the legal firm that backed onto the alley, not those from the raid.

Hirschfeld had his investigators canvass both sides of the street without success for anyone who could testify they saw a woman walking that night with or without a bag.

Ms. Blucher, the woman with the Dalmatian, turned out to be a widow of seventy-nine. After the investigators interviewed her, it was Hirschfeld's opinion she'd embellished her affidavit at the urging of the government. He doubted she would be called, and said he hoped not. Impeaching a little old lady on the stand was not something he wished to do to win the jury's goodwill.

Most crushing, the defense investigation failed to locate a picture or video that showed Denise's shoes the night of the raid. The framing was too high.

The FBI surveillance team remained on watch in Villamay.

Wednesday, August 15
Alexandria

Michael James and Arnold Porter convened with Assistant US Attorney Paul Fleming and two of his associates to discuss a proffer.

"Thank you for coming," Fleming began in his not-quite-in-sync accent. "What we would like to do today is work out an agreement with you and your client that would satisfy the government that he is telling the truth in this matter."

"That's fine, Paul. What did you have in mind?"

"After a great deal of careful thought on this matter, the subject being how to satisfy ourselves that Mr. James is indeed an innocent party, we would like to proffer two proposals. If you'll allow me the analogy, one is a basic no frills used pickup truck, and the other is a brand new Cadillac. We favor the Cadillac, but we feel the Cadillac will require more careful consideration for Mr. James here to drive off the lot."

Porter looked at his client. "Please continue."

"First, let me say that the government does not really know whether Mr. James knows where the money is or not. We consider the possibility that he's telling the truth to be quite high. What we do know is that his wife knows where it is. We'll be proving that in court. We'll get a conviction against her first, and under current statutes and case law, we believe we can obtain a conviction against Mr. James afterward under the theory of willful blindness."

"What does 'willful blindness' mean?" asked Michael.

Fleming defined it. "Technically, the charge will be 'willful blindness as an accessory after the fact.' It means you could have known, or should have known, that a crime was committed, or had been committed, and you willfully chose to do nothing to disclose it, or discover it. Willful blindness carries with it the same sentence as if you were convicted of committing the crime itself."

Porter turned to Michael. "Most willful blindness involves money laundering, as in passing dirty money through a legitimate business."

"Judge Smert has expanded its scope," said Fleming.

"And he's our judge," said Porter.

"Anyway," said Fleming, "the no frills pickup truck is to reduce the charge in the plea to the least felony for which statutes dictate no

185

jail time, no halfway house, and no home confinement, just probation for a term as approved by the court. This plea would be an admission of guilt, in effect, his confession of knowledge of the crime after the fact. In return, he agrees to being debriefed by the government now, and in said debriefings, he must agree to tell the complete and unvarnished truth concerning all he knows in this matter."

"So your basic pickup truck is some kind of felony confession," stated Michael. He turned to his attorney. "If I plea to anything, doesn't that make Denise guilty?"

"Just listen," advised Porter.

Fleming said, "This proposal also contains the provision that Mr. James not discuss the agreement he has regarding the plea with his spouse. If he does so, and we find out about it, the deal is off, and he gets prosecuted. Here again, this is a voluntary plea. Nothing is being forced upon your client."

"Nothing being forced?" said Michael. "Why isn't this blackmail?"

"Because if you're innocent, you don't plead to anything," said Porter. "If you're guilty, you negotiate."

"But if I'm innocent, I still get prosecuted. He's giving me net-zero unless I'm guilty."

"Just hear him out."

"That's the first proposal," said Fleming. "The Cadillac involves full and complete immunity for your client up front."

"How far do I have to bend over for that?"

"Michael," said Porter putting his hand on his shoulder. "Please just listen to the man. All right?"

"All right, I'll listen. But he's not a real man. Without the power of the government behind him, he isn't fit to carry—"

"Hush!" ordered Porter.

Michael fell back in his chair.

"The second proposal," Fleming droned, "would provide your client with immunity from prosecution even if he's been lying all along about his knowledge of, and involvement in, this case."

He cleared his throat.

"This proposal has, shall we call it, features."

He opened his file and began reading.

"First, Mr. James agrees within the body of the agreement that he has entered into said agreement without coercion and of his own free will.

"Second, Mr. James agrees that the terms of the agreement are confidential, and that he will not disclose the terms of the agreement to anyone, public or private.

"Third, Mr. James agrees to extend the time for trial." He looked up. "Quite frankly, we need more time, and it's still within the Rocket Docket."

"What's the 'Rocket Docket?'" Michael asked.

Porter said, "The Eastern District of Virginia is called the Rocket Docket because trials are set so quickly. In other districts this could take a couple of years. Here the defense has less time to prepare. Advantage government."

Back to the list.

"Fourth, Mr. James agrees to fully disclose all he knows about this affair, good and bad. If he doesn't know anything, he doesn't know anything. If he does know something, he has to tell us. A minimum of three and a maximum of six polygraph tests will be administered to verify to our satisfaction that the truth is being told.

"Fifth, Mr. James agrees to testify in court as to what he discloses to us, should we, in our sole discretion, require it. This would mean testifying against his wife if that is what the truth entails. Again, we don't know what the truth is, so we're prepared to be disappointed if he doesn't know anything that can help us.

"Sixth." His eyes rose to Porter's. "And please hear me out all the way on this before you start jumping up and down. This item is the reason the government is willing to consider the possibility of complete immunity." He took a long look at Michael. "He doesn't have to follow through on it all the way, but it might save him time in the long run."

He read.

"Of his own accord, we want Mr. James to file a complaint for divorce against Ms. James based upon irreconcilable differences. Mr. James is not to discuss the reasons for filing the complaint with his wife or with the press. If he does so, and we find out about it, the deal is off, and we prosecute.

"It will be necessary that he separate himself from her physical person. By that I mean he has to move out of the marital domicile. The government realizes there are small children involved, so we suggest he move in with his parents and take the children with him."

Fleming raised his eyebrows to Porter.

"We know, we really know, she has the money, and this action is designed to induce her to give it up. We want the complaint filed no later than thirty days before trial, hence another need for an extension of time. After he files, he can tell the media that the stress has been too much for him, and that it's caused him to seek this resolution for himself, and for the sake of the children. He can't say it's part of a plea with the government.

"In the unlikely event the woman turns out to be innocent, then she'll be acquitted at trial, the petition can be withdrawn, and the James family can go on about its business. They can write a book, or do afternoon talk shows, whatever. In the event the woman turns out to be guilty, and we know she is, she will be going to prison for a long time, and Mr. James will no doubt wish to consider the virtues of a divorce in any event." He offered both hands palms up. "If the woman is guilty, we get our conviction. If she's innocent, then no harm done. No matter how it turns out, your client goes free."

"Are we talking transactional immunity here, Paul?"

"Yes. Full and complete transactional immunity."

Porter looked at his client, then back to Fleming. "Give us a few minutes, will you?"

The government attorneys closed their files and left the room.

Porter spoke in a soft voice.

"Michael, taking this offer assures your ability to raise your children and be with them no matter what. To go any other way will be expensive and risky. At worst, the consequences for you and your children are unthinkable."

Michael glared at him. "And what if I'm innocent? My marriage hasn't been going all that well lately. Filing divorce will kill it."

"This is the real world, Michael. I'm not going to tell you what you want to hear. Innocent people get hurt all the time. This is a good resolution for you as an individual and as a father. You should consider it with care."

"I have to terminate my marriage because the government tells me to, or I go to jail? Arnie, she's the mother of my children. She's a good woman. How can I stab her in the back like this?"

Porter leaned against his chair. Seconds passed. He breathed a sigh. More time passed. He looked at his watch. Michael sighed.

Porter said, "There are a number of ways to look at this. From a selfish point of view, my job is done. My client goes free no matter what, so long as he tells the truth and abides by the agreement.

"Second, an audience of disinterested observers would say that you, Denise, Tommy, and Sydney are all in the line of fire. Disregard any moral issues because the government has convinced itself there are no moral issues, and they write the rules. We need to conduct ourselves with that in mind. The bottom line is that if you agree to this and abide by the agreement, three out of four of you are out of harm's way. It's the best I could do."

Michael fixed him with a stare.

"You mean you knew about this in advance? You talked to them and discussed strategies for presenting it to me?"

"There was no client management plan, but I listened to them. The government just wants the money, and more than that, they want Denise James. They know she has it, and they think they have the evidence to prove it. As your attorney, I don't want you to have to pay for what she's done."

"But how can I do this, Arnie? How can I face her? What do I say?"

"Maybe you don't face her. Maybe you move out of the house, go to a hotel, or go to your parents. A restraining order can be placed on Denise restricting her contact with you."

"Good God! Another restraining order?"

"From a practical standpoint, it would make the government happier if you officially limited contact with your wife from the time she's served until trial is over. The wording can be crafted in such a way that the government is satisfied and the pressure is off you."

"They're blackmailing me." Malevolence coated every word. "They're holding the children hostage. Denise is the ransom."

"If you don't do this," said Porter, "the James family could be finished, even if you're both innocent. Juries around Washington are less suspicious of big government than in any other part of the country because so many jurors work for the government. We drew a very pro-government judge. There is strong evidence against your wife, and Paul is correct in that the government has had increasing success in convicting people under willful blindness. If Denise took the money, she alone pays the penalty, and that's fair. If she didn't take it, at least she's the only one on trial. That might not be fair, but that's how it is."

"What if they find the money?"

"Maybe that would help Denise, but it doesn't matter for you. You get immunity up front, as long as you tell the truth and abide by the agreement."

"If what I say hurts her, I have to testify?"

"Yes. The government will call you."

"What if my testimony helps her? Can I testify on her behalf?"

"If her counsel deems it proper. If your testimony doesn't help the government, they won't call you."

"What's to prevent Denise's attorney from putting me on the stand and having me expose this whole sorry scheme?"

"That won't happen. The government wouldn't have made this proposal if Judge Smert wasn't on board."

That surprised him.

"Isn't that called tampering with the judge?"

"There are many ways to learn a judge's position on a matter. There are intermediaries, hypothetical situations, and communications through clerks. Believe me, Smert has already decided the question. He'll rule that any plea agreement you've made is irrelevant as to whether or not she committed the crime."

"What if I expose it right now?"

"Then they prosecute you with no hope of cutting a deal."

Porter could see he was making progress. Time for a lawyer's trick.

"Look, the government wants to wind this up without trial. They know you're surprised, even shocked. Let's do this. I'll ask them for a couple of days so you can think about it. I'll make them understand you need a little time. I'll also work on drafting some language. The actual document may not read as bad as it sounds. In the meantime, go home and think about it. Turn it over in your mind. Make a list of questions. We'll talk in a couple of days."

Porter gave him his best look of reassurance.

"You need to face up to the responsibility you undertook as a parent when you chose to have children, Michael. Every parent has an obligation to protect them from danger, any danger, even from their mother. Try to look at it for what it is, a short-term pain, but in the long run, a huge gain for you and your children. You'll see I'm right. It's for the best."

"What about the polygraph?"

"What about it?"

"I don't want a polygraph. Just coming down here makes me jumpy. I don't think I can pass."

Porter studied him, wondering what that might mean.

"It's possible I can get them to back off."

"How?"

"Polygraphs are useful indicators for things like employment and background checks, lower stress situations than a federal prosecution. Under high stress, it's less reliable, hence not accepted as proof in court."

"Ask them."

"Okay. I can't promise anything, but I'll ask."

"Good."

"Don't talk to your wife about this, Michael. If you do and it's disclosed, I can assure you the offer will vanish."

"I can connect the dots."

"Then it's settled. I'll call you in a few days when I have a draft document."

Friday, August 17

When Michael saw the Immunity Agreement, he was appalled at the length to which the language focused on the voluntary nature of his action. Three double-spaced pages were devoted to the fact that even though Michael Sidney James would be exposed to the full wrath of the federal government at trial if he did not enter into the agreement, he was, nevertheless, not being influenced by the benefits of immunity. The document stated in several ways that he felt no duress, had been fully advised of the terms of the agreement by his counsel, had given proper consideration to it as a legal document, was of sound mind, and would keep its contents confidential.

"So under this agreement I'm not being forced to do anything I don't want to do. It's entirely voluntary, as long as everyone understands I don't have any choice in the matter."

"Look at it any way you want," said Porter. "Just sign."

The following Tuesday, debriefings began on the second floor of Courthouse Square without a polygraph. Arnold Porter attended. Michael denied knowing anything about the money. There were three subsequent meetings, the results of which the government considered inconclusive. Recordings from the James home remained unremarkable.

As far as Denise knew, Michael was at work during the Courthouse Square debriefings. Having withdrawn Tommy and Sydney from childcare, her time was spent tending to them, rehearsing magic tricks, playing guitar, maintaining the household, receiving no good news from Hirschfeld, and worrying.

Money would fast become a problem. Only Michael's incoming paychecks were available to cover expenses; her final check had been paid. Hirschfeld's fees, private investigators, and efforts to have the restraining order set aside or modified to free assets eroded the funds Hirschfeld had. The government objected to every motion for relief of the restraining order in a battle of attrition. She supposed Fleming and Kludge wanted her in bankruptcy before trial.

Hirschfeld informed her that the government and Michael's counsel wanted her consent to move the trial date to the second of October, still within the hundred-and-twenty-day speedy-trial time limit. She viewed Michael's consent as unfortunate. He could have joined her in an objection to try to force the government to allow their retirement accounts to be freed from the restraining order so the mortgage could be paid before the loan became delinquent. Faced with a *fait accompli*, she consented.

Hirschfeld presented her with a fixed fee agreement requiring one hundred and seventy-five thousand dollars for the duration. Faced with a fate worse than debt, she signed, prepared a promissory note in that amount to her parents, and tendered the full amount to the firm.

Hourly charges didn't stop until the fee was paid, and no credit was given for hours already billed, or private investigators. The next billing cycle would tell her if anything was left from her retainer.

She and Michael had grown as far apart as they'd ever been. By order of their respective counsel, neither discussed any aspect of the case. Each felt an undefined time urgency that could not be slowed or allayed by anything they could do. Denise stayed upstairs with the children most of the time. Michael paced downstairs, television on, computer on, unable to find anything to do to pass the time. Conversation was impersonal, distant, and functional. Play and laughter ceased. Neither slept well. No meetings were convened with the shower running, and lovemaking had ceased weeks before. She didn't want him, and he felt it inappropriate knowing what was to come.

Monday and Tuesday, September 11 and 12

Michael went to work Monday without a kiss good-bye, the first time either could remember that happening. Tuesday dawned overcast to match their moods. Denise left for a meeting with Hirschfeld, telling Michael she would be home by noon so he wouldn't miss a full day's work watching the children.

As soon as her car and surveillance van were out of sight, he began packing. Two suitcases would suffice for clothes, a third being for the money.

He checked the street out front. His surveillance van was there, the gas tank no doubt topped off to follow him to Charlottesville.

His heart beat faster.

They weren't supposed to interfere with him. He'd have to take his chances they wouldn't search his bags.

He moved the coffee table and end tables to the far side of the living room, and dragged each end of the sofa until it was well away from the wall. Two Lego pieces were on the carpet where the sofa had been. The corner had a spider web Denise had sprayed with a can from her magic props. She'd been meticulous matching that area with the other corner of the room. When the agents from the search warrant team flipped and examined the sofa, they'd seen the Legos and dust and moved on.

Michael used a screwdriver to wrestle the carpet from the corner tackle-board and get a grip on it. He yanked at it from his knees. A foot on each side pulled free. He stood, and ripped it from the wall until the black plastic underneath was fully exposed.

There it was. Cash laid flat inside trash bags, the world's most expensive carpet pad. Water and steam cleaning couldn't have gotten inside. God, she was good.

He picked up one of the bags, ripped the plastic, and shook out its contents.

Newspapers fell to the floor.

Hirschfeld had been somber, the meeting unproductive. His investigators had uncovered nothing positive on any front, and the government stood pat behind its indictment. Jury selection was to begin October second and could not be changed. The ordeal of trial loomed large, and she could stomach only half the sandwich Hirschfeld ordered in for lunch.

By one o'clock, she and her government van returned to Villamay. Michael's car was gone. No note was taped to the refrigerator indicating where he had taken the children. Her calls to him went unanswered.

In the living room, the carpet rippled between the coffee table and the sofa skirt.

He tried to take the money!

She ran upstairs to the children's room. Sydney's diaper bag was gone. Clothes were missing. So were Michael's toiletries.

He'd cut a deal, she thought. He was going to confess.

She looked out the window at her surveillance van.

They'd be coming to get her. She was going to prison.

She rushed to the bathroom and delivered Hirschfeld's half-sandwich into the commode.

When the doorbell rang, she expected federal marshals. Instead, a stoop-shouldered man stood squinting at her with the semi-startled look of someone who'd lost his glasses.

"Denise Elizabeth Lang James?"
"Yes?"
He held out papers. She took them.
"You are hereby served."
He walked away.

She read the documents word-for-word sitting on the stairs, sounding out each syllable with her mind's voice. The Bill of Complaint was for divorce. It cited irreconcilable differences as cause, a get-to-the-point document of four pages. She allowed it to fall to the floor. In six pages, the Restraining Order prohibited her from seeing or telephoning Michael or the children without Michael's prior consent.

She picked up the Bill of Complaint and refolded the papers.
She called Hirschfeld.
He said he would call back.

Possibilities flowed as she worked to even the newspaper padding across the floor and stretch the carpet flat against the wall.

Michael couldn't have turned against her she thought. He had more courage than that. They'd been too close for too long. Something else was happening.

She was staring at the portrait of the First Couple and her family in its silver frame when Hirschfeld telephoned.

"There have been developments. We need to talk. Come down here."

Alexandria

Hirschfeld had the ashen look of the slow dying.

"The Bill of Complaint and Restraining Order were properly noticed, filed, and served. Both are valid. If divorce is pursued after one year of separation, it is only a matter of time before it is final. You should consider it constructive notice. In addition, charges will be dropped against your husband. The government informs me he will testify against you."

195

She was right. Michael cut a deal.

"Where is he?"

"With his parents. You are prohibited from seeing or calling him or the children."

"This is part of the government's attempt to pressure me, isn't it?"

"You think so?"

"There's nothing for him to say against me. Did he get immunity?"

"Charges are to be dropped. That is all I know. Witness lists are not yet due, but I can guarantee that whatever he says can and will be used against you."

His tone made her queasier than she already was.

"Is there something else?"

"I do not have it on firm authority, but word is the FBI lab lifted a fingerprint from one of the bags in the alley." He paused. "And guess what?"

"It's J. Edgar's."

"No, Denise. It is yours. It matches your thumb. With the footprint and hair, this is a third piece of damning evidence that places you in the alley."

He sat.

"You have to get serious about this. Three pieces of physical evidence are impossible to overcome."

She'd never seen him so discomposed.

"They're going to say I went into the alley and picked up the money, took it home, and hid it. They have a shoe cast they say came from the alley that matches a shoe from my closet. They have hair samples they say match my thermo-nucleic acid. Some old woman walking a Dalmatian at two o'clock in the morning claims she saw me carrying a bag. And now, just before trial, they say they have a fingerprint on one of the bags left in the alley that matches mine?"

"And your husband is testifying against you."

"Your investigators canvassed every homeowner from the alley to my parking space that night, and no one saw anything. They've also searched for a picture showing what shoes I'm wearing. They can't find one. We've still got the frozen ground expert. And yes, there's one other thing. They've searched everywhere and haven't found the money."

"Listen to me, Denise. They have the footprint, the hair, and the fingerprint. You have divorce, separation, a restraining order, your husband testifying against you, terminated employment, a motivated task force, and Emil Smert. I would say chances are good that if you go to trial, you may be found guilty. If they have not found the money, it means you hid it well."

She paced the floor, then stopped at the window to look at the sun heading down over the courthouse tower where trial would be.

"Do any of the photos taken in the alley show this footprint?"

"No. The lab report will say the print is light, and the cast has been enhanced for depth so as to strengthen its material, but the impression is valid. The report's conclusion is that the shoe is the same as your brown one, but it is not one hundred percent, it is not as irrefutable as a fingerprint or DNA. It is, however, conclusive their way into the high ninetieth percentiles."

"The hair. Have you found out when it was taken from the alley?"

"It was found among debris in the alley taken by Alexandria police the morning after the raid."

"Do you have Alexandria's evidence list from that day? Is hair specified on it? If it is, I'll bet it's the last item listed, the last item written down."

"We can get what there is."

"Interview the police officer who picked up that debris. See if he specifically remembers picking up hair."

"You cannot say the hair was planted, Denise."

"Why not?"

"Because the DNA report on the hair found in the alley is dated prior to the search warrant on your house."

"That's impossible."

Hirschfeld nailed it down. "They could not have planted hair in the debris before they had access to hair acquired during the search. The hair had to have come from the alley. And they made the cast of the shoe imprint before the search as well."

"They couldn't have had the hair and the shoe before the search. Could those reports have been backdated?"

"No. They have procedures in place to prevent that."

"The fingerprint. When did they find that?"

"Unknown. One of our paralegals heard about it from one of their people."

"When the government wants something kept quiet, it's kept quiet isn't it? And if they want something known, they leak it, right?"

"I suppose."

"So when do we get access to all their evidence, including the evidence they haven't leaked yet?"

"Five days before trial. ·That is the time under the rules. They could give it to us now if they wanted, but it is not in their interest to give us more time to examine it than required. They would prefer to present it for the first time in court if they could."

"All in the interest of getting to the truth."

"Truth has nothing to do with it."

"As you're so fond of saying—it's who wins that counts."

"Correct."

"Well, the fingerprint's fake."

"How can you prove that?"

"I wore gloves that night. It was freezing."

Hirschfeld's chin fell to his chest.

"That is not proof."

He remained motionless, eyes closed. "If we wished to bargain at this point, I am uncertain what options might be available." He cocked an eye at her as she stared out the window. "Would you like me to ask?"

"Wouldn't do any good. I don't have three million dollars."

Hirschfeld got up and stood beside her. Together they gazed at nature's daily closing curtain in silence. The sky was brilliant: reds, pinks, oranges, and violets reflecting off clouds, rays of sunlight streaming through from behind.

"I believe you, Denise. I do not know why, but I do. I would tell you to take the four years if you had the money. At this point, with Michael and the children gone, and this new evidence, I believe you would take it, would you not?"

It was as though she hadn't heard.

"How can we find out if the government ever does searches without warrants? A neighbor saw a security company surveying our house before the vandalism. That would have been at about the right time. And when was the fingerprint discovered? This is late in the game for evidence like this to be coming out. It's as if they needed one more piece."

If she'd had any doubts about the validity of the footprint or the hair, the fingerprint erased them. She'd worn gloves in the alley, and didn't touch any of the bags. She'd thought about that while she was prodding them with her toe.

"Three pieces of physical evidence are going to be difficult for the jury to disregard," said Hirschfeld.

Morton Mieske was right, she thought. She didn't know what the government could do.

"What chance do I have if my defense rests on saying the government is so mad at me that they fabricated all this evidence?"

Hirschfeld took off his glasses.

"I would say take a good look at this sunset."

Self-pity hit hard with those words. Self-pity: the most debilitating of emotions. Denial had been her ally against it, that and keeping active. Ride faster than the black dogs of despair could chase you down, someone once said. Be always up and about, keep your wits, and never be afraid. Well, she was damn sure afraid now.

Michael was gone. Hirschfeld's initiatives were exhausted. She was alone.

What could she do? How could she cope if she couldn't do anything? There had to be an alternative. Even spreading confusion was an alternative. The only tool she had was her brain. But she'd already been through all that. So much time to think, so much time to think and she had nothing. She had to act, do something desperate, something unconventional, something almost magical.

Wednesday, September 12
The Washington Post - Regional Briefs - Virginia - Page B4

Captured Fugitive Slain

Jason C. McCullough, exposed informant from the January 16th Old Town drug ambush, was found stabbed to death Monday night in his cell at the Alexandria Jail. McCullough was scheduled for arraignment next week in federal court on charges stemming from his role in the raid. The Alexandria Police Department's Internal Affairs Division and federal authorities are investigating.

Chapter Fifteen

Thursday, September 13
Villamay

She began with the Office of Protocol. From there she was transferred and placed on hold. The connection was empty, no music. Every few minutes someone would ask for more information or request that she please remain on the line while verifications were made. She was thinking a speakerphone would be good for calls like this when a man picked up the line and said, "I'm putting you through. Thank you for waiting."

The line clicked.

"Hello, Denise How are you?"

"Oh!—Hello. I never thought I'd get through."

"When I heard it was you, I decided to take the call."

"I appreciate that very much. Thank you."

"You've become quite infamous since I saw you last. Every few months it seems you're in the news in some near tragedy. Now I understand you have legal trouble."

She recognized the voice. She had to be speaking to the First Lady.

"Yes, ma'am. Jury selection starts in a couple of weeks. And my husband has filed for divorce and taken the children."

"I'm sorry. I didn't know about the divorce. With all that's been happening, how are you holding up?"

"Rationalizing the best I can. At least Michael's parents call and I get to talk to the children."

"Well, be strong. I'm no stranger to controversy, politics being what it is. Despite your best efforts, it can sometimes be an absurd world."

"That is so true, ma'am, so true. And that's why I'm calling, to ask your advice in an absurd world situation."

"I'll try to help if I can."

"You might remember I was threatened by a drug dealer."

"Yes, I do. You played a message from him at your Tea Party."

"You saw that?"

"You're quite a character, Denise. And I've always loved characters. So many people lack that quality these days."

"Well, thank you—I think."

She could almost see her smile.

"Yesterday I received another call from the drug dealer. He got my unlisted number again, and he's threatening my children. Bad things happen when I ignore him, so I was wondering—do you think if I called someone at the DEA, they might be able to catch this man? Maybe agree to give him the money he thinks I have, and then arrest him? That would get my family out of danger."

"It might also affect the jury pool for your trial."

Astute woman, thought Denise.

"I suppose it might, but I'm more concerned about my husband and children. I've learned surveillance isn't the same thing as protection. As for the jury pool, as I understand the process, both the plaintiff and the defendant have to agree on each juror to make it fair."

"The plaintiff is the complaining party in a civil suit. Yours is criminal."

"I stand corrected. I just want to make this drug dealer go away before something bad happens. The threat was left on my machine. He'll call again."

"You don't want to use the FBI on this, do you?"

"No, ma'am, I don't."

"I understand."

She could hear the First Lady breathing into the receiver.

"You *do* feel you and your family are in danger, don't you?"

"After the vandalism, the kidnapping, and a shot at the house, yes, ma'am, I do. I'm desperate."

Denise wondered if Kludge and Penes would get a transcript of this call.

"Why don't you wait a couple of days and call Archer Adler at the DEA. Archie might help. I can't promise anything, but it can't hurt."

No need to ask for the number. If the Office of Protocol could get through to the First Lady, they could find anyone at the DEA.

"Thank you very much, ma'am."

"You and your family were charming. I do so much wish we had more time to get to know each other."

"Again. Thank you."

"Keep your chin up, Denise. Remember, things seldom have a bad end if you never give up. I wish you luck."

"And good luck to you too, ma'am. Thank you so much for your help."

"I haven't done anything, but you're very welcome. Good-bye."

"Good-bye."

Two days later she called Archer Adler and received a warm reception.

Sunday, September 23

"Hello?"

"Denise James."

It was the electronic voice.

"Yes."

"I got you in my sights."

"I know."

"I gonna kill you."

"I'm ready to talk."

"Good. Go to the pay phone at the car wash at the corner of Beacon Hill Road and Route One. Wait for my call."

"Okay."

He hung up.

The DEA had given her a cassette recorder wired to a microphone she was to place in her ear and cover with the receiver. She got in her car wearing it, and led her surveillance van to the lot.

"Hello?"

"I whack the snitch in jail. I gotta long reach."

"So you do. Listen. The police aren't at my house anymore."

"I know that."

"And the surveillance stops after the jury's picked. Some kind of anti-harassment rule. I need to make a deal."

"You got my money?"

"It'll take a week to get. It has to be shipped."

"You taking this good. I hope the FBI not involve."

"I'm on trial for taking the money, *stupid.* If the FBI found out what I was doing, they'd confiscate it and show the judge. Case closed."

She sensed nothing from him.

"Now, before I give you anything, you have to get me off the hook with this trial. You have to announce *you* took the money, and that you've had it since the raid. You figure out how to do that between now and next week. It has to be convincing. And I don't want you holding a grudge because of the kidnapping. For what you were going to do to me, we're even."

"We businessmen. This is business. I call you next Tuesday. Get the money."

"Trial starts that day. Call after eight."

She hung up and drove to Villamay. Within an hour of making a call, a DEA agent appeared at the sliding glass door and took the cassette.

Tuesday, October 2
Villamay

Denise stared out the kitchen window, coffee mug in hand.

She still didn't know how the FBI got the hair or the fingerprint. Hirschfeld and his investigators determined neither had been enumerated in the evidence tabulated by the Alexandria police. Both had been "discovered" by the FBI after the Bureau became involved. The hair was inside a bag labeled "Miscellaneous Debris." Nothing in the evidence description contained the word *hair.* According to the lab report, the fingerprint was found just before indictment. Hirschfeld said it pushed the case over the edge as far as the government was concerned. He and Antaramian had both seen it. The print matched her right thumb. There wasn't much to attack.

Morton Mieske had been singularly unhelpful in trying to ascertain whether the FBI ever executed searches without warrants. As it was unreasonable to expect anyone in an authoritative position at the FBI or the Department of Justice to take the stand under oath and testify that the chief law enforcement authority of the United

States government broke the law prohibiting illegal search and seizure, attempts to find another qualified witness proved fruitless.

Gus Gordon's belief that a security company had surveyed their home led nowhere. Hirschfeld told her he considered any testimony from Gordon about as reliable as that from the woman walking the Dalmatian.

The defense submitted a witness list of seventy-two names including police officers at the raid, authors of the lab reports, FBI agents, Treasure Chest employees, and the woman with the Dalmatian. Everyone justifiable as a witness was named.

Denise asked Hirschfeld how he was going to call all these people in the time he'd told Judge Smert the defense presentation would take. He said he intended calling no more than fourteen witnesses depending on the government's case. The list of seventy-two would mask the defense, and make the government's life more difficult by forcing them to waste time interviewing people the defense never intended to call.

"Every good attorney does what I am doing," Hirschfeld told her. "I do it to others, and they do it to me. But what you have done to the task force has hurt you. A typical defendant is too terrified to leave his residence. Few, if any, hold press conferences or spill coffee on the agent heading up the investigation. Few have a television correspondent debate the case in the media the way Mattison does for you. My actions are standard and expected. Yours make the government more determined to convict you."

Pressure mounted during the days preceding trial. Time seemed to pass more slowly. Getting through one day at a time became too much, and reduced itself to getting through one morning or one afternoon or one evening at a time. In court, she imagined she might learn to live from moment to moment.

Jury selection would begin today. Hirschfeld didn't want accountants, scientists, military veterans, or anyone dealing in a profession involving exactness. He wanted libertarians, independent thinkers, and humanitarians, as many as he could get, and people of any age who might feel empathy for the client personality he intended to paint. All Denise had to do was sit and watch.

One thing she knew for certain: the task force was better at planting evidence on her and covering its tracks than she and

Hirschfeld and his investigators had been at proving the evidence false.

Despite all the negatives, she'd slept well. Her isolation and loneliness were about to end. The Langs were flying in from Ohio on Saturday, and Bret and Marianne James would be bringing the children later the same day. Allies would be with her through the verdict.

"We'll circle the wagons," her dad had said.

Courthouse Square

Moses Hirschfeld and Vartan Antaramian were already seated in the second floor snack bar when Denise came around the condiment stand.

"Morning, gentlemen."

Antaramian stood. "Good morning, Denise."

"Good morning," said Hirschfeld seated. "I've asked Vartan to join us for jury selection and the prosecution's presentation. I want his feelings on both."

"Good." She removed her coat. "Let me get some coffee."

She did and sat.

"This is what we know," said Hirschfeld. "The jury is to be sequestered for the duration. The government has filed a motion, and Judge Smert will grant it this morning."

"So?"

"So sequestration takes away one of your future grounds for appeal if it should come to that," said Antaramian. "No tainted jury, no jurors poisoned by outside influence like the media. The press will be here in force once trial starts."

She nodded.

Antaramian continued. "Also, while there is to be no live broadcast, Smert has agreed to allow videotape to be released at each break. Never before has any federal court in this district allowed that to be done. This means highlights will be on the news every night."

Hirschfeld sipped coffee, then removed his glasses and began polishing them with a handkerchief, though not the one from his breast pocket. His face had the look of polished marble.

"For today, you sit and pay attention. Do not say anything. This is the most important part of the trial for you."

Antaramian said, "Moses says whatever we're doing on any given day is the most important part of the entire judicial process." He smiled. "Associates get tired of hearing him say that about scheduling hearings."

Hirschfeld put a hand on her arm. "You may look at the jury pool, at the judge, whatever. Do not scowl, and do not look down. Keep your head up. Get used to the environment of a courtroom in session. Let us handle everything. Be still, and be attentive."

They were ready. Homework completed, they were now only wary of something unforeseen, some surprise, like something untoward from their client, or some new information their client had kept hidden.

At nine-thirty sharp, court was called to order. There were introductions, instructions, motions, and administrative matters. Then the first pool of prospective jurors was brought in, and Smert began weeding out those who said they could not objectively hear the case and arrive at an unbiased decision because of what they'd seen or heard in the media. This included the raid itself, the State of the Union Address, the Tea Party, the "involuntary abduction of the person of the defendant," the bullet through the window, and any and all interviews or written materials. Only those without preconceived notions need apply.

The attorneys then had at them. The government and the defense could eliminate any juror for cause if Smert agreed. Each side had twelve pre-emptory strikes they could exercise without cause. Denise learned the art of jury selection was to use pre-empts with care so as not to let the other side get ahead and force a bad choice. It was slow going. Smert took ten minutes and read the same instructions to each new pool and excused the twenty-percent or so who said they could not be objective. Twelve jurors and two alternates had to be agreed upon by both sides.

That evening, a DEA agent with the entrancing name of Billy Freep came to the Villamay house to monitor the anticipated call for the money. He entered through the sliding glass door and asked Denise to pull the drapes closed. A second man arrived.

Both agents were black, weighed in at well over two hundred pounds, were dressed in civilian clothes, and didn't move or speak with the officiousness to which she'd become accustomed at Courthouse Square. She liked them.

The electronic voice called on schedule.

"Go to the pay phone outside the supermarket at Belle View and wait."

He hung up.

She drove to the center a mile to the north and parked. Her surveillance van followed in her wake. She headed toward two telephone kiosks along the store's exterior wall. One phone rang as she approached. She was being watched.

"Hello?"

"You got my money?"

"I'll have it Thursday and be able to deliver it Friday. What about the announcement that you've had the money the whole time?"

"I make some calls."

"Making some calls isn't good enough."

"It gotta be."

"Look," she huffed, "if you don't make an announcement, my husband goes to Brazil with the money, and I go to jail for fifty years. I have nothing to lose. You don't get anything until I'm satisfied you've done all you can do to get the charges against me dropped. This is not negotiable."

The voice said, "I do what I can."

Her words came out heavy with disappointment. "You know, I've always thought of myself as an honest crook. I guess you don't. I'll be saying goodb—"

"No!"

Pause.

"What you want me to do?"

"Maybe send a tape to Dan Mattison at Channel Three. Show a table with three million dollars sitting on it. Use your electronic voice and say you and your gang have had a laugh a day because the government is prosecuting the wrong person. Normally you'd keep your mouth shut, but you want to get in on embarrassing them like I do all the time. Be original. Ham it up. You don't have to name names or show faces, but there has to be something in it that convinces them that you are who you say you are. When Dan Mattison broadcasts it, I'll give you your money, not before."

Rasps of the man's breathing came through the line.

"Think about it. This is a good deal for you. I have the money. From your standpoint, all you have to do is make a one-minute tape. You have no risk, and I get out of a jam. Without that, there's no reason for me to talk to you."

She waited.

"Get the money. I call back Friday."

He hung up.

Back at the house, she handed Billy Freep the recorder. He listened to the tape, and cracked a neon-white smile.

"You did good, Denise. Let me know when you're back on the job market. I could use you."

"Fat chance me working for the government."

"Aw, don't say that. It's all how you look at it."

"I suppose there's truth to that. But in my case, it's how they'd look at me."

He nodded to her point, and set the recorder aside.

"From the sound of that, I'd say Channel Three is going to get a tape sometime Thursday. Let's assume they do. In that case, we can either set up inside your house, or we can go remote with our team. We're going to want six men in here Friday when he calls in case he tries to make a grab for the money when you get home. You never can tell with these guys. They do stupid things sometimes. After he calls, and we send out our team, we'd like to leave two men with you, just in case."

"Is that why there's two of you here now? Just in case?"

"That's right."

She handed Billy a key to the house.

"I'd feel a lot better if you camped out here until after trial," she said.

"No can do, but expect six of us Friday. It may take a couple of days to do this. These people spook easy."

"That's fine. Just arrest them. Any special requests for food?"

"Coffee, chips, jalapeño cheese dip, and coffee. That should do it."

"You sound like me before my last baby."

"Hey, hon." He pulled in his stomach and pulled up his belt. "Fat jokes are out of bounds."

She smiled watching him.

"Thanks, Billy. I'll stock the refrigerator. Help yourself till I get home."

Friday, October 5
Courthouse Square

Jury selection proceeded without fireworks, both sides wanting to please Judge Smert. For lunch, the defense adjourned to a witness room and ate nutrition bars. There was no time for a real meal, and Antaramian said a heavy stomach led to a dull mind.

Friday before noon, both sides had settled on eight women and four men for the twelve jurors, and two men for the alternates. Hirschfeld and Antaramian seemed pleased. They didn't get everyone they wanted, but they thwarted the government's effort to get most of the candidates that didn't meet the defense profile. Only two jurors gave them heartburn. They got four they liked.

Antaramian summed up the selection up with a Grinch-like smile.

"Two guilty, four innocent, six undecided. We need to hold one of those four to hang the jury."

When word went out trial would begin that afternoon, the eighth floor was overrun with reporters. Hirschfeld and Antaramian offered no comment as they pushed their way across the hall, Denise silent between them.

Chapter Sixteen

At one-thirty sharp, all eyes focused on Judge Emil N. Smert and his medieval robes as he floated to the judge's chair from his entry on the left. He smacked the gavel, and court was under way.

Both sides affirmed their readiness to proceed. The jury was brought in and instructed. They were not to discuss the case among themselves, or to read newspapers or magazines, watch news reports, or in any way acquire knowledge of the case except from the presentations and witnesses in court. Any violations must be reported. Any willful violations could be punishable under federal law. If any juror did not feel he or she could perform their assigned duties, including informing the court of violations or suspected violations of the rules of the court, that juror was free to be excused. None volunteered. They were sworn.

The jury was to be sequestered. They'd been apprised of this and were so prepared. Witnesses were to remain outside the courtroom so they could not hear testimony. Witnesses could not discuss the case or their testimony while waiting. Smert outlined the rules for the two permitted video cameras, the primary one being that members of the jury were at no time to be seen.

All preliminaries completed without objection, Judge Smert read the eight charges in the indictment against Denise Elizabeth Lang James, and the government was asked to make its opening statement.

Assistant US Attorney R. Paul Fleming, III walked to the lectern and laid a sheaf of papers under the microphone. He removed a binder clip from their top. He adjusted the microphone. He looked at the faces of the jurors in the box; then lowered his head to begin slow, blurry reading.

He introduced himself with title, and he introduced the members of his team at the table beside him with their titles. Then he thanked the jury for taking the time from their busy lives to serve in this most sad proceeding.

Sad?

Yes, sad.

He and the government felt sadness to have to prosecute the defendant in this particular case. But duty is duty, and he and the other staff members at the government table, and those many more not present in court, were doing their jobs, distasteful as they were in this instance.

They had all heard of the now famous Denise Elizabeth Lang James. She'd headlined news in January when she'd assisted police in the capture of a later convicted drug felon. In recognition, the President of the United States had presented her to the joint Congress and a national television audience as a heroine of the first order.

Unfortunately, the money brought to the raid to purchase the drugs was missing. A net had been thrown over the event, and all possible suspects within it scrutinized. Anyone who could have taken the money, three million one hundred and fifty thousand dollars, was examined, and, according to proper and time-tested investigative procedure, eliminated. Police officers, passersby, neighbors, television and press people, and the drug dealers themselves, everyone within the suspect net was examined and discarded.

"Except one."

Fleming looked up at the jury.

"That is why this is so sad. That one suspect, now subject to an eight-count federal indictment handed down by a grand jury, is the defendant, Denise Elizabeth Lang James."

The stenographer rolled his eyes as Fleming reread the eight counts and amplified their meaning in language fit for middle school.

"But that can't be true you say. She's our heroine, and she's pretty, and she has a handsome husband and two adorable children.

"It is sad, isn't it?

"The investigation went where it had to go, ladies and gentlemen of the jury, and it centered on a woman who has received every accolade except a tickertape parade down Fifth Avenue. Evidence was found that contravened public statements she made over and over again. She said she never went into the alley.

"A footprint was found at the site where the money is known to have been that matches a shoe belonging to Ms. James. Hair samples from the alley match the DNA of her hair. A fingerprint belonging to the defendant was found on a bag in the alley. There is no mistake.

"But this is our superstar, a real-life Wonder Woman who risked her life to bring down a dangerous criminal who had just shot at police.

"Despite being a superstar, incontrovertible physical evidence speaks for itself. That is why this is so sad ladies and gentlemen. The defendant picked up the money on her way home after the raid and hid it. The footprint, the hair, and the fingerprint will prove it. In statements the defendant made to the Alexandria police, the FBI, and in countless interviews, she said she went straight home, not back into the alley, as the evidence will prove. Denise Elizabeth Lang James practiced not heroism most brave, but treachery most foul."

Throughout this plodding and pedantic presentation, Moses Hirschfeld, Vartan Antaramian, and Denise James sat looking from Fleming to the judge and the jury. There wasn't much the defense could do except watch "How-could-you?" expressions cross faces in the box. Told often enough the sky is green by an authority figure, even people who otherwise regarded themselves as having more than average common sense sometimes became tempted to go outside for a confirmatory look.

Fleming concluded by thanking the jury for their anticipated clear thinking and future verdict. He took his papers to his seat.

Moses Hirschfeld moved to the microphone and requested the court's permission to make his opening statement at the conclusion of the prosecution's case. This brought an immediate objection, leading to a sidebar, followed by a conference in chambers. Court sat in silence for ten minutes before resuming. When it did, Smert granted Hirschfeld's request.

The government was asked to call its first witness. Fleming stuttered out a request for adjournment. Smert noted the early hour and the long Columbus Day weekend. Only four sessions would be available the following week. Fleming said the government had anticipated hearing the opening statement of the defense today and calling its first witness on Tuesday.

"Do you mean you are not prepared to proceed?" asked Smert.

"The government only wishes further time to confer with itself on strategy, Your Honor."

Smert gave him an acid look of understanding and granted the request.

The jury was reminded of its sacred duty not to discuss the case or view anything about it from the media. Court was adjourned.

Denise arrived home, surveillance van in tow. Billy Freep, four men, and a woman were set up on the first floor with their equipment. They introduced themselves by first names. They carried automatics on their belts, and shotguns lay in open carrying cases across the arms of chairs. Billy made a call, and the van out front drove off. Denise was impressed.

"Ambush team to position," he ordered.

Three men gathered up utility belts, helmets, and shotguns. They positioned themselves on the first floor covering the entries.

Denise felt a rush of adrenaline. They meant business.

"Let me show you the tape," said Billy. "I got it cued up."

He pressed Play on the remote.

"...and in an exclusive, Channel Three has received a video purported to have been made by the drug traffickers that may put into question the reason for continuing the Denise James trial."

The screen cut to a picture of a card table stacked corner-to-corner six inches high with cash. The bottom of the frame read, "October 4th - 1:32 P.M."

"This is not," said a raspy voice, "I repeat, not the money we got after the Old Town raid. That money been spent."

The room was sterile, no windows or doors, perhaps a basement. The camera walked in over the cash.

"This is proof I am who I say I am, an' I got the money. Denise James didn't get it. I got it. The feds is gettin' back at her for the tequila. It's a frame."

That was it. Billy stopped the tape.

"What do you think?"

Denise thought the voice could have said the other gang didn't know he'd gotten the money. That would explain the attacks on her.

"It's good enough for me, Billy."

"Works for me too." He spoke into a hand-held radio, his black eyes twinkling. "It's a go. Bring the money."

The woman in the group turned out to be Denise's body-double. Arlene was her name, a physical look-alike, perhaps twenty-five, with dark pageboy hair, brown eyes, and a ski-jump nose. She and Denise went upstairs to change clothes.

"The DEA has a pretty tough reputation," Denise said when they were alone. "Your team isn't as formal as I thought it would be."

213

"Every unit's different," Arlene replied. "We're loose 'cause we've worked together a long time and know each other real well. We want you to be loose too, hon."

Arlene took off her fatigues and showed Denise the waterproof locator taped to her back.

"That's so they can track you?"

"Yep. GPS can peg me within ten feet. Global Positioning."

Without a second's thought, Arlene put on the clothes Denise had worn all day.

"How long have you been doing this?"

"Four years. First two training."

"How often do you go on missions?"

"More than you might think. The hardest part is traveling so much."

"You go all over the country?"

"Pretty much. The case has to be important.to get us."

Back downstairs, Arlene pulled on a sandy brown wig the length of Denise's hair, brushed it until it approximated her style, then fixed it with spray. Billy inspected them standing side-by-side.

"That's a real good match, hon, but lighten your face a little. Yours is too tan."

"Delivery arriving," said an agent in front.

"Everyone into position," Billy ordered. Then to Denise, "This is when the show starts."

Out front, a panel truck pulled up, and a uniformed deliveryman got out. He went to the back doors, opened them, took out a hand truck, and manhandled a metal storage trunk to the pavement. He slid the hand truck under it, and wheeled it to the front door. Arlene signed the receipt. He rolled the trunk inside.

When he left, Billy opened the trunk.

The bag wasn't the same as the one that actually contained the money, but Denise thought it unnecessary to point this out. Inside it were bundles of color-copied bills. They looked good at first glance, but fuzzy up close.

"How much is that?" she asked.

"About three million," said Billy picking up a packet. "Some of the bills have transmitters in them so we can trace them if they get separated from the bag. And the bag's been sprayed so we can see it in the dark."

"How? You have special glasses?"

"Special binoculars."

Billy picked up an aerosol can and sprayed Arlene's wig and shoulders.

"You can see this same as the bag. It shows up from the bird."

"You have a helicopter?"

He handed the can to an agent and told him to spray the Firebird's roof.

"Yeah. We love all this spy-stuff. See, it's likely they'll separate Arlene from your car, make her get on a bus or a subway, something like that. They might make her change clothes, X-ray her, make her go for a swim, there's lot's of stuff they could do. We have to be ready for about anything."

"What's the name of the guy you're after?"

"We think it's Nick 'The Knife' Rivera. He carries a big blade all the time. First-class bad news boofer. Every year we bust some of his guys. We just ain't busted him yet."

So it's not just Nick Rivera, she thought. It's Nick "The Knife" Rivera. That fit.

"While we wait for the call, let Arlene listen to the way you talk. She has to be you on the road. I think she's pretty close." Billy grinned. "But all you white girls sound alike to me."

After it was fully dark, the telephone rang.

"Hello," answered Arlene.

"Go to the pay phone outside the bar-b-cue place at Beacon Hill Road and Route One. You know where is it?"

"Yes."

He hung up.

"Let's roll," said Billy.

The team unwound from their ambush positions and exchanged their shotguns and gear for other equipment. Denise had never seen such menacing machineguns with so many attachments and wide-lens scopes.

Arlene gave herself a final look in the mirror and said she was ready. Billy handed her a hearing aid she fitted into her ear.

"That must work the same way as the tape recorder you gave me," said Denise. "You send telephone conversations by putting the receiver on that ear."

"Yeah," said Billy. "It transmits to a booster unit she has in your purse. We can hear everything she hears, and she can hear us."

A final transmission check of everyone's equipment was completed. Arlene made sure she had a map.

"Good luck, hon," said Billy. "We gotcha all the way."

Arlene hoisted the bag's strap onto her shoulder, turned off the lights, and went out the door to the garage. The covering agents stole out the back at intervals. They would join the shadow team forming up while Arlene waited for the call on Route One. Billy and a second agent stayed with the radios, a recorder, the Mr. Coffee machine, and the bathroom.

Billy put Arlene's conversation on the speaker.

"You got the money?" the voice asked.

"Yes."

"You got it with you?"

"Yes."

"Okay."

They listened to his instructions.

The radioman kept the channels straight for Billy, who monitored Arlene's movement and acted as backup for the communications van on the road. Billy called it the AWACS. Denise couldn't tell how many vehicles were involved. She guessed four, but had to ask. Billy said there were two cars, the AWACS, a helicopter above the sound cone, another standing by on the ground, and two motorcycles. Motorcycles had greater mobility on assignments like this where the probability of pursuit was high.

The scrambled voice ran Arlene through three counties from pay phone to pay phone. Each time she took a call, the anticipation of capture rose in Denise, and lasted until it became clear the other side wasn't ready to meet. While Arlene drove, the agents drank coffee, snacked, answered her questions about Rivera, and told war stories in the dark.

Near midnight, Arlene was left hanging on Route 50 near Fair Oaks Mall.

"Okay Billy. I've been here almost an hour. Maybe something scared them off. I haven't seen anyone, and I'm running low on gas. How much longer do you want me to wait?"

"I think it's a bust already, but it's your call, hon."

A half-hour later, Arlene started back to Villamay.

"They saw something," said Billy, "or it was a planned dry run. If it's a dry run, we'll get another call. If the phone rings as soon as she gets back, the house is being watched. We should be ready."

Denise looked at Billy. "You guys are staying here till this is over, right?"

"As long as they think the money's here, we'll be here too."

The telephone rang as soon as Arlene turned on the kitchen light. "Hello."

"Tonight was practice. Sunday we do it again. Wait for my call." He hung up.

"He'll call us Sunday to do it," said Arlene.

Denise turned to Billy.

"The money's going to be here for two days?"

"So will we, hon."

Even with two-way scramblers, Johnny Murphy seldom called Nick Rivera by telephone. Saturday morning was an exception.

"Did you see the tape on the news?" Murphy asked.

"See it? I made it. I gotta deal with the woman."

"She has it?"

"Course she has it."

Murphy covered his surprise.

"I get half."

"Bullshit!" Rivera snapped. "I been doin' all the work. Whadda you done?"

"This is a share-and-share-alike business, Nick."

"Not when the snitch was on your side an' you couldn't find him. Not when your man pick up my money and lose it. All you doin' is sit on you fat ass. Hear what happen to you snitch when he get back?"

"I heard." Murphy lowered his voice. "Look, Nick. You and I don't need to get into a pissing contest over this. We go back a long time. We can work it out."

"I takin' care of my business and fixin' yours."

"You're making a big mistake. If you don't split, I'll cut you off."

"Go fuck yourself."

Rivera slammed down the receiver.

Denise picked up the Langs at Reagan National Airport and almost cried seeing them exit security. Her strain must have shown, for there was no end of compliments about her appearance, her clothes, and from her mother, her posture.

"Nothing's going to get you down, girl," Palmer assured her. "We'll get you through this."

On the drive to Villamay, she explained about the DEA agents and why they were at the house.

"Thirteen people will be with us tonight, Mom. I'll put you and Dad in my room."

Ever affable, Billy Freep welcomed her parents with his luminous grin. He introduced his team and explained a few common sense rules that would make life easier in the cramped quarters they would occupy.

Bret and Marianne arrived in their SUV. The children filled the house with screams of delight seeing their mother for the first time in almost a month, and Denise, hugging and giving kisses, almost forgot about Courthouse Square and trial.

When things settled, Billy went through his performance again, this time adding points of strategy the team would employ when the time came. He concluded saying he wanted everyone to feel confident the operation would be over safely.

"Sounds like you have things well in hand," said Bret James. He turned to the family. "Why don't we all go out to dinner? Get our minds off all this." He faced Billy. "We'd be happy to bring back something for you and your men if you want."

"Not a good idea," Billy warned. "Now that Denise's car's back, they think the money's here. You can't all fit in her car. If you take your vehicle, we're vulnerable. We have minimal surveillance as it is so they won't know we're here. We can't be on red alert all the time with the people we have."

Quiet fell hearing this from the man in charge.

"Having a lot of people in the house helps, though," Billy added.

Marianne told Denise they'd brought Michael from Charlottesville and dropped him at a motel pending completion of his testimony. He'd be joining her as soon as his attorney was satisfied his immunity agreement had been fulfilled. She gave Denise a hug and said, "Everything will work out between you two." She wanted her son's marriage to survive as long as hers.

Linda busied herself in the kitchen with dinner. Still water ran deep in her.

Palmer had just turned sixty-four. He'd been looking forward to retirement and believed most of his worries behind him until this. He loved his two sons, but he loved his daughter like no other. The thought that she might go to prison was crushing.

Bret James sat silent, fingers intertwined, head down.

That night, trial was never mentioned.

Sunday, October 7

The call came just before noon, and directed Arlene to a pay phone outside the Howard Johnson's on Route One South. From there, she was sent to the general aviation terminal at Dulles International Airport where she picked up a radio headset left in an envelope at the reception desk.

"Put the receiver on the opposite ear from me," Billy told her. "You might be deaf, but we can't risk him hearing me."

In the car, she adjusted the headset and turned it on. No more chasing pay phones across Northern Virginia. Now she was in direct contact with the voice.

"Go to the Vienna Metro Station and park," the headset told her. "Take the train into D.C."

"Okay," said Arlene. "Vienna Metro Station and park."

Once on the Dulles Toll Road heading east, Arlene tapped the hearing aid transmitter with her fingernail.

"Dialing now, hon," she heard Billy say. "Get ready to hear my best white man imitation."

The car phone rang.

"I have to get this," said Arlene.

"No," said the headset.

"You can listen. I'll put it on the speaker."

She hit the pickup button.

"Hello?"

"Denise. Vartan Antaramian. There's been a breakthrough. Judge Smert has called a meeting at one-thirty in chambers. Where are you?"

"On the Toll Road. What happened?"

"Either your case is going to be continued until this video can be examined, or it's going to be dismissed. Moses will explain. How far away are you?"

"Maybe forty-five minutes."

"I'll call chambers and tell them you're on the way. You'd better hurry."

"Fuck!" screamed the headset. "You can't do that now!"

Arlene pressed the accelerator.

"Okay. I'll be there. Bye."

"Bye."

Billy hung up.

"You heard that," Arlene said to the headset. "I have to get to the courthouse. My case might be over."

"You bitch! I gonna kill you for this!"

"Listen. I'll give you the money. Are you following me?"

"Not now."

"You want to meet me on the way? I'm going to the Telegraph Road exit off the beltway. You have at least half an hour to get there."

He didn't answer. A minute passed. She could hear muffled talking in the background.

"Get off the beltway at Van Dorn," he told her. "I tell you where to drop it. You don't do it, I gonna—"

"The beltway exit at Van Dorn," Arlene repeated. "You'll tell me where to drop it."

On the exit ramp, the headset told her to turn east on Eisenhower Boulevard, a wide avenue paralleling the beltway with industrial buildings and vacant lots on both sides.

"I got somebody can see you, now. Don't fuck this up. On the right is a lot with a red 'For Sale' sign. Put the bag under the sign."

"Okay. Vacant lot. Red 'For Sale' sign."

The car phone rang.

"Goddamn!" said the headset.

She punched the speaker button.

"Hello?"

"This is Gary Griffith, clerk for Judge Emil Smert. Judge Smert wants to know if you're on your way to meet him."

"Yes, I am."

"I wouldn't keep him long. He's not in a good mood."

The sign was coming up, two cars parked facing hers on the opposite side of the street. She could see people inside them.

She drove past.

"Sonofabitch!" yelled the headset. "What the fuck you doin'? You fuckin' missed it!"

"Tell the judge I'll be there," said Arlene and disconnected. The headset voice screamed obscenities.

She pulled over at a vacant lot further down.

"Listen," she told the headset "You said you could see me."

She got out of the car, walked to the trunk, and took out the bag.

"There's a fence around this lot. I'm throwing the money on the other side."

She hoisted the bag up with both arms, and rolled it over the six-foot chain-link. It thudded into knee-high brush.

"I'm leaving the headset on the fence to mark where I dropped the bag."

She looped the earpiece in the chain-link at waist level, got back in the car, and drove off.

Agents could see the bag from six thousand feet overhead. They fixed its position on a map, and radioed the coordinates to the DEA where it was matched to the GPS readings from transmitters in the money. The shadow team stayed out of sight.

Down by the red sign, one of the cars U-turned up Eisenhower and almost stopped as it passed the bag. Minutes later it returned, and its passenger picked up the headset from the chain-link.

The tactical team was deep into prep before the helicopter was back on the ground.

The same two cars passed up and down Eisenhower Avenue. One would park within sight of the bag, wait and watch, then drive off, only to return a few minutes later. Both were ID'd as stolen. Hours passed and darkness fell, the bag glowing with iridescence only DEA lenses could see. All night they waited, and the next day.

Penetration came near two in the morning Tuesday. Two men scaled the fence on the beltway side of the lot and stole across its width to lie face down in the scrub. Night-vision equipment picked up their presence. Two cars closed on the fence, and the men inside raced to the bag, picked it up, and pushed it over. They climbed after it.

The trap began closing as soon as the intruders were seen inside the fence. From both ends of Eisenhower, chase cars drove past designated roadblock perimeters a half-mile away and stopped, lights extinguished. Behind them, DEA vehicles lined up side-by-side between fenced lots or knolls or ditches, engines forward, a half-car width apart. No Red Rover breakthroughs allowed.

The bag-nappers who'd climbed the fence put the money in the back seat of one of the cars and got in. Both cars drove east. The driver of the lead car saw the chain of vehicles first, and didn't know what to make of it. Then their high beams came on in a ragged line. The driver squinted at the lights and braked. So did his companion. Chase cars moved forward, not too fast, colored strobes and sirens on.

The lead driver turned around and headed west. His companion did the same. They floored the gas and were topping seventy in the mile stretch between choke points when the high beams from the second roadblock lit. Its chase cars closed.

As the tactical team planned, both drivers slowed, jumped the curb, ran their cars across an open stretch to the tree line where they had to stop, and fled on foot into the woods.

K-9 squads tracked all four to arrest.

Villamay

Billy Freep monitored the operation to the end. He didn't wake Denise. She had court in a few hours and good news could always wait. He told the radioman to shut down the equipment and get some sleep.

Denise was curled up on the sofa in the living room. Billy adjusted a fallen blanket across her feet.

"You're a pretty little thing, Denise James," he whispered. "I hope you come out of this okay."

He stretched out on the floor with a chair cushion.

"We got all four," Billy told Denise over coffee.

"Was Rivera one of them?"

"No. We have to get him through the gofers we got."

Parents and in-laws gathered around as Billy recounted how it was done.

"The dogs were a good idea," said Bret at the end, hinting he would have thought of that had he been in charge.

Even without Rivera's capture, the effort was deemed a success, and the tension under which they'd been living eased. Bret was convinced the dealer threat had been broken. They now knew the DEA was on the case and closing in. Those arrested would name names, and the dealers would have to leave the country, go south. Linda thought the capture would look good in court. Denise had helped the government catch four more dealers. Hirschfeld would cite that. Clearly the other gang had taken the money. Palmer pointed out the FBI had been scooped. People would wonder why the DEA had become involved.

Nothing concerning the capture was on the morning news.

When would the media announce it?

Billy said he didn't know. Probably when the higher-ups chose to make it public.

Denise listened to everyone's opinion and smiled to herself. Like a well performed magic trick, it was a question of how to make the audience look at a distraction while the rabbit was being moved elsewhere. She'd done it. She was going to have a good day.

9:30 A.M.
Courthouse Square

Judge Smert scowled at the defense table as he spoke to a packed courtroom without the jury.

"It has come to my attention through communications from the Department of Justice and the news media that certain events occurred over the weekend that the court must address for the record.

"A videotape, originally broadcast and disseminated by a local television station, declared itself to have been generated by certain individuals who claimed they were in possession of the missing funds from the January sixteenth drug raid, said funds being the instant cause of this action.

"In addition, the defendant, Denise Elizabeth Lang James, was involved with elements of the United States Drug Enforcement Agency in the apprehension of suspects who were arrested early this morning in an operation conducted by the DEA.

"Because this operation was a success, and based upon information supplied to this court from the DEA, the tape aired previously must be considered counterfeit, in that the operation would not have been conducted and the suspects would not have been captured had they, or persons known to them, been in possession of the original payment funds from the January raid.

"Any role the defendant may have played in the DEA action that resulted in the apprehension of these suspects, who may or may not have played a role in the original raid, is considered inadmissible based upon information at present available to the court. There are four grounds for inadmissibility. First, the jury has been sequestered, and these events are post-sequestration. Second, witness and evidence lists are closed. Third, these events are prejudicial to the defense in the view of the court, because, taken together, they appear at best an effort by the defendant to muddy the waters and create confusion, and at worst, an attempt to tamper with the jury and this trial through undue and unfounded influence. Fourth, these events are irrelevant to the issue before the court, which is whether the defendant committed the crime or crimes for which she is being charged. Any attempt by the prosecution or the defense to bring before the jury the events of this past weekend are prohibited, and will be dealt with severely by the court. The jury is not to know about them. The prosecution has made its opening statement and the court does not wish to restart trial because of a tainted jury.

"Is this understood, Ms. James?"

It was apparent her day had taken a serious turn.

"Yes, Your Honor."

"Clearly?"

"Yes, Your Honor."

"Mr. Hirschfeld?"

"Yes, Your Honor."

"Mr. Antaramian?"

"Yes, Your Honor."

"Mr. Fleming?"

"Yes, Your Honor."

"Now, as to you, Ms. James. Be advised the court is very close to sanctions against you for your involvement in activities that the court finds at best manipulative, and at worst, illegal. I have a mind to revoke the generous bail I have granted you. You must be guided by the advice of your counsel in matters of conduct. The court is shocked and appalled at your actions, and views them as an attempt at improper influence. As such, this court does hereby censure you for your conduct. If the court finds any further activities done by you to be beyond what is considered to be within the scope of proper behavior by a person in your position, you will be held in contempt, bail will be revoked, and further sanctions may be imposed.

"Do you clearly understand this, Ms. James?"

"Yes, Your Honor."

"Good. Be warned. The court is not happy.

"Mr. Hirschfeld. Mr. Antaramian. I am relying on you for the proper behavior of your client."

"Yes, your honor," said Hirschfeld.

"Yes thank you, Your Honor," said Antaramian.

Smert shot Antaramian a second look for that.

"Mr. Bailiff, please bring in the jury."

Alexandria Chief of Police Joan C. Harris took the stand and described the raid setup. A four-by-six foot poster diagrammed the streets, car locations, the drug bag, the moneybag, and the positioning of the dealers at the time the raid began. A second poster showed who went where, what they took with them, and whether or not they were arrested. It was correct as far as everyone knew.

To whom does the drug money now belong? Under forfeiture law, it belongs to the United States government, the Commonwealth of Virginia, and the City of Alexandria. So, if this money *were* stolen, it is considered stolen from federal, state, and local government?

Yes.

Hirschfeld had no questions.

Police Officer Robert Armstrong was next, then Officer Stephen Johnson, both nervous. Each described his position before the raid, his pursuit of a suspect, the chase down the alley between Lee and Fairfax, the shots, and subsequent resumption of pursuit. The government used another poster to detail what occurred in the alley. Each officer described how he saw the defendant point for the suspect to go to his left, and then kick him in the stomach as he passed. Fleming had the officers emphasize their belief that they felt the fleeing suspect's bag was heavier than the one retrieved beside the car, and that the suspect was out of sight in the alley for a few seconds before the officers rounded the corner and saw him.

On cross, Hirschfeld established that neither officer saw any money anywhere at any time. Neither knew what bag contained money, or if any money was on site at all. The officers said they did not search the path the suspect took through the alley, and that they were given no indication by the defendant that anything had occurred other than what they themselves had seen.

Victor Barracks followed. In accented English, he outlined his criminal history and admitted he was serving ten years four months at a Virginia state prison for his role in the crime associated with the raid. His affidavit was entered into evidence. Fleming read it aloud, and then led Barracks through its events.

At the pickup point in Baltimore, Barracks said he saw Jason McCullough open a bag of drugs, close it, and place it inside a trash bag. Two other similar bags filled with shredded paper were put in the trunk of the car. At the exchange site, the bags were removed and placed on the ground beside the car. The drug bag was swapped for another, purportedly the money, and the drugs were taken to the back of the buyers' car for examination.

226

When the police dropped the hammer, Barracks picked up the moneybag and ran west. He knew officers were in pursuit, and ran into the alley to switch the money for a bag of paper. The legal firm whose rear opened into the alley always had bags out on garbage night.

He saw a woman at the far end, switched the heavy bag for a lighter one, and kept running. He was out of breath. He heard the police come around the corner and order him to stop. He pulled his gun and fired over their heads, not to hurt anyone, but to slow them down. This had been held against him during sentencing, and he felt the enhancement was unwarranted. Smert told him to answer the questions without editorializing.

The woman at the end of the alley hadn't moved. He ran toward her, his only means of escape. The woman told him to go to his left and pointed that way. He thought she was helping him. The woman, the defendant, then attacked him by kicking him in the stomach, at which point he was arrested.

Was anyone designated to retrieve the bag left in the alley? Not to his knowledge. Why not? They just didn't. Nothing had gone wrong before, and nothing was expected to go wrong this time. So you left it there? Yes. And the woman, the defendant, saw you make the switch? Yes.

Your witness.

Hirschfeld established Barracks never saw any money. The bag he took from the park was heavy, and as far as he knew, could have contained sand. Hirschfeld had him say this twice. Yes, it was possible the bag he left in the alley might not have contained any money at all.

You ran a considerable distance with a heavy object, and you were looking for a row of bags in the alley with high intensity, were you not? I suppose. No, it was more than a "suppose," wasn't it?

Hirschfeld referred to the plan of the alley provided by the government.

You were tired, and you knew if you passed the exchange point you could not stop and go back. It was dark. You had to look with care to find the correct place, correct? Yes. So you were looking down and to the left, were you not? Yes. There was no light ahead of you; the light was behind you. Yes. You were running into the dark,

227

were you not? Yes. So, it is a fact you never saw anyone standing at the end of the alley watching you make the switch? I saw her. You could not have seen her if you were looking down and to the left. She had to have seen me. How do you know what she saw if you could not see her? Are you clairvoyant?

Objection.

Withdrawn.

After you say you made the switch, you resumed running with the legal firm's bag. Yes. You heard the police officers come around the corner and order you to stop. Yes. You turned and fired your gun at them, or above them, as you say. Yes. How many times? Three. You say they took cover on the sides of the alley? Yes. Then you continued running. Yes. And you did not see the woman in front of you until you got near the exit on Fairfax Street, did you? Well, I know I saw her. But you did not see the defendant until after you made the switch and fired over the officers' heads, did you? I don't know. Why did you not shoot the woman standing at the end of the alley if you knew she saw you make the switch? I don't know. Be honest with the court, Mr. Barracks. You did not see her until you were right on top of her, did you? And you did not shoot her because she was a woman, and she told you which way to go, and you thought she was helping you escape. Yeah, I guess. The defendant could have been out of sight around the corner and been drawn to the alley by the sound of the shots, could she not? I suppose. So you *cannot* testify that you saw Denise James see you make the switch, can you? No. That statement contradicts your sworn affidavit read into evidence by the government earlier, does it not? I suppose. Does it, yes or no? Yes. Yes what? Yes it disagrees with it. Your testimony just now disagrees with your sworn affidavit? Yes.

"Then there is little value to your testimony either, Mr. Barracks." Hirschfeld shook his head. "Your witness."

Fleming asked how many times Barracks had made the drug run to Alexandria. Lots of times. How many times in round numbers? Fifteen to twenty. Did you ever check the moneybag? No. The drugs vary in quantity and type each time don't they? I suppose. Does the amount of money vary accordingly? I guess so. Has the money ever been wrong? No.

"Your witness."

Hirschfeld asked, "So the amount of money is a matter of trust?"

"Yeah."

"Honor among drug dealers? Who is the person who heads up your organization, the supplier organization?"

"I don' know."

"Because you are out of the loop at that level?"

"Yeah."

"As I said, honor among drug dealers."

Before Fleming could object, Hirschfeld said, "No more questions," and sat.

The next witness was William Clark, who testified he was serving seven years ten months for his involvement in the raid on behalf of the buyers. He stated the moneybag contained three million one hundred fifty thousand dollars. He saw the money before the buyers left for Old Town.

Hirschfeld established Clark didn't count the money, and didn't know whether it was counterfeit.

The next witness was also serving time under a plea. He said he was on the buyers' side and had seen the same amount of money inside the bag before taking it to Old Town.

To this witness, Hirschfeld had only sour commentary.

"So, you are the second witness now serving a prison sentence who was told there was three million one hundred fifty thousand dollars on site. You are the second witness who did not count the money and does not know if the money was counterfeit. You are the second witness who admits he is a convicted felon testifying on behalf of the government under a plea agreement dependent upon that testimony."

The witness did not answer.

"The defense considers the jury need hear nothing further from these quality witnesses, Your Honor. I hope there are not many more to follow."

After a pause, Hirschfeld said he had no further questions and returned to his seat.

Fleming next offered FBI expert-witness Conrad Peterson, who had given the first videotape demonstration to the Flytrap task force. With an egret's gait, he took his time walking to the witness stand and getting settled. Considerable background information was elicited at

Fleming's direction on the science of pixel enhancement. Then Peterson stepped from the stand and showed the court two videos on television consoles set side-by-side so the judge, jury, and court could see them. One set showed the Channel Three tape freeze-framed on a close-up of the alley. At this point, the video had been enhanced into a greenish glow. On the other set was the Alexandria Police Department tape taken just after daylight. An extra bag lay on its side in the light-enhanced video.

"What did you conclude from this?" asked Fleming.

Peterson pointed with a laser pen.

"Since this bag is present at night here, and not present in the morning here, I conclude someone took it."

Hirschfeld asked Peterson if it could be determined from the tapes that Denise James had taken the bag in question. No it could not. Could it be determined what was in the bag? No it could not.

The next government expert testified that the bag recovered by the police from Victor Barracks contained shredded paper from the law firm whose service entrance backed into the alley. This had been verified by reconstructing shredding inside the bag into documents that could be identified. The expert said fingerprints found on Barracks's bag matched fingerprints on the other five bags in the alley, all from a staff member who worked at the firm. Technical discussion revolved around the difficulty of obtaining fingerprints from plastic bags. Not all prints were identifiable, many were smudges, but the same law firm's staff member's prints were on all six bags. So, it is certain that the bag of shredded paper Barracks was arrested with had originated from the legal firm? Yes.

Hirschfeld asked what evidence there was in this presentation to indicate Denise James had taken the money. The expert said none.

Smert called a halt for the day. He reminded the jury of their responsibilities and outlined again their overnight rules. It was six o'clock.

In the witness room, Antaramian summed up the first day.

"They're proceeding in the customary fashion. You'll end up the only suspect. Then the hair, the footprint, and the fingerprint will be entered. If this goes the way the government wants, Fleming is going to put you in a cell, Smert is going to close the door, and the jury will lock it and throw away the key."

Wednesday, October 10

Assistant US Attorney Paul Fleming called an FBI agent to describe the net spread over anyone who could possibly have taken the money between the time it was left in the alley and the time the video showed it missing later that morning. Once the yellow tape went around the bags in the alley, the area was guarded. Trash pickups were halted. The bags were examined, and data and debris around them gathered. All neighbors, police officers, and members of the Channel Three television crew were interviewed.

The final list of possible suspects included the drug dealers, Officer Armstrong, Officer Johnson, and Denise James. A spokesperson named them as suspects. All individuals reported receiving telephone calls from someone demanding return of the money. What was the FBI's conclusion? The dealers were looking outside of themselves for the money. They didn't have it.

Based on personnel interview analysis, location reconstruction, and timesheets, the agent testified neither Armstrong nor Johnson could have taken the bag. They were not present at the site after they ran through the alley chasing Barracks except for their television interview with Channel Three. The officers' sworn statements and those of the television crew with them indicated the officers never went back into the alley. That left one suspect, the defendant.

Hirschfeld got the agent to say that for the first five days after the raid the Alexandria Police Department conducted the investigation. It wasn't until after the FBI took over the case that it was learned from the videotapes that a bag was missing, was it? That's correct. The initial search by the police was a cursory one; they didn't know where the money was, so they poked and prodded all the trash bags in the neighborhood looking for it, did they not? Yes. Did they take footprints from them all? No, the FBI found the footprint. Did the Alexandria police take debris samples from them all? No, they took them only from the alley. Why only the alley? Because it was proximate to the arrest of Barracks. Who actually tied the hair and the fingerprint to the defendant? The FBI lab. Is it not true that the FBI inherited all the evidence collected by the Alexandria police? Except for the footprint, yes. Does it seem odd to you that such a cursory search by Alexandria would turn up so many pieces of evidence the FBI lab would later find? Not when the FBI knew the drug dealer ran through the alley.

Why did the government call an FBI agent to tell the jury what the Alexandria police did? Because the FBI became the controlling authority for the investigation. All right then, for the sake of argument, the money, if it was in the alley, lay there unprotected from the time the police left the area where Mr. Barracks was arrested until the barrier tape was put up in the alley and a guard posted the next morning, a period of about eight hours. During that time, would it be possible that someone unknown could have picked it up? Yes. Someone did.

The agent admitted the FBI profile worked up after taking over the case indicated an eighty-percent-plus chance that the drug dealers had retrieved the money after the raid. The agent further admitted it was the FBI's belief that if one of the three named individuals took the money, that individual would not report a threatening call. All three individuals reported threats, including the defendant.

Hirschfeld asked at what point was the area inside the police tape in the alley considered part of the crime scene. The witness was unsure how to answer. When was the yellow tape put around it? Sometime just before sunup. Why so late? Because it wasn't until then that all similar areas near the waterfront were being taped, guarded, and searched to find the missing bag. When did the police know to look for a black plastic bag? Immediately after the ambush was executed. Why? They saw it on site. And this was at what time? Eleven forty-five, or so. So from eleven forty-five at night until just before sunup the next morning, the moneybag went from the park at the waterfront to the alley and then disappeared. Yes. How long did we say that was? Eight hours. So, for up to eight hours, three million one hundred and fifty thousand dollars sat unclaimed in an alley in Old Town. How do you know a drug dealer did not come back and pick it up, and then not tell the rest of his gang he had it? The investigation followed standard procedure. That is non-responsive. Other evidence not yet presented will show why the investigation led elsewhere. You have been a sequestered witness. How do you know what evidence has been presented? He didn't know, but he knew the general outline of the government's case, and that part had not been presented.

The area was taped off where the defendant apprehended the drug runner almost immediately was it not? Yes. Who guarded the guards left there? No one. How do you know the guards did not take it? They didn't know it was there. The police knew they were looking for a trash bag containing money, you just said so. How do you know the guards did not go into the alley, move the bags around, note one of them did not feel like the others, and take it? Because the investigation led elsewhere. But you do not know for an absolute certainty that the officers on guard did not take the money do you? Not to an absolute certainty. How long were the guards there? About an hour.

After the area in the alley was cordoned off, what was the first step taken when the tape was crossed by police officers? Each of the bags inside the tape was examined. Were the officers wearing gloves? Yes. What about their feet? What about them? Their feet trod the ground inside the tape to approach the bags, correct? Yes. How many officers conducted the examination inside the tape? Two. That would make four feet? Yes. Four feet inside the tape examining five trash bags and five trash cans? Yes. They had to have taken many steps across that ground. Yes. Was the ground wet? Not wet, no. Would those officers' feet leave imprints in the ground? They might. So if someone took plaster casts of all the footprints inside the tape, they would include the shoe prints of the officers? Sounds logical, although a print laid in wet soil might not be overlaid later after the soil dried.

"A hint at evidence to come," said Hirschfeld. "Please note frozen ground does not receive imprints either. And why is there only one imprint of one shoe? Is it the only one needed for evidence? Where are the others?"

"I don't know."

An Alexandria police officer testified that neither the homeless nor the city's vagrants frequented the alley in question. The night was cold, and there were no heated areas nearby. There was no reason why anyone would be there.

On cross, Hirschfeld asked what the temperature was that night. The officer didn't know. Would it surprise you to learn the defense will provide evidence that will show the temperature was twenty-two to twenty-five degrees? No. Hirschfeld questioned the witness for another five minutes and got him to say he could not positively testify that there were not half a dozen people sleeping in the alley.

They broke for lunch.

When the afternoon session resumed, Hirschfeld had the officer repeat that no one was guarding the alley for eight hours. During that time, was it possible for one of the drug dealers, the police officers on guard for an hour, a homeless person, a vagrant, a neighbor, or someone else to have taken the money? Yes, that was possible in the strictest sense. Before he stepped down, Hirschfeld got him to say that by itself, the focusing of the investigation on Denise James did not make her guilty, it only meant she was the prime suspect.

Fleming took the rest of the week introducing the search warrant, footprint, hair, and fingerprint. He set up an easel and placard between the judge's bench and the speakers' lectern. As each piece of evidence was introduced, he taped a preprinted slat under the title at the top. By Friday morning, the easel's words were etched into the jury's psyche:

Evidence Denise James was in the Alley

Footprint Matches James's Shoe
Hair Matches James's DNA
Fingerprint on Bag Matches James's Thumb

During one of the breaks, Denise asked Hirschfeld when the government was going to put Olsen, Iacob, or Kludge on the stand. He told her the government wouldn't present anyone more knowledgeable than they had to be to get across the point they wanted to make. He likened it to suing a corporation. If you wanted specific testimony, you had to subpoena someone by name. A corporation would respond to a non-person-specific subpoena in the correct technical sense, but any witness it chose of its own accord would be next to clueless on case-specific knowledge. If the defense wanted Olsen, Iacob, or Kludge, they would have to call them.

"Why does Fleming read everything?" Denise asked.

Antaramian answered.

"Because appeals are based on transcript reading, not courtroom performance. Reading prepared text reduces mistakes. Besides, Fleming isn't that quick on his feet."

Over Hirschfeld's objection, Smert allowed Fleming to enter a video reenactment of the events in the alley as the government believed they occurred. The witness, the producer of the tape, was from Accumulation at the Hoover Building. The scene was taken at night from where Denise James had stood on Fairfax Street looking down the alley. The lamppost on Lee Street silhouetted a man carrying a bag and running toward the camera. He stopped at the wall, dropped the bag, picked up another, and continued running toward the camera. Two men ran into the alley from Lee Street and shouted for him to stop. The man carrying the bag turned and yelled, "Bang! Bang! Bang!" Those chasing took cover. As the figure with the bag approached the camera, he fell to the ground. The men ran up from the alley. The tape went blank, and then from the same camera position, a woman was seen walking into the alley. She examined the bags, picked up one, and walked back past the camera with it.

And, that's how it happened ladies and gentlemen of the jury.

Hirschfeld got the witness to declare the tape did not show Denise James taking the bag, and although it was well produced and depicted some events already stipulated, it had no bearing on the defendant's possession of the money.

All the while, the poster showing the footprint, hair, and fingerprint etched itself into the minds of the jurors like some creeping toxin demanding refutation.

The government concluded its case mid-afternoon Friday, still calling it sad. Fleming had presented quickly, a surgical strike, in and out so as not to confuse the jury. As Hirschfeld had predicted, the woman with the Dalmatian had not been called.

After a break, Hirschfeld made his opening statement.

"The government of the United States obtained an indictment from its own grand jury, subject to its own direction, accusing Denise James of taking three million one hundred and fifty thousand dollars from a drug raid. This does not mean that Denise James committed the act.

"A grand jury sees no defense evidence. A grand jury determines 'probable cause,' the lowest level of proof under the law. An indictment should not be considered evidence of guilt. It is more akin to a rubber stamp for cases the government chooses to prosecute. Some call it a remnant of the Spanish Inquisition.

"The government's case is predicated on the theft of money. Where is the money? Denise James was there, that is certain. At her own peril, she halted a felon in the act of fleeing the scene of a crime. Ms. James was interviewed at the park after the event, and then interviewed any number of times by the media, radio, television, newspapers, and magazines. The President of the United States introduced her to the nation during the State of the Union Address. You will see these interviews. You will get to know Denise James. You will get to know her as unique, hell for leather, a real piece of work.

"Would you have stopped the criminal that night? Most of us, if not all of us, would have run as soon as shots were fired. I would have. Would you expect a woman to do what she did? I would not. Law enforcement should handle such situations. For all Ms. James knew, the man running at her could have leveled his gun and pulled the trigger.

"But she did not jump aside or cower behind a car. No indeed. She struck him, and brought him down so police officers could make an arrest.

"What type of person does something like that?

"A woman who would do that is the type who would nickname two FBI agents Mulder and Scully. She is a woman who would stage a televised press conference where it appears that she and her husband are drinking tequila. FBI agents arrive and arrest them. The tequila turns out to be tea, and the Bureau is forced by public opinion to let them go.

"Ladies and gentlemen, if there is one thing I have learned both as a former prosecuting attorney for the government and as an attorney in practice for myself, the one thing I know is, you never make the government angry at you.

"That is what Denise James did. She broke all rules of common sense. She calls Assistant US Attorney Paul Fleming, the distinguished gentlemen presenting the government's case sitting at the table to my right, she calls him *Mr. Flaming.* She spilled coffee over Assistant Director Roscoe Penes, the man who reports to the Director of the FBI on this case. I was there and saw it. Her hand tipped the top of his cup, by accident I believe, and coffee went all over him. Then she pulled the handkerchief from his pocket and said, 'Here, let me spread that around for you.'"

A few jurors smiled.

"I saw it myself, ladies and gentlemen. It was masterful. And Ms. James called Assistant Director Roscoe Penes—well—you can imagine for yourselves what she called Roscoe Penes."

Suppressed laughter rose in the court.

"One of my chief concerns in the defense of Denise James is what she might say when she goes on the stand. She has a smart mouth, and I do not believe she has much control over it."

Hirschfeld could have made a living as an actor, a politician, or an evangelical preacher. He was authoritative, convincing and sincere. Denise thought it not for nothing he'd been so well recommended by Morton Mieske.

"While Ms. James's personality permits her to take action against a fleeing criminal and become a hero, that same personality permits her to ridicule FBI agents to their faces, humiliate the Bureau on national television, and embarrass an Assistant Director in front of fellow agents.

"As a result, some few agents and Department of Justice officials are in a blood-feud with her. They dislike her because she shows them no respect. They formed a task force whose sole purpose was to prosecute her. The defense will show you how this animosity has festered and grown into a persecution by introducing into evidence FBI reports, and you can read between the lines yourselves to determine what you think their true feelings are about the defendant. She gives them no respect, and they have given her no quarter.

"Ms. James does not have the money. The government, make no mistake, has looked for it. They have been through the alley in question and through every building around the alley. They searched the Jameses' neighborhood and home. The shores of the Potomac have been dragged. They searched storage facilities, baggage lockers, Federal Express records, UPS records, and United States Postal Service records looking for packages. They looked in Ms. James's locker at her gym. They searched her parents' and siblings' homes. They have had a surveillance team watching her for months."

Hirschfeld took on an expression of thinking out loud.

"I must tell you that Ms. James has taken my advice regarding her behavior to some extent. She wanted to lead her surveillance team on a marathon run down the bike trail near her home in an attempt to blister their feet. She wanted to plant empty boxes in storage lockers where they could be found. She wanted to send packages through the mail the task force would have to locate and open. She wanted to open safe deposit boxes with notes inside that said, 'Dear Mousetrap: The money's not here. Have a nice day. Very truly yours, Denise.' She wanted her husband to build a concrete slab in her backyard the task force would have to dig up in hopes of finding the money underneath.

"I convinced her these actions were not in her best interest."

The jury ate every word looking from Hirschfeld to Denise and back.

"Why would anyone contemplate such harmful activities? *That* is a very good question.

"My chief concern is every defense counsel's worst nightmare: lack of client control. I tell her not to speak to the media, yet she does so. But then, why would anyone face down a man pointing a gun at her he had just fired at police officers?

"Why does she bait the task force?

"She baits them because the task force named her as a suspect without warning. They could have said, 'We are going to announce that you, the police officers, and the drug dealers are suspects. If the dealers have the money, nothing will happen, and the case will move along different lines. If the dealers do not have the money, they may call you. Let us know if you hear anything.'

"But the task force did not do that. If they had, the defendant, and the police officers, would have had warning that their property might be vandalized. Ms. James heard the announcement that she was a suspect on television, she received threatening telephone calls, she asked for protection, she was denied protection, and she was vandalized. She felt outraged she had been placed in such a position. Her property was attacked. So was that of the police officers who were with her the night of the raid. Ms. James was later kidnapped, beaten, and almost raped before she fought off the attackers and escaped. A rifle shot was fired into her home when she and her children and husband were present. Who could believe that could happen?"

Hirschfeld shook his head.

"Without that devil-may-care personality of hers, it is doubtful she would have survived the kidnapping to be with us here today.

"I admit, Ms. James has been foolish to toy with the task force as she has. She has tweaked their noses, pulled their ears, and made them look bad in public and in private. This prosecution has become a vendetta, in large part, because it is Denise James's nature to have made it so. Nobody does what she does and gets away with it. As a result, every resource available to the task force has been applied to this case.

"And with what result?

"There is no proof Denise James took the money.

"There is no proof because Denise James did not go into the alley that night, and she did not retrieve a bag from it, and she did not take the bag home. And even if the government should prove Denise James *did* return to the alley, that in itself does not prove she took the money allegedly left there.

"Now. The legal basis for this case had to manifest itself in hard physical evidence against Ms. James. Evidence had to be found where it needed to be found in enough divergent forms so that at least on the question of whether or not Ms. James went into the alley, there could be no doubt. If the task force could prove Ms. James lied about being in the alley, if they could prove she lied about that, then she could have lied about taking the money.

"Denise James has always maintained she did not take the money. The task force tapped her telephones and bugged her residence and office without her knowledge, and they have no evidence from these many hours of secret recordings that she took it because she did not take it.

"I am not sure Ms. James can prove to you that the evidence listed on the government's easel was fabricated by some few rogue officials bent on a mission to make something look as if it happened that did not happen. But she does not have to. The government must *prove* she took the money. She has no criminal history and no criminal ties. She is a mother, with a loving husband waiting to testify on her behalf. They have a three-and-a-half-year-old son and a nearly two-year-old daughter. She is a lone woman pitted against the combined professional law enforcement powers of the United States that have been corrupted against her by a small group.

"Remember, implications and innuendos are not proof.

"Please follow the defense presentation with an open mind, and you will reach the correct conclusion in this matter. The government cannot prove Denise James took the money. To convict, they must.

"Thank you, ladies and gentlemen."

Hirschfeld turned to Smert.

"Your Honor, with the kind permission of the court, the defense requests a recess for the balance of the day. It is now half past four. Ms. James's defense should take no more than five days. You should be able to charge the jury with this case next Friday."

Smert looked to the Assistant US Attorney who looked at his watch.

"No objection, Your Honor," said Fleming.

Smert turned to those impaneled.

"The jury is reminded, no television, no radio, no newspapers, and no discussion of the case among yourselves. Court is adjourned until nine o'clock Monday morning."

Thwack!

In the witness room the defense team huddled around the table.

"We have presented the outline of our case," said Hirschfeld. "All we can do is give the jury the idea and let them draw their own conclusion."

"If you were the prosecution, how would you feel right now?" asked Denise.

"Confident. Confident because of Smert. We drew the worst judge in the district."

Chapter Seventeen

Saturday, October 13
Villamay

Denise welcomed a weekend's respite after five days of trial and the somber opinions of her counsel, but her parents and in-laws were now heavy into the proceeding and discussed it without end. They poured through newspaper accounts and tuned to television commentary. Bret and Marianne, home with the children all week, recorded the broadcast tapes. Bret played them ad nauseam offering never-ending angles of defense.

An IRS "Notice of Audit" for the last three tax returns arrived in Friday's mail. Denise and Michael would have to call for an appointment within thirty days and bring in their backup information for those years. She supposed this to be another inadmissible post-commencement action that would be suppressed if voiced in court.

She'd had enough. She'd get burned out if she didn't do something to get her mind on something else. So while trial analysis continued inside, she took Tommy outside to toss a plastic football on the front lawn.

The morning was mild, dew gone from the grass, the air clean and refreshing. Trees were changing color around them. The maples were already brushed yellow and heading fast toward the flaming reds of peak season.

The ball kept landing between Tommy's elbows, dribbling down his stomach, and rolling onto the grass. Once in a while he'd catch it against his body. When he did, she'd raise her arms as if he'd caught a touchdown and shout, "Score!"

"Now, when you catch the next one say, 'Touchdown!' just like that."

It took four tosses from six feet before she made a perfect lob. He grasped the ball against his chest, smiled at Mommy happily, then thrust his arms in the air and screamed, "Touchdown!"

The ball fell at his feet.

"You spiked it!" she laughed. "Good boy! Now throw it back."

With the exuberance of his touchdown catch, he picked up the ball and heaved it ten feet behind him, releasing on the cock instead of the throw. He stood mystified not seeing the ball arcing toward Mommy.

"It's back there," she said pointing.

He spun three-quarters around before spying the ball. With wild arms and flailing legs, the run of a two-hour fawn, he took off in a capering skip of scattered limbs, and fell face forward on the grass.

She took a step toward him.

Phet!-Phet!-Phet! sounds like slingshot marbles smacking bricks.

Instinct took her down as fast as gravity could work, faster than she could think.

Phet!-phet!-phet!-phet! against the side of the house. Holly leaves falling to mulch beds out of the corner of her eye. Brick dust rising in the sun. A car accelerating away.

Tommy lay still. Her heart shuddered.

"Tommy?"

He looked around, surprised to see her on the ground.

"Are you all right?" she asked in panic.

"Yeah."

In four strides she was to him. He raised his arms to circle her neck. As she reached for him, she saw blood on her hand. She snatched him off the ground in a bear hug and turned to the house. The bricks looked as if they'd been ice-cream-spoon dipped.

She ran with him.

"What was that?" asked Palmer at the front door. "The house shook."

She pushed past him.

"Get the FBI in here, Dad."

She sat Tommy on the kitchen counter next to the sink and asked again and again if he hurt anywhere. He said no. Linda, Marianne, and Bret were with her. She wrapped her hand in a paper towel, and looked him over, head to toe. He said he was okay, and she couldn't find a mark on him. He just seemed quiet and looked away from her.

"He's fine," said Bret.

"Tell me what's wrong, Tommy. Please."

His face told her he was about to cry. He was afraid to say something, something important.

"Please tell Mommy what's the matter, honey?"

He held up an arm and pointed to her hand.

"You bleeding," he said, an apparent revelation. "I didn't know mommies bleeded."

She removed the blotchy towel and examined her fingers.

"Yes, Tommy. Mommies bleed."

The flesh between her middle and third fingers was bloody, a gash across her wedding ring. She took off the ring and rinsed her fingers in the sink under Tommy's watchful eyes. She pulled off excess skin.

"It's hardly worth two Band-Aids," she said putting them on.

"We've called in a ballistics team, Ms. James," an agent from the surveillance van told her. "It would appear your house was fired upon by an automatic weapon."

"The house?" Her eyes pierced him like pins through an insect for mounting. *"They tried to kill us!"*

"From the count on the bricks," he said unperturbed, "it was seven shots. Had to have had a silencer."

That afternoon, the FBI moved Denise and the children into protective custody at a suite they maintained in Landmark.

Michael arrived furious.

"You can cram your Immunity Agreement right up your rosy reds," he told the agents in cold blood. "I'm staying with my wife and children."

Fixed in her mind and replaying without end were the images of Tommy running and falling, the sound of marbles striking bricks, dust rising, leaves falling, and Tommy lying still on the grass.

During the children's afternoon nap, Michael took Denise into the bathroom and ran the shower.

"Where's the money?" he whispered.

She couldn't believe these were his first words in private.

"Is that all you can think about?"

Unfazed, he waited for an answer.

"It's safe," she said. "What were you going to do with it?"

He ignored the question.

"I had to agree to divorce and take the children to get immunity, Denise."

"I know. But you've become obsessed with the money. You tried to take it."

"But you *did* take it."

"Yes. *Twice.* And if *I'm* caught with it, you and the children are safe. If you're caught with it, we're both goners. Your having it proves I took it. Then who'd raise the children?"

"You're not going to give it to that thug, are you?"

She suppressed the anger that rose with that. He wasn't seeing the point, even after this latest assault.

"I'm probably going to be convicted, Michael. If I go to jail, I'll be murdered on orders from that 'thug.' He had that informant killed in his jail cell, you know." She held up her left hand. "A bullet clipped these two fingers today. One step not taken toward Tommy, and I'd be dead right now."

"What are we going to do?"

She wondered if he meant with the money or in general. She gave him the benefit of the doubt.

"I'm going to play it out, see how it goes. I have a plan."

"What is it?"

"I'll tell you when you need to know."

She'd never seen so many emotions cross his face in so short a time.

"That wasn't what I wanted to hear," he said with little inflection. "I thought we were a team."

"I'm doing everything I can to keep you and the children safe. To do that, I have to keep some things to myself."

She prepared herself to hear him threaten to go to Kludge or Fleming and tell them everything in an attempt to get her to tell him what her plan was and where the money was. All the lies, trauma, and physical threats had hardened her, had taken away that part of her that needed someone close, even Michael. She waited, expecting the worst.

He sighed. "This is like a heist movie where the team that took the diamonds conspires against each other and brings the whole thing down. They argue over shares or try to take the prize for themselves, and they all get caught. I don't want that, Denise."

He stared around the room.

"You're right. The children come first."

"Taking the immunity agreement was the right thing to do, Michael. You're out of it."

"I felt guilty as hell about it, though."

"And you felt cheated when the money wasn't under the sofa, didn't you?"

"They were making me do something I didn't want to do, and then the money was gone. I was livid."

They looked at each other.

There was nothing else she could say.

She turned off the shower.

Monday, October 15
Courthouse Square

Moses Hirschfeld addressed the court without the jury.

"Your Honor, this information has been in the media, but I feel compelled to say it for the record. Two days ago, Denise Elizabeth Lang James and her three and a half-year-old son Thomas were victims of an apparent murder attempt at the defendant's home. Despite government surveillance, an automatic weapon was discharged at them, and the automobile containing the assailants escaped.

"Needless to say, Ms. James finds herself incapable of presenting herself in court this morning. She has been devastated by this attack.

"In view of this near tragedy, and the relative short duration of this proceeding to date, the defense requests a mistrial, Your Honor. My client is unable to proceed."

Judge Smert leaned toward his microphone.

"For my own information, Mr. Hirschfeld, do the authorities have any idea who did this thing?"

"I have heard speculation that it might have been the drug dealers, Your Honor. Both the FBI and Fairfax County police are investigating."

Smert sat back.

"Mr. Fleming?"

"Your Honor, the government wishes to be understanding and compassionate in this matter, and regrets this incident, and hopes that justice will soon be done. The government can assure the court, all law enforcement efforts are being employed to locate and apprehend those persons responsible.

"However, the jury is impaneled. The prosecution has concluded its case and rested. The defense has made its opening statement, and has declared for the record that they need perhaps five days to complete their presentation. No one has been injured. The government does not see why we cannot proceed with defense witnesses toward the end of this week."

"Your Honor," protested Hirschfeld. "My client intends to take the stand in her own defense. She is emotionally unable to do so today, or this week, perhaps not for a long while."

"I can't hold the jury idle for a month counselor," said Smert. "It's difficult enough to be sequestered through a weekend without feeling like a prisoner. To hold them in their rooms on regular weekdays will require an explanation."

"Then declare a mistrial, Your Honor," said Hirschfeld. "If we were to continue without pause, my client would have grounds for appeal due to her quite justified inability to defend herself. She does not care about her defense at this time. A new trial would eliminate that."

"Where is your client now, Mr. Hirschfeld?"

"Under the protection of the government at an undisclosed location, Your Honor."

Smert appeared to review papers in front of him.

"Today through Sunday to rest and recover. Reasons of health. Back here at nine o'clock next Monday morning, October twenty-second. Mr. Bailiff, bring in the jury."

"Your Honor," said Hirschfeld. "Decency requires an objection for the record."

"So noted, counselor." Smert held his chin low on his chest making his eyes bug out. "Have your client here Monday morning an hour early so I can take a look at her. Bring her doctor if you like. The court will examine the situation at that time."

"Thank you, Your Honor," said Fleming.

Chapter Eighteen

Six Days Later - Sunday, October 21
Landmark

Moses Hirschfeld came to visit.

"Smert will delay no further. Tomorrow he will deny a motion for mistrial."

"I'm prepared for that," said Denise.

"Please understand, the jury for any new trial will know of this shooting. This jury does not, and will not. My feeling is that a future jury will feel more empathy for you with that knowledge than without it."

"What are you suggesting?"

"I will not put you on the stand. We will prepare for appeal."

"That's your strategy? Play for appeal?"

"It is a good strategy, Denise. Hear me out. If the jury knew you had allied yourself with the DEA and helped apprehend more drug dealers, and then those dealers tried to murder you in retaliation, it is indeed more plausible that an unknown third party took the money. I can engender sympathy and additional doubt. The government wants to proceed with this jury untainted by your DEA involvement or the gang's retaliation. Smert and Fleming have them sequestered. I must advise you that until the task force evidence can be proven false, you are most likely to be found guilty whether or not you testify. This way I have a chance, not a great chance, but an improved chance, to obtain a new trial through appeal by reason of your inability to provide an adequate defense. To evidence your emotional inadequacy, I will not put you on the stand."

To her not taking the stand was tantamount to giving up.

"Is this the way it's supposed to be, Moses? Set up the judge you don't like in a trial you don't like so you can do it all over again? To throw this trial to get another judge and jury is—is—*immoral.*"

"There is no moral aspect to it. I am giving you the best professional advice I can. That is why I am compensated."

She looked at him, a small man with granny glasses, dressed in a fine suit, every hair in place. A dandy if she ever saw one.

"You're just a mercenary paid for specialized services. Is that what you are? A gun for hire?"

Hirschfeld studied her a moment before he answered.

"Yes. A gun for hire undertaking a professional risk in the pay of others."

"But no personal risk."

"Correct. No personal risk. I do not go to prison if I lose. I provide legal services."

"What about doing what's right and correct and noble? What about strutting through life with the sound of trumpets in your ears and dancing every day as if no one was watching, and knowing all the while that no matter what, you're fighting the good fight?"

Hirschfeld assumed the countenance of a father explaining the IRS to a teenager with his first paycheck.

"I felt noble enough through law school, even the first years I was in practice as a prosecutor. I was going to save the world, or at least change it for the better. But the world is gray and grinds you down, wears you out, erodes your spirit little by little. The nobility of my youth was overtaken by the reality of the experiences I had, and the need to find a way to survive in my chosen profession knowing I could change little about it."

"So as a prosecutor, you realized the system wouldn't change no matter what you did. You saw defense attorneys making more money, and you crossed over to the dark side. If you couldn't change the world, at least you'd go where the money was better."

He hesitated before he said, "True."

"Self-interest rules."

"To a large extent."

"Now you view yourself as an instrument, disinterested and unfeeling. You fulfill a need someone else has. In my case, the need for the best defense, regardless of guilt or innocence."

She seemed not to expect a response as her eyes wandered and her voice trailed off.

"In the main," he said.

She was thinking that the man in the car doing the shooting was an instrument fulfilling someone else's need. Nick Rivera wouldn't pull the trigger. He'd hire someone with the expertise to do it. Nick Rivera. Without him—

"Denise," said Hirschfeld breaking into her thought. "I hesitate to tell you this." He was grave. "If you are convicted, you will have been judged guilty of having three million one hundred and fifty thousand dollars in cash, a worthy sum with which to flee. You will be held in custody pending sentencing, perhaps through appeal."

She put her hand on his.

"Why do you think I'm in this suite, Moses?"

After Hirschfeld left, she watched Tommy and Sydney sleep.

Like all little children, they believed their parents were gods. Parents could fix anything, and they didn't bleed. Learning the truth would come soon enough, and take away a safety net they thought would always exist that had never been there in the first place. There were no safety nets.

She watched them for some time.

She called Billy Freep on her cell. When she was finished with him, she called Baltimore information, and then a number for an address. She opened the business card program on the suite's computer and began playing with it.

Chapter Nineteen

Wednesday, October 24
Courthouse Square

Over strenuous objections from Moses Hirschfeld, trial proceeded after a further two-day delay. Without the jury, Smert lectured to the effect that the defense about to be presented had better be of the quality to which the federal court system had become accustomed when the incomparable Moses Hirschfeld was before the bar. If the court felt or suspected any holding back of his finest effort, there would be serious, though unspecified sanctions.

All uncalled witnesses were reminded not to talk to each other about the case or their testimony. Counsel were instructed that the jury could be told that Michael James had filed divorce against the defendant, but it could not be told or hinted that its filing was linked to anything relating to the trial. Michael James's Immunity Agreement and Statement of Facts were considered separate from the present proceeding and sealed. The bullet through the window and the kidnapping could be mentioned, but the defense was cautioned to tread lightly as there was no proof those events were connected to the charges in question.

Smert noted defense witness Jason McCullough was deceased.

Nothing would be permitted regarding assistance provided by the defendant to the DEA or the government as regards the apprehension of the suspects captured during the early morning of October 9th.

No information concerning the attempted murder of the defendant, or her son, would be permitted, no oblique reference, no hint at all. Without connective proof, the alleged attack was irrelevant to the question of whether or not the defendant committed the act or acts for which she was being charged. The event was post-witness and post-evidence list, post-sequestration, emotional in its nature, and liable to influence the jury unfairly. Any such reference, again in the sole discretion of the court, would be dealt with in the same stern and vague manner as violations of other rules.

The jury was brought in, reminded of its solemn duty, and given no explanation for trial delay other than it had been warranted by circumstances of health, the details of which they would learn when their obligations were fulfilled.

Smert asked Hirschfeld to call his first witness.

Alexandria police Captain Tyrone Washington took the stand. He disclosed the Alexandria police did not know of the FBI's involvement prior to the raid and vice-versa. Alexandria did not, in fact, learn that a bag was missing from the alley until after the FBI took over the case a few days later. Hirschfeld wanted to give the jury the idea that the investigation was rife with confusion from the start.

What is the role of the Alexandria Police Department in this case at present?

Watching it on television and reading newspapers answered Washington.

Your witness.

No questions.

Clayton Stevens was called. He identified himself as the supplier who fled north and was later apprehended.

How many people on your side knew about the drop site in the alley? The four who were at the site itself. How many people in the entire organization knew about it? Maybe eight, including the four at the site. How many of them are still at large? The four not at the site. So four individuals not now in custody knew about the alternate drop site? Yes. Any of four people could have colluded with deceased informant Jason McCullough to return to the alley and retrieve the bag after the raid? Yes.

Fleming had no questions.

Hirschfeld called one of the three agents from the Flytrap stakeout team present the night of the raid, and established through him that the FBI was unaware of the Alexandria Police Department's involvement prior to the raid. The agent also admitted participating in the ongoing investigation.

"Are you familiar with the suspect list compiled as part of the investigation to locate the missing money?

"Yes."

"Are you on it?"

"No."

"Are the other two agents who were at the site the night of the raid on it?"

251

"No."

"Why not?"

"As federal employees acting within the scope of our employment, we have immunity."

"Was there no effort to eliminate you three agents from the suspect list?"

"Not that I'm aware."

"So the suspect list included everyone at the site except members of the agency conducting the investigation?"

"Yes."

Fleming asked if any of the three agents went into the alley between Lee and Fairfax. No. What did you do after the raid? When the police moved in, we reported what we saw, and we were ordered to leave the scene.

Next up was a subpoenaed witness from the FBI to speak on efforts to locate the money. This frail and wispy woman described searches of the defendant's home, cars, office, parents' and siblings' homes, river dredging, bulk carrier package searches, and the examination of every hiding place the Bureau could imagine. She admitted efforts to locate the money were, in effect, exhausted.

Fleming had the witness agree that the investigation's failure to find the money was not evidence that the defendant had not taken it.

Hirschfeld called a subpoenaed FBI technical expert to speak about the content of the taps at the defendant's home and office. How long a period did this encompass? From April 25th when the taps were installed to the present. What kinds of conversations were recorded? Normal, everyday ones. All of them? Yes. And you personally listened to every recording? Someone did. Are you authorized to speak for all the recordings? I believe so. Had any conversation been recorded that indicated Denise James had taken the money? No. Was anything ever heard that would indicate that either of the Jameses knew the calls were being recorded? No. What kinds of clues did you receive as to the location of the money from these clandestine, though legal recordings? None.

Fleming asked, "How did the defense learn that the government had placed listening devices at the James home?"

"The government must turn over all evidence to the defense and did so."

Hirschfeld asked, "When were the transcripts of the wiretaps turned over to the defense?"

"Five days before trial."

"Why five days?"

"It's the rules."

Special Agent Joseph Stitch, senior agent in command at the Tea Party arrest, was called next, and the Channel Three video shown. The jury already knew the tequila was tea, and it was hard for them not to smile during the viewing.

When the tape ended, Hirschfeld entered a viewer ratings survey that showed the national audience had topped five million on all channels, up from twenty-two thousand on Channel Three before the special report interrupted regular programming.

"Describe to the jury how you felt when you learned the Jameses were drinking tea and not tequila?"

Stitch cleared his throat. He'd been on the stand over an hour and this was the first question put to him.

"I felt they had played a trick."

"What was your impression of how the Bureau felt?"

"I cannot speak for how the Bureau felt."

"You must have some sense of their reaction?"

"The Bureau felt it was an unfortunate incident."

"With whom have you discussed your testimony?"

"The United States Attorney's Office."

"Were you advised to hide your emotions, to cover up your feelings?"

"No."

"No one has ever humiliated the FBI on national television like Denise James did, have they? Is not one of your duties to preserve and protect the integrity of the Bureau, to avoid its disgrace? All agents have high standards in that regard, do they not?"

"Yes, yes and yes."

"Were you not angry at the Jameses?"

"Any anger I had was controlled by professionalism."

"So you were angry, yet you controlled it?"

"Yes."

"Are you on the Mousetrap task force?"

"No."

"There was public support for the defendant vis-à-vis the government after the vandalism and the Tea Party. What did you think of that and the publicity that appeared in support of her after the broadcast?"

"I have no opinion as to what other people think."

"No, I suppose not. Do you believe the Mousetrap task force was angry with her?"

"My opinion on anything anyone else in the Bureau felt would be speculative on my part."

"Yes. I'm sure Mr. Flaming instructed you to answer that question that way."

"Objection!" said Fleming standing.

"To what?" asked Hirschfeld. "The name?"

"To the question and the name, Your Honor. It's Fleming, not Flaming."

Hirschfeld said, "Your Honor, could the statement be read back?"

Smert nodded.

The stenographer read. "Mr. Hirschfeld: 'Yes, I'm sure Mr. Flaming instructed you to answer that question that way.'"

Hirschfeld said, "Is that a question, or a statement?"

"I object to the statement, Your Honor."

"Withdrawn. Far be it for me to conspire in a trick that would incite anger controlled by professionalism."

This drew a response from the courtroom at large but no pounding gavel. The jury was instructed to disregard what they'd just heard as though so ordering made it fact.

"Whose decision was it to make the arrest?"

"It was mine as senior member of the team."

"And you alone made that decision?"

"I take responsibility for it. Children were watching cartoons before the stations cut in."

"Did you yourself make the decision?"

"Yes."

"You were in contact with a superior officer by telephone during this so called Tea Party, were you not?"

"Objection," said Fleming. "Your Honor, this is irrelevant. The government will stipulate this agent ordered the arrest."

Hirschfeld said, "Goes to the state of mind of the agents handling this investigation, Your Honor."

"I'll allow it," said Smert. "Please answer the question."

"Yes, I was in contact with a superior officer."

"Who?"

"Special Agent in Charge Eric Kludge."

"Does Agent Kludge head the Mousetrap task force?"

"Yes."

"Did you advise Agent Kludge you intended to arrest the Jameses prior to doing so?"

Stitch thought about his answer for a moment. With care he said, "I made the decision when the woman said the FBI had the money."

Hirschfeld rewound the tape and played the last minutes before arrest.

"Agent Stitch. Your testimony is you were in direct contact with a superior officer, you received no order from him to arrest, you did not advise him you were going to make an arrest, and you made the arrest on your sole authority."

"Yes."

"As the tape shows, the agents moved simultaneously from both sides to circle the table. You are at the center of the picture giving the orders we heard."

"Yes."

"What we saw occurred on a moment's notice of your command?"

"Yes."

Hirschfeld replayed the arrest again.

"That is instant field coordination, Agent Stitch." Hirschfeld faced the jury. "I commend you for your loyalty. Your career should advance unimpeded after this testimony."

"Objection," said Fleming on his feet.

"Withdrawn," said Hirschfeld. "Your witness."

Fleming had no questions.

Olsen was called. Then Iacob. Each in turn admitted being a primary field agent for the Mousetrap task force. Each admitted being tagged either Mulder or Scully. They claimed they thought the names no more than childish humor. Any personal animosity they felt was overcome by their professional attitude and training. No, they didn't care if the nicknames stuck.

Each admitted being briefed in advance by the United States Attorney's Office. No admissions were made of a personal vendetta, or that the task force was "out to get" the defendant. As far as the two primary field agents were concerned, they acted properly in all respects.

"Was the defendant's home surreptitiously entered into at any time prior to the legal search of April 25th?"

This was asked in turn to Olsen and Iacob, then to Kludge who followed. Each responded with the same pat answer: "Not to my knowledge."

To Kludge, Hirschfeld asked, "You were in telephone contact with Special Agent Joseph Stitch during the so called Tea Party of February 10th, were you not?"

"Yes."

"Who gave the order to arrest the Jameses?"

"Special Agent Stitch."

"You did not concur in this decision?"

"I was not asked."

"You knew nothing of it prior to it occurring?"

"No."

"Did your conversation go through the communication system at the Bureau?"

"No. I was on my home phone with Agent Stitch in the field."

Hirschfeld removed a cassette tape from his coat pocket and examined its label. He tapped it against his palm.

"So there is no recording of your conversation that could shed light on who made the decision to make the arrest?"

The witness did not answer.

Hirschfeld laid the cassette on the defense table beside him and looked at Kludge.

"Well?"

Kludge looked pasty.

"To my knowledge there is no recording."

"Would you object if I played one for the court?"

Kludge heaved a heavy sigh.

"No."

Hirschfeld picked up the cassette, and stood motionless at the lectern staring at the witness.

"No further questions."

Next was a forensic weatherman to place into evidence the fact that the ground was frozen and there had been no measurable wind. He produced National Weather Service documentation as proof. A rainfall graph showed no precipitation during the prior eight days. The expert estimated the ground had been frozen hard for two days. A sketch of the area and a blowup photograph indicated no landscaping and no water faucets. He testified that if water had been present, it would have been ice.

The same expert opined that if a person possessed gloves that night, they would probably have been worn, and that if they were not, the air was too cold to allow a fingerprint to be laid onto an object that was itself twenty-five degrees or so in temperature. Existing moisture and oils on the fingers would evaporate, and the pores would be sealed by the cold. Hirschfeld entered Denise's gloves as a defense exhibit.

Fleming got the expert to say he could not swear an idling car engine had not heated the ground. This would have allowed enough warmth for the soil to accept the defendant's footprint and then be frozen so the prints of police officers searching the area later would not be present.

Intense questioning by Fleming concluded with the witness saying he agreed it was possible for someone to leave fingerprints on a plastic bag on a freezing night if her hands were inside gloves long enough for oil and moisture to form on the skin. Then if the gloves were removed and the fingers touched the bag, prints could be left.

On redirect, Hirschfeld made it sound absurd that the ground had somehow been artificially heated, or that anyone would remove gloves she was wearing on a freezing night to touch a plastic bag with her bare hands.

At quarter of six Smert announced, "Court is in recess until nine o'clock tomorrow morning. The jury is once again reminded not to discuss this case with each other, and not to listen to any radio or television, or to read newspapers, magazines, or other materials relating to this case."

Thursday, October 25

Michael was next.

"Good morning, Mr. James," Hirschfeld began. "How old are you now?"

"Twenty-seven."

"How old is your wife, the defendant?"

"Twenty-seven."

"It hasn't been a very happy six months has it?"

"Not entirely."

Hirschfeld showed the jury the Channel Three interview taken the night of the raid and had Michael point out the hat, coat, and gloves Denise was wearing. Hirschfeld entered the hat and coat as defense exhibits. Hirschfeld then took him through the prepared script.

Michael described the first morning after the raid, and how proud Denise had been about her assistance to the police. Since that time, she had not given him a hint she had the money. He had been indicted with her and had agreed to an immunity agreement that resulted in debriefing sessions with the Department of Justice. He was not a prosecution witness because he could provide no testimony that helped the government. Charges against him had been dropped. He'd filed divorce citing irreconcilable differences resulting from the trauma and scandal of his wife's prosecution, but he hoped to reconcile when she was acquitted. A bullet had been shot into their home while the family was present. Government surveillance had been on duty outside. He felt the drug dealers had done it. The agents had referred the matter to Fairfax County. He'd been upset by the incident, and the FBI's reaction. No one had been apprehended. And the kidnapping? He'd been very upset, though proud of his wife for how she'd acquitted herself. Again, he believed the drug dealers were responsible. No one had been apprehended. No, he never knew the house or the telephones were bugged. Yes, he and his wife taunted Special Agents Olsen and Iacob with the names Mulder and Scully. Why?

"Because it was fun. We never imagined it would come to *all this*—" He held up his arms to encompass the courtroom.

"Answer the questions without physical movement, Mr. James," said Smert.

What event made the Mousetrap task force angriest? The Saturday morning Tea Party. Why did you do it? To tell our side of the story and to try to embarrass them because of the vandalism they caused. Did you invite the FBI to attend? No. Did you know they were there? No. Did you know the interview was being broadcast? We were told it was being taped. You didn't know it was broadcast? Not at the time. What else did Ms. James wish to do that would have further angered the task force? She wanted to lead them on wild goose chases with fake packages—Objection. Hearsay from this witness. Sustained. Did Ms. James ask you to assist her in these proposed wild goose chases? Yes. Did you? No. Why not? Advice of counsel. What else?

We got notice of an IRS audit. Objection. No basis for connection. Sustained unless you can show a connection, counselor. The defense is unable to show that, Your Honor. The jury is to disregard what it just heard.

What else?

"Arrest reports, evidence in the case, and the status of the investigation were leaked to the press from unnamed sources. No response was provided when we received threatening telephone calls. Denise's job was terminated after the task force interviewed her employer, and we've been unable to have the post-indictment restraining order relieved."

"And what have you concluded?"

"I believe certain members of the task force investigating this case are out to get her. After she embarrassed them, they did what they had to do to obtain an indictment. Now they're doing what they have to do to get a conviction and put her in jail."

"How do you explain the evidence?"

"It's made up. I know how my wife dresses. When she wears that blue pantsuit, she wears black shoes, not brown ones. Brown shoes don't match. We've searched everywhere to find a picture that shows what color shoes she's wearing, and we can't find any."

"What about the fingerprint?"

"She wore gloves. You can see them on her hands in the video. If she's wearing gloves in that interview under the lights, why would she walk into an alley and take her gloves off before she picked up a bag?"

"And the hair?"

"The hat covers her head—"

"Objection," said Fleming. "There is no foundation for this, Your Honor."

"Sustained," said Smert. He looked at the prosecutor. "I'm surprised the government allowed the fingerprint testimony, Mr. Fleming." He turned to the lectern. "This witness was not present in the alley, Mr. Hirschfeld. There has to be a basis for his statement that the defendant was wearing something at a time when he wasn't there to see her wearing it."

Hirschfeld at least looked apologetic.

"Perhaps if I approach another way? In a general sense, Mr. James, who had a motive to plant evidence against Ms. James?"

"The task force. Denise has admirers, you know. Kludge and Olsen were really embarrassed by the Tea Party. Every time I turn on the TV someone is telling a joke. Like how many FBI agents does it take to—"

"Enough," cut in Hirschfeld. "What about means? Who had the means to plant such evidence?"

"The task force. They have access to scientists and laboratories and such. They couldn't find the money, and they looked hard. Denise kept getting in the news. Bits and pieces of evidence that only they had access to kept getting released, like witness interviews and police reports. They employed every procedure they could against my wife, some standard, and some going right up to, if not over the line."

"Like what?"

"Like releasing her name to the public as a suspect without giving her warning. She got threatening phone calls. The house and cars were vandalized. She got kidnapped in the Treasure Chest parking garage. The house got shot up. After indictment, they put her in shackles and chains when they arrested her, and paraded her in front of television cameras. That was to get back at her."

Hirschfeld played the video of Denise being hustled in body cuffs from her front door to the van.

"And isn't it strange we would be audited while Denise is on trial?"

Judge Smert cleared his throat. Michael left the subject of the IRS.

"The Department of Justice has fought easing the restraining order at every hearing. My job paid some of the bills, but now I'm living in

Charlottesville, and the paid portion of my leave has expired. The mortgage is delinquent. I believe the task force is trying to force us into bankruptcy."

"How is the loan being handled?"

"Right now we're talking to the mortgage company. They know about the restraining order and what's happened to us. They know there's equity in the property. We're doing all we can, but we haven't been able to have the restrictions on assets lifted. That's hurting our credit when we could make the payments."

"Please continue."

"So when nothing conventional worked, the task force, not the whole FBI, just the task force, used their professional capabilities to frame my wife."

"What about opportunity?"

"The task force has been running this investigation since they took it over from the Alexandria police. If we hadn't made them so mad at the Tea Party, they wouldn't have taken the steps they did to put us in this position. They've had ample opportunity to work all this up." He began to raise his arms, thought better of it, and put them down. "We're talking about one person against the combined resources of the United States government when those resources have been mobilized by a task force determined to nail her."

"Objection," said Fleming. "The witness cannot know the motivations of a government agency."

Hirschfeld said, "The witness has the right to express his opinion concerning the task force. The defense will stipulate it is his opinion, Your Honor."

"I'll allow it."

"Please continue, Mr. James."

"The task force has had the opportunity to fabricate evidence from the time they took over the case. I believe our residence was entered and evidence taken prior to the legal search. They took hair samples and fingerprints when we weren't there. They made a shoe mold, but did it on the wrong shoes. That could have happened during any weekday when we were working."

"Your witness," said Hirschfeld.

Fleming took his time getting to the lectern and arranging his papers.

"Mr. James. Do you have any factual proof that the fingerprint has been manufactured?"

"Denise was wearing gloves. She didn't go into the alley. Those are the facts."

"Where were you at the time of the incident, at the time of the raid?"

"Home… with our son… Tommy…"

Smert turned his head to the witness. If information were to be spilled about the attack on the defendant in the front yard, either the husband or the defendant would do it during cross-examination. Hirschfeld would arrange it that way.

"Does the witness wish to have a sip of water?" asked Smert. "Or take a few moments to compose his thoughts?"

"Thank you, no."

Fleming continued. "You don't know whether she wore gloves, do you? You weren't there."

"I know she wore gloves. She had them on in the video."

"But you weren't there to see her in the alley, yes or no?"

"I can't prove I love my son, but I do."

Smert cleared his throat. "Mr. James. Let me remind you to answer the question with a direct, not obtuse, answer."

"Yes, sir."

Fleming asked, "Did you see Denise James wearing gloves as she walked home after the incident or not?"

"I know she was."

Fleming looked to the bench.

"Your Honor."

Smert addressed the witness.

"Mr. James. Did you see Denise James wearing gloves as she walked to her car after the television interview the morning after the January sixteenth raid while you were at your home some miles away? Yes or no?"

"No."

Smert nodded to Fleming.

"Thank you, Your Honor." He turned to the witness. "Do you have any evidence that the hair found at the site in the alley is anything other than what the government says it is?"

"I must compliment the government. I don't know how it was done."

"Please answer the question, Mr. James. I don't wish to have to ask Judge Smert to intervene again. Do you have any evidence that the hair found at the site in the alley is anything other than what the government says it is?"

"No."

"And the footprint?"

"I can't prove she didn't wear the brown shoes, but she didn't."

"So the answer is no?"

"The method has been well hidden."

"Is the answer no?"

"Yes."

"Yes, the answer is no?"

"Yes—the answer is yes—the answer is no."

He paused.

The court became still.

He leaned to the microphone and whispered, "Could we do that again, please? You're obviously a very smart man, Mr. Flaming, and I'm just an accused co-conspirator with a frightened wife and child."

A murmur rose from the gallery.

Smert crashed down his hammer, surprising the court, and glared at the man on the stand.

"The witness is warned not to be too clever!"

The jury thought this harsh. Voices were now audible from the gallery.

"Quiet in the court!" ordered Smert. "Quiet!"

The room settled.

"I will not caution the gallery again," said Smert pointing his gavel and scowl at those behind the bar. He waited for silence. "You may proceed, Mr. Flaming—uh—Fleming."

From his position behind the microphone in the center of the room, the Assistant US Attorney went crimson. The gallery behind him stifled itself. Jurors hid smirks. Fleming gaped at Smert in disbelief. Smert played with papers on the bench. Fleming poured himself a glass of water and took a sip.

"Can that be stricken, Your Honor?"

"Yes," said Smert. He looked at the stenographer. "Strike that."

Fleming reviewed his papers for some seconds, perhaps hoping for an apology.

"Please proceed," said Smert.

"Just one final question, Mr. James. Yes or no will suffice. Do you have any physical, tangible evidence that the fingerprint, the hair, or the footprint were planted at the site by the government?"

"Not the whole government, and not the whole FBI. Just the task force."

"Do you have any evidence, Mr. James?"

"My resources are more limited than those of the task force."

"Why can't you answer yes or no?"

Head down, Michael said, "All right, Mr. Assistant United States Attorney, no."

"No further questions of this witness, Your Honor."

Hirschfeld had nothing further.

"You may step down, Mr. James," said Smert. "Call your next witness."

Hirschfeld went to the lectern.

"The defense rests, Your Honor."

Smert blinked at him from atop his altar.

In the witness room Hirschfeld said, "I do not like Smert's tenor. The jury may be—"

"Jesus Christ, Moses! How can we prove the evidence is planted? We can't file charges against a dozen FBI agents, have them indicted, tell them they're all going to jail for thirty-two years if they don't cooperate, and wait till someone breaks. These people are blood brothers!"

"Enough," said Antaramian. "Let's get out of here. Stretch our legs. We can discuss this over drinks and dinner." He stood. "Come on Denise. Real food. My treat."

Gathering up her purse and papers, Denise wondered if this was her Last Supper. If not, she wondered how many more good sit-down meals lay ahead before a cafeteria line of USDA "Grade D" food selections became her staple.

Friday, October 26

"The court trusts the parties are prepared to proceed," said Smert.
Fleming moved to the microphone. "Yes, Your Honor."
"And the defense?"
Hirschfeld went to the lectern. "Yes, Your Honor."
"Good. Mr. Bailiff, please bring in the jury."
Fourteen people entered from the right and sat in the box. Smert
welcomed them, and told them their work should soon be completed.
As was the custom, they were asked if anyone had seen, heard, or
read about the trial through any news media or other source. None
volunteered. Had anyone discussed the case with any other juror, or
another person, including family members? None had. Smert asked if
any juror was aware of any other juror having violated any of the
rules of the court. When no one spoke, the jury was cleared for the
record.

Smert polled both sides for further testimony. The government
and the defense confirmed completion of their presentations. The next
phase was closing arguments.

Assistant US Attorney Paul Fleming stood at the lectern and
began reading a laborious reconstruction of the government's case
with practical emphasis on statements made by the defendant that she
had not entered the alley versus finding the footprint, hair, and
fingerprint in the alley. For nearly two hours he enumerated the
details of the eight charges, each being a foundation building on the
next. There could be no doubt of guilt. She had motive, means, and
opportunity. All suspects had been eliminated in a systematic manner
by investigators employing standard procedures, all tried and
adjudicated legal by the courts. It was she who had lied, and the
government had proven it. She had taken the money, the money that
rightfully belonged to the government through forfeiture. He took it
all the way to lunch.

At half past one, Moses Hirschfeld began his summation. He
stressed Denise James's impish character, her career as a banker and
law-abiding citizen, the government's failure to locate the money, and
the media inflation surrounding her after the Tea Party. This singular
public embarrassment had resulted in a handful of individuals going
to any length to prove guilt. Certainly the FBI would never condone

manufacturing evidence, but certain praetorian agents within the Bureau could have done so. Hair could have been planted, lab reports could have been backdated, a fingerprint could have been discovered where needed, and a footprint mold could have been created. With the cooperation of a half-dozen individuals, just enough hard evidence could be developed to put doubt out of reach and sentence Denise James to prison. It had not been a vast conspiracy, just an overzealous vendetta by a few gone too far. If the jury could not find overwhelming doubt, there was reasonable doubt. Without locating the money, a fair-minded person could not convict, even if the jury determined Ms. James had returned to the alley as she denied doing. No one could steal seventy pounds of paper and hide it from the talents of an exhaustive federal, state and local search.

In thirty minutes, Hirschfeld made his points and sat.

There was a short break, and Smert delivered his instructions.

The jury's decision on each of the eight counts in the indictment must be made based upon facts presented by witnesses and physical evidence alone.

The failure of the defendant to take the stand in her defense is not to be held as a sign of guilt or innocence on the part of the defendant. She has that right under the Constitution.

That the defendant has not shown evidence of having the funds in question is not to be construed as evidence she did not commit the act or acts for which she is being charged. If the defendant took the money and donated it to charity, she is still responsible for the crimes for which she is being charged.

The fact that the money has not been found is not evidence the defendant did not take it. The money need not be found to convict.

The jury must decide whether the evidence presented proves the defendant physically returned to the trash bag area in the alley. If so proven, this would be in contravention of statements made by her and entered as evidence on her behalf.

The cost and depth of the government's investigation is irrelevant to the jury's decision.

The jury must ignore extraneous matters such as emotional pleas, charm, looks, family position, hero status, prior acts, and presentation by the President of the United States.

The position of the defense that evidence was manufactured is a theory. It has not been proven. In deliberating, theories without proof have no basis. The jury's decision must be made based upon fact. No proof has been presented by the defense indicating the government's evidence is other than as presented, and the decision of the jury must be made on evidence presented. To do otherwise could necessitate the court's intervention.

Smert advised the jurors of the procedures for having transcripts read to them, how they should address any questions that arose, and guidelines for completing the final ballot.

The verdicts must be unanimous. Please use every effort to earn the faith the people of the Eastern District of Virginia have placed in you.

Smert dismissed the jury at three twenty-five.

After the jury door closed, Smert ordered those present before the bar to be available to reconvene when given notice, or as otherwise directed by the court.

They were adjourned.

Her attorneys huddled around her in the witness room. Hirschfeld said, "I believe with those instructions, the jury will be forced to find you guilty, Denise."

"And if they should find you innocent," said Antaramian, "Smert may set it aside with a directed verdict."

"That's when the judge throws out the unanimous vote of twelve of my peers and reverses their decision based on his power as a judge."

They nodded. She offered a thin smile.

"I've seen that on television."

"When the jury renders its verdict," said Hirschfeld, "if it is innocent, you will walk out a free woman unless Smert sets it aside. After the language we just heard, a set-aside is a viable possibility. If the verdict is guilty, your status will change as of that moment from a person presumed innocent to a convicted felon. Smert will order marshals to escort you to a holding cell downstairs."

"Thoughtful, though unnecessary," said Denise. "Please inform Judge Smert I already know my way to the courthouse jail."

Saturday night's edition of "Dateline" aired the results of an NBC poll: Guilty 44%—Innocent 56%. The network provided no commentary. Neither did the two agents on duty with the James family.

Hirschfeld telephoned Sunday to inform Denise that the jury had agreed on its verdicts. Court would be brought into session Monday at nine for the reading. He also said he would arrive at her suite at five-thirty the next morning so that he, Denise, and Michael could arrive at Courthouse Square well ahead of the expected crowd.

Chapter Twenty

Monday, October 29

The morning air was dense and murky, low clouds, cold fog. At Courthouse Square, media trucks and trailers crowded the plaza and service roads. Since no electronics were allowed inside the security perimeter of the first floor, television coverage was limited to the exterior, hence the milling throng of reporters and crews outside the main entrance.

On the eighth floor, the elevators opened onto a marbled corridor with windows on one side, and courtrooms and judges' chambers on the other. Judge Smert's courtroom was on the right beyond two sets of heavy wooden doors.

As soon as a verdict was rendered, observers inside the courtroom would signal or sign to others behind the windows in the first set of double doors. They would pass the message through the windows of the second set of doors to those in the corridor who would repeat it to someone at the exterior windows. Telephoto lenses eight floors below would focus on those windows to record and relay the result. News anchors would be told, and the verdict announced. Some teams considered using lip readers in case a verdict turned out to be more complex than a simple "guilty" or "not guilty," but telephoto lenses couldn't pick up lip reading at that distance. Semaphore was discussed and rejected. One wag suggested white or black smoke.

Late-morning television was devoted to the story. Experienced court observers predicted the verdict would be read ten to twelve minutes from the opening "Oyez." Once the results were known, each network had a prepared storyline that would carry to at least the top of the hour. An across-the-board "not guilty" would occasion an interview with Denise on a podium set up for the purpose on the plaza outside. A victory tea party was prepared. If any verdict was "guilty," it was anticipated Moses Hirschfeld would make a statement, as would Assistant US Attorney Paul Fleming.

Outside the courthouse, a carnival-like crowd was kept behind bicycle rack barriers. News teams waded into them seeking opinions, especially from those who sported the season's hottest Halloween mask, a rubberized Denise James head.

An ABC News camera focused on the windows of the eighth floor as the anchor provided commentary from the news desk in New York.

"We are told Judge Emil Smert will bring court into session within the next minute or two. There will be preliminaries, then Judge Smert will bring in the jury, and the eight verdicts will be read.

"Our spotters are in place and have been testing signals so that you, our viewers, will know the results as soon as possible. Altogether the twelve jurors and two alternates spent about ten and three quarter hours in deliberations, approximately half an hour last Friday, seven hours Saturday, and the balance Sunday morning. As of this moment, there are only fourteen people in the country who know the fate of Denise James."

As he spoke, the picture zoomed in enough to pick up the movement of hands against the glass, though mist still obscured the image. Earlier, the anchor had broached the possibility that the air might clear before the verdicts were announced. Now that nine o'clock approached, the media and the viewers would have to make do as best they could. Someone was seen spraying and wiping the glass. "No need to leave fingerprints inside a federal courthouse needlessly, I suppose," quipped the anchor.

To the consternation of the networks expecting a prompt start by the punctilious Emil Smert, nine o'clock passed. The anchors ad-libbed, repeating the same information for those who might have joined late. The stations had already commercial-upped in preparation for a long uninterrupted segment, though some considered cutting away during the gap. Word came at nine-ten that court was being called to order.

"This has been a bizarre case to say the least," said the ABC anchor. "No money found, and no proof positive presented that Denise James did, in fact, take it. Yet persuasive physical evidence located at the scene indicates that she was indeed where she said she was not. To this the defense has responded: it has all been fabricated.

"Does the jury believe there is a conspiracy to frame Denise James because the task force could not otherwise obtain a conviction against someone they are convinced committed a crime? Or has Denise James been lying to everyone all along and"—he put his finger to his ear—"I am now told there may be a further delay—it would appear Denise James is not in the courtroom."

"Where is your client, Mr. Hirschfeld?" asked Smert from on high. "Under the bail agreement, you are responsible for getting her here."

"I do not know where she is, Your Honor."

A flurry of signing hands appeared in the gallery.

"And I beg to differ with the court," continued Hirschfeld. "In this instance the government is responsible for producing the defendant. The Federal Bureau of Investigation has been chaperoning Ms. James at a suite they control, holding her there under virtual house arrest. The government is therefore responsible for assuring her appearance."

Rapid signing behind the bar. A woman approached the exit doors. A marshal motioned her to return to her seat.

Smert was not pleased. He'd arrived at seven and been told the government could not locate the defendant. Efforts to find her were then three hours old. He'd gone to chambers and monitored the networks until shortly after nine, at which point he'd been forced to call court into session to give them something to report.

So here they were, all ready to go, and no defendant.

"What about that, Mr. Fleming?" asked Smert. "Where does the government think she is?"

Fleming took his time getting to the microphone.

"It appears as if Ms. James fugitized herself from the premises of her own accord sometime during the night, Your Honor."

"Am I to assume the defendant has voluntarily fled?"

"Apparently so."

"Do you have any information about this, Mr. Hirschfeld?"

"No, Your Honor. I do not know where Ms. James is. All I can say is that she was distraught concerning her circumstances."

"She will be worse than distraught when she next appears in this court."

"I would suppose that is true, Your Honor."

"Counsel in chambers."

Thwack!

271

Smert was furious at Hirschfeld for not getting his client to court, furious at Fleming and the agents at the suite for letting their charge slip from confinement, and furious at Denise James for putting him in the position of being the star judge in a national drama with no script.

"What's being done to find her?"

"The Bureau is on top of this, Your Honor," answered Fleming. "Her automobile is in the Landmark lot. Her husband is here with his car. He says he doesn't know where she is. Immigration, airlines, trains, bus lines, they've all been alerted. All police jurisdictions in the Greater Washington region have been notified."

Smert rose red-faced from his chair.

"We have the world waiting outside, and we don't have the defendant!" He glared at Hirschfeld. "I sense sanctions, counselor."

"We return now to Dan Mattison of our ABC affiliate in Washington, D.C., who is outside the Eastern District of Virginia's federal courthouse."

Mattison faced the camera on the west side of the building, the white pergolas of the square visible through the mist behind him.

"The same message has been received and verified from our relay team inside the courtroom. Denise James is not present, and neither defense counsel Moses Hirschfeld, nor prosecutor Paul Fleming, knows where she is. Court was brought to order twelve minutes after the hour and is now in recess while Judge Smert confers with both parties in chambers. Anything we could say beyond that would be speculative."

"Is Denise James considered a fugitive?"

"We just don't know that. We'll have to wait until court resumes and further information in made available from official sources."

"Thank you, Dan Mattison, live from the Eastern District of Virginia's federal courthouse."

The anchor then turned to experts on hand to provide a summary of law enforcement procedures to locate Denise James, if indeed she were declared a fugitive, and to outline the range of sanctions she would face when she was apprehended.

Judge Smert brought court back into session and had the jury seated.

"At the present time, it would appear that defendant Denise Elizabeth Lang James has voluntarily absented herself from this proceeding. Until otherwise advised, this court must consider her in fugitive status."

Signs flew and voices rose in the gallery. Camera conscious, Smert chose to wait for quiet rather than command it.

"Madam Foreperson."

A middle-aged woman stood in the box.

"Has the jury reached agreement on the verdicts?"

"Yes we have, Your Honor." Her voice was strong, sure.

"Verdicts on all charges?"

"Yes, Your Honor."

"You have the verdicts written on the proper form?"

"Yes, Your Honor." The papers were in her hand, folded in half.

"Please place the verdicts in this envelope." Smert handed it to a bailiff who handed it to the woman. "Please seal the envelope and write on it the date, the time, and the words, 'Original Verdicts, US versus DELJ.' Then hand it to the bailiff who will hand it to my clerk."

All eyes watched as this was done. When the clerk received the envelope, he initialed it, and nodded to Smert.

"Ladies and gentlemen of the jury, I am sorry for this inconvenience. I must ask you to indulge this court with your services a little while longer. We will recess until eleven-thirty this morning. Whether or not the defendant has been located at that time, the verdicts will be read, and you will be dismissed, you duties here concluded. Again, I apologize for the delay.

"Court is adjourned until eleven-thirty."

Thwack.

Roody Packwurst and Chief of Police Joan Harris approached Eric Kludge and other agents on the second floor of Courthouse Square just outside the snack bar.

"Hello, Eric," said Packwurst.

Kludge fixed him with a look reserved for unwanted pests.

"What are you doing about this?"

Packwurst dropped his politician's face and stood to his full height before the towering Kludge.

273

"Right now we have people at her house, her former office, the Landmark suite, the airports, metro stops, bus stations, and train stations. Her car and her husband's car have been booted. Every jurisdiction knows what she looks like. Every tollbooth operator has been advised. We're preparing to go public with an appeal for information."

Kludge said, "Hold that up until our announcement is complete."

"What do you have for me?"

"We'll tell you when you need to know."

Packwurst must have expected that answer. He took a step under Kludge's nose and said, "You're a fucking bastard."

Kludge blinked at him in surprise.

Packwurst walked away.

The report from Landmark was that both nightshift agents had verified the woman was asleep at midnight. At two o'clock, one agent checked the bedroom and told the other she was present. The proper procedure was that both agents were to check. At four they did and found the apparent person in Denise's bed a sham made of blankets and sofa pillows. Without disturbing the scene, they awoke an astonished Michael, searched the suite, then the outside corridor to the vending machines and stairwells. To their credit, at five after four, they called it in.

Kludge was summoned to Landmark, as were Olsen and Iacob. The building became silly with agents. Called at home, Hirschfeld and Antaramian had no information. Michael appeared as stunned as everyone except Tommy and Sydney who slept through it all.

Both automobiles were found in the lot and searched. The metro system began operation at five, but the nearest station was a distance too far to walk. Taxi companies were contacted.

Until nine o'clock, Kludge harbored a vague hope that either the woman would show up at the courthouse on her own, or they could find her before her escape became public.

Smert remained in chambers reviewing the law on fugitive flight.

Court was called back into session at eleven-thirty.

"Mr. Hirschfeld. Have you located your client?"

Hirschfeld moved to the microphone. "No, Your Honor." He sat.

"Mr. Fleming. Has the government located the defendant?"

Fleming took his place at the microphone. "No, Your Honor." He sat.

"Is there anyone in this courtroom who knows the location of Denise Elizabeth Lang James or can provide information that might lead to her location? If so, please indicate your presence."

Smert surveyed the room paying special attention to Michael James in the pew behind the defendant's empty chair.

"Let the record show there is no response."

The stenographer nodded.

"Despite the unscheduled absence of the defendant, the court can no longer hold the jury. The verdicts must be rendered, and the jury must be released from the duties their government has asked them to perform, and that they have so ably executed.

"Clerk of the Court."

"Yes, Your Honor."

"Do you have the envelope containing the verdicts given to you earlier this morning by Madame Foreperson?"

"Yes, Your Honor."

"Hand the envelope to the bailiff. Mr. Bailiff, please hand the envelope to Madame Foreperson." It was done. "Madame Foreperson, is this the envelope in which you sealed the verdicts?"

She examined it.

"Yes, Your Honor."

"Madame Foreperson, please open the envelope and remove its contents."

She did so.

"I ask you, Madame Foreperson, are these the verdicts reached by the jury in the matter of the United States versus Denise Elizabeth Lang James, Criminal Number Seventeen-zero-one dash twenty twenty-seven-A?"

She took a moment to review the papers.

"Yes they are."

"Please hand them to the bailiff."

She folded the papers and held them out. The bailiff took them to the bench and handed them up.

Smert's eyes bored into each page for some seconds. He refolded them without betraying their content and handed them to the bailiff who returned them to Madame Foreperson.

Smert turned to the defense table.

"In the absence of the person of the defendant, would defense counsel please rise and face the jury in her stead."

Hirschfeld and Antaramian faced the twelve impaneled members.

"Madame Foreperson. What say you?"

"In the matter of Criminal Number Seventeen-zero-one dash twenty twenty-seven-A, United States of America versus Denise Elizabeth Lang James, count one, Title Eighteen, Section two B, one-point-one, theft of stolen property, we the jury find the defendant, Denise Elizabeth..."

Hand signals flashed in the gallery. Spotters behind the windows between the double doors signed the message to those behind them in the corridor. They signaled to others at the exterior windows, who signed for the cameras below; a manual bucket brigade of information in the telecommunications age. Viewers at home saw a flurry of hand movement behind the eighth floor windows.

CBS was first.

"And the verdict on count one, theft of three million dollars, should be—now is—guilty! Guilty to theft on count one. Denise Elizabeth Lang James is found guilty of theft. Now for count two, Title Eighteen, Section two D, one-point-one, drug trafficking as an accessory after the fact, the least likely charge for which analysts believe a guilty verdict could be rendered. That should be next—count two—we're waiting, ladies and gentlemen—it is—guilty again! Count two, drug trafficking also guilty. Denise James is found guilty of drug trafficking. Now for count three—"

The margin of CBS's first "guilty" was three quarters of a second ahead of the first runner up.

"...we find the defendant, Denise Elizabeth Lang James, guilty," concluded Madame Foreperson.

Smert could only have been more pleased if the defendant had been present.

"Mr. Hirschfeld, do you wish to have the jury polled?"

"Not necessary, Your Honor."

For the first time since proceedings began, Smert contorted his face into a smile. Some jurors evoked smiles themselves at this mark of favor, believing they'd voted correctly in the eyes of the judge.

"Ladies and gentlemen of the jury, your duties have been concluded with success. Please accept the profound thanks of the court.

"Sentencing in this case will be November twenty-ninth whether or not the defendant has been located. Memoranda on sentencing are due by November twenty-second." He looked at Hirschfeld. "At that time, I will further examine the ultimate responsibility for the defendant's fugitive status."

Smert looked to Fleming.

"I order all law enforcement agencies of the government of these United States to find and arrest Denise Elizabeth Lang James as a fugitive felon convicted this day on eight federal counts so rendered, and to do so at the earliest possible time.

"Court is adjourned."

Thwack!

"Eric. How are you?" asked the FBI Director.

"Fine sir, fine. And you?"

They were on a secure line.

"Great. Great. I understand we have a new fugitive. Bring me up to date."

It was not unusual for the Director to bypass the chain of command to get first-hand information from the agent in charge of a case. Statements from the Director would set public tone.

"The woman was found guilty on all eight counts. She's been declared a fugitive. She made her escape from our Landmark location under the custody of two agents at seventeen minutes after midnight according to the exit cameras. We have a tape of her leaving the suite and going down the stairway. The suite's alarm was never set. Quite frankly, the agents were complaisant. They didn't think she would flee."

This was Kludge's first time speaking to the Director one-on-one on a case. He waited for a reaction and got none.

He said, "We're going to take some heat on this, sir. It's already started."

"That can't be helped, Eric. What's happened has happened. The quicker the woman is apprehended, the less the damage. Tell me about that."

"All law enforcement agencies have been notified. Within the hour we'll be running public service bulletins on all major stations in the Greater Washington region. All standard protocols are being engaged.

"She has no fugitive experience, no known contacts with criminal elements, no transportation, no weapons, no clothes, no aliases. DMV reports no automobiles in her name except the two impounded. Relatives, friends, and acquaintances are being contacted. Her face is well known. The belief is she panicked.

"Analysis believes the chances of finding her by midnight are twenty-five percent, by tomorrow, twenty percent, and the next day fifteen percent. We have a sixty percent chance of finding her in the next three days. It goes down each day from there by ten, six, four, and two. By this time next week, there's an eighty-two percent probability she'll be in custody. Lasting a month is impossible."

"Quicker is better."

"No one will sleep until she's apprehended."

"Thanks for the update, Eric. Let me have some good news when I get back to Washington. See me tomorrow in my office."

"Yes, sir."

Office of the Commonwealth's Attorney

Roody Packwurst, Joan Harris, and the Director of Public Relations watched the "Most Wanted Alert." The FBI-Department of Justice logo appeared first.

"The following is a special bulletin from the Federal Bureau of Investigation's Criminal Apprehension Team." Full face and profile photos from the indictment booking came on the screen. "Denise Elizabeth Lang James is being sought in connection with her failure to appear in federal court on October twenty-ninth." Vital statistics flashed next: HEIGHT: 5' 9", WEIGHT: 135-145, AGE: 27, HAIR:

LIGHT BROWN, EYES: GREEN, ETHNIC BACKGROUND: WHITE CAUCASIAN, DISTINGUISHING CHARACTERISTICS: EVEN FEATURED. "If you have seen Denise Elizabeth Lang James, please call the toll-free number on your screen."

Packwurst muted the set.

"I want a public service announcement like that under our logo. Use more pictures, lots of them, and our hotline number. Start by saying, 'Virginia Commonwealth's Attorney Roody Packwurst asks the public's assistance in locating Denise James.' The description has to match the FBI's. Bring me a demo as soon as you can."

"Yes, sir."

The Director of Public Relations left the room.

Packwurst sat behind his desk.

"Are you ready for my officer now, Roody?" asked Harris.

Packwurst smiled.

"Send him in."

Harris went to the door.

"Come in, Officer Johnson."

In full dress uniform, Stephen Johnson entered looking sheepish. Most officers ended their careers without seeing the inside of the Commonwealth's Attorney's office.

Packwurst rose to meet him and shake his hand. They were the same height.

"Chief Harris tells me you have some very interesting information for me, Officer Johnson."

"Yes, sir. I hope I did everything right."

"If what Chief Harris tells me is true, I'm sure you did. Have a seat. Let's talk about it."

Packwurst's smile broadened as he listened to what Johnson had to say.

Chapter Twenty-One

That Evening
Northern Virginia

Wall speakers played Salsa music in the El Condado Restaurant, a sleazy wicker and plastic eatery off Route One South. Being Monday, there were few patrons, conversation private. At a corner table sat seven men under a dim overhead bulb.

"It took four months to break even after January," said the accountant. "It hurt when we couldn't add the garage on time, but now that we got it, it's running okay. By the first of the year we should have enough cash to buy another one at the same price."

This was the regular Monday night meeting of those who ran drug distribution and cash accumulation from Fort Belvoir to Reagan National and from the Potomac to I-95.

"Excellent," said Nick Rivera. "I gotta garage in Skyline and another one in Crystal City. I play one against the other and see who accept the better deal."

Discussion so far had been on the positive side. Rivera hadn't mentioned Denise James since the DEA debacle, and despite her disappearance and guilty verdicts that morning, those at the table were loath to bring up her name.

Appetizer plates were cleared, another round of beer and lime served. The waitress told them the entrées would be ready in a few minutes.

Rivera pointed to the trellis in front of the bathroom doors. Without a word the bodyguard got up and went into the men's room. When he came out, he gave the okay to Rivera.

"I be back," he said getting up.

Heads nodded. No one wanted to be the first to have to go, at least not before the boss.

The bodyguard pushed the door open for Rivera and stood outside.

Stained yellow tile and dirty grout covered the floor. Rivera stepped to the sink to wet a paper towel and wipe the oil-shine from his face.

After the double-crossed money exchange, it had no longer mattered to him whether the woman had the money or not. He wanted her dead on principle, and his first attempt to have her killed failed. Now, as soon as she was arrested, he'd arrange a jailhouse death and go on with business.

Out in the restaurant, a gray-haired Hispanic used a cane to get up from a chair. He had a weak leg and swayed in baggy clothes as he walked to the men's room door.

"Hold on, hombre," said the bodyguard.

"Emergencia!" croaked the old man.

The bodyguard caught the reek of tequila.

"Not now."

"Emergencia!"

Leaning against the wall within easy range of the bodyguard's leg, the man pulled down his zipper and reached inside.

"Jesus Christ, you old fuck!"

The bodyguard wanted to throttle him. Failing that, he was running out of time.

"Go ahead," he said and pushed open the door.

Reflected in the mirror over the urinal, Rivera saw his man give a frustrated shake of his head as the old drunk shuffled in. This had happened before.

The door closed.

Denise James launched her foot at the middle of Rivera's back, slamming his solar plexus against the protruding flush-valve above the urinal. His body bounced against her heel, and she thrust again. Hands at his stomach, Rivera rolled against the corner wall, urine dribbling, legs splayed, and slid to the floor.

She spoke in a low coarse voice.

"I have a message from Johnny Murphy. You're through."

She pulled his right wrist from his stomach and wrapped it tight with a thick rubber band.

"You violated Murphy's Law."

She drew his signature knife from its sheath.

"He's taking over. You're finished."

She held his arm out from his body. With a high-arced sweep of the blade, she lopped off his hand at the wrist. It fell to his lap.

281

Even with his face contorted from pain in his diaphragm, at the feel of the blow Rivera opened his eyes to see his arm stop just beyond the rubber band. He gaped in horror at white bone, yellow fluid, and oozing blood. He tried to scream, but had no breath.

"Your people will be reporting to Baltimore or not reporting at all."

She sank the knifepoint an inch and a half into Rivera's eye and twisted, optic fluid bursting across his face. His arms jerked.

She picked up his hand and tossed it to the back of a metal storage locker against the wall, gold rings skittering across its top.

She wrapped a paper towel around the knife hilt, wiped it well, and rammed its point deep into Rivera's abdomen giving the blade a wide turn and leaving it.

"My boss's card," she said drawing it from a pocket and laying it on the urinal.

Rivera lay inert on the stained yellow tile and dirty grout, his good hand twitching.

"Nothing personal, just business."

She zipped her pants, picked up the cane, and shuffled out the door.

The bodyguard watched the old drunk reel past him and go into the parking lot, glad to see him leave. At the table, the entrées were served. Rivera must be doing number two he supposed.

The music ended.

Before another trumpet intro began, he heard a groan that took him through the men's room door.

"Call 911!" he shouted at his table.

Rivera was sprawled on the floor nipping air in short shallow breaths. The bodyguard knelt beside him, not sure what to do. The accountant arrived first, saw the empty eye socket, and vomited.

"Get an ambulance!" ordered the bodyguard. "Go! Now!"

There was little blood. The wrist stub had a tourniquet, and the knife acted as a stopper. Rivera's good hand shook its way toward his eye. The bodyguard took his wrist and checked for a pulse. He had one.

The bodyguard picked the paper towel from the knife handle and laid it across Rivera's forehead to cover the hideous socket. He zipped up his fly and took his wallet and jewelry, some of which had fallen to the floor from his wrist. When he stood to pocket everything, he saw the card on the urinal.

JOHN C. MURPHY it read with a Baltimore address and telephone number.

The bodyguard handed it to the accountant who looked at it and passed it to the man next to him.

In the dining room, the lights were turned up and the music stopped. No one said anything in the men's room, no words of comfort, no reassurance.

EMT's arrived and shooed everyone away. Police came and started taking names. Rivera was stabilized and wheeled out on a gurney.

No one found his hand until the next day.

Twenty Hours Earlier
Landmark

Michael had taken a sedative. According to schedule, the agents checked beds every two hours. After the midnight visit, Denise stole into the bathroom and dressed in casual clothes and running shoes. Leaving the door ajar, she crept to her bed and lined sofa pillows and a blanket under the covers as though she were sleeping on her side facing away from the door. She took care with her toiletry bag, placing it half-exposed as her head.

Michael was lying on his back, breathing a light snore. She didn't know when she would see him again, or how she would feel when she did. Bending down, she kissed his forehead and whispered, "I love you."

Moving to the crib, Sydney slept face up, Tommy beside her sprawled on his side. Here was a picture that would change. How pristine they were. How delicate. If she remained free for any length of time, she might not recognize them. She etched into her memory their hands, fingers and nails, chins, mouths, noses, eyes, and hair. She kissed her finger and touched it to Sydney's head, then Tommy's. She might not see them again. She took a deep breath and said, "I love you, babies."

Turning off the bathroom light, she made her way in darkness to the bedroom door. Cracking it, she stepped into the hall and closed it behind her. The agents watching television couldn't see her from the living room, but they could see the foyer she had to cross to get to the front door.

Creeping to the corner, she leaned around until she saw the backs of their heads. Whatever they were watching was in a slow part. Even the air handler was cycled off at the moment.

She waited.

"More after these messages."

A used car salesman began a pitch.

"Come on down! We'll beat any price in town!"

She leaned forward. Both heads were watching the set. She faced the door and walked to it, freed the chain with both hands, turned the handle, opened the door, slipped through, turned the outside handle, released the inside handle, closed the door, and released the striker back into the plate.

The corridor was empty.

She walked toward the stairwell anticipating a shout or alarm. She made the stairs and descended to the outside exit, walked across the parking lot, unlocked a gray Volvo, started the engine, and drove away.

The car's cup-holder held a Styrofoam coffee cup. At the first traffic light she pulled a beret from the glove compartment and put it on. It wasn't much, but it went well with the Volvo. Any police officer next to her would see an artsy-craftsy commuter sipping coffee in the most suburban of automobiles. And if she were pulled over, she'd be Cora Stephanie Masters.

She'd had good reason for visiting her Treasure Chest construction sites during her sabbatical. Four were phased townhouse developments nearing completion. If what she needed wasn't available at the first stop, there were others.

At the second project she found what she wanted, loose security. In a first floor bathroom, she flipped the switch and was bathed in light. The brightness made her blink.

From a backpack she removed a video camera, an electric razor, and one of her *Magic Central* makeup kits.

Not long after the verdicts were read at Courthouse Square, a platinum blonde checked Mr. and Ms. Drexel Masters into a luxury hotel near the Convention Center in Washington, D.C. She paid with traveler's checks. She ordered room service for two and monitored her disappearance on CNN throughout the afternoon.

An old Hispanic left the hotel that evening, bought a cane, and returned after a visit to the El Condado Restaurant on Route One South.

By nightfall, immigration, airline, railroad and bus terminal personnel, taxi drivers and metro workers, all had been given pictures and been briefed. Police checked hotel registration lists, especially low and moderate priced motor inns and lodges. Drivers who met age and gender specific profiles were pulled over, their identities verified. Merchants were advised to take a careful look at anyone presenting hundred dollar bills for payment.

Hotels with the technical capability to do so provided authorities with guest information on discs. Their names were run through a computer to corroborate identities with known addresses. Drexel and Cora Masters checked out.

Wednesday night was Halloween. Denise James masks triggered a horde of false sightings, hundreds of leads; far too many to follow up quickly.

Friday, November 2
The Washington Post - The Federal Page - A4

> Virginia Commonwealth's Attorney Roody Packwurst announced yesterday that he had filed a sworn affidavit with the Office of Professional Responsibility at the Department of Justice alleging information from a material witness in the Denise James trial had been withheld from defense counsel and the federal court in Alexandria.
>
> FBI Special Agent in Charge Eric Peabody Kludge headed the investigation. Assistant US

Attorney R. Paul Fleming, III prosecuted the case, which ended in eight guilty verdicts against James on October 29th.

Defense attorney Moses Hirschfeld declined comment.

Denise James continues to be sought by authorities.

Monday, November 5
Courthouse Square

Michael James, Bret James, Moses Hirschfeld, and Vartan Antaramian were in the main conference room at Hirschfeld's firm. The mail that morning had included a package addressed to Michael and a letter in Denise's hand to Hirschfeld instructing him to deliver the package to Michael.

"Thank you for coming," said Hirschfeld. "Before we start, I must tell you I believe this package is from your wife. If so, Vartan and I are bound by attorney-client privilege regarding its content. It will remain confidential."

Michael had yet to move back into Villamay. He had circles under his eyes, his expression wan. It seemed an effort for him to move. Bret had driven.

Hirschfeld said, "As such, I feel bound to ask your father to wait outside."

Bret gave Michael a pat on the shoulder before leaving the room.

Hirschfeld continued. "We can stay if you like, or we can leave. Again, what is in this package is confidential as Denise remains under attorney-client privilege."

They were studying him, trying to be sure he understood.

Hirschfeld said, "As counsel for Denise, we cannot advise you what you should do. You may wish to discuss this with your counsel."

"I see."

"Michael." Antaramian's tone made him look up. "It's important you understand that if you disclose to your counsel what's in this package, your counsel may be required to disclose it to the authorities. Any information relating to illegal acts or activities regarding

286

individuals other than you, including any such acts or activities of your wife, would fall into this category."

"That's because Arnold Porter represents me, not Denise."

He wasn't so far out of it as he appeared.

"That's correct," said Antaramian.

"I understand."

Hirschfeld tore the perforation strip across the top of the box.

"And you represent Denise," said Michael. "Not me." He held out his hand. "I'll open it alone, please."

Inside were bundles of hundred dollar bills, Denise's wedding ring, and a videotape. He counted out a hundred and sixty thousand dollars before putting it back in the box and sealing it. The ring he put in his pocket.

He slid the tape into the conference room's player and turned it on.

Denise appeared.

"Hello, Michael. It's just after one in the morning on the twenty-ninth. I'm not sure under what circumstances you're watching this, whether I'm in jail or still on the run. I might be dead, and if that's the case, you need to know what I did and what I plan to do.

"Last March, I thought the best place to hide the money would be in a car somebody else owned. To do that, I needed to create a legitimate alias, one that could stand up to the DMV. I did some research. It's called 'Alternate ID' and it can be had for as little as thirty dollars by mail. One ad for 'Legal Alias' in the back of a military magazine said to call a certain number and have two thousand dollars cash available for strictly confidential services. I called from a pay phone, gave its number, and got a call back with an address in Maine.

"I used the name Lee Gardener to rent a mailbox in Prince William County. I made passport pictures wearing a prop box wig from *Magic Central* and took a bundle of cash from under the carpet. I mailed two thousand dollars, the pictures, a physical description, and my age to the Maine address with a return to Lee Gardener at the post office box. The box number I wrote as an office suite.

"A Canadian driver's license, passport, social insurance card, credit cards, and pictures, all in the name of Cora Stephanie Masters of Ottawa, Ontario arrived. A note said she was married, had twin boys, and for my purposes, should consider herself a tourist in the U.S. The cards were worn, so they looked like the real thing. Cora Masters died of cancer. Her husband must have needed the money.

"Cora purchased a used car for cash and applied for plates using the box number as an apartment number at the mailbox street address. The Commonwealth seemed happy to put another vehicle on the personal property tax rolls because ten days later I had plates in her name.

"I took all the cash from under the sofa and put it in the car with a few other supplies and things, then parked it in a storage lot in Lorton under the name of Masters. I didn't really plan to become a fugitive. The idea just grew, and it was a better hiding place. It's not that I didn't trust you. It's just that I didn't trust you enough to tell you. Something about my loose tongue and your fixation to keep the money. By the time we came under surveillance, it was all done.

"As you know, things deteriorated. I couldn't leave you and the children to the mercy of the drug dealers after what happened with Tommy, so I got as much information as I could about Nick Rivera from Billy Freep. Billy told me who his Baltimore contact is.

"The biggest problem was getting the car to the Landmark lot while the agents were with me. You might remember I went to Hirschfeld's office each day during that last two-day break. The second day, they followed in their van and waited outside like they did the day before. I went to the ladies room, reversed the jacket, changed the skirt for spandex, put on sunglasses and a cap, and exited out the side door. I walked to King Street Station, rode the Metro to Lorton Station, retrieved the car, and drove it to the Landmark lot. The bus took me back to Courthouse Square, and I went through the side entrance, reversed the jacket, and changed back.

"As soon as Moses told me Smert's jury instructions all but assured a guilty verdict, I knew I would have to disappear. When he said the jury had reached a verdict, I knew it would have to be tonight. Good God, it was close."

Her eyes became slits.

"One problem still has to be cleared. I have to be sure you and the children are out of danger from this murdering thug Rivera. He did everything to us. I can't prove that in court. I don't think the government could prove it well enough to get an honest conviction, but Rivera's the one who kidnapped me, and he's the one who ordered the shootings at our house.

"Billy told me where Rivera and his gang meet for dinner. I'll be there the next few nights. If things work out, the pressure will be off. If they don't, I may be dead, and that's all right too, because you and the children will be safe."

She looked at the floor.

"You'll have to raise Tommy and Sydney by yourself, Michael. I can't imagine a worse time to leave, but Moses told me I'll probably lose this trial. If I do, Rivera will have me killed in jail."

She looked at the camera.

"I suppose this is why fictional heroes aren't married or have children. It makes them too vulnerable."

She gulped.

"I've signed a half-dozen attorney-in-fact forms in your favor. Moses has them. When you get the government to release assets, you can sell the house and cars.

"Another thing. The post office box key is in the kitchen taped under the plastic holder that separates the knives and forks." She told him the address and box number. "I'm going to mail more packages like this one to Lee Gardener. You'll need to check the box every week or so. I think it's safe. See that my parents get their money back. The rest is for you.

"Take care, Michael. I love you. Always will love you. I'm sorry it turned out this way. Give my regrets to Tommy and Sydney. Tell them I love them every day. I'll be in touch, God willing. I love you. Bless you always. Be careful. Your luck has got to change. I'm so sorry about everything."

She leaned to the camera. The screen turned blue.

Michael pressed the Rewind button. When the machine stopped, he pulled out the tape. He didn't bother to see Hirschfeld or Antaramian on the way out. He got Bret from reception and they drove back to Charlottesville in silence.

Denise Elizabeth Lang James made the FBI's "Most Wanted List" a week after the verdict. Initially a reward of ten thousand dollars was offered. Four days later it was increased to fifty thousand in time for billboards and ads featuring her picture, description, the reward amount, and a toll-free number.

Campgrounds, trailer parks, vacant buildings, junkyards, warehouses, and places frequented by squatters were searched. The homeless on the streets and in shelters were scrutinized. Vans and cars and commercial carriers were stopped and searched. Sides of buses carried her picture. Retail merchants asked large bill customers to produce picture identification. No one bothered to review luxury hotel registries in Washington, D.C. after the first three days.

Thursday, November 29
Courthouse Square

Judge Emil Smert smoothed the pleats in his robe, irritated the media had tied his name so closely to the embarrassment the government was suffering for the latest buffoonery carried out by that woman Denise James. He wanted this hearing short and sweet.

"Are there any objections to waive reading charges and verdicts?"

Assistant US Attorney Paul Fleming went to the microphone and said, "No, Your Honor."

Moses Hirschfeld did the same.

"Let the record show both government and defense counsel waive reading."

Smert folded his hands in front of him and began his formal remarks.

"I'll make this brief.

"In the matter styled United States of America versus Denise Elizabeth Lang James, Criminal Number Seventeen-zero-one dash twenty twenty-seven-A, Denise Elizabeth Lang James was found guilty of eight felony counts by a jury of her peers October twenty-ninth last. Denise Elizabeth Lang James is at present a fugitive from justice having chosen to voluntarily absent herself on October twenty-ninth prior to the reading of verdicts in the referenced case and has not since surrendered. Efforts to locate her have proved unsuccessful. This sentencing is in regard to those eight verdicts. Other charges are accruing and will become active upon her apprehension.

"Denise Elizabeth Lang James shows no remorse and no acceptance of responsibility for the crimes for which she has been justly convicted. Denise Elizabeth Lang James played the solitary role in these crimes, and she has failed to mitigate damages created by these crimes. The cost to the taxpayer continues to rise due to the government's efforts to locate her. The court's displeasure is extreme.

"Individual calculations for the eight guilty verdicts are detailed within the Sentencing Report, hereby made a part of the record and described as Sentencing Exhibit A."

He handed a dozen bound-binders to the bailiff who handed them to the clerk, the government, and the defense.

"To summarize, the range of sentence under mandatory minimum sentencing guidelines is from seven hundred and ninety-one months to one thousand and twenty-one months.

"The court finds this range appropriate.

"I do hereby sentence Denise Elizabeth Lang James to the maximum of one thousand and twenty-one months in a medium security federal penitentiary without possibility of parole. Sentences are to begin and run consecutively as soon as Denise Elizabeth Lang James is apprehended and remanded into the custody of the United States Marshals who will process her into the Federal Bureau of Prisons.

"The range of fines available to the court under the guidelines is from nine million dollars to twenty-seven million dollars.

"The court finds this range appropriate.

"I do hereby sentence Denise Elizabeth Lang James to pay a fine in the amount of the maximum of twenty-seven million dollars to be imposed through enforcement against her real and personal assets as applicable under law.

"The court re-charges all members of the law enforcement community to locate Denise Elizabeth Lang James, and to bring her to justice before this court at the earliest possible time. Denise Elizabeth Lang James must not be allowed to remain at large."

Thwack!

Sunday, December 2

An interview with Michael James and FBI Assistant Director Roscoe Penes aired as the first segment on "60 Minutes." In a point-counterpoint exchange spliced from multiple interviews, Michael reiterated his wife's innocence. The footprint, hair, and fingerprint were manufactured. He admitted he had no proof, but held out hope based upon the inquiry that had surfaced through Officer Stephen Johnson.

"How can I get proof? I have no resources, and the government is forfeiting our assets. Without my parents, I'd be bankrupt. Thank God the shoe issue is working its way through the system."

Assistant Director Roscoe Penes declared all evidence had been gathered in the course of standard investigative procedure and stood on its merit. If joint assets had to be liquidated to carry out the sentence, it was being done in accordance with the law. He would offer no comment on any pending investigation.

Michael claimed he and the children had suffered enough from the actions of the task force in that their home had been shot up, his wife had been kidnapped, and his wife and oldest child had escaped being killed by sheer chance.

Penes responded that those incidents were indeed unfortunate. Notwithstanding, Denise James had broken the law. As such, linkage was inappropriate.

Michael was asked why he thought the evidence was manufactured and who he thought manufactured it.

"Certain members of the Mousetrap task force did it. They couldn't get a conviction any other way. First we had the Tea Party, then the bullet through the window, then the attempted murder of my wife and son with agents sitting in front of the house. There was that unfortunate coffee incident. And now she's walked out of their special suite, right under their noses. Denise got 'em again."

Penes said straight-faced it was unfortunate Denise James had done things that might have embarrassed government agencies, but the Federal Bureau of Investigation was not subject to succumbing to embarrassment by resorting to personal vendettas.

"It is Denise James who has made a terminal sequence of errors," he said.

"What do you plan to do now, Mr. James?"

"I'm being forced to sell the house and cars. Denise's share of those assets and her IRA are being applied against the twenty-seven million dollar fine. That makes a thimbleful of payment against an ocean full of debt. I'm working through it, trying to view these events as hurdles, not obstacles. It's hard, but life goes on."

"You filed a divorce action against Ms. James."

"Yes."

"What's the status?"

"It's being withdrawn as soon as I receive consent from my attorney. There is information concerning the divorce in my immunity agreement that I am unable to disclose without putting myself in jeopardy of losing that immunity."

"Does that mean your immunity agreement was subject to your filing divorce against your wife?"

His eyes said yes.

"I don't feel comfortable saying anything further on the matter."

The same reporter asked Penes, "Was it a condition of Michael James's immunity agreement that he file divorce against Denise James?"

"The government has no comment on that question."

"The same type of 'no comment' you made about the shoe problem?"

Penes assumed an expression of patience.

"I'm here to maintain an open policy of communication with the American people. If evidence has been withheld, and it can be proven, the appropriate action will be taken against the appropriate people. That's how the FBI works, according to the law. However, there are some things on which I am unable to comment, and the content of any sealed agreement comes under that purview."

"Mr. James," asked the reporter. "If you could tell Denise something on this broadcast, what would it be?"

Michael turned to the camera and said, "I love you very much, Denise. Press on regardless."

To Penes the reporter asked, "If you could tell Denise James something on this program, what would it be?"

Penes kept his eyes on the reporter.

"I'd tell her that while it is unfortunate she failed to make an appearance at the federal courthouse as she was required to do under the law, and that while it is unfortunate she has chosen to become a fugitive, one thing is certain. Her freedom is a temporary condition. She will be apprehended, and she will begin serving her sentence in a federal penitentiary. More than anything else, her freedom is a short term circumstance."

The picture switched back to Michael. He cocked an eyebrow and said, "Does it sound personal to you?"

The ticking stopwatch led to commercial.

Thursday, December 6
The Washington Post - A2

Federal Officers Suspended

Three Special Agents of the Federal Bureau of Investigation and an Assistant US Attorney were suspended with pay yesterday pending further investigation relating to suppressed evidence in the Denise James trial.

In a sworn affidavit, City of Alexandria Police Officer Stephen P. Johnson alleges that during the James trial he informed FBI Special Agent in Charge Eric Peabody Kludge that on the night of January 16th he saw Denise James wearing black shoes with brass buckles.

Shoes presented by the government at trial were plain brown.

Michael James, husband of Denise James, claimed in his testimony during trial that much of the government's evidence was manufactured, including that of the shoes.

Contacted by the Post, Johnson said, "After I ran up to the suspect, I was leaning over to catch my breath. I was looking straight at her shoes. I know those kind of shoes because my girlfriend was after me to buy her the same pair at Christmas last year. They were Guccis."

Johnson said that during trial he approached Kludge about the shoes, and was told how unreliable eyewitness accounts could be.

"Trial was almost finished," Johnson said. "Kludge shrugged it off. He said something about going along to get along."

Johnson's affidavit also charges Kludge told him the FBI would look favorably upon his application to join the Bureau at a later date.

Assistant US Attorney Richard Paul Fleming, III and Special Agents James Edward Olsen, Jr. and Marvin Herbert Iacob were also suspended.

Calls to the FBI and the Department of Justice were not returned.

Denise James remains at large.

That Same Morning

Leaves were off the trees completely now. Not a whiff of wind breathed as the baldheaded woman crept along in a line of cars and trucks. She had no visible hair, no eyelashes, no eyebrows, nothing on the backs of her hands.

The "60 Minutes" broadcast had been four days ago. Already she'd seen a bumper sticker that read: DOES IT SOUND PERSONAL TO YOU? On a T-shirt a month ago was her favorite: DENISE JAMES - HIDE AND SEEK WORLD CHAMP!

She'd been freezing in an abandoned coal country cabin in West-By-God-Virginia for the past five weeks. From time to time she'd gone into town to get clothes and supplies and warmth. It was in town she'd read that Nick Rivera and his colostomy bag had been moved from intensive care to one of the hospital's coach-class beds. His organization had disappeared, much of it wounded or killed in a drug war with Johnny Murphy. The Baltimore-Alexandria connection lay in ruins. Commonwealth's Attorney Roody Packwurst claimed credit.

At least twelve were known dead. No mention was made of her involvement.

While in town she'd also mailed boxes to Lee Gardener, nearly a million dollars worth, enough to keep Michael going for a long while.

Cora Masters looked at herself in the mirror and hardly recognized the face she saw. She looked like a genetic error.

Facing forward, heart beating fast, she stared at the back of the truck in front of her. New Hampshire had the best plate motto in America: LIVE FREE OR DIE. The truck pulled ahead. The gate barrier fell behind it. She eased the car up to a uniformed inspector and held out her wallet and passport. He looked at her and blanched.

"Chemo-therapy," she said. "Oncology unit. Sherbrooke Center."

"Oh."

Inside his booth he entered her name, address, and social insurance number into a terminal. He flipped through her wallet and passport.

She sat motionless, hardly able to breathe.

The computer in the booth beeped. She turned her head to watch the inspector as he looked at the screen.

He stamped her passport.

He came out of the booth and handed the wallet and passport back to her, waving her on as though her condition were contagious.

She moved to the next stop and handed over her identification. This inspector didn't look at her face. He went into his booth. Another inspector asked her to pop the hood and trunk. She did. A handler led a sniffing dog in and around her car.

She waited, eyes staring at the top of her open hood.

The trunk clapped shut and she jumped. The inspector walked around and closed the hood.

The booth inspector returned.

"Welcome home, Ms. Masters."

He handed the identification to her.

"Thank you. It's good to be back."

The barrier rose.

She headed across a two-lane bridge passing under a billboard. Across a waving blue background covered in fleurs-de-lis were the words, BIENVENUE AU CANADA!

The LIVE FREE OR DIE truck was stopped at a light. She braked behind it, able to breathe again. When the light changed, the truck turned left and drew away. Cora Masters was going straight, or nearly so. She pressed the accelerator and moved ahead.

Sam Skinner

About the Author

Sam Skinner is a freelance consultant living in Sterling, Virginia. He received Bachelor of Arts degrees in French and Foreign Affairs from the University of Virginia and a Masters in Business Administration from California Coast University. He is a former banker, real estate executive, and Executive Administrator of a licensed Home for Adults. *The Moneybag* is his first novel.

Printed in the United States
6224

Printed in the United States
6224